STORMSONG

Also by C. L. Polk

Witchmark

STORMSONG

C. L. POLK

A TOM DOHERTY ASSOCIATES BOOK

New York

This is a work of fiction. All of the characters, organizations, and events portrayed in this novel are either products of the author's imagination or are used fictitiously.

STORMSONG

Copyright © 2020 by Chelsea Polk

All rights reserved.

Edited by Carl Engle-Laird

A Tor.com Book
Published by Tom Doherty Associates
120 Broadway
New York, NY 10271

www.tor.com

Tor® is a registered trademark of Macmillan Publishing Group, LLC.

Library of Congress Cataloging-in-Publication Data

Names: Polk, C. L. (Chelsea L.) author.
Title: Stormsong / C.L. Polk.
Description: First Edition. | New York : A Tom Doherty Associates Book, 2020. | Series: The kingston cycle; 2 | "A Tor.com Book"— Title page verso.
Identifiers: LCCN 2019042696 (print) | LCCN 2019042697 (ebook) | ISBN 9780765398994 (trade paperback) | ISBN 9780765398987 (ebook)
Subjects: LCSH: Witches—Fiction. | Magic—Fiction. | GSAFD: Fantasy fiction | Science fiction.
Classification: LCC PR9199.4.P6563 S77 2020 (print) | LCC PR9199.4.P6563 (ebook) | DDC 813/.6—dc23
LC record available at https://lccn.loc.gov/2019042696
LC ebook record available at https://lccn.loc.gov/2019042697

Our books may be purchased in bulk for promotional, educational, or business use. Please contact your local bookseller or the Macmillan Corporate and Premium Sales Department at 1-800-221-7945, extension 5442, or by email at MacmillanSpecialMarkets@macmillan.com.

First Edition: February 2020

Printed in the United States of America

0 9 8 7 6 5 4 3 2 1

TO ELIZABETH BEAR,
WHO WAS THERE ALL ALONG

STORMSONG

ONE

To Fly a Kite

Fourteen days after Miles, Tristan, and I broke the aether network, I dreamed the Cauldron brewed a storm. I watched a vast, many-armed spiral of clouds from the highest reaches of the sky. Half-awake, half-dreaming, I opened my eyes, but all I saw was the vision.

The storm pinned down my arms and legs as it grew larger, larger, impossible as it swelled, hundreds of miles wide. A weight pressed my chest, denying me breath. The storm forced me to watch as it moved east. It was coming, and I couldn't move, couldn't speak.

A low, wavering wail sounded—me, mewling and weak. I forced a breath for another small, helpless whimper. Again. I sucked in a gulp of air and screamed.

The sound set me free. The storm winked out. I could see my tent, smell the air drowsy with the last traces of dream-resin. A full night's sleep tasted sour on my tongue.

While I tried to convince myself it had been a nightmare, I opened a trunk, pawing through it for clothes. It was just a dream. Just a dream.

But what if it wasn't?

I dressed in splendid garments the Amaranthines had given me, rich with color and proven against the cold. Outside, the sun rose on the white-shrouded world of a winter come too early, dazzling my eyes. The vision gnawed at my gut, driving me to ask the craftsmen for the makings of a kite. I took sturdy twine, dowels, glue, and wings of bright yellow paper up the stone-crowned slope of Bywell Rise.

My fingers knew the task by heart, even if they numbed in the too-chilly air. I'd been making scrying kites since childhood, under my father's watchful eye. As I waited for the glue to set, I stood in the wind and put my back to the sunrise. Below me, the Amaranthine camp ringed the hill with colorful domed tents dyed saffron, scarlet, summery green, and the largest pavilion dyed in deep indigo and patterned with a scattering of stars.

Aeland's final harvest lay under last week's snow, destroying what should have carried Aeland through winter in comfort and plenty. I hadn't been with the Circle the night they stood against the storm. Aeland had needed me, and I hadn't been there.

The soft crunch of snow under heavy-soled boots pulled me from my thoughts. Tristan Hunter climbed the hill to crouch by my side. I glanced at him, but turned back to the horizon as he pulled a carafe from a leather sling.

"Good morning, Tristan."

"Good morning, Grace. I see you roused from a screaming nightmare to climb the rise and fly a kite." Tristan opened a glass jar filled with the roasted root tea Amaranthines used to stay alert. Steam caressed my face as I took a sip, the bitterness of the root mellowed by the spices that joined in its brewing.

"It's for a spell." The tea warmed my stomach. "I'm being foolish, but I have to know if I had a dream or a vision—oh Solace, I needed this."

Tristan waved off my thanks. "And you need a kite for that? Tell me more about this spell—wait."

The air took on the scent of summer grass and meadow flowers, a smell that spread from the Waystones behind me. Tristan loosed his sword and dagger, moving to face the stones.

"Who approaches?" Tristan asked.

A man emerged from behind a sentinel stone at the top of the hill, pausing with his hands well away from a hip quiver. A winter breeze set the hems of his scarlet-and-saffron robes to fluttering. "Tristan. What is this? Did the Grand Duchess send a party after you?"

Another Amaranthine. I stood up, ready to bow my head in greeting at my introduction.

"The Grand Duchess came herself," Tristan said, lowering his bow. "But why have you come?"

The stranger swiped a hand over his face. "Does Her Highness know what these monsters are doing in Laneer?"

"She's been informed." Tristan shifted his weight—a casual gesture, but it put him between me and the other Amaranthine. "Why did you come here from Laneer, rather than go to Elondel? It's dangerous."

The stranger swept it aside with a careless gesture. "To find you. To bring you back and warn the Grand Duchess about— Wait." He looked at me, narrow-eyed. "Who are you?"

Tristan stood aside to let the man have a look at me. I swept back the fur-edged hood of the felted Amaranthine tunic I wore, and he recoiled. His hand came up, a balanced dagger pinched between his fingers.

Tristan raised his arms, blocking the way. "Aldis, stop. She's a friend."

A friend. Soft warmth spread across my face to hear Tristan call me so. But the stranger's face puckered in scorn.

"She's no friend. She's an Aelander. Do you have any idea what they've done in Laneer? What they're doing here?"

"We know now," I said. "And it's horr—"

"Don't speak to me," Aldis said.

"Stop that. She had no idea," Tristan scolded. "When she learned the truth, she helped destroy the aether network. Her brother nearly lost his life, undoing what was done in their name."

I nodded, while Aldis stared murder at me. "It's over," I said. "The abomination is destroyed."

"Let's try this again," Tristan said, "only we're going to be civil. Aldis, this is the Liberator, Dame Grace Hensley. Grace, this is Sir Aldis, Hunter for the Grand Duchess."

They shared a name, but they didn't look like brothers. They were both handsome, but where Tristan's finely boned face and fair hair made him beguiling, Aldis's auburn brown hair fell in loose waves around sharp cheekbones and a square chin in a blunter, more angular face. He eyed me with open dislike, but the knife went back in its sheath.

"How do you do?" I asked.

Aldis ignored me. "What justice is the Grand Duchess considering? I have a few suggestions."

"The Grand Duchess will enter diplomatic communications with the Queen," Tristan said. "There's a lot you need to know before you can really form impressions of this place."

Aldis glanced at me one more time. "Where can I find her?"

"The indigo tent. She'll want to see you."

"Right."

Aldis marched straight for me, forcing me to step aside for him. I spared a glance at his retreating figure and hoped his toes froze off.

"Well. He seemed pleasant."

"We have to assume that Aldis discovered Aeland's true purpose in conquering Laneer." Tristan watched the saffron-and-scarlet figure trot across the camp, headed for the deep blue tent that housed Grand Duchess Aife. "He'll argue in favor of punishing Aeland, and Aife trusts him. He needs to be countered."

How could we counter against Aeland's abominable motive for the Laneeri War? There would never be a day when remembering the soul-engines in the basement of Clarity House wouldn't flood my system with the horrified lurch that made me want to retch. Aife hadn't spoken to me of the abomination, preferring instead to see me as instrumental in the liberation of the dead. But Aldis had been in Laneer. He had seen the atrocity of war, understood that Aeland was responsible for every drop of blood that soaked its ground. He would tell Aife those things, and I couldn't see her looking on me with kindness after that.

"Aife trusts you," I said.

Tristan pressed his lips together. "Indeed. Shall we continue?"

"Let's." I steadied my grip on the kite and climbed the rest of the way.

A dead child waited for us at the top of the hill. I could see right through his sore-covered skin and the holey tunic that hung off one skinny shoulder. He stared at the kite under my arm before looking at me. His lips moved, but I couldn't hear him.

"Ahoy." I crouched just as if he were alive and showed him the kite. He reached out, but his fingers slid right through the paper, and he vanished.

The child ghosts were the worst of all the apparitions to appear from the broken soul-engines that fueled the aether network. They deserved it least of all, and I couldn't do anything to help them, had no talent that would serve them. They were cut off from the Solace, all the pathways between here and there stopped up by the Amaranthines in camp.

"Poor lad," Tristan said. "Life wasn't easy on him, either."

But he should have had the comfort of the Solace when he died instead of the fate he'd suffered.

"All right." Tristan scuffed his way to a tall stone and leaned against it. "How does the kite spell work?"

"A bit of witchcraft. A little blood, and I'm linked to the kite." I stripped my left hand of its glove and mitten, fished my white-handled bolline out of my pocket, and spilled three drops of my blood on the kite's nose.

Soon a cheerful bit of yellow flew in a clean blue sky, stretching a thread of my soul between me and the blood I'd shed on the paper. The kite dipped and swirled in the upper breezes, caught its breath, and steadied as I emptied my mind and sent my senses out. Westward, crossing polar breezes. Westward, pushing upwind over the ocean, where the air dampened and swirled around the depressed air from the north. And where they fought . . .

The kite dipped, diving to the ground. I hauled on the line, caught the wind again, and what I saw strained belief:

A storm spread out miles wide, spinning away from the Cauldron off the coast. It was wrong: too vast, too violent. The storm came east even as it swelled with fury. East to Kingston, where millions huddled in the dark and cold with no aether.

I reeled the kite in with shaking hands.

"A tidy trick," Tristan said. "You should have eaten first."

"Yes, Mother." My head spun with the turning of the land, my hunger multiplied by my wind-reading. I hadn't been dreaming. I wasn't mistaken. The storm I sensed in my half-wakeful daze was real. And if it broke on the shore, I couldn't count how many it would kill.

Tristan caught my shoulder, steadying me. "But really, you're green around the edges. What did you see?"

I shook my head, trying to clear it. Maybe I was still dreaming. Maybe this was still a nightmare. "A storm. It's bad. It's—I have to go."

"Go where? Grace? What are you—?"

I laid the kite in the snow and set off, my feet slipping along the slope. Tristan called my name, but I kept my course, aiming for the long tent that served as a stable.

"Grace." Tristan caught my arm and held fast. "Explain yourself and let me help."

"I have to get to Kingston. There's a storm. It's huge, and it's headed straight for us."

"And you need to be there."

I swept my arm in a wide arc. "Look what happened when I wasn't there."

"You can't blame yourself for that. They kicked you out of the Invisibles, remember? Besides, Miles needed you."

"You're right," I said. "But being rational never stopped guilt before. This storm that's coming, it's worse than last week. I have to get back—"

Tristan caught my hand. "And then you'll be taken in for treason. And what good will you do then?"

"I can't just sit here!"

"No one is asking you to. Miles can be moved if we pad a wagon. Aife sits on the cusp of a decision. Help me convince her to move the camp. It's time we went to Kingston anyway. Come on," Tristan said, heading toward the Grand Duchess's tent. "The less time Aldis has to whisper venom, the better."

Two sunrises after I flew my weather kite, I came home to picketers gathered in the parade square in front of Mountrose

Palace. They carried signs that voiced the anger and fear of the people, painted in hand-high letters: "Bring us the light" and "We are hungry—We are cold." Most of the signs had one word, lettered in black: "Shame."

It pooled in my gut, sour and hot. I couldn't tell them why Kingston was dark, their wireless stations and telephones silent. If they knew the truth, Aeland would burn with their fury.

I had come as quickly as I could with the company of the Amaranthines. When I had burst into Aife's tent to tell her of the storm, she agreed to strike camp so quickly I wondered what Aldis had been saying when Tristan and I arrived. But the storm, still hundreds of miles away, had grown in speed and ferocity as the ocean winds shoved its fury toward us. There was no more time.

But just now, Kingston was astonished at the sight of us. We stunned newsboys out with their stacks of the daily paper, confounded wagon drivers and constables, amazed the shift change of assembly workers walking home from a night of work. Some of them abandoned their tasks to follow us, jostling for position and a better look at the procession. And now the protesters stared, their angry signs askew.

Mingled among our witnesses were the dead. Their lips moved, but no sound escaped them. The light shone through their transparent forms as they groped for the living, who flinched from their skin-crawling touch. They were the first to crowd around us, and Aldis clicked his tongue, moving his mount closer to the center of the procession. He caught sight of me and scowled, turning to radiate his disgust at the people who came nearer.

The Amaranthines riding around me glanced my way, their expressions tight with disapproval. I shrank in my saddle and turned my mount to walk beside the wagon that carried my brother. He sat up and tried to see past horses and riders, but gave up with an exasperated sigh, flopping back down onto the pallet.

Miles caught my eye and tried to wheedle me with a smile. "I can ride."

"No you can't," I said. "Besides, we're finally here."

He sighed and stared at the sky. "And you're going to rush off and do something stupid."

"I'm not," I said, and winced as the weight of the air pounded against my head.

Someone carrying a photographer's tripod mounted with an enormous camera and flash torch ran toward us. She set the contraption down as Amaranthines peered at her with curiosity. She shot a picture, and the whole company reared in surprise, shocked exclamations sounding all around me.

"What is that?" Aldis asked.

Tristan spoke loudly enough to be heard. "It's a camera. Amazing little things. They capture a subject's image perfectly."

The photographer straightened up, peering at the crowd. "Sir Tristan?"

I knew that voice. I stood in my stirrups to get a better look.

It was her. My memory cast back to her striding into the Starlight Room at the newly opened Edenhill Hotel, garbed in scandal. She had rebelled against the iron-clad code that restricted unmarried women to white, her freshly cut hair dyed bottle-black in a sleek, short style that curved around her cheekbones to point at her mouth, painted red as the ball gown draped from her shoulders, her pale arms sheathed in black silk opera gloves.

I had stood rooted to the spot as my heart thrilled to see

her, and then in horror as her furious father threw a white tablecloth over her head and dragged her from the room so violently she cried out in pain.

This was her: same black hair, same angled cheeks, same heart's blood lipstick. Her fur-trimmed coat had been fashionable two winters ago, her hat a pinch-fronted topper favored by reporters. But it was her, and she froze me in my tracks just as she had on New Year.

Tristan raised his hand in greeting. "At your service, Miss Jessup."

Avia Jessup had been an heiress, the eldest child of three girls in line to reap the fortune of Jessup Family Foods. I watched her float about at parties, laughing and glamorous and glittering, wishing I could talk to her. Now she was a one-eye in a secondhand coat, and I couldn't imagine it—she had persisted, refusing to go back to the velvet life so she could work at a newspaper. She had chosen her own desires, her own ambitions, herself. It was shocking. She was interesting. I wished I weren't surrounded by Blessed Ones, that I could find something clever to say to her.

My mount swung its head to whicker at another beast coming nearer. I tore my gaze away to greet Grand Duchess Aife with a nod. She smiled at me, and a breeze caught her spiralling golden locks, making them float around her angular, brown-skinned face. She moved to my side and tilted her head, watching Avia slam another plate into her camera and shoot, the flash torch giving one last flare of light before it extinguished with a smell like burning wire.

Aldis put his hand out, blocking the view. "Stop that. It's rude."

"A little," Avia admitted. "But you're news, you see."

Tristan pushed Aldis's hand down. "She's come to get the story of our arrival. That's her job."

Aldis eyed Tristan. "She's a herald?"

Tristan shrugged. "Close enough."

Aldis grunted. He directed a stern gaze at Avia and spoke too loudly. "We follow Grand Duchess Aife of the Solace, heir to the Throne of Great Making, most blessed daughter of Queen Eilidh the Watcher. Make sure to tell them that in your song, herald. Tell them we come with our blades ready. Tell them we come to set your people away from the evil you have done."

Tristan sighed, loud and annoyed. "Enough, Aldis. She doesn't know about that."

Avia let go of her camera and reached inside her coat for a pad of paper and a pen. "Aife of the Solace, Throne of Great Making . . ." She dropped her pen in the snow. "You're Guardians. You're Amaranthines. You're real."

Gasps erupted from the protesters behind her. A woman shoved Avia aside, falling on her knees. "Blessed Ones. What have we done to bring your justice down on us?"

"You didn't do anything wrong." I guided my mount with nudges and gentle hands to move in front of Aldis. "The blame is not yours, people of Aeland. Please remain calm. These are the Blessed Ones, and they have come to speak to Queen Constantina. Let them proceed into the palace in peace."

I let myself look at Avia Jessup one more time. She watched as I turned toward the cohort of scarlet-coated guards, my ears bitten by the icy air.

"Grace, stop!"

Miles's voice. I kept my mount's gait steady and rode with my hands up. "Ahoy," I said. "I'm Fiona Grace Hensley."

The guards raised their rifles in one motion. "You are wanted on suspicion of treason," the guard captain said. "Surrender."

"Please see the Blessed Ones to comfort and hospitality.

I need to speak to the Queen. It's life or death." I spread my
empty hands, imploring.

Bolts pulled back in a chorus of slides and clicks. A shout
went up from the company of the Amaranthines, and Tristan
rode forward, one hand raised for peace.

"The Liberator is protected by Grand Duchess Aife of the
Solace," Tristan called. "She is our guest, and we will defend
her from insult and violence."

They could fight. Right here. The guards and their rifles
against the Deathless and their magic. Would they be stupid
enough to spill Amaranthine blood?

I wouldn't let them fight, not over me. I planted one hand
on the saddle and dismounted. "Tristan, stand down. Please. I
have to do this. She has to know right away."

Tristan shook his head. "You have the protection of Grand
Duchess Aife."

I held my hands up, palms out. "Should I insult my Queen
by staying under that protection when a loyal subject would
trust her monarch's wisdom? I throw myself on her mercy. I
have every faith that she will hear me out."

"Queen Eilidh would expect the same," Tristan said.

Something in his tone made me look at him, to read his
face. But his expression was still as a pond, and he stepped
back, allowing me to surrender.

"Take her," the guard captain ordered, and scarlet coats
closed in on me. One of them wrapped copper-lined manacles
around my wrists. Cold flames shuddered over my skin. My
lips tasted like metal. The world warped and snapped back
with a clang. My empty stomach shuddered, and two more
guards seized me before I could fall.

I couldn't react. I couldn't scream, or retch, or indicate in
any way that I couldn't bear the touch of copper against my

skin. They'd know what I was, and no one could save me from the examiners.

"Gently," Aife said. "She surrendered. Treat her with respect."

The guard captain regarded Aife with a worried pinch to his brows. "She's wanted for treason, Your Radiance."

"'Highness' will do," she said. "I am Grand Duchess Aife of the Solace, Hand of the Throne of Great Making. I wish to see your Queen immediately. Will you go and tell her?"

The captain gave an order and an underling ran, kicking up chunks of snow as he sprinted through the gates.

The others marched me away, turning down the snow-tamped path to Kingsgrave Prison.

"I must see the Queen," I said. "It's the fate of the kingdom."

"We have our orders, and they don't come from you," a guard said. "Now shut up and march."

I held my tongue. We passed under an ash tree, its boughs draped in snow. A flight of scarlet jays circled the rough gray stone of the prison tower as the heavy doors swung open, ready to swallow me whole.

It was time for a meal in Kingsgrave Prison, and I couldn't stay here another minute. The awareness of the storm pressed on the base of my skull, tying knots in my stomach and twisting my dreams in the dark. The others had to have felt it by now. They had to have come to the Queen with the news. She wouldn't leave me in here, not when she needed me. I could convince her if I could just speak to her. She would understand everything. If she would see me, even for a minute.

The door opened with a rusty groan. Prince Severin strode into the cell block, his fashionable attire incongruous in the rough stone and stink of the prison. From the shiny toes of his shoes to the hand-eased shoulders of his suit to his dark hair dressed and gleaming, he was every bit as handsome as the last time I'd seen him. A satin-woven orange silk tie-dyed the same shade as the Hensleys' heraldry descended from under the collar of his shirt. After a day and a half, my hair hung in my eyes. I was unwashed and clad in the shapeless undyed hemp of prisoners.

"I came as soon as I could," he said. "I can't believe you brought the Blessed Ones to us."

"Your Highness. Please. A storm is coming—" I lifted my head and groaned. "Sorry. It hurts."

"I know about the storm. The others sent messages an hour ago, and they all say the same thing."

I fought to sit up. "There's no time to waste. It's the biggest storm I've ever seen. Did Her Majesty send you to get me? No one else can lead the ritual."

He came closer to the copper-plated bars. "Listen to me. I can help you get out of this cell, but I need something from you."

I stood up and swayed, but I stayed on my feet. "If it's in my power."

"Whatever she says, no matter what she says, agree to the Queen's terms." Prince Severin spoke so quietly I had to watch his lips to understand. "But after, I need you on my side. Aeland is in deep trouble with the Amaranthines because of this mess with aether and the asylums, and she won't listen to me."

I came as close to the bars as I dared. "What kind of trouble?"

"They want things the Queen doesn't want to give. I'm trying to compromise, but she can't be convinced to bend."

"And you want me to help you convince her?"

"I want Aeland to survive this storm and the Amaranthines'

pronouncement of justice," Prince Severin said. "We must surrender to their word and do as they tell us, but Mother won't
do it. But it's even worse than that. The people are angry."

How angry? I hadn't any idea what had happened in Kingston since we discovered the truth deep in the basement of Clarity House. Was it more than just protesters standing in the
parade square? "They should be angry. The lights are out."

"We'll have plenty of time to discuss this when you're released. Will you support me?"

"What do the Amaranthines want that Queen Constantina
won't give?"

Severin counted one point on his finger. "Reparations for
Laneer, for Aeland's aggression against them."

"Oh." The old tales were clear. An Amaranthine's justice
cost the punished what they least wanted to pay. Queen Constantina prided herself on the success of her reign, measured in
millions of marks. "Is that all they want?"

"No." A second finger joined the tally. "They want the
witches freed, and reparations paid to them."

And once freed, they would tell their stories. That knowledge would have the people in a rage. Constantina could lose
her crown over that revelation. Maybe even her head. "She'll
never do it."

"She must," Prince Severin said. "Lastly, they want Aelanders to know the truth of what has been done in their name."

I stared at the third finger counting the point that would
destroy us. "Aeland will burn to the ground if that happens."

"We might be able to control that part, if we can convince
Mother to agree," Severin said.

"But if she doesn't?"

"Then I need you."

To turn my back on the Queen, he meant. Severin suggested
that I promise to commit treason as a condition of acquitting

me of that same charge. How hard would he try to preserve his mother's place if I stood with him? How could I turn against the rightful monarch? How could I turn generations of service to the Crown to dust as I betrayed her?

"Must you ask this of me, Your Highness? Is there nothing else I can pledge?"

He wrapped his hands around the bars, his chin raised to meet my eyes. "I don't want to do this. But it's the Amaranthines, Grace. It's them. Here in the palace."

His eyes shone with awe and wonder. I understood that. It hit me too, sometimes, when I remembered they knew the faces of the Makers. I found it easy to forget—but the Prince attended temple. He kept his book of meditations. He saw them differently. "Is it strange, sometimes?"

"It's a blessing," Prince Severin said. "The fact that they're granting us the chance to beg them for mercy can't be wasted. She doesn't understand that they could simply take their justice, and what that could mean for Aeland."

"What will they do?"

Severin's shoulders came up. "You know the Blessed Ones better than I do. One of the Grand Duchess's courtiers is no friend to Aeland. Do you know who I mean?"

"Aldis." His advice to Aife wouldn't favor us at all. "What does he want?"

"He argued that they should take the royal family and all the Royal Knights prisoners, and make us a vassal state to Laneer—"

"They can't!"

"And if we refuse," Prince Severin said, "he's asking that we be withered."

I stopped breathing. Poets sang of the Amaranthine who cursed King Randulf, his twenty heirs and bastards, and his sixty-eight grandchildren: *You will wither.*

His wife had miscarried on the spot. A year later, neither he nor his children nor the children of his children proved fruitful. Ten years later, brides were returned, treaties broken, the land taken or emancipated as Randulf's line grew old and powerless, and died, vanished from all but poetry and legend.

I understood why Severin looked so pale. I had to get out of here.

"The Grand Duchess said she would give us her decision after she has seen the truth of Aeland for herself, but I fear she won't be patient with Mother's resistance."

Queen Constantina would choke to death before she apologized to Laneer and admitted the war was a criminal act. If she learned of the Prince's plans, she wouldn't hesitate. He would hang, and his accomplices with him.

But if she brought Aeland to ruin, could I really stand by and plead loyalty? Never. I would never let Aeland fall, if I could help it.

And so I committed treason, in truth. "All right. I'll support you. And if it comes down to it, I will stand with you."

Severin let out a long-held breath. "Thank you. Let me get you out of here. Guard!" he called. "Unlock this door. I am taking Dame Grace into my custody immediately."

TWO

The Spider's Web

Severin let me have time and privacy to dress in my borrowed Amaranthine garb before he offered his escort through the chilled halls of Kingsgrave. I matched his unhurried pace even though I wanted to run. I had so much to do, starting with rallying what was left of the Circle of Invisibles. But I could use this time if the Prince would inform me on what had happened while I had been in Bywell.

"The Queen arrested them all?" My voice bounced off the stones and resounded in my ears. I lowered it to a murmur, turning my head to point the words in Severin's ear. "The entire Cabinet?"

Severin inclined his head in my direction, already familiar with the stone hallway's acoustic tricks. "They're all imprisoned."

So that was why it had snowed so hard a week ago. The entire First Ring was in chains. They certainly deserved it. They were absolutely guilty. But the storm made my skull ache and tied knots in my stomach, and I needed their power and skill to fight it. "Since when? Oh, I apologize, Your Highness. It's only that this is so urgent—"

He covered my hand, curled around the crook of his elbow, with his. "Severin. I rely on your candor, Grace. Please don't withhold it from me, not when I need it the most."

"Severin," I said.

He gave me the smile that half of Kingston sighed over, the one that featured in so many photographs of him with Aeland's most famous beauties in the news. "To answer your question, about three days after the lights went out."

"That's before the storm on the eighth," I said. "And that one was a mere blizzard. It wiped out the last of our crops."

"We always reap a surplus," Prince Severin said with a shrug. "We can manage."

It wouldn't be that easy. Hundreds of tons of food lay rotting under the snow. Thousands. "I mean that this coming storm is worse. The eye is enormous. I must have the First Ring in ritual. I need every Storm-Singer I can get."

"I know you do. But Mother's in a rage. I'm not sure she'll let you have them." Severin led me around another corner, deep into the twisting maze that would confuse anyone trying to escape. But weren't we going the wrong way? The Prince turned right where we should have gone left. He didn't have the Cauldron boiling in his senses forever to the west, but he knew the palace better than I could ever hope to.

I tried to find a graceful way to ask, but Severin turned another corner and spoke again. "I thought Sir Christopher the Younger was dead."

So much for my brother's attempt at freedom and privacy. "He wanted it that way," I said. "And he uses Miles, now."

That curled the Prince's lips in a smile. "An alias? How dashing."

"He deserves all the credit for doing the right thing and staying the Amaranthines' wrath. He was the one who acted. I just helped."

"Did you hesitate to help him?"

I shrugged. "No. He was right."

"Then you deserve credit too. Many people wouldn't have moved to do the right thing so quickly. But you made the hard choice, for the good of Aeland."

His approval warmed my cheeks. "Thank you, Your High—Severin."

He patted my hand and led me around another corner. "You'll get used to it. But about the Amaranthines."

I wasn't the only one who needed information. "What do you wish to know?"

Again he smiled at me, crinkling the skin at the corners of his fine dark eyes. "Is it true they can't lie?"

"I have never caught an Amaranthine lying."

"That doesn't mean that they always tell the truth, does it?" He nudged my arm, guiding me to a wide set of stone stairs that curved upward.

I stopped in my tracks. "This is the Tower of Sighs."

"Yes," Prince Severin said. "Someone wants to see you."

I fought the urge to pull away from his arm. "My father."

"He's in the tower with the rest of the Cabinet, awaiting judgment."

"And what will that judgment be?" My voice bounced off the stone, louder than I had intended. He didn't know what Father had done, how close he'd come to killing his own son. Severin probably thought this was a kindness—and I had to accept it as such.

"It's a complicated case. All conspiracies are. It will take time to unravel exactly who knew what, when, and what they did about it. One must be careful and sure, when delivering a punishment. And sometimes, one has to be swift."

We halted on a landing next to a window. Outside, gray-coated soldiers cleared off the stair of a gallows, sending clumps of snow cascading to the ground.

Prince Severin spoke, breaking through my awful fascination with the scene outside. "How long do we have before the storm comes?"

I set my gaze past the execution grounds, letting the horizon blur as I sensed beyond sight to read the wind. "If I had the full Circle, it would be in reach today."

"And without the First Ring?"

"Tomorrow evening. It might shed some of its power in that time, or it might get even stronger."

"You'll do everything you can," Prince Severin said. "I know it. So does Mother."

He led the way past cells walled with bars. At these lowest levels, the Laneeri delegation who had come under the guise of surrender languished in bare cells, their long, bleached hair bound in plaits and wrapped around their heads, attempting to hide the dark roots growing from neglect. Their eyebrows were growing back in, and their faces were bare of the complex, colorful makeup they used to signal their rank and importance. They hovered near the copper-plated bars and watched us pass, silent and hateful. Some of them glowed with magical talent, their auras dotted by witchmarks.

Outside their cells stood Sir Aldis Hunter, vibrating with fury.

"What is the meaning of this mistreatment?" he demanded.

"Good morning, Sir Aldis," Severin said with a bow. "I didn't expect to see you here."

"Her Highness wished a report on the status of the diplomatic envoys Laneer sent to this place," Aldis said. "And you have caged them, humiliated them with these rags. You have denied them all but the meanest of necessities."

Severin's expression went blank. "They're prisoners."

Aldis took a step toward Severin, close enough that he towered over the Prince. "They are ambassadors. Your imprisonment was supposed to be ceremonial. They should have been released days ago."

"We're in a state of emergency, Sir Aldis," Severin said. "We had to increase coverage of guardsmen and police throughout the city to keep order. We haven't the personnel to spare to watch them."

Aldis seethed, every muscle stiff with repressed ire. "I will report this to Her Highness."

He pushed past us and stalked off.

"He's really not happy with us," I said.

"He's wrathful," Severin said. "He's a test."

I wasn't sure what that meant, so I kept silent as Severin led the way.

We passed cells decorated with carpets, silk quilts, feather pillows, and even paintings, paid for with bribes. Money was no object when it came to the comfort of the patriarchs and matriarchs of the Royal Knights. They glared through the bars at me, puzzled at my royal escort. I nodded acknowledgment and followed Prince Severin to the peak.

My father's cell had braziers for heat, a comfortable bed, a small dining table, books on shelves, and a window. A portrait of me at sixteen hung on the wall just over his bed. The window was little more than an arrow slit, but a plump gray messenger dove perched on the windowsill, pecking at millet.

Father had always liked birds, and the affection was mutual. I knew many of them from walking with him, learning their names along with the exports, imports, industries, and laws of Aeland—all the things I had to know so I could become Chancellor after him. It wasn't supposed to be like this. Father wasn't supposed to be a traitor. He wasn't supposed to be a monster.

I wasn't supposed to hate him, but I did.

The Prince opened the cell himself, holding it open for me. I stepped inside the copper-barred cell, and he closed it. Locked it. And then walked away, taking the key with him.

I was alone with the last person I wanted to see.

Father rose unsteadily to his feet. "Grace."

He coughed, great wracking whoops that should have knocked him back into his chair, but he stayed on his feet. Still so tall, even as the cancer eating his body made him thin, his skin pale, a little blue around the lips.

I reached for the coughing tonic and unscrewed it before I knew what I was doing. He drank straight from the bottle, held in a trembling hand.

"Thank you."

I didn't want his thanks. I shouldn't have come with Severin. I should have made a scene. "I don't want to talk to you."

He leaned on his cane, knuckles white with his grip. "You have one chance with this storm, Grace. Do you really want to tackle it alone?"

"You couldn't help me even if you were free." He didn't have the strength to channel into a working. He was too weak to direct the power of the Circle and tame this storm. He would die if he tried.

"Fight the wind by diluting it. You can't force it to slow. Force it to spread. Spread it as wide as you can. Hundreds of miles. It's your best chance."

He had no idea. The storm probably plagued him, but he didn't dare exert his talent to see the scope of it for himself. It was already hundreds of miles wide. We'd have to spread it all the way across the coast, north and south. "That would work better if we had more reach."

Father leaned on his silver-headed cane, moving to a padded chair next to a table covered in paper. "You're right. But
you can't stop it, so don't even try. How is Christopher?"

"Miles still breathes. No thanks to you."

He gave me a sad look. "Do you think I wanted to kill my
own son?"

I folded my arms in front of me. "I'm sure you were just
doing what you had to do. How do I signal that the visit is
over?"

Father's lips thinned the way they always did when I'd exasperated him with stubbornness, or an unwillingness to see what
he believed to be reality. "He was going to destroy Aeland's
power. And now he has. Look at what he's done, Grace. Look at
the harm he's done to innocents."

I made a disbelieving noise. "How can you sit there and
speak of innocence to me? You knew exactly what powered
aether. You and Grandpa Miles worked together to make this
happen. And you never breathed a word."

"We had to stop using coal." Father pulled his chair out, and
slowly lowered himself into it. "You don't know what it was
doing to the weather, how it was changing the atmosphere,
how smoke hung over Kingston like soup. Gas wasn't any better. We needed an alternative."

"So you picked *souls*?"

Father picked up a glass teacup and sipped. He was ignoring
my outburst, the way he had when I was a child taken wholly
by anger or excitement or despair. "They were just energy,"
Father said. "Just energy, going to waste. That's all magic is.
Your personal power. We have an excess and the ability to use
it according to our will, but unburdened from the task of power-
ing a body, even an ordinary soul has amazing power."

"It wasn't yours to use!"

Father set the half-empty teacup on its saucer. "Do you

think the Amaranthines don't use souls for their own ends? They were right there the moment you broke the aether network and played into their hands."

That wasn't how it happened! "They were looking for Tristan."

"And why was he here?"

I clamped my mouth shut and watched the dove on the windowsill. The days of telling Father everything were over. We weren't a team. Not anymore.

Father gave me a patient look. "He was looking for those souls, Grace. The Amaranthines wanted them badly enough to break the compact of Menas the Just."

"You speak of a Maker, Father? I thought you didn't believe in the gods."

He shrugged. "The Age of Miracles is long over. No one had been touched by the Makers or the Deathless. We have no new stories of them since the Abandonment. What was there to believe in?"

"The Amaranthines are real. The Solace is real. We turned away from them—"

His fist struck the table. "They turned away from us."

Tea sloshed from the cup, over the rim of the saucer, and onto the *Star,* unfolded to show a picture of me and the Amaranthines on the front page.

The guardians wore glamors that made them appear human—unbearably gorgeous, but mortal all the same. But the camera, having no mind to fool, captured them exactly as they were: unearthly and beautiful with their huge eyes and high-bridged noses, mounted on antlered steeds called heera that had looked like horses to the naked eye.

Grand Duchess Aife held the center of the shot, looking the camera dead in the eye with a calm smile, the wind playing in her golden curls. Beside her hovered dark-skinned, black-clad

Ysonde, the secretary who went everywhere with her. Tea spilled across Aldis's scowl, and Tristan's hand pressed heavy on Aldis's shoulder.

Father's journal lay to the left, his pen capped across a page half-filled with notes. Father had taken note of news every day, from the front page to the shortest column, sometimes even from the tiny print in the classified ads. He was taking notes now. What good would they do him, rotting here in prison?

"They turned away from us," Father said. "They left us without their miracles or their mischief. Even if they were real, why honor a god who has abandoned you? I will not. I owe them nothing."

"You owe the souls you imprisoned in the network to be consumed and destroyed. That's beyond horrific, Father. There isn't a word for what you've done. And what of your own soul, now that you'll go to the Solace you denied to thousands?"

"I can't say. But I deny them. Now and hereafter. But to you, I apologize."

I lost my tongue. I stared, slack-jawed.

Father didn't bow his head or touch his heart. Just the admission was more ground than he ever gave. "I kept the truth about aether a secret from you. I knew what you'd think of it. I wanted to find a substitute power source. A way to supplement our growing needs. But then Stanley found a solution and pushed the Laneeri War."

"Blasted evil reason to fight a war." It was unspeakable. How could he have done it? How could he have done any of it?

"Don't be hostile, Grace. You have a terrible task ahead."

"Thanks to Sir Percy botching the spell-web, I'll be chasing storms all winter."

Father shook his head. "It's not just controlling the weather. The Invisibles are a mess without the experience and skill of the First Ring. Aeland needs its power back. The people are shocked, but soon they'll be looking for someone to blame. These are dangerous winds to handle alone. But you can ride them, Grace. You can turn the wind to your own use."

"All I have to do is obey your every word. All I have to do is trust you." I had always trusted Father. He knew so much and saw so far—he was the one who'd taught me to explore the implications, to delve for the underlying motives. He had a way of making everything come right in the end.

Well, not this. I stepped back. This tearful reunion wasn't for his apologies, after all. "I don't need your help, Father. And you don't deserve my trust."

He sighed. "If you change your mind, I'm right here."

"How do I leave?"

"There's a bell-pull behind you."

I rang it twice before Severin came to let me out.

Severin waited until I took his arm and strode past the Laneeri as if the cells were empty, but he glanced at me with worry. "You have to understand what's at stake here, Grace."

Everything was at stake. His future, mine, everyone's— between the storm headed for the coast and the judgment Aife would deliver to us after observing our country for fourteen days, we were on the edge of a very tall cliff and edging closer still. Naturally, he would turn to Sir Christopher Hensley for guidance. Who wouldn't?

Me. "You can't trust my father, Severin. You can't. He's the reason we're in this mess. And he never, never does anything without the guarantee that he'll benefit."

Severin sighed. "I know you're angry with him. And you have reason. But he loves Aeland. He swore to serve it. And he's ready to give everything to remedy what the Royal Knights and Grandfather Nicholas did."

"Everything?" I barely held back an indelicate, skeptical noise.

"He'll go to the gallows, if that's what it takes. And it might."

"And you believe him."

"He made a terrible mistake," Severin said. "One I don't even have words for. But he wants to make it right. He wept, Grace. He tried to hold it back, but he broke when I told him that Christopher the Younger still lived."

"He tried to kill Miles. I was there. I know what he did."

"He told me," Severin said. "He repents everything."

The skeptical noise huffed from my lips. "He didn't seem repentant to me."

"I think it's different, for you." Severin stroked my hand, soothing. "He spent his whole life with you looking up to him. He was strong. He knew everything, guided you in everything. He couldn't stop being strong for you."

Father had always been that. Always strong. Always wise. Always clever, inventive, insightful—and he had taught all that to me, while never breathing a word of secrets I had to learn if I was to succeed him. What if he had wanted a different way to power aether, as he said? It would be just like him to never let me know that he had faltered. To never let me see anything but strength and certainty.

I dashed the thought away. I was trying to understand him. I was trying to find a way to forgive him, and I could never do that, never. But one thing bothered me nearly as much as the headache that heralded the cyclonic blizzard headed our way. "Why did you take me to him before the Queen?"

"He wanted to see you."

And he obeyed my father's wishes rather than his mother's? I didn't have to grope around for a reason. Almost anyone would have done the same. Father had a reputation as one of the finest minds in Aeland, with an ability to see to the heart of a matter and a knack for sussing out the weakness in an opponent.

Only Miles had ever defied what Father had planned for him. He had dealt Father's reputation a blow, giving his rivals something to sneer about. Father had done his best to drag my brother back to his place, but Miles wouldn't bend, wouldn't break.

Father had tried to kill him in order to preserve the nation's most horrible secret. I wouldn't ever forget that. I would never forgive him. "Please be careful, Severin. Father always finds a way to get what he wants, in the end."

"Then that's all to the good," Severin said. "Your father wants safety for Aeland. If he always gets what he wants, then we're halfway there."

I stretched my face into a smile. "As you say."

My father did want safety for Aeland. Naturally, he wanted that. But there was more. I knew it, even if Severin didn't.

The Prince guided me along the complex route through Kingsgrave to the long breezeway connecting the old castle to the "new" palace, built two hundred years ago. Stone floors gave way to golden, waxed wood; the air warmed as we made our way up stairs and along carpeted hallways to the Queen's private office.

Cold winter light poured through the circular window in the wall behind a tall, upholstered purple chair behind a wide desk. Queen Constantina rested in that chair, clad in a cleanly tailored violet wool suit, fingers tapping on the desk as she tilted her head.

"You're three minutes late."

Three minutes late. Severin had lied to her in order to take me to my father first. I didn't let my thoughts cross my face. My knee touched the floor. I bent my head, hand over my heart, and waited.

"Rise. We know why you have come," Queen Constantina said. "A number of our other prisoners have warned us of the storm brewing in the Cauldron to the west. But you left the protection of Grand Duchess Aife of the Solace to bring me the news of this storm, risking your own neck with the news a full day before the others mentioned it. What did you hope to gain, Dame Grace?"

I returned to my feet. Severin moved away from me to lean on the Queen's desk, perched by her side.

"Your Majesty. It's worse than anything I've ever seen. I fear the Circle didn't quite manage to power the spell to gentle the Cauldron on Frostnight."

She paged through a stack of letters on good paper, their envelopes weighted by wax seals. I saw the teal of the Blakes, the deep muddy brown of the Pelfreys, caught a glimpse of dark green that could have been the Sibleys. All of them from the new leaders of the Hundred Families, trying to be the first to warn the monarch of the danger only her Invisibles could guard against. "You would have been the one to shape that spell, if Sir Percy hadn't succeeded with his vote."

If she wanted to blame him, that was fine by me. I folded my hands in front of me and quit peering at her correspondence. "Yes, ma'am, though I can't say if that would have changed our fortunes."

"They tell me you have power to match your height, girl. Is it true?"

I nodded. "It's true. But even if Sir Percy had succeeded, this storm would have torn it apart. It's too powerful."

Crown Prince Severin touched the Queen's shoulder. "It's as I said, Mother. They couldn't all be lying. Dame Grace was brave to give herself up like this, and she says the same as the rest."

"I don't know if we can stop it," I confessed. "And without the power of the First Ring . . ."

Queen Constantina gave me and her son a scowl. "And you would have me free them after I called for their arrest?"

I shook my head as Severin shifted his weight off his mother's desk. "No, ma'am."

"Obviously you can't," Severin said. "But you can free Grace, establish her innocence, and she can Call the storm to calm. She can help us."

"There's more," I said. "Do you recall the ritual you witnessed at Frostnight, the one where my brother and I were ousted?"

"Nothing makes me wish for a book more fervently than the Frostnight Ritual," Queen Constantina said. "Tradition demands my presence, but it bores me to tears. But I remember your expulsion, girl. What of it?"

"We had come to warn you about an attack on your person," I said. "My brother was attempting to unravel the mysterious condition some of his patients suffered—patients who had served in the Laneeri War—"

"Yes, yes," Queen Constantina waved it aside. "Skip to the point."

"It was a spell. Necromancy," I said. "Most of the veterans were carrying a spirit of a Laneeri soldier they had killed by their own hand. There would have been a thousand of them present when you accepted the formal surrender of the Laneeri delegation. That would have been more than enough to overcome the rest and—"

"Reenact the Revenge of Lucus," the Queen said. "And you told the First Ring this."

"Yes, ma'am."

Her jaw squared as she swallowed. "And they didn't believe you. As a result, no one told me. It is only sheer luck that caused me to postpone the surrender after the lights went out."

"We neutralized the threat, ma'am. Miles tapped into the power of the aether network and used it to dispossess the veterans. Then we destroyed it, to keep it from consuming any more Aelander souls—"

"Enough." The Queen silenced me with a gesture. "The Laneeri. I want them executed for this."

Severin leaned on the desk again, balancing his weight on one spread-fingered hand. His nails gleamed with a recent buffing. "Mother, one of the Amaranthines is particularly solicitous of the well-being of the Laneeri delegation."

"Which one?" the Queen demanded.

"Sir Aldis Hunter," Severin said.

The Queen gusted out a sigh. "The unreasonable one."

"Yes."

"Blast it."

I stuck my tongue to the roof of my mouth. Queen Constantina the First, cursing? She picked up a handmade wooden pen, its grain shaded by purple dye and then lacquered to a high shine. "We'll need irrefutable proof that they committed this atrocity. Do you understand me? It must be undeniable."

"Yes, ma'am."

"Good." That pen pointed at me now, as the Queen gave me a wry look. "I'm about to run you ragged, girl. Are you ready?"

I touched my chest, just over my heart. "I am."

The Queen lifted the pen as if it were a scepter. "You are hereby granted the Voice of the Invisibles. I assign you to the post of Chancellor. You are to advise me in matters public and unseen."

Warmth suffused my skin. I stood up taller. She had given

it to me. I'd thought I would have to wheedle and beg, but all it took was her word. "Yes, ma'am."

"As Chancellor, you are my chief inquisitor into the matter you have brought before me concerning the Laneeri delegation and their plot to bring down Aeland from within. You must keep the details of this investigation secret. Do you understand?"

Oh. I blinked and groped for words. "I do, but there's a problem, ma'am."

"What is it?"

"I don't speak Laneeri."

That didn't stop her for one moment. "Your brother served in Laneer, did he not?"

The blood drained from my face, leaving behind a chill. "He did, ma'am."

"Did he learn to speak their tongue?"

Oh, no. No, no. "He did, ma'am."

"Use him."

I couldn't do that. "Ma'am—"

She gave me a look that stopped my tongue. "Is there a problem, Dame Grace?"

I didn't even have time to appreciate her not calling me "girl." "Your Majesty, Miles was a prisoner of the Palace of Inquiry for months before the Johnston Rescue." A rescue our father had engineered, because he'd known perfectly well where his son was. And when Father had been ready, he'd moved all the pieces in position, allowing me to find Miles again, ignorant of the truth. Miles had earned freedom and rest. I couldn't drag him into this.

"Then here is his chance to bring justice to his captors," the Queen said. "Include him in your plans."

"My brother suffered grave injuries at Clarity House," I said. "He's still weak. He tires easily. He needs to recover."

"Grant him every possible accommodation," the Queen said. "But I don't want the truth of this to come out until I am ready to present it. Do you understand me?"

Once Queen Constantina made up her mind, she was impossible to budge. Beside her, Prince Severin caught my eye, and gave the tiniest nod. He believed it was the best idea, then.

I'd have to ask my brother to walk back into that nightmare, by royal order.

THREE

To Serve Aeland

No. I couldn't do it. I wouldn't do it. There were hundreds of people in the palace. I could find one who could translate and stay quiet about our assignment.

I headed toward Government House, where the office of the Chancellor—my office—waited for guidance and instruction. I would set someone to researching suitable candidates immediately. It would probably take all week. Janet, Father's—my—secretary, could prepare a press statement, and we had to build the beginnings of a top-level plan to handle everything that was about to come flying at the office. That schedule would probably have me home in time for a late supper. I already wanted to kick off my boots and steal a nap somewhere, but I had to get notice to what was left of the Circle—no. That could wait until morning.

"Grace?"

I halted in my tracks and turned to bow. "Severin."

The Prince moved to my side, hardly noticing the people who halted in their progress in the corridors to bow their heads until he had passed. "Grand Duchess Aife wants to see you."

"Now?"

He smiled and offered his arm. "It would go better for me if I brought you to her, so she could see that you are well. It shouldn't take long."

"I will be happy to meet Her Highness, but I can't stay." I took hold of his elbow and fell into step beside him. "I have to get to work."

"This is work," Severin said. "The Grand Duchess won't go a minute in session without bringing up your incarceration."

Was it Aife's advocacy that had freed me from Kingsgrave? It could have been. I would go and speak to her, but I had too many things to do. "Then I will put her at ease. Where are we going?"

Severin guided me along a hallway lined with masterwork paintings. I barely gave them a glance. "We gave the Amaranthines the ambassador's wing."

I had passed it many times on the way to Government House, the doors always locked, the corridor behind it silent. "I've never seen it."

"I used to explore it as a child," Severin said. "I used to pretend a delegation had come, and all the dust covers would come off all the furniture and the place would be full."

Aeland had closed its borders so long ago the furniture and decorations in the diplomatic wing were ancient by fashion's standards—heavy, dark wood, no spring-padded seats, all of it carved into busy, gaudy excess. I glanced at pedestal tables holding urns filled with hothouse blooms—carefully grown in one of the palace's smaller, shyer sisters to the Kingston Royal Gardens, crowded year-round by the public—

A heavy weight pressed on my shoulders. The Gardens depended on aether to heat the glasshouses and their faraway, exotic specimens. The innocent plants of the public gardens couldn't have survived, or the jewel-colored birds or the butterflies of unreal shape and hue that depended on that splendid glass cage to live.

I had destroyed so much. I had so much I had to mend and make right. How could I undo everything I had done, and what the First Ring had done? The task spread out before me, so vast that I shrank before it.

Severin glanced at me. "All right?"

"Just a passing melancholy," I said. "It's gone now."

Severin nodded. "We're here."

Two dark-skinned Amaranthines, armed and armored, stood sentry by a pair of heavy, black lacquered doors, carved all over with birds in flight.

"Crown Prince Severin Mountrose and Chancellor Dame Grace Hensley to see Her Highness," Severin said, and the guards opened the way to us.

We walked into a room of glass, faceted like a jewel between panes of black ironwork. A butterfly as bright as a flower bumbled toward us, its tiny wings an azure and emerald blur as it wound its way back to where others frolicked under a glass dome. Music thrilled its way over my skin—a melody that made me think of the sparkling reflections of sunlight on a shallow brook.

Aife sat on a guitarist's perch. Her skirts draped over the floor as she played the music that filled the room. Amaranthines gathered in clumps, working on craft or art—I spied spinners, weavers, and a man who tatted lace so quickly his shuttle blurred. One woman draped in nothing but a length of cloth and black hair like a river stood statue still for another woman painting her likeness, and I shivered in sympathy before sending out tendrils of power to warm the air.

A few of the guardians glanced my way and smiled their thanks. I smiled back and waited for Aife to notice our arrival. She stopped playing when she caught sight of us, and the

troop of butterflies vanished in the silence. She set the ebony
guitar on a stand and moved to greet us, catching me in a hug
I didn't have to bend to return. Her hair smelled of luckgrass
and violets, her tight golden curls brushing light fingers over
my cheek.

"You are well," Aife said. "My fears can rest."

I smiled. "I could use a change of clothes and a decent
night's sleep. But yes. I have been freed and assigned the post
of Chancellor. Unfortunately, my duties begin now, so I have
to run—"

She took my hand and squeezed it. "Nonsense. When did
you last eat? The palace staff will be here soon. Stay and take a
meal with us."

I had planned on ringing for a tray while I strategized, but
refusing to eat with an Amaranthine was a sign that you dis-
trusted them. "I will—if there's a spare lap desk and some material for correspondence."

"You can borrow Ysonde's," Aife said, and led me to the
Grand Duchess's black-clad secretary, who stood by a perch
near the glasshouse's doors while hand-feeding his beloved,
raven-black doves. He was the tallest Amaranthine in the
party, his long, braided hair and dark-skinned features so arresting that I had to remind myself not to stare. He nodded at
me in greeting, offering a dove to Aife.

She stretched out her hand, and the dove hopped to her finger. "What news from our friends?"

"The temples are full," Ysonde replied, pushing a silver-
beaded braid behind one elaborately ornamented ear. "People
attempted to gather in the parade square this morning, but a
squad of Queensguards forced them out. There are people lining up for hours to get inside shops that sell food, people begging
in the street for coins."

I listened to this recital with a hollow pang in my stomach. Severin cleared his throat. "Without aether, the people are disrupted. Factories are at a standstill, and there's no work. They're worried about putting food on the table, about being able to keep their homes—it's an enormous problem."

"Grace." Miles rolled to a stop beside me, tucked into a rush-backed wooden wheelchair with a colorful tapestry blanket draped over his lap. "Excuse us, please," Miles said, and Aife nodded her permission for me to go.

Tristan beckoned to me, and I followed them to an unheated corner of the room where the glasshouse met the palace's stone walls. We settled next to the view of an ash tree. It stretched out snow-covered limbs dripping with flame-red berries.

Miles still looked too thin, but he wasn't in Death's arms any more. I smiled through the warm rush suffusing my limbs. "Should you be out of bed?"

Miles rolled his eyes. Around his head, a crown of witch-marks glowed to my Sight, filled with power feeding the intricate spell knitted over and inside his body. When Cormac had first laid the magic on him, it had done the work of breathing, of making his heart beat steady and true. Now the threads of magic were fewer, softer in intensity. "I should be moving more. I'm eating like three horses, I'm putting on weight, I'm getting better—"

"And healers are the worst patients," I said, echoing what the Amaranthine's healer had said in response to Miles's impatience with rest and recovery. "You have to give it time."

Tristan looked up, alerted by movement coming our way, and Prince Severin stopped beside us. "Ahoy, Sir Christopher. 'Miles,' I'm sorry. Your sister told me you preferred 'Miles,'" Severin said. "My thanks for your service."

Miles took the Prince's offered hand. "I gave what I could, Your Highness."

"And for your future service," Severin said. "Grace hasn't had a chance to talk to you about that yet, of course. Still, I wished to express my gratitude."

. Miles's smile had a polite, automatic curve. "I am honored, sir."

I wasn't sure if I could keep my dismay out of my voice. "I still have decisions to make about my plan."

"Miles can help you make them," Severin said. "He's as important to this task as you are."

He patted Miles's shoulder and walked off, pausing long enough to snatch a few pastry puffs from a tray before leaving the gathering. I would have thrown something at his head if it wasn't treason. I laid a hand over my quivering stomach and met Miles's eye.

"Grace," my brother said, almost too quietly to hear, "what was the Prince talking about?"

We left the music and phantom butterflies behind. My stomach growled as Tristan wheeled Miles up the hall to a smaller black lacquered door, this one carved in concentric rings. Miles leaned forward in his chair to twist open the knob, and Tristan pushed him into a chamber decorated in deep blue, ivory, and gilt. A fire slumbered in the grate, and Tristan left Miles's side to wake it with another seasoned log.

I perched on one end of a settee while Tristan draped himself in a chair next to Miles, one leg hanging over the armrest. "What's going on?"

I pressed my lips together and watched the fire. "Severin presumed too much. I wasn't going to say anything. I'm so sorry, Miles. It's nothing you need to concern yourself about."

"Best to just say it outright," Miles said. "What service am I supposed to be performing for my country?"

No help for it. I petted the velvet nap of the settee's upholstered seats and tried to think of the right words. "I told the
Queen about our hypothesis concerning the possessed veterans. She wants proof, and she wants me to get it. Only—"

"Only you don't speak Laneeri, and I do," Miles said.

"Impossible. No," Tristan said, sitting up properly. The heel
of his boot thumped on the antique Falondari carpet. "It's out
of the question."

"I agree," I said.

"He talks in his sleep," Tristan went on. "You know perfectly well that he dreams about that place."

I didn't know Laneeri, but I had a good guess at what Miles
whimpered from the depths of a nightmare. I probably knew
the words for "no," "stop," and "please."

"That's why I wasn't going to say anything. Miles. You don't
have to do it. I wasn't going to ask you. I wasn't going to let you
near it. I wasn't even going to tell you."

Miles wrapped his arms around his middle, staring at something none of us could see. The gently swaying gaslights in the
chandelier above lit the pallor of his skin, his cheeks still too
hollow, his shoulders too sharp, too bony. I clenched my hands,
balling them up to keep from trying to touch him, trying to
comfort him. He could be startled by touch.

"Miles," Tristan said. "You're in Mountrose Palace. You're
in Aeland. Not there. Here. I'm here."

"I know," Miles said. "I know I'm here. I know you're here."

"Tell me five things you see," Tristan said.

I bit my lip and kept silent while Tristan slowly, gently
pushed Miles away from the horrors that would haunt him
for the rest of his life. I swallowed the lump in my throat as
Miles named the things he could hear and smell and feel. He
stretched out his hand to Tristan, and Tristan cradled it like
priceless glass, tracing a spiral in the middle of Miles's palm.

The color returned to Miles's face as he raised his hand and cupped Tristan's jaw.

"I'm here."

"And you're not going anywhere."

"That's right." Miles let his hand drop to Tristan's knee, and turned his attention back to me. "What do you plan to do?"

"I was going to pull personnel records and interview candidates—"

"You need to isolate them," Miles said. "For the interviews. No contact with each other, no way to communicate. Each one needs to be alone. If you keep them together in the initial stages they'll draw strength from each other, solidarity and resolve—"

"No. Miles. This is not on your plate," I said. "You don't have to have anything to do with this."

"I know. And I understand that you wanted to protect me. But I'm the best tool you have."

"Miles, no," Tristan said.

Miles ticked off the points on upraised fingers. "I speak Laneeri. I know how to interview subjects who are trying to hide things from me. I know what tactics you can use to break their silence without stepping over into torture. You won't find anyone else who can do all that."

He was right. We all knew it. But hadn't he sacrificed enough? "They hurt you. They kidnapped you and locked you away and—"

"Used the foulest magic to attack us," Miles said. "And I want to know why. I deserve to know why. You're stuck with me, little sister. I'll do it."

Once I made it to the Office of the Royal Chancellor, all three of my secretaries hopped to their feet and chorused "Good morning, Dame Grace" before the door clicked shut behind me. Janet picked up a clipboard with a neatly typed document.

"Good morning." I took the clipboard and scanned it. Bless Janet. How could I do this job without her? "Thank you, all of you, for continuing to keep operations here flowing in my absence. What do I need to know first?"

"Member Albert Jessup has called an emergency session of the House on the twentieth of Frostmonth to discuss rationing," Janet said. "Do you have anything you wish to add to the agenda?"

"Not at the moment." I crossed the reception room and opened the door to my office, a golden oak-paneled room lined with bookshelves on every space that wasn't a window. The feeders mounted outside the windows were visited by a flock of messenger doves, the feral descendants of the birds used in the days before aether and telephones made their service obsolete. "Is there anything to eat? I've a hole in my stomach."

"Right away, Chancellor. I just updated that report an hour ago." She nodded at the clipboard in my hand. "The relevant source documents are in your tray."

"Thank you." I smiled at her and skimmed the report when she left. Some of it I knew—the arrest of the entire Cabinet, the aether outage shutting down factories, the arrival of the Amaranthines. But there was a report on citizen unrest, from protests and demonstrations to increased incidents of vandalism and heightened crime—culminating in a quickly suppressed riot. I read a truly alarming report about the estimated loss of crops due to the storm on the eighth of Frostmonth.

I had been reviewing the progress of the trial of Sir Percy Stanley when Janet brought me tea and enough lunch to feed three women. I ate it all while she brought me up to speed on the chaos that had run wild in the days while I dawdled in Bywell. We made lists, prioritized tasks on a wheeled black slate chalkboard, and tapped two dozen minor scribes to copy the messages I needed sent by post, restored by royal order to deliver five times a day. The sun cast long shadows across the small square in front of Government House when I finally left my office, weary beyond measure.

It had been a productive day. Janet had been a brick, handling my absence with her usual omniscient efficiency, picking up from when I had only been my father's proxy. She had me up to speed in an afternoon. There were reports to read and people to meet, but not until tomorrow. Not until I had a proper meal and a hot bath and as many minutes sleeping in my bed as I could manage before it all began again in the morning. My sled waited for me at the foot of the stairs, bright and bold, orange as a pumpkin even in the blue-tinted shade that fell on it from the peaked rooftops of Government House.

A dark figure popped out from behind a pillar. I caught the full force of a flashbulb right in the eyes. I put up my hand, blocking another photographic assault, and a familiar face emerged, discolored by the green spots in my vision.

Avia Jessup let the camera hang around her neck. "Sorry! Are you dazzled?"

"Quite," I replied. She wore the same gently threadbare coat, but her hair swung free, dark as a magpie's wing and flashing the same deep blue that glinted off their feathers. I breathed through the flutter in my stomach. "How did you know to wait for me?"

She shook her hair back into place. I blinked, trying to clear the spots that fouled my view of her charming, red-lipped smile. "Pure luck. I was here for the press statement from Member Clarke. I noticed you weren't present."

I sorted through the flurry of motions, memos, appointment requests, invitations, and came up with nothing. "I was in my office, trying to catch up on everything during my absence."

"And imprisonment," Avia noted. "But you're free now. And if you're playing catch-up, do I congratulate you on your formal position as Chancellor?"

She was fast. "There was to be a formal announcement tomorrow."

"Oh, I love a scoop," Avia said, and it sparkled in her eyes. "Congratulations, Chancellor."

"Thank you. But you were explaining how you knew to . . ." I trailed off as I recalled the presence of a bright orange lacquered sleigh, pulled by a team of four, with William and George waiting for me. "Oh."

"It is distinctive, isn't it? Add the boars on the horse blankets, and I knew you were free."

"And you were here for a press statement."

Avia nodded. "Not a lot of interest, by the turnout. A number of the shadow coalition have formed a subcommittee to investigate claims by abolitionists about the validity of the Witchcraft Protection Act."

I hoped the quickening of my heart didn't show on my face. I thought of still, tranquil waters, relaxing my expression. "I didn't know of this subcommittee. Maybe it's in the next pile of memos."

"I have the press statement and a photo, but I think it'll barely make the back pages," Avia said. "Though now I'm bound back to the *Star*. Your appointment shall be in our morning edition."

She was every bit as vivacious as I'd thought she would be. She was a figure of action, staying still only long enough to wait for my dismissal so she could charge back to the paper and drop another headline winner. I wanted to be near her energy and ambition, to bask in the freedom she had carved out for herself. Like my brother, she had given up everything to chase a dream, however risky, whatever the sacrifice. "I'm passing right by it. Hook your bike onto the back and ride with me."

Avia leapt for a black lacquered bicycle that had rust spotting the frame and fenders and lifted it on the bike hooks herself. My footman William helped us into the back seat, and I spread a wool-filled sled blanket across our laps. "We'll have to share the foot-warmer."

"I don't mind," Avia said. We squeezed closer, sheltering against the chill. We pressed together from hip to knee, ankles bumping as we perched our toes on the warming box. Up close she smelled like spiced apple tipsy blended with the floral bouquet of her perfume. "That tunic looks warm. How was your stay in Kingsgrave?"

"Mercifully brief," I replied. "Don't eat the millet. Listen, do you have a smoke? I'm dying."

"I do." Avia regarded me with an impish smile. "I'm mercenary enough to trade it for a few questions on the record."

"Then let's bargain. One smoke, one question."

She laughed, throaty and rich. "Five."

It caught me up, that laughter, making me smile. "Three, like in the stories."

"Done." She slipped a battered tin cigarette case from her pocket and had a pair of ready-mades between her lips in an eyeblink. I reached for the wind and stilled it as she swept a matchstick along the rough side of a matching tin box. She watched the unwavering flame for one surprised moment, then set both cigarettes alight, handing one to me. "So. You're back in business."

I closed my lips over the red-stained end she had held in her mouth. The smoke rushed through my blood, and something in my head unknotted with a grateful sigh. "The Queen appointed me her Chancellor. That wasn't a question."

Smoke trailed from Avia's mouth as we turned left onto the King's Way and passed a temple whose steps were crowded with seekers, their heads covered in short white veils. "It wasn't. But here's one. How did you come to return to Kingston with a procession of Amaranthines?"

I had rehearsed for this one. "Pure coincidence," I said. "I was in the area with a physician who studies battle fatigue in veterans; he needed my influence to visit Clarity House in Bywell, which is where the Guardians first appeared. Their arrival was astonishing. I shall remember it for the rest of my life. My compliments on your photo, by the way. I had no idea cameras would ignore the veiling on their true appearances."

"Thank you," Avia said. "That gave me quite a shock in the darkroom. I have no idea why it happened, but it made the most arresting photographs I've ever shot."

"You'll be famous forever," I said. "That one photograph alone, the rights must be worth thousands of marks."

Avia's smile faltered. "I shouldn't doubt it. Next question. The Amaranthines' arrival coincided with the country-wide blackout, and it begs me to ask: Are the loss of aether and the arrival of the Blessed Ones connected?"

She had good intuition. I had a drag and a long exhale to gather my thoughts. "This is a difficult question to answer. I don't want to imply that the Amaranthines are responsible for the loss of aether. But they are intensely interested in the power that lit Aeland's homes and businesses. More than that, I cannot say."

The horses made it up to trotting speed, matching pace with a peloton of cyclists on their way home from a day's work. Yellow ribbons bannered from their left arms, and some of them gave me and my sled a dark look. Avia leaned toward the small urn meant to catch ashes. I turned my gaze away from glowering cyclists to focus on her.

My response to her next question was poised on the tip of my tongue as she wrote with a sleek silver-trimmed ebonite pen. She raised her head and looked into my eyes, catching me staring. Hers were night-dark, lined with long black lashes shadowing her keen expression as she spoke:

"After the institution of the Witchcraft Protection Act, the first people arrested under the new law were Deathsingers, witches who could communicate with and compel the dead. Around the time the lights went out forty-two years later, thousands of ghosts appeared throughout Aeland."

She pointed. A transparent woman in a white gown and no shoes walked through a clump of pedestrians waiting for the traffic light to turn blue. They shied away from her as she stepped into the street. Cyclists shouted in alarm and horror as they rode right through her.

Avia went on. "You were in an asylum that housed Death-singers at the extraordinary moment when aether stopped working and the Guardians of the Dead set foot in the mortal realm for the first time since the Age of Miracles. What is the connection between these three events?"

My breath stopped. My mind screamed at me to lie, lie. "I have no comment."

She caged me with her stare. "So there is a connection?"

Every rattle and bounce of the sled's runners jarred my bones. "I cannot confirm or deny a connection between the events you have mentioned."

"It's so easy to say 'No, there is no connection' when that's the truth." Avia crushed the coal burning at the end of her ciga-rette in the urn mounted in front of us. "But you didn't."

"The newspaper is no place for sensationalist speculation," I said.

The corners of Avia's mouth turned down. "I'm not in the habit of publishing wild guesses, Chancellor Hensley. I will find corroboration—maybe not from you, maybe not today. But I will keep looking."

"What makes you think there is a connection?" I asked. I could have bitten my tongue. Fool!

"I don't really believe in coincidence," Avia said. "This is where I get off."

The sled had come to a halt on Main and the King's Way, parked in front of a sandstone-fronted building that rose a little taller than its neighbors. At the end of the block, the Eden-hill Hotel soared into the sky, its windows dark and empty of guests. As one of the first buildings fully powered by aether, it stood abandoned and useless in the wake of the blackout.

Avia lifted her bicycle off the back of the sled. "Thank you for the ride, Chancellor Hensley. When I have more questions, I'll look you up."

She shot me a wink and wheeled her bicycle to a rack, where she was still chaining it while George drove the horses around the corner and out of sight.

I tucked the sled rug around me and planted both feet on the warmer, but I felt as if I would be cold forever. Avia Jessup had made the connection. She'd keep poking around until she found the answer—an answer that could leave Aeland devastated if the people learned the truth.

My stomach gnawed at me as I shivered in the back seat, weariness banished by a single question: What was I going to do?

FOUR

An Election

The question gnawed at me through the evening and the rest of the night. The next morning, I bade George stop at the intersection of Halston and 17th and give two cents to a newsboy whose stacks of the latest edition of the *Star* rose to his waist. William brought it to me, and my face peered out at the reader under the headline "Hensley Scion Appointed."

I scanned the story. Avia hadn't written a word connecting the asylums, the loss of aether, the appearance of Aeland's dead, or the arrival of the Amaranthines. I could breathe for today, at least.

I set the paper down on the bench when we pulled up to the headquarters of the Kingston Benevolent Society, the city's most exclusive charity club. A cruel northern wind chilled the citizens waiting to apply for relief programs, who shivered in a great huddle.

I searched the crowd for the green caps of Society workers. "Hasn't anyone come out to take your names?"

They shook their heads. Someone should be out here, talking to these people.

"I'll get someone."

I handed my coat to a woman and put in a request for workers to see to the people waiting outside. The lift was out, so I took the stairs past appointment rooms and clerks' offices, climbing above the larger boardrooms and suite clubs officers used when forced to meet with the public. The private floors smelled of breakfast. I ached with hunger.

I'd cause an uproar when they saw the royal writ declaring me the Voice of the Invisibles. It would be as much work as quelling a thunderstorm alone, but the others weren't unreasonable or stupid. They'd see I was the only clear choice. I wove my way past dark-stained pedestal tables flanked by horseshoe-back chairs. Gaslight chandeliers brightened the room enough to read the fine print on the day's paper, but the scent of newspaper ink wafted as people lowered their pages to stare.

It wouldn't do to rush inside and trot from table to table, wheedling the others into coming upstairs. The scent of coffee carried me across the room to the buffet. I filled a plate with every kind of cheese on offer, tempered by sliced fruit and goose sausage. I smiled at a young man who dropped his gaze to the jacquard squares covering the arm of his chair when I looked at him.

His name bubbled up in my memory. Sir Richard Poole, barely twenty years old, a Second Ring Link from somewhere up north. I knew all the faces in this room. I hadn't talked to them much, as they were mostly Links and Third Ring Callers, mostly young and untried—

Wait.

There wasn't a single Second Ring caller taking breakfast. If they weren't here, if not a one of them was here, then they had to be upstairs. And if they were upstairs, I had to be upstairs. Now.

I set my tray full of breakfast down on an empty table and

walked out of the breakfast lounge. When the door clicked behind me, I took the stairs two at a time, grasping the door-knobs to the sky room to fling the doors open.

The faceted glass dome set in the ceiling was covered in snow, dimming the room enough to need the gaslights. The callers of the Second Ring filed up to a row of three black glass bottles with black and white voting balls in hand. I strode into the room, hand inside my jacket.

"An election is a good idea, friends, but wholly unnecessary." I produced the thick vellum reserved for declarations of law and royal writ. "Queen Constantina has made her decision already. She has chosen me."

Voices babbled one over another—I clearly heard "She can't do that!" among the exclamations and annoyance. I couldn't stop myself—I rolled my eyes.

"Of course she can do that," I said. "She's the Queen of Aeland."

"But she doesn't." Brandon Wellesley ducked his head. "I mean, she never does that. We elect a Voice. Then we inform her."

"We elect the candidate for Voice and humbly offer the choice for her consideration," I corrected. "She's already chosen me for Chancellor—"

Elsine Pelfrey scoffed, shaking her long-chinned head. "The practice of one person holding both the post of Chancellor and the Voice is by no means ancient tradition. It only began when your own great-grandmother manipulated her way into holding all that power. There's no reason why we can't have one person for the Voice and another for Chancellor."

"The Voice *is* chosen by ancient tradition," I said. "We choose the most experienced, the most capable, and the most talented to be the Voice, do we not?"

Elsine's face creased in a most unattractive way when she didn't like what she was hearing. "And that's you?"

As far as arguments went, it was pathetic. "I'm not going to be humble, as there is too much at stake. That person is plainly me. And with the storm on our doorstep and the First Ring in prison, we don't have time to test out an untried Caller."

Elsine folded her arms and slung her chin forward. "We won't follow you."

That was really quite enough. Elsine had been eager to shackle my brother to her side for a chance at more influence in the Circle. "Are you going to go home then, Elsine? Are you going to squint at your needlepoint while this storm makes landfall right on Kingston? Fine. Go." I pointed at the exit. "And any of the rest of you who won't lift a finger against what's coming, you may as well go too. I'll let the Queen know you're staying home that day."

And the others spoke out. "Why should we let you come in here and take over?"

"How do we know that writ of yours is even real?"

"I don't care if it is real. You were ousted! You can't walk in here and expect us to—"

"Grace is right."

The voices stilled. All eyes turned to Raymond Blake. He stood up, buttoning the top button of his jacket. Ray was defending me? Ray, who had given me back Grandpa Miles's engagement ring the night I'd been kicked out of the Circle?

I'd gotten over Raymond's abandonment already, honestly. We knew why we were marrying, and love wasn't even on the list. But what would he get from supporting me now?

He spoke into the silence he had commanded. "This is no time for petty bickering. Grace led us for months before Sir Percy played politics. And then look what happened when the job was his. Frostnight was one blunder after another, and you all know it. You were there. And when the little storm blew in on the eighth—"

"It wasn't that little," Elsine objected.

"I don't know how you can say that when snow cyclone Mabel is pounding on our heads," Ray said. "If Grace had been here, we probably could have saved the last harvest."

I eyed Raymond. "You named it Mabel?"

Ray shrugged. "We needed a code."

"But she wasn't here," Elsine said. "Where were you, Grace?"

"I was in the company of the Amaranthines in Bywell," I said. "Since Sir Percy had ousted me, not just from the First Ring but from the entire Circle, I had no reason to sit around Kingston while he mucked it up. And when the Blessed Ones arrived here, they were not happy. It's a lucky thing I decided to go out of town."

"Lucky, indeed," Ray said, supporting my tattered story. "So now that you're back, we need you to lead us."

"We could hold another vote," Elsine said. "That would be fair."

"The election's over," Raymond said. "I recognize Dame Grace as the Voice of the Invisibles. You should too."

Chaos take him, he was *rescuing* me.

Elsine's mouth was a thin line. "There's obviously a place in the Circle for Dame Grace, but to deny us the chance to elect our free choice—"

Raymond scoffed, his lips curling into his usual humor. "Oh, chin up and take it, Elly. I know you were hoping to be elected."

"Against you? Not likely," Elsine said. "If we count those votes, Ray, you'll be the clear winner."

Ah. The fog cleared, and I could see exactly what I'd stepped in.

"And I recognize Dame Grace as the Voice," Raymond said. "So support her. We've some work to do, reckoning when to meet the storm with the Circle. Let's stop fighting and do it."

I kept my smile on and spoke up. "We have to be ready the moment the storm gets close enough. I did the calculating last night. We begin the working at eleven tonight."

A few people twisted to retrieve satchels, but others sat still, looking uncertain.

Raymond nodded. "Tonight. Let's prepare."

Now everyone moved, capping pens and getting on their feet. Raymond touched my shoulder. "May we speak privately?"

"Of course."

I followed Raymond into a small office. It wasn't like I had a choice.

He shut the door and pinned down a thin pane of magic where wind would roar in the ears of any would-be listener. This smaller meeting room had a view of the street and a cold hearth. Raymond swept out one arm, inviting me to sit. The ghost of Hiram Carrigan lounged on the settee, unaware of us both. He'd collapsed in the card room five years ago.

"It's dark as a tomb in here. Should I ring for anything?" He pulled the curtains all the way back, moving around old Hiram. "Coffee, perhaps?"

I stood where I was. Letting Ray play host would give him the advantage. "No time. I have to talk to the Emergency Relief Program manager and find out if we can help everyone standing in line outside. What do you want, Ray?"

Ray flopped into a deep blue horseshoe-back chair, his head resting against the tufted velvet. "We really should screen those people more thoroughly."

"How many people do you think are jobless right now because of the power outage?" My power outage. I had denied these people the work they did to put food on the table. I had taken away their wages, disrupted the transport of goods they needed to survive. Would they understand? Would they agree that we had done the right thing, taking their miracle away?

Raymond cocked a finger at me. "That's exactly my point. Those are the people who deserve our help."

"I'm not going to argue the philosophy of charity with you. This is a national emergency, and the people who were desperate before this crisis are a sign of how we failed them—"

Raymond scoffed, propping one ankle up on his knee. "If they'd just make an effort—"

"Just tell me what that show of support to the others is going to cost me."

"Nothing." Raymond spread his hands and shrugged. "You're the best person to be the Voice. I'd be a fool to try and stand in your place. I'm good, but I'm not that good."

Oh, this was trouble, and I was in it up to my knees. "And so I'm supposed to believe you're stepping aside for the sake of us all?"

"Yes. Because that's exactly what I'm doing."

And horses could fly. I didn't even bother trying to hide my skepticism.

Ray didn't quite squirm in the silence. "We need to rebuild government. We need a new Cabinet."

There it was. "You want your father's job. Finance Minister."

"And we don't have time for the usual process. It would have to be done by writ."

Meaning I had to convince the Queen to incite a riot in Government House by skipping the usual scrutiny the elected men and women in the Lower House would normally demand of a prospective Cabinet member.

"Do you think the Elected would stand still while an entire Cabinet was appointed without their approval?"

Raymond's gaze flickered away from me, and then he looked me square in the eye. "We don't have time to let the Elected bicker over Cabinet positions. It has to be done by writ. This is an emergency."

He was correct, but my scalp prickled. Something wasn't right. What?

I turned my head and looked out the window. Street maintenance was out rolling down a fresh layer of snow, crushing the track marks of bicycles, skis, and sleigh runners into a uniform surface. Cyclists went around the heavy tampers on winter wheels, continuing on their business, gray and black smudges topped with a dash of color—often yellow ribbon around left sleeves, a sign of their frustration. And stretching taller than my window was the Edenhill Hotel, Raymond's triumph of architecture.

The Edenhill had cost millions to build. It hadn't been open even a year. It stood silent and dark, nonoperational due to the loss of aether power. There wasn't a bank in Aeland that would wait for their loan payments. The Elected would want to see Ray's finances. If the Blakes were in money trouble, he'd never stand against the scrutiny of the Lower House. And everyone would know why within a day.

Raymond's face was sheet-white when I turned back to him. He unflexed his fists and shrugged. "I know you can handle everything on your own. But I can ease the way with the others."

He'd scooped up the Second Ring in the handful of days between the First Ring's arrest and my arrival. His support meant joining his supporters to my cause, exactly as it would have been for our marriage. I'd needed the Blakes' popularity against Percy Stanley back then. Now Ray needed my pull with the Queen to hide the truth about his family's overleveraged wealth.

The real work was convincing Queen Constantina to en-rage the Lower House. But what choice did I have?

"I'll get you your writ," I said.

Ray was going to be a thorn in my side if I didn't do something about him. The Storm-Singers left free were young enough and foolish enough to throw their vote behind a personality rather than the facts, and Ray had been making friends with his peers all through his school days.

William handed me into the sleigh, and the foot-warmer blazed with new coals nestled inside it. I lost count of the num-ber of people in line at the Benevolent Society, now attended by workers in green caps. But my thoughts strayed back to Ray. He and his voting bloc could push me into doing what he wanted rather than the right thing to do for Aeland.

I didn't have a voting bloc. I hadn't attended college, so I was never a member of the Sticky Pudding Club or any of the associations they'd formed while carousing across the cam-pus of Queen's University. Instead of scavenger hunts and se-cret parties, I had been learning how to guide a nation by my father's side. I'd remained in the company of my elders during winter balls and parties, discussing trade and policy, while the others drank too much and danced all night.

I hadn't regretted it. I even congratulated myself for keep-ing my focus on important matters while the others got into all kinds of mischief and forged their friendships. I didn't have any friends my own age, and that was now biting me around the ankles. This was ridiculous! I was twenty-eight years old, and I didn't have any friends?

The sled veered around the corner onto Main Street. People dashed in and out of the building that housed *The Star of Kings-ton*. I looked for a glimpse of bottle-black hair, but it was silly of me to hope for the sight of Avia. She was dangerous. She was looking for the truth. And once she found it, the nation would know what their leaders had done.

I gazed out at the world from the back of my family's luxurious sled, pulled by fine horses and attended by the most solicitous men, and felt the walls of my upbringing closing around me. I needed a friend. Someone who understood what it was like.

I let William and George drop me at Government House, but I walked through the warren of hallways and doors that housed the clerks and bureaucrats who kept the wheels of government turning, across the threshold that marked the border between Government House and Mountrose Palace. I paused at the doorway guarded by Queensguards and Amaranthines and was granted entry into the wing where the Amaranthines guested in the hospitality of Queen Constantina.

The cut flowers had been replaced by fragrant boughs of evergreen whose scent mingled with the smell of burning sweetwood. Each table held a censer that leaked fragrant smoke, filling the hall with the gentle, calming aroma. I moved to the door of Miles and Tristan's suite and waited to be allowed in.

Miles had company taking tea with him in the sitting room next to a blazing fire. The ghosts of two Samindan women stood by the door as if they were guards. Miles looked up at me, lowering a bone-clay mug from his lips. "Grace. There's someone I want you to meet. This is Robin Thorpe."

I turned my attention to his companion on the settee—a short Samindan woman dressed in a smart wool walking suit. My attention went to pure envy at the sight of the spirit-knitted weskit she wore under her gray tweed jacket. The cables of knitting bent and wove over each other, the pattern said to be a protective magic that confused the deadly spirits of the waters and kept their sailors safe. I would have loved to own one, but I wasn't Samindan, and it wouldn't have been appropriate. Dangling from her left sleeve was a yellow ribbon, the long ends hanging to her wrist.

That gave me pause. Miles's friend was one of those who wore their grievance on their sleeve, silently counting themselves among the rebels who wanted to overturn all order and normalcy. I inclined my head, the politest greeting appropriate for a commoner.

"How do you do?" I asked.

"How do you do," she replied, but she didn't answer my smile with one of her own. She bore a face that could have been twenty or fifty or even older, with strong cheekbones and a softly curving mouth, her eyes dark enough to hold starlight in them. But it was her aura that made me stand up straight.

It was normal. But too normal, too uniform, with none of the iridescent flicker that made even a mundane aura appear to breathe and flex around the person. I never would have noticed with a passing glance, but hers was wrong, all wrong, and she tilted her head at my long, silent inspection of her person. Heat rushed to my cheeks.

"I am so sorry," I said. "I adore spirit-knitting. I'm quite entranced by yours. Perhaps I'm actually a water spirit."

"It's a clan pattern," she said in reply. "In case you were wondering."

"I was," I said. "I'm Miles's sister, Grace Hensley."

"Oh, I know who you are, Madam Chancellor. Congratulations on your appointment."

She made me feel as if I stood on the pitching deck of a ship, fighting to stay balanced. "Thank you."

"Robin used to work with me at Beauregard Veterans'," Miles said. "Then she left me for medical school."

Robin shrugged, her smile bemused. "Alas, classes are canceled due to the blackout."

Miles picked up his mug. The scent wafting from it was pungent, medicinal. I recognized it as a fortifying brew meant to strengthen the blood. He sipped and grimaced at the taste. Father never liked it either. "Not even lectures?"

She scoffed. "The entire first year, crammed into an auditorium that was only meant to hold two hundred people? You couldn't hear yourself think. But you didn't come here to hear about the woes of an ex–medical student, Dame Grace."

Miles set down the cup, coughing. Robin reached for the silver water jug. He shook his head. "No, it's all right. She might be able to help."

I didn't have time for chitchat with a stranger. "Miles, there are things happening at the Benevolent Society I wanted to tell you—"

He ignored me. "Robin, tell her about the movement."

Robin grimaced. "Thank you, Miles. I came to get your help precisely so you could reveal my secrets."

"Robin's instrumental in the efforts to end the persecution of witches in Aeland," Miles said. "But she could use some support from the establishment."

Robin's face went as smooth as polished sculpture, her expression carefully blank.

"Is that what the ribbon means?" I asked. "It's a sign that you support freedom for witches, isn't it?"

"It means we all stand under the same sun," Robin said. "The ordinary people of Aeland should have the same rights as our rulers. The vote. Legal protection from exploitation, incarceration, and persecution. Fair taxation. Representation in Parliament that serves us, not just the landowners and bosses who work us to the bone and drain our pockets after. And it means putting an end to the malicious, systematic persecution of witches."

Ah. The talk of university students, arguing for Uzadalian utopia.

It had the ability to capture the imagination of the young—stories of distant nations and their idealist principles, their practice of letting all citizens over the age of sixteen vote for free. They exchanged drinking tales of workers who only worked seven hours a day and were paid a share of the company's profit atop high wages. They wrote of the freedom to travel to any nation in the league. And sometimes, even though our government had done their best to suppress the information, they whispered that witches were free citizens.

Fine talk to excite a first-year student away from family for the first time. Stories of Uzadal were sincere and earnest, but the lore lacked the understanding of the rippling consequences of change, and how even the most carefully planned reform had unexpected losses.

"Especially that," Miles said. "You know it's wrong, Grace. She was there at Clarity House," he explained to Robin. "No one could ever support the asylums after witnessing that."

Father had. He'd built them in the first place. I wasn't like him. I wouldn't ever be like him. But Miles was promising too much, talking of freeing the witches. They would tell people what had become of them, what they had been forced to do . . . and how could we withstand the fury of the people after they learned that?

Robin sighed at Miles. "You're sure she's all right."

"Positive."

Miles was friends with an agitator guided by ideas and dreams, but with very little concept of reality. I attempted a friendly expression. "You have a difficult battle ahead of you. Do you want my advice?"

"No. I want freedom. You can't give me that even if you wanted to."

Makers, how I wish it were that simple. But I could help her. Miles was right. "There are things I can probably do, but it will go better if you call off the protests. They alienate the people, and you need them on your side if you want them to—"

Robin cut me off, her tone and expression cool. "I didn't say I wanted you to save me, Dame Grace. I said you can't give me freedom. We will take it for ourselves."

Oh, Solace. "Change is slow," I said, as gently as I could. "When you set a goal, you can't just grab for the end results. It's a journey of small victories."

She gave me a patient look. "Gradual change from within. I have heard that before, Dame Grace."

"The work you do today will help your children, your grandchildren."

"It will. Because the work I do today will help my friends, my neighbors, and the hundreds of witches unjustly stolen to languish in asylums, because I'm going to free us now. That you would take people from our families to rot—"

"It's worse than that," Miles said. "They were locked away so we could—"

I gripped the arms of my chair. "Don't you tell her that! Miles!"

Miles glanced at Robin, but he spoke to me. "She needs to know, Grace. They all do."

"They can't know," I whispered. "If they knew what our parents and grandparents did, they'd never forgive us."

"Do we deserve forgiveness?"

"We didn't do this! But it's on us to put it right."

Robin watched us argue, the furrows on her brow deepening. "What did you do?"

"We broke the aether network," Miles said. "Me. Grace. Tristan. We destroyed it. That's why the ghosts are wandering."

"You mean the spirits were— Oh Makers." Robin's face went ashy. She covered her mouth with one hand, but she held my gaze, staring into me. "How could you do this?"

"You see? We had to break it," I said. "If we had walked away from that, we would never sleep again."

She shook her head slowly, her gaze never leaving me. "How can you sleep now?"

"Pure exhaustion," I snapped. "Oh, I'm sorry. That was uncalled-for. Miss Thorpe, I don't know how we can help you, but—"

She cut me off with a shake of her head. "I think your people have helped enough."

"Then why did you come to Miles?" I demanded. "He's one of us too."

"He turned his back on your wealth and power. He had to hide from the courts, run scared just like us, trying to help people without getting caught—he's more of a witch than one of you, Chancellor."

She said that last with such scorn I jerked upright. "How dare you."

"Grace," my brother said. "Be polite."

It was cold water dashed in my face. "I won't be insulted by some renegade witch—"

"We took her grandmother. We ripped out entire branches of her family and forced them into a nightmare. She has the right to be angry. I thought you'd understand that."

How could he take her side? My brother, scolding me after everything she'd said? And I wasn't the one who'd done those things, Father and Grandpa Miles had—

And in a different future, where I was ignorant of the truth when Father died, when I became the Voice, when I locked myself in his office dressed in a white veil and wore butterflies on my shoulders, I would have read his journals. I would have learned the secret. And what would I have done then?

I cringed away from the answer.

"I apologize for my rudeness," I said.

"Thank you." But she didn't smile. I wasn't forgiven, even though I'd apologized. What more was I supposed to do?

I rose, smoothing my trousers. "I should come back later. Too much strain can't be good for you."

"I'm fine," Miles said. "Come by when you're ready to start our inquiry."

Miles couldn't help me anyway. He could offer sympathy, but I needed solutions. I had no one to confide in, no one to look over my shoulder and help me plan my next move.

And I needed more power. More knowledge. More skill and experience. I needed the First Ring, and they were locked up in the Tower of Sighs. But so was the man who had the power to shove them into helping me.

That was the only advantage I had against Ray. I needed to use it.

I passed tall windows flanked by heavy blue curtains. Against the snow-covered grounds, a college of red-winged jays took flight in search of better shelter. A dead woman in servant's livery passed me in the hall as I stopped a page to ask for directions. At his word I turned my steps south, toward the Tower of Sighs.

FIVE

Articles of Incorporation

Building a tower to hold Aeland's more distinguished prisoners was a notion couched more in romance than practicality. My thighs burned as I climbed past the cells holding shivering Laneeri nobles unused to the chill of an Aeland winter.

I steeled my heart against their discomfort. These men and women had come to seize power in the aftermath of the terrible vengeance they had planned for Aeland. I stepped around ghosts gathered by the cells, more Laneeri with the unbleached hair of commoners, all of them dressed in their army's uniform, all of them glaring fit to kill. Ghosts could only affect the physical world with monstrous effort, but my show of nonchalance as I strode past covered a churning stomach and palms gone clammy.

I passed by the cells that held the First Ring, interrupting the pastimes of the men and women who had ruled Aeland until Queen Constantina had closed her fist. They read. They wrote. They listened to music on hand-cranked audiophones. Dame Joan Sibley glared at me while she stabbed a needle into tapestry canvas stretched on an oak frame. Sir Johnathan Blake pointedly turned his back on me.

The dead were here too, garbed in the stuffy clothing of the past decades, gazing at the living invaders of their cells. I climbed higher, each prisoner rising in power with my steps. I faltered at the empty, luxury-stuffed cell that belonged to Sir Percy Stanley but climbed onward, toward the highest cell of all.

My father awaited me from his place at the table, a half-eaten luncheon pushed out of the way of his journal and the newspaper.

"You came."

I had. I shouldn't have. I didn't need him.

My father closed his journal, screwed his pen shut. "Have you eaten? It's quail in butter sauce."

The tip of my tongue curled as if the delicately herbed sauce was in my mouth, all the flavors of a beloved dish haunting my tastebuds. "I'm not hungry."

He folded up the newspaper. "Tea, then? I admit that I could use the company. The Amaranthines toured the tower this morning."

"So you met them."

"Prince Severin was with them. A woman, two men. An amanuensis and a bodyguard to the woman, from what they carried."

"Did they speak to you?"

Father's teacup clattered as he set the delicate glass vessel down. "I don't see how anyone could take one look and not see how uncanny they are, how implacable and cold. They hate us."

"They hate what you did."

Father gave me a look full of reproach. "I taught you better than that. You know the old stories. They're lovely creatures, but still monsters."

"Not monsters," I said. "Just dangerous. It seems they're treating you well. You have everything you need. Your comfort is seen to."

"I know you didn't come up here to make sure I was comfortable." Father pushed his chair back, fingers laced over his belly. "You want something from me."

"I want something from all of you," I said. "The storm of the century is breathing down our necks."

"No."

He said it quietly, but it still slapped my cheek. "No?"

"Queen Constantina needs to understand the cost of locking us up like this," Father said. "It pains me to refuse you, but in this we are united. How do the commoners put it? We are on strike."

"People could die," I said. "Don't you care about that?"

"Very deeply. But Constantina refuses to see what she's done without proof. She needs a dose of reality. Ask me for anything else."

If he wouldn't give this, I was sunk. "There's nothing else."

One side of Father's mouth quirked up, a gesture so like Miles I had to swallow a gasp. "You want to know how to gain a solid footing with the remaining Invisibles."

"I can handle it." Oh, chaos and void, why couldn't I keep my mouth shut? Why did I tell him everything, still?

"Don't try to win them over. Don't make deals with them. Don't make promises. You can't deliver anything yet. You don't have that kind of power." He tilted his head and sighed. "But you already did. What did you promise?"

I shook my head. "It's fine."

"What did you need so badly you made a deal you don't know how to keep?"

He rose from the table, as if he could ruffle my hair the way he did to show that he wasn't angry, just sad. And it worked. I spilled the truth, just as I had when I was his fledgling.

"Ray's too popular with the Invisibles. They were in the middle of electing him Voice when I showed up, and then when everyone was bickering at me, he declared his support."

"And they fell in line," Father said. "They belong to him. And he wanted to be Finance Minister."

Even trapped up here, with nothing but a tiny window and the daily papers, he knew the shadows and secrets of the Invisibles. "That's exactly what he wanted."

Father nodded. "Don't try to win the rest over. You don't have what they want. And you don't need them."

Support of the Invisibles was my first priority! I needed them to follow me. "I do."

Father lifted a finger, ready to interject his point. "You have Raymond Blake. He'll tell them to do what you want so long as he thinks you can get him what he wants. Don't be obvious, Grace. He'll be waiting for you to try and wheedle his devoted away from his influence. You need something greater than that, something Ray can't possibly do."

I hovered near the copper-plated bars separating us. I pressed closer, straining to hear his soft voice. "What?"

"Gain the goodwill and love of the people," Father said. "The public's trust. Aeland is a match head, waiting for someone to strike it alight."

"They're frustrated," I said. "They need a champion. Someone who hears them and understands their plight."

Father smiled. "That's my girl."

I hated the swirl of warmth that coiled around my head when he said that.

"Gain the love of the people, Grace, and no one in the Invisibles will be able to stop you."

I slipped a small pad and a pen from my pocket and started

making a list. Reports, appointments with bureau chiefs, and a new idea lifted its head and unfurled—to gain the love of the people, I needed access to the voice of the people.

I had a reason to see Avia Jessup again.

Movement in the corner of my eye halted my rush down the stairs. White-capped thrushes startled off the ledge of the window, drawing my eye to the sight beyond, down in the execution grounds.

A crowd dotted with the red caps of palace scribes and the stiffened lace collars of court officers gathered around the gallows. A flock of reporters in gray felt hats wielded cameras and notepads, ready to report on the event and fly away to their newsrooms.

I searched for Avia in the crowd, unable to help myself. But it was the women in white who made me pause in the cold radiating from the glass. One stout, the other lean, their shoulders bowed in weeping. I knew them by their postures: Sir Percy Stanley's wife, his barely gifted daughter. They stood out of the general crowd near an auburn-haired man who wore no hat, who stood up straight in gray velvet robes, his chin raised to watch the noose swaying above them all.

Sir Aldis Hunter stood still, witness to a traitor's death.

I laid my hand on a pane, pressing my forehead to the glass. I watched until the executioners marched Sir Percy up the stairs, until they draped the black hood over his face and looped the rope around his neck. Sir Aldis watched every moment, unflinching even when the others averted their gazes as the floor opened under Percy's feet and let him fall.

Percy's legs kicked. I covered my mouth, riveted to the smudge of his aura sliding away from his body, gathering into a tiny ball of light floating by Sir Aldis's head.

When it was over, Sir Aldis looked up and over his shoulder toward the window where I stood, his brand-new witchmark shining. I drew back from the window and pressed a hand to the pang in my chest: a flutter of guilt, a thread of anger, the spilling of relief. My enemy was dead. Aldis had taken his soul—what need did an Amaranthine have for a witchmark?

I didn't know, but I was cold all over at the execution. Queen Constantina had picked a man to die for the Cabinet's sins. Once begun, there would be more. Would that soothe the rage of the Amaranthines, or feed it to greater intensity?

It was one more thing to worry about as I navigated the winding halls of the prison and made my way through the wide, art-lined corridors of the palace. The Queen must have ordered Percy's death. What would it gain her? I hugged myself for warmth in the long corridor that led from the palace to Government House. The people despised Percy Stanley. They blamed the Laneeri War on him and had nicknamed him "Minister No." It would be hard to find someone who was sorry he was gone.

But the Amaranthines were opposed to killing. They wouldn't appreciate what the Queen had done. Severin would have to handle their opinion of the Queen's move, as if he didn't have enough to do—

I paused before the door of my office. Avia Jessup rose from her perch on the stairwell, wearing the rakish pinch-fronted hat favored by journalists. The brim dipped low enough to shade one eye, highlighting her crooked smile.

"Miss Jessup." I gripped the doorknob as she walked toward me.

"I told you I'd look you up if I had another question," Avia said. "Are you going to invite me in?"

The delicate, springlike scent of peonies brushed over me

as she came near. I twisted the doorknob and held open the door. "Please come in. Would you like coffee?"

"I'd love some." She rested one gloved hand on my shoulder and tugged me a little closer to murmur in my ear, the breath of her words wafting over my skin. "And some music? I don't think you want this overheard."

Janet wheeled in a cart bearing two bone-clay mugs of strong black coffee and a plate of butterbread cookies, their edges leaking caramel filling. She regarded Avia with a suspicious eye but closed the door behind her without a word. A moment later music poured through the air, the sound protecting us against listening ears.

Avia stood in the middle of my office's sitting room and turned in a slow, awed circle, gazing at the bookshelves filled with sets of identical volumes. "Law books?" she asked. "Oh, thank you."

I handed her a cup balanced on a saucer. She cradled it in one hand, the gesture trained by years of etiquette drills. She picked up the cup and sipped, watching me over the rim.

I stepped backward, putting a safe distance between us. "They're records of law and Parliamentary meetings, mostly."

Avia drifted toward the elegantly carved hearth, basking in the warmth from the fireplace. She smiled in delight at the company of winter birds gathered at feeders outside the windows. "You like birds?"

"My father put those feeders up," I said, "but I can't imagine looking out the window and not seeing them. How did you manage to penetrate Government House? There are guards stationed in the rotunda."

"They took the whole lot of us through. All I had to do was hang back. I'm supposed to be covering the execution."

"You missed it."

Avia dismissed it with a shrug. "John Runson will handle it. I thought my time was better spent here."

"I was going to write to you," I said. "I have a favor to ask you."

Avia set down her cup and picked up a cookie. "Oh?"

"The Lower House of Parliament is holding an emergency meeting tomorrow. For the moment, they're all we have for government. I want to introduce a suspension of the Oil and Gas Consumption Penalty. It's not fair to charge the people for using gas when there's no other choice."

Avia nodded thoughtfully, munching on her cookie. "That means we're not getting aether back anytime soon."

I had an answer for this. "Damage to the national network is too extensive, and the weather conditions too extreme to effect repairs. But even charging the people once is too much."

"True," Avia said. "You'll look good to the people, asking for relief. Is that what you want?"

"I want what's best for Aeland's people," I said. "I want to ease their burden in hard times."

Avia held up one finger, asking for me to wait until she swallowed. She dabbed her fingers on the linen napkin resting under her coffee cup. Her lipstick left a crescent of red on the rim, marking it as hers. "If you really want to do that, you need to stop these crooks from price-gouging at the grocers. A quart of milk is going for seventy cents."

Seventy cents was a lot, then? "What does it usually cost?"

Avia looked up at the ceiling and laughed. "Dear me, Dame Grace. It's usually a dime."

I couldn't help my shock. "That's outrageous."

"That's why we need price caps. Most people pay a mark a month for the smoke tax, but the food situation is utterly criminal."

I studied her. "Jessup Family Foods owns the biggest grocery chain in Aeland."

"Why, so they do," Avia said.

Aha. "And your uncle Albert, who sits in Parliament for East Kingston-Birdland—"

She nodded. "—will throw a fit at the very idea. But if you really want to help Aeland, this will save more people more money."

And it would poke her estranged family in the eye. I didn't like Albert Jessup. Getting a dig in for Avia's sake made me feel like I was defending her. "I'll do it. Would you run a story in tomorrow's paper announcing my intent? I'll have a messenger deliver the particulars to you by end of day."

She grinned and set her cup down. When she straightened up, she lifted her camera. "They'll praise you in the streets, Dame Grace. It might soften the blow for the real story."

I set my coffee cup on the cart and stood for the brilliant flash. "Is this the matter that brought you to my door?"

"Yes. It's . . ." She bit her lip. "It's possibly incendiary. No. It's definitely incendiary. It concerns your father, and your grandfather."

I took a sip of coffee to buy a moment. "What is it?"

"I found the articles of incorporation and the minutes of the first official meeting of the board for Aeland Power and Lights."

She drew photographs from the satchel at her hip. I scanned images of the original documents, properly hand-scribed as all legal records must be. I skipped over the carefully written words to find the signatures at the bottom, a suspicion boiling in my middle.

Grandpa Miles's name was on the document, just under King Nicholas's signature. Father's was the third signature on the list of original shareholders. The other photograph was a record of how many shares each investor had purchased. Grandpa Miles's and Father's shares were considerable.

I lifted my head to watch Avia's expression. "What's this about?"

"Most people think APL is a Crown corporation. The presence of the crowned lamb on the company seal certainly implies that. But it's functionally a monopoly, because the owners can use the government to preserve it. Do you mind if I smoke?"

I gestured toward the smoking set on the low table in front of the settee while I scrambled for a way to dissuade her. "Don't you think that story would only serve to agitate already unhappy people?"

"Well yes, I do," Avia said. "But if I'm looking into it, someone at the *Herald* probably had the same idea. They'll find this information—and since your grandfather's dead and your father is in the tower, you're the one who'll take the blow. I know a thing or two about how the bad actions of one's father reflect on his children."

She had been the Jessup heiress, next in line to receive a fortune and an empire. The papers had called her the Sugar-Sack Princess and had followed her glamorous hijinks with breathless admiration. Sometimes her escapades succeeded in distracting the press from the ongoing struggle between the company and their workers. It wasn't like inheriting the helm of a nation, but if anyone was in the position to understand, it was her.

I swept a hand through my hair, breaking the careful wave set my maid had styled that morning. My hair flopped into my face, and I gritted my teeth. "I have no idea what to do about this. It should be a Crown corporation. But I don't think the nation's treasury can buy these shares back from the owners—and with the network's catastrophic damage—"

"It might be the right time to talk about it." Avia leaned on the mantel, her weight on one foot. "If you look at the names on this shareholder list, most of them are in the tower right now. The crown could confiscate those shares, couldn't they? It'd be a blow to your fortunes, though."

"No. No, you're right again, but proposing that would get me shot," I said. "Do you want a job in my office? If I had someone ferreting out all the skeletons in all the closets, I could really do something about setting Aeland right."

Her answering smile ignited an ache in my heart. "I like the job I have," Avia said. "What do you say to this: I run the story with what I discovered, and quote you as acknowledging that the deal was crooked from the start? Then I'll float the opinion that the shares should be confiscated. It's blood in the water, but you'll look sympathetic."

"You would do that for me?" I stared at her with wonder.

"You've got a tough job," Avia said. "Do you know, you're the youngest person ever appointed Chancellor?"

"Yes. But really. Why?"

"I saw you in the hall before you saw me." She came closer, moving in slow, deliberate steps. I stood where I was, heart in my mouth as she came within arm's reach. "You looked so troubled, alone with your thoughts. You're carrying too much. And when I confronted you with a scandal that would light Aeland on fire, you admitted that what your family did was wrong. It's more than what I did in your shoes."

Warmth spread over my skin at her word. "Maybe you can help me set Aeland right anyway. I know people are unhappy. They want the sun to rise on a better Aeland. I want that too— and that means admitting wrongdoing where I can."

Avia tilted her head and shifted her weight, and somehow she was scarcely a foot away. "What about the wrongdoing you can't admit?"

I really had to watch my tongue around her. "Some things are . . . Solace, everything's hanging by a thread. There are secrets I have to keep, Miss Jessup."

"Call me Avia. Or Avey. Friends call me Avey." She skimmed one hand down my arm, soothing and warm. "Sometimes secrets won't be contained, no matter how hard you try. I'm not the only one looking into the strange happenings Aeland has suffered since the first of Frostmonth."

I shook my head. "I know it's your job to find the real story behind an event."

"It is," Avia said, her voice soft. "I want the real story, but I don't want to destroy you by telling it."

"So you'll stop looking into it?"

"No," Avia said. "The wheels are turning on this story. I can't stop that any more than you can. Let me tell you what else I discovered while I was researching. Ghost sightings were regularly reported in the news and written about in personal correspondence until about forty years ago. Nothing like the Great Haunting we have right now, but it did happen. Until it stopped."

My stomach did a slow, nauseous roll. "That doesn't seem like headline news."

"It's not," Avia said. "Not on its own. But as part of a fuller picture, as one piece in a very peculiar puzzle . . . a puzzle whose pieces are joining as we speak . . ."

I wished I had a cigarette. I wished I could breathe in its steadying calm, give myself a way to gather my thoughts. She was right. Too much had happened, and I didn't have a way to head it off.

I wished, suddenly, that I could tell her everything. That she would share my secret and understand what was at stake if those secrets came out. That I could tell her all the things I had once believed in, now shattered at my feet.

"I can't," I said, and Avia stroked my arm again.

"You'll tell me when you're ready, or when I know so much that trying to keep mum is ridiculous. I will keep looking. I will find the truth. And when that happens, I'd like to run it by you," Avia said. "But I don't know if I can sneak back into Government House again."

"Not without a pass."

She tilted her head and smiled up at me. "Would you grant me one?"

I had to keep an eye on her. I had to keep her safe from my father. I needed to see her again. I moved past her and opened the door separating my office from the reception area. "Janet, will you draw up a permanent guest pass for Miss Avia Jessup? She'll give you all the particulars."

Janet dropped what she was doing to put a pass together. I turned back to Avia, and she stuck out her hand to shake.

"Thank you, Chancellor Hensley."

"Grace," I said. "Janet will take care of you. Good afternoon."

She went out. I stood before the windows, watching a messenger dove feed until I was sure she was gone. She was close to the truth. How could I keep it from her? I couldn't.

Maybe I shouldn't. But it was too much of a risk. I couldn't get that close. I would keep this under control. Mind settled, I turned away from the windows and stepped out of my office.

"I'm out for the rest of the afternoon," I said to Janet. "I'm off to see my brother."

Miles and I had to get started interviewing the Laneeri. The sooner we found out the truth behind their attack on Aeland, the better.

SIX

The Lady of Oaks, Attempt Seventeen

I desperately wanted something to eat, and the stone-walled room we had claimed for interrogation was too cold, too damp. It made the man in front of us shiver, his lower jaw chattering. Our cloudy breaths mingled in the air, and Miles spoke to the prisoner again. I had written only his name for our records—Niikanis an Vaavut, the head priest of the bogus surrender delegation. Like the others, he hadn't uttered a word.

He remained silent, and we didn't have any more time for him.

"That's enough," I said, and Miles wheeled his chair away from the table. I opened the door for him, and we went out. "It's not working."

"They're all trained to resist interrogation, and that was their Star Father," Miles said. He spun his chair in a tight little circle, facing me. "It will just take longer. Especially because we won't resort to their methods. In the Palace of Inquiry, each of them would be cradling an injured hand by now."

I shuddered. Whatever they had done to him, it hadn't been that. "You're sure isolation will work?"

"Isolation is a cruelty all its own," Miles said. "They're alone in rooms that don't allow them to reckon how much time has passed. In a few days—"

"We might not have a few days," I said. "The Queen wants this information now."

Miles shrugged and drove his wheelchair to the next cell. "That might be a problem. For now, we follow the plan."

He stopped before a heavy timber door.

"How are you getting along?" I asked. "Do you want to stop for the day? Do you want to eat?"

Miles looked up. His smile was reassuring and brave, and I didn't believe it for a minute. "This is the last of the diplomats. Let's just get it over."

"We can take a break. Eat something—"

"No." Miles's voice cut like a knife. "When I'm done here, I want a bath. And a drink. And Tristan's arms around me. Let's get this done."

He nudged his wheelchair back. I stepped in front of the door and shoved the long, sturdy key into the lock. Miles guided his chair through the doorway. He halted at the sight of the next woman, who raised her head to stare at us.

Miles stiffened in his chair. "This one. I recognize her from the parade. She smirked at me." Miles spoke to her then, a rapid string of syllables and tonal stresses that made her swipe at her eyes and glare at him. Miles scoffed at her reply.

"She's insulting my accent."

"That's not very nice."

Miles shrugged one shoulder. "Notice that she's speaking. The others didn't. It's a way in. What do you want to ask her?"

"What's her name?"

Miles asked.

"Sevitii an Vaavut," she replied.

"Any relation to Niikanis an Vaavut?"

Miles asked and Sevitii nodded, her reply curt.

"Her father. Vaavut means 'Moon'. It's one of the most common surnames on Laneer."

Miles regarded the young woman—very young, with the unlined face and thick, lush hair of youth. She hadn't grown into her face yet—true beauty for a woman didn't develop until she was past thirty—but she had fine hazel-green eyes made startling by the dark ring around her iris. Still, it was interesting. The delegation Laneer had sent had to be the people they wanted to control the country after the occupation. Why send someone so young?

I thought I knew why. "She's important. Born important," I said. "She's too young to be part of this if she hadn't been."

Miles pressed his lips together and shot a question at her, and she gripped the table and snarled back. "Dead in the black. She's ninth in line to the Star Throne of Laneer."

He paused to listen to her impassioned speech, translating on the fly. "We will of course suffer the most agonizing torments for eternity after our deaths for harming the destiny of the shining family, but she will bargain for the release of her diplomats and Star Priests."

"Oh, child," I murmured, shaking my head at the girl. "How frightened you must be right now."

Her face went white as Miles translated my words to fit in her ears. I went on, watching a tiny line between the stubble of her plucked eyebrows crease and deepen. "This entire delegation is your responsibility, and you must protect all of them. That's the obligation of your birth, isn't it? They're your people, even though you're the youngest of them. They were sent to guide and advise you through the occupation, but you're the true leader of the delegation. Aren't you?"

Miles had the trick of translating on the wing, speaking my words half a moment after I said them. Sevitii's eyes went wide, and then she glanced away, dropping her chin as I explained her situation. Then she raised her chin and spoke.

"I am, by the grace of my destiny and the honor of the star lords who shone on my birth. I am the only one who has the power to parley with you, the only one whose word can be bound into law," Miles translated. "This child is their leader? She can't be any older than nineteen."

"She has an experienced staff, and she's probably been training for the responsibility since she was in pigtails," I said. "King Philip was nineteen when he took the throne, and he didn't do too badly."

She squinted at us, and Miles spoke her words to me. "What do you want in exchange for our freedom?"

"We want the truth," I said. "We know that your country launched an atrocious attack on ours using rankest necromancy, that you ensorcelled your own soldiers with a ritual that would bind their souls to an Aelander soldier, gradually taking control of that Aelander's body. In this way, you brought tens of thousands of murderers to Aeland's shores—"

"You prattle at me of murder," Sevitii growled, her face red. "You killed ten times that number, and then trapped their souls in your foul death temples. You accuse me of necromancy, Soul-Eater? You, who devised a way to deny every soul their destiny in the Kingdom of Solace?"

I ignored this outburst. "I want to know who devised the plan. How you learned the spell. How you passed the knowledge on to your mages. Tell us that, and we will arrange to have you transported back to Laneer."

Sevitii clamped her mouth shut. I slipped my hands into my pockets and waited, but she might as well have been a statue. But I had gotten a great deal from her, and I knew just how to press on her sense of responsibility and her fear of making a major mistake to start the flow of words again.

Miles gazed at her, calm and expressionless, but he kept his hands still, laced together across his stomach. I had to get him out of here. He deserved that bath, and the drink, and the comfort of Tristan holding him. I folded my arms and gave Sevitii an appraising look. "All right. She's talking, and she has the authority to talk. Do we leave her in here?"

"No," Miles said. "Let's try honey rather than vinegar. Do you ever use the Chancellor's suite?"

For naps. For silence. I'd planned on sleeping here instead of going back and forth between the palace and Hensley House, but I let it go. "Only occasionally."

"Can we borrow it? Find her clothing and personal effects?"

"We'll have to take out the weapons. We'll need guards. But I can have her situated in a few hours."

Miles nodded. "Let's do it. We'll put the other Laneeri back in their cells. Sevitii is the key, and if the others think we're doing something barbaric to her, maybe they'll bargain for her safety."

I rose, and together we left Sevitii without a word, locking the door behind us. "Thank you, Miles. I couldn't have done that without you."

Miles nodded, rubbing his stomach. "I never imagined I'd become an inquisitor. It's hard on the gut. How's the storm?"

He knew a bit about how it felt pounding across my scalp. If he'd dared, he would have held my hand and eased the pain like he used to when we were children. He knew how it hurt. But I couldn't tell him that fear surged in me, chilling my hands and stealing my breath. I couldn't tell him how tiny I was, how insignificant I felt against the immense, whirling power coming to bury us. "We're facing it tonight," I said. "I need to sleep. And eat. And a hundred other things."

"Sevitii wanted to talk to us," Miles said. "That's good. We can find out the truth about— Oh, Your Highness."

Severin Mountrose had just come around the corner, sack-suited and elegant in stormy gray flannel. "Sir Miles. Dame Grace. All is well?"

"Very well," Miles said. "We're ahead of schedule. I thought we'd need a few more days. But their leader is eager to speak to us."

"Excellent," Prince Severin said. "That will give you plenty of opportunity to get the truth. Grace. Will you eat with me, after the session tomorrow?"

"I'd be delighted," I said.

He nodded to us. "Excellent work, both of you. Please excuse me."

He continued on his course, strolling through the prison as if it were a garden path. I lingered in the intersection and watched as he turned left, his footsteps' echo getting fainter and fainter.

"What are you doing?" Miles asked.

"Shh."

I listened, and the rhythm of his steps changed as he climbed the stone stairs to the Tower of Sighs. Severin was visiting the mages of the First Ring—no. I knew better.

Severin was going to see my father.

I grasped the handles jutting out of Miles's wheelchair, pushing him through the halls. "Do you mind if I run off and arrange Sevitii's transport? I want her in comfort before sundown."

I had seven hours before I had to lead the ritual. It would have to be enough. All I had to do was put in the request with the guards to station sentries outside the doors to the Chancellor's suite, with a list of who was permitted inside, down to the last servant. I'd have to walk all the way through the palace to put in the orders, so I dragged weary feet along the passages connecting Government House to Mountrose Palace until a hallway full of tall, elaborately dressed Amaranthines blocked my path.

I regarded the backs of long coats over heavily embroidered tunics, the ornamented braids their fashions preferred. I shuffled along behind them, listening to the warm murmur of their conversation—not quite Samindan, but frustratingly close. I fancied if someone would speak slowly, I could pick up a word here and there. What did it mean that the Amaranthine tongue sounded like the first language of literature and mathematics?

"Grace!"

I shook off my thoughts and smiled at Aife. She had broken through the crowd to clasp my hands and draw me into the center of the procession. "We're going to the Gallery."

"I had no idea a visit had been scheduled."

"It's a sop." Aife swept it away with a dismissive wave. "I told the majordomo that I wished to saddle my mount and ride through Kingston, and he was beside himself. He said there were too many logistics involved, and he couldn't possibly arrange anything without proper planning."

The hallways were lined with servants on their knees. I tried not to look at them. Aife saw a young girl in a starched cap and veered away to touch her head. The girl looked up, radiating awe. She stared as we continued past. "I can push for a formal parade if you want one."

Aife groaned. "I don't want a parade. Or a pageant. Or even the upcoming ball, to be honest. I ask the servants if they're happy and they assure me that they are, but I remember those people in the square when we arrived. Ysonde's reports from the birds talk of ragged people, cold and hungry and lining up for food. I want to know what's truly happening."

And hiding the truth from Aife might not be so good an

idea. "I could bring you some of my reports," I said. "I don't have anything that covers the past few weeks. Do you get newspapers? You must be getting newspapers."

Aife gave me a scowl. "I can't read them. I understand you because of a spell. Your writing is meaningless to me."

We stepped past the hallway and into the soaring, well-lit rotunda that housed the Aeland National Gallery. A ten-foot stone statue of Queen Agnes bore the weight of the heavy golden crown of the Aelish kings, restored at last to her rightful head. She wore a sword at her left hip, a symbol of her ascension through battle. Bare toes peeked out of the gleaming folds of her gown and cloak, curled against the cold damp of the King's Stone. Leaning against her leg was a curly-coated lamb, signifying the Queen's childhood as a shepherdess who learned the ways of war and the sword.

Aife craned her neck to stare at the statue's sober expression.

"Good Queen Agnes, the founder of Aeland's restoration," I said. "The Hundred Knights arrived to her keep after their exile and swore to fight and serve her, if she would consent to give them a home. She did—and the Hundred Knights are the ancestors of the Hundred Families, who continue under the same oath as their elders."

Aife had turned to me halfway through my recitation. "And where did the Hundred Knights come from?"

"A kingdom lost to legend," I said. "It was said to be a series of islands erected by magic in the middle of a vast lake. It was supposed to be a beautiful place, where the knights only drew their swords for sport and no one ever died. No one has ever found it, not in years of searching."

Aife's expression went from curious to carefully, eerily blank. Her golden-brown skin lost the rosy glow that made her look so radiant. She remained silent a heartbeat too long before she said, "You're speaking of a place that exists only in stories. An explorer could circle the world a thousand times and never find it, or the ruins it left behind."

She regarded the statue, tense enough that the cords of her neck stood out. I dared to touch her shoulder. "Are you all right?"

"Yes." She blinked twice and nodded, flashing the tiniest reassurance of a smile. "I was taken by the sadness of it. You and your fellow Knights don't know where you came from."

"We came here. This is our home," I said. "We swore it a long time ago."

Aife nodded one more time and turned away. "And these landscapes?"

"A seasonal exhibition," I said. "They're mostly from in-country."

I didn't want to look at them. These squares of peace and abundance put a knot in my stomach. Aeland was under two winters' worth of snow, with a major storm pounding on my skull. The ouranologists had issued warnings this morning, and Kingston dashed about trying to find food and firewood to wait out the storm.

The Blue River had frozen as if it were the month of Snow-glaze, halting the last cycle of trade from in-country to the city. We were getting hungry, while the people in-country had plenty. Whatever fury we couldn't stop here would blanket Aeland in more snow. Come spring, snowmelt would rush through their cheerful river valley towns, sweeping their homes and crops away in floods.

"What are they all looking at over there?" Aife asked. She moved to join the crowd of Amaranthines surrounding a painting. I knew which one it was.

"*The Lady of Oaks, Attempt Seventeen*," I said. "By the master Briantine."

Aife's brow furrowed, and then her eyebrows shot up her forehead as she came close enough to see it.

The subject was a woman draped in the rich silken folds of a garnet-red sheet, the powerful color a complement for the flawless, deep bronze skin of the woman herself. Her hair was a cloud of brown-black curls, so richly detailed they seemed to sway and bounce. Her face bore the high-bridged nose and elongated eyes of an Amaranthine, set in a haunting, sorrowful expression. All around her, oak leaves in the brilliant shades of autumn fell, one of them about to land in her outstretched hand.

Aife's jaw flexed as she gazed on the greatest masterpiece of Briantine's life. She folded her arms and stared at it as if she could light it on fire. Amaranthines scattered as if the wind had blown them away, all of them gazing at their Grand Duchess with deep, silent dread.

She turned blazing dark eyes on me. "Tell me the story of this painting."

"It's considered the greatest work of painting in Aeland," I said. "Briantine was a prodigy. A genius. *A Study of the Human Figure and the Means of Its Capture* is the cornerstone of every artist's education. Briantine wrote and illustrated it at fifteen—"

"This painting."

"Right." I tried to banish the quivering in my limbs with a deep breath. "At age nineteen, Briantine had famously declared that the Maker Halian's gift had come to rest in his body when he was named the royal portraitist by Queen Mary-Henrietta. He was unpacking his new studio when a veiled woman came in the night, wanting her portrait done. He tried to refuse, but she drew off her veil and he could think of nothing but painting her. He toiled for hours and produced what he swore was his greatest work. But when he woke up, she and the painting were gone. She left a bag of golden oak leaves as payment."

She didn't take her eyes off that painting. "And then what happened?"

I drew in a breath. "He tried to duplicate it. He would do nothing else. He couldn't talk about anything else. He went into deep debt, he angered the Queen, but he could do nothing but paint her. This was his last attempt. They found it drying on the easel next to his dead body. He had put out his eyes, then killed himself."

"And so Halian's gift destroyed, as it ever had . . . but not without help." Aife shook her head, softly, sadly. "Leave me here. I wish to be alone."

I bowed my head and backed off. I turned and nearly collided with Aldis, who took my arm and led me away, pausing before a painting of children playing in a sleepy, sunny peach orchard bursting with fruit. He looked nearly as angry as Aife did, but this time it was at me.

He jerked me around to face him, his face furious. "What have you done with the Laneeri?"

"Unhand me." I wrested my arm from his grasp—without applying the shin bruising he all but begged for. "What were you doing, binding Sir Percy's soul to you at his execution?"

"My duty to the Hand of the Throne of Great Making," he said, "not that it's any business of yours. I am a shepherd of souls. We did not wish to lose track of this one."

That had to mean the Amaranthines had some other plan to get justice from the people who'd had the asylums built. Aldis didn't have to tell me that. But that didn't mean I could confide in him like a friend. "The move is temporary. The cells are being cleaned and made more comfortable, and then the Laneeri will be returned."

"How long?"

I'd just made another job for myself. I would write it when I made it home, and it would be on Janet's desk first thing in the morning. "Two days."

"Unacceptable."

"You asked for this," I said. "You said they were being kept poorly. Now you're angry because we're improving their cells. I could give you a bag of gold and you'd complain that it was heavy. If you don't like it, take it up with the Grand Duchess. I'm sure she's in the mood to hear it."

His nervous glance at the Grand Duchess standing alone before *The Lady of Oaks* warmed me, however petty it might be. I walked away from him and past a portrait of Princess Mary, letting my feet carry me all the way to the guard station where I should have been an hour ago.

SEVEN

Sing Down the Storm

The storm-headache, a bruised arm, an endless list of tasks that needed my approval—hours were eaten while I tried to settle enough issues at Hensley House to reassure the servants and get some sleep. But though the smooth silk sheets were infused with a fragrant herbal blend meant to encourage slumber, the bed cozy from a half-dozen warming pans, I couldn't relax. My thoughts dashed from one problem to the next, denying me peace. Sleep came, but it had to be banished minutes after it arrived.

William and George packed in extra warmers for the short trip to the pale moonlit building that stood on the edge of a cliff and gazed at the confluence of the river and the sea. The Knightshall was the westernmost point of Kingston, our bulwark against the fury of the Cauldron. I leapt from the sled and dashed into the building, passing long buffet tables groaning under the weight of enough food to supply three times our number. Not a scrap of it would go to waste. I hurried past white-robed Secondaries gobbling down pasties and threw open the door of the Hensley suite. I would eat when I was dressed—

Teal curtains stopped my headlong rush surely as a brick wall. Had I gone the wrong way? I hadn't. I knew the path from the front door to the finest of the dressing suites. That was our fireplace, though Great Grandmother Fiona's portrait had been taken down. The windows showed the proper view, though they were curtained with teal velvet instead of orange—

I stared at the portrait that had usurped Fiona's. A wide-browed man with thin wisps of ashy hair, that particularly sensual curve of the upper lip, but the nose told me who had taken my suite before the movement of the room's air announced the presence of a visitor who didn't bother to knock. Of all the—

"Grace."

I turned to confront Raymond Blake, pointy nose and all. "Why did you take my suite?"

He smiled, a cajoling, come-along smile. "That was a mistake. The election . . . well. They were just trying to show initiative. Everything will be put back."

Did I believe that? No, but I had to let it go. "I'd like to make some changes to the reception room anyway."

"Of course," he said. "I'm sure you have a grand vision."

Trip and fall in a hole, Raymond. I used a well-rehearsed smile. "Is everyone in attendance? Have we gathered everyone we need?"

"You were the last. But where is your Secondary? You haven't lost him already, have you?"

Blast it to pieces. "Miles has sustained serious injuries and recovers in the care of the Amaranthines," I said. He also wasn't bound to me anymore, but I wasn't about to start that conversation.

"I'm sorry to hear that he's unwell, but I'm glad to hear he hasn't run away again," Raymond said. "That would have been too embarrassing."

"Indeed," I said. "I'll let him know you wished him a swift recovery."

The others would expect Miles in tow, attending me during Storm-Singer business. I had forgotten that Father had forced us to bond. That was going to be a problem, but it could wait for another day.

I retreated to the dressing room with an open door illuminated by the gaslight. Hanging on the valet stand was the robe of the Voice. Black silk, beaded all over, subtly sparkling like the night sky. Dozens of small jet buttons closed the front all the way up to the standing collar. It was a masterwork.

I had imagined the first night I put on the full vestments of the Voice of the Invisibles. In all my imaginings, it had never been like this. It had meant something. It had felt like something. I should feel different.

A bell sounded in the corridor, calling the Invisibles to the ritual hall. I turned my back on the Voice's robe and found a kettle full of water that had cooled to lukewarm. I bent over a basin to wash my face before shrugging into the robe's full, shimmering folds. I had to re-earn the respect of the Invisibles, and this ritual would be a step forward—or back.

It was time to do magic. I banished doubt and hurried to the ritual hall.

The Sky Chamber looked empty without the First Ring. Secondaries sat scattered around the padded red bench built along the curving walls, their white robes the only teeth left in a poor man's mouth. Links stood in their places on the inlaid floor patterned in the interlocking pentacles that was the template for dozens of mages weaving their power together, and our place inside it.

The storm swirled in my awareness. The path would

scythe over Kingston and continue south, where it would strike the coast and its scattering of islands, shredding the ribbon of Samindan-settled towns that fished and sailed and gathered pearls, then drive farther south to become Edara's problem and not mine.

I took my place on the violet tile that marked the center of the room. Through the dome above me, fast-moving clouds driven before the storm churned as we sang the ritual. By the first chord, they parted and let starlight fall on us.

The song wasn't the power. The song guided each singer to cast their power, first into a coil that melded the raw energy of their bound Secondary to their trained skill, then into the work that braided the lines together. I would spin their magic into a force that could dissipate a squall, bring moisture to dry earth, change the path of the wind across miles of ground.

The power grew with every voice. In the Sky Chamber, a hundred twenty-six mages and as many Secondaries put their power into my hands, and it wasn't enough.

I dragged them all with me to meet the storm's arms, fighting its force to reach the center. My stomach growled. Unfortified, I pressed on, guiding us through the unreal cold and furious wind. Where should I start?

Stretch it, Father had said. We didn't have the power to do that. Maybe with another hundred mages on the other side of the storm—I had thought it immense, when I sensed it. Miles across. It was at least as wide as Kingston itself, just in the eye. We didn't have a hope of stopping it and never had, and that wasn't what made me want to weep.

I could barely hold our power inside the storm. I couldn't split it—not even in half, or we'd all get knocked aside, blocks tumbling from the swipe of an angry child. Whatever I did, it had to be with our power united.

"Why aren't you doing anything?" Raymond asked. "Do something."

The whole construction wavered at Raymond's words. Curse the man to void and chaos. No one would forget that I had met the eye of the storm and faltered.

But I wouldn't let him drive me into foolishness. I wouldn't act until I was ready. We were in the eye, and my joints ached as if I stood in it, the pain throbbing in my forehead and temples. This was the storm's engine, the heart of the destruction that moved steadily toward us, and I couldn't stop it, couldn't stretch it, couldn't slow the cycle—

I couldn't slow the wind, but I saw a way.

"What are you doing? You have to do something!" Raymond exclaimed. "Try, you have to try!"

"Ray. Please be quiet. On your toes, everyone." I teased out the strands of our magic into the eye, spreading across the air warmed by the Cauldron. "Chill the air in the eye."

The Storm-Singers from the country Circles understood immediately and set to work. The storm was the battle between warm air and cold, and it would rage until cold won. The country mages who brought the rains and calmed cyclones every summer knew exactly what to do. The rest watched for an instant before copying the rainmakers.

The winds howled, but didn't the eye narrow somewhat? I stretched out my awareness. The storm spiraled around its center, the difference barely noticeable. We had hit on the solution, but we didn't have enough power. We needed double the mages we had if we were going to halt it. There was nothing left to do but pray.

O Guardians, you deathless ones, watch over us—it was a prayer for the already dead, a wish that our loved ones would find comfort in the Solace. It was the only prayer I had ever learned, living in my father's house. *Please. Please, help us.*

I didn't know who I prayed to.

I didn't know who answered.

A line of power stretched into my awareness. It was wound into a cable of power that staggered me. It wasn't just the immense might of that energy, but that each line was equal in strength and talent . . . this was two mages linked together, rather than a mage and a bound Secondary.

It wound around our lattice, and strength filled my bones. My knees stopped wobbling. And the power—that bright and glorious power—spread into the eye and joined our efforts, freezing the air to match the cold winds that churned around the center of the storm. It shrank a little more, like the pupil of an eye shying away from the light.

This had been the first. Another storm would come. And another. How long would we last against the Cauldron? Without the First Ring's power, how long could we stand?

One of the Links fell to the floor in a faint, and then another, closer to me, collapsed with a little cry. We had pushed to our limit. The storm had degraded, but it was still coming for us. One by one, the mages arranged around me withdrew their power from the Work, unable to go on. But the mage duo worked until only I remained, then withdrew, retreating back to the boundaries of their bodies.

I fought dizziness to trace their path back.

As I watched the trail of the mages who helped us, sparks of light ignited on the southern border of Kingston—witches, risking discovery to meet the storm that threatened us. More than a hundred witches clumped in the middle of Riverside, rising to meet the winds. It shivered over my scalp. They had waited until we were done. They had watched us weave power and then had plunged in to help after we expended ourselves— how many times had this secret Circle risked discovery when Kingston was in danger?

I didn't need to know. If I brought attention to them, the Examiners would swarm Riverside looking for people to lock up. And I couldn't spare them a moment, not when I needed to know who had helped us meet the storm.

I swayed dizzily and fell to my knees. Sickness roiled through me, and the shrinking, trembling weakness in my limbs couldn't hold me up anymore. I hit the floor, exhausted. But still my senses extended past my body as I chased that bright, unnatural power as it disappeared inside the multilayered, ancient wards set on the seventeen domes of the palace.

Our saviors had been Amaranthines. They had helped us all the way from the palace while the elders of the First Ring sat in their cells and did nothing.

Then I was back in the Sky Chamber. It spun and tilted so wildly I had to close my eyes, breathe, and wait for one of our attendants to get to me.

Many hands eased me onto a stretcher. "Send a message," I said. "To Her Highness Aife of the Solace. I humbly request an audience—"

No one listened to my ravings as they took me somewhere to sleep.

EIGHT

A Wall of Secrets

Kingston was blanketed in our failure by morning. Three feet of snow had landed on the city, but there was an emergency session at Government House, and I had been the one to call it. I had William search out a waxed pair of skis and my old boots, and I selected the quilted tunic that had kept me warm in the Amaranthine camp to wear on my expedition.

Workers had already ventured out, attempting to tamp the snow down into dense layers. People were digging their way out their front doors, helping each other clear snow, sharing hot drinks that steamed in the chilly air. I was cheered by the resilient determination of Aelanders. I skied along, warm from my exertions, and made it to a near-empty Government House.

I passed through the quiet corridors intent on the palace. Two Amaranthines had helped us fight the storm last night, and I meant to find out who. But when I arrived in the wing of the palace where the Amaranthines quartered, a red ribbon was tied to the doorknob of the room where Aife received guests. Not available, then. I turned to Miles and Tristan's quarters and knocked. Miles answered the door. He was already dressed, a gleaming olive silk tie snugged against the collar of his shirt.

"I knew you'd come, even after exhausting yourself last night." Miles rolled down the hallway, and I scrambled to catch up. "That storm was a monster. I've never seen so much snow in my life. I don't even know why you showed up to work today."

We nodded at the Amaranthine guards and hurried into a corridor lit by temporary gaslamps casting a pale green glow on the walls and floor. "It's an emergency session, and the day I let Elected Members go wild in Parliament without me is the day of my death."

"Ah, clarity." Miles glanced at me with a little grin. "So Sevitii's had a night in comfort. Now we see if she's grateful for the luxury, or whether it inflames her sense of importance."

"Which do we want?"

"A little of both— Oh." Miles rolled to a halt in front of a flight of wide marble stairs.

My face flushed, hot and embarrassed. "Blast it. I didn't think."

"It's all right. I can make a flight of stairs, if you'll handle the chair."

It was awkward, but I pulled it up the stairs while Miles took the obstacle at a walk. "See? Nothing to it."

He was doing much better than I feared, his breathing only a little labored when we reached the top. He planted himself back in the cushioned seat and propelled himself down the hall. "Is it still the same suite?"

His wheels slowed as they met a long, narrow carpet meant to muffle footsteps. "Can I push you?"

He sat back with a sigh. "Go ahead."

Soon we stood before a golden oak door flanked by guards, who didn't know which of us to look at.

"Who has seen the prisoner?" Miles asked.

The guard with two golden bands of rank on his sleeve

answered. "Only the two maids you assigned, and never without guards. Will you be going in alone?"

"Yes. Thank you."

They unlocked the doors, and I led the way inside.

Sevitii was transformed. The dark roots of her hair still showed, but her astonishingly long hair shone from a recent washing, fastened in a braid as thick as her wrist and hanging down to her ankles. Instead of undyed hemp she wore saffron and rose in light, floating layers. Her face was painted ivory, her eyebrows plucked and repainted in an exaggerated arch over eyelids powdered in rose and lined in gold. A gold line ran straight up the middle of her countenance from the base of her throat to her hairline.

She looked like one of the full-face masks the Laneeri painted to represent ancestors, and the return of her clothing and cosmetics had bolstered her confidence. She swept her arms open in welcome, as if the room were her property and not her prison. "I have water for flower tea. Please make yourselves comfortable."

Miles translated that line with a half-amused expression. "I think she chose arrogance."

"You said that wasn't necessarily a bad thing."

"She's had time to think. Play along, let's see what she says."

"Thank you for your kind offer of tea," I said. A glass tea set rested on the table, the pot already filled with blooms that had been rolled into balls before they were dried. One of the chairs had already been pulled aside, and at the seat in front of the window, Sevitii had written documents in the curving, utterly puzzling alphabet of Laneer.

I took the seat opposite, resting my hands on my knees. Sevitii poured, and the blooms spun in the water, ready to unfurl. "The wind howled all night," Sevitii remarked, setting the kettle down. "And the world is vanished under 'snow.'"

That last word had been Aelander. "This is a storm the likes of which we have never seen," I said. "I notice that you have written something. The composition is beautiful."

"It is my offer," Sevitii said. "Do you wish to know what is written?"

"I'm very curious." I wasn't sure if I was following the politest conventions, but Miles was no doubt compensating for my lack of manners.

"They are simple. I know the truth behind the plan to usurp Aeland. I want you to understand that our action was a means of defense, not just for our land but for the souls of our people. I tell you this freely, but for the rest, I must be satisfied with our bargain."

Miles shook his head. "She wants something big."

"So I gathered," I said. "What would satisfy you, Honored Sevitii?"

She sat back, draping her arms across the back of the settee. "Laneer is a free land. We have been ruled by the actions of the stars for centuries, enjoyed prosperity and happiness through the guidance of the Star Throne for all that time. My country cannot flourish without the true rulership of the Star Throne and the horoscopes. We must continue our way of life, with the freedom we have always known."

I navigated through this circuitous talk and drove for the point. "You want Laneer's independence restored," I said.

"I will give you the truth for nothing less," Sevitii replied.

Miles knew about interrogation, but this was not that. We were firmly in my domain. Sevitii wanted the impossible. She had to know that if she had been trained the way I had.

I paid attention to the unfurling blooms of Sevitii's untasted tea for a moment before looking at her. "That's not going to happen, and you know it."

She remained unbowed. "Nothing less. Here is my offer."

Sevitii let one hand drift to the seat cushion where the document rested and leaned forward to offer the paper. Only the right half of the page had been written on, using a pen with a nib that widened according to the pressure the writer exerted on it. I wondered if she'd used my father's gold pen to write this document. She liked gold. I supposed she had. The left side of the page featured a diamond shape filled with stylized letters. It was something one would order for a signet, for stamping a family mark in wax, but she had hand-scribed it with skill.

I took it in careful hands. "Can you read it?"

"Yes." Miles stretched out his hand. He read the single page and nodded. "It says exactly what she wants: information in exchange for Laneer's sovereignty. Are you going to take it to the Queen?"

"Severin."

Miles nodded. "A better choice. Is there anything else you want to tell her?"

"I think we've said everything, honestly. Oh. Thank you for your offer. I will take it to the royal family and see if they can forgive your plot to murder them and usurp their rule."

Sevitii's expression went stormy at Miles's translation, and my heart skipped a beat. She was so young to be in this position. Young, and alone, and probably frightened. But she said nothing, staying firm on her demand. Part of me admired that resolve. It was brave. What would I do, in her place? I was suddenly glad I had never needed to know.

I rose to my feet. Miles wheeled his chair toward the door, and we made our way back to the main floor of the palace.

Miles took the stairs down much more easily and settled himself back in his chair with barely a gasp. "Back to work with you?"

"In a moment," I said. "There's something I want to ask you."

He started the chair rolling, skimming his hands along the wheel-hoops. "Go ahead."

I quickened my step. "Not here."

He caught up and kept up, not letting me push him. We hurried back to Miles's suite, where he spun his chair around to face me. "What is it?"

I glanced around the room, but we were alone. "You know we did a ritual last night."

Miles nodded, but something in his eyes went wary. "That had to have been one deuce of a storm."

"We drained ourselves. But I saw something."

The corners of Miles's mouth pulled in. Just a little, but my senses went on alert as I went on. "Two mages in the palace helped us. Their power was staggering. It had to be Amaranthines."

The color returned to Miles's fingertips, filling in with pink. "Do you want me to ask Aife?"

"Please. I have so much to do today, I'm not sure I'll get the chance."

Miles nodded. His shoulders sank into a relaxed position. "I'd be happy to."

He smiled at me, his guard lowered, and I smiled back. "And what can you tell me about the Circle of Storm-Singers down in Riverside?"

It had been a mistake. I knew that the moment Miles glowered at me. He spun the wheel hoops in his hands and rolled to the fireplace, where he caught up a poker and assaulted the fire.

"It was a dirty trick. I'm sorry," I said. "I shouldn't have gulled you like that. It was wrong to treat you like someone I needed to take advantage of, Miles. I will just tell you straight out when I want something."

"I won't deny knowledge of what you're talking about," Miles said, his voice flat. He took up tongs and laid more wood on the coals. "But I won't tell you anything."

"Good. Don't," I said. "But get a message to them. Tell them I spotted them. And I thank them for their risk and sacrifice, but they must be careful, even when we desperately need their help."

Miles eyed me. "You won't tell anyone?"

"Solace! No. The last thing I want is Storm-Singers carted off to asylums in the middle of the worst storm season in history."

Miles turned his head, and the look he gave me made my knees turn to water. He wasn't angry—that would have been bearable. He looked at me with sadness. Disappointment.

It made my insides flutter with the need to fix it. "What?"

He stared at me a moment longer before shaking his head. "You don't see it."

"See what?"

Miles put the fire tools back and rolled closer. "I can't tell you. You need to see it for yourself."

Oh, I hated feeling like this. I had done something, said something wrong. But I didn't want the Riverside witches caught. What was wrong with that? "I have no idea what you're talking about."

"I know." He pulled the hand brake and pushed himself to his feet. "But I think you will."

He drew me down so he could kiss my brow. "Go govern Aeland, little sister. I'll pass on your message."

I had barely enough time to read any motions that the others wanted, but I could nap after—no, I'd told Severin we'd eat after. And I had to tell him about Sevitii's audacious negotiations. It was going to be another long day.

I rounded the corner and spied a pair of skis leaning in the wall rack next to my office. I studied them for a moment, as if my inspection would allow me to intuit who'd left them there. They weren't the new style, by the bindings, and that left out the presence of the fashionable set. An Elected Member would have left their skis to dry at their own offices. That meant someone who had business in the building, but who wasn't staff—

I didn't know if my heart leapt from happiness or fear. I pulled open the door regardless. The clatter of typewriters stopped as I walked into the office, Janet and her staff of secretaries rising to attention as I walked in. Another figure rose as well.

Avia Jessup was dressed for a day of winter frolic in long-toed ski boots with felted gaiters buttoned from her ankles to the cuffs of tweed knee-breeches. A matching jacket swung open over a peerie knitted vest, the tiny patterns knitted in black and white over a gray background. She bore a newspaper tucked under one arm, then drew it out and showed me the headline below the fold on the front page: "Price Caps on Necessities—Chancellor Hensley's Proposal in Parliament Today."

"Oh that's gorgeous," I said, and her grin answered my own. "Did you come all this way just to give me the first glance?"

Avia tossed her head, and her hair fell exactly in place. "I'm hoping you can give me a statement about the closure of the Royal Gallery yesterday."

"I'd be happy to." I moved in to pat the quilted shoulder of her jacket. "Do you have time to talk?"

"That's why I'm here," Avia said. "Thank you."

Philip was already at the bench of the pianochord and ready

to play music to muffle our conversation. I ushered Avia inside my office, inviting her to sit, but she wandered from the library to the room that held a long table suitable for dining or small meetings. She trailed her fingers over the gleaming, waxed surface and raised her head.

"I know the Amaranthines were in the National Gallery yesterday. Were you there?"

"I was." I moved to the nearest chair, but she picked her way around the table until she was at my side.

She leaned on the table, swaying closer. "The public was kicked out without notice. I imagine that the expedition wasn't scheduled."

"It wasn't. Grand Duchess Aife is restless. She wants to see Kingston and meet its people, but the word of the palace is that it's too dangerous."

Avia rolled her eyes. "They're Amaranthines."

"And thousands could trample each other for a chance to get close," I pointed out.

"Hm. You're right." She studied a point below my chin. "You're rumpled."

"I am?" I froze as she raised her hands and flipped up the collar of my shirtwaist, her fingers gliding around my neck. She felt all around my tie, pulled gently on the silken knot, and resnugged it.

I stood absolutely still, riveted to the intent look on her face as she folded my shirt collar down and smoothed it over the neck of my knitted vest. She concentrated on her task, fussing over the lay of my lapels. She stroked her fingers along my shoulders and then looked up, her dark eyes sparkling over a gentle smile.

"That's you put to rights."

I trembled. "Thank you."

She touched me again, her hand curled on the knob of my shoulder. "You wouldn't let me walk away with my collar askew like that. Do you think she'll get the trip into Kingston that she wants? The Grand Duchess, I mean."

What could I rumple, so she would volunteer to fix it? The sensation of her touch clung to my skin, even though she had only handled my clothing. "No. Oh, they'll take the Amaranthines out, but it won't be the way Aife wants to do it."

Her smile widened. "You call her Aife."

I flushed. "She likes me."

"I'm not surprised. You weren't what I thought you'd be at all."

I cocked my head. "You thought I'd be different?"

"I thought you'd be all smile and no substance," Avia said. "But instead, you're serious. You're conscientious. You listen to criticism of your ideas—and you are dangerously honest, for a stateswoman."

I glanced away, trying to hide my smile. "I thought you would sell my soul for a headline," I confessed. "It wasn't a very nice thing to think."

Avia winked. "That was before I understood what a complicated situation you're in; otherwise I would have parceled it out in ink for two cents a copy."

I wanted to laugh, but she went serious, her mood turning on a dime. Her hand slid down my sleeve and left fuzzy warmth in its wake.

"You're in something deeper than I know." She looked down, her long eyelashes sending fringed shadows over her cheek, and then she tilted her face up, so close it made my heart pound. "You're in it alone," she murmured, and it sent shivers racing across my scalp. "It's painful to be alone."

She must have felt it. Maybe after she had been cast out

of her home. Maybe when she started her first day with the paper. Maybe as she rose from "Star Staff Photographer" to "Avia Jessup, Star Reporter."

The truth fell from my lips before I could stop it. "I hate it."

"You don't have to be." Her hands were on me again, stroking, soothing, calming me even as they fed the flame that lit whenever I saw her, the fire I had to keep covered, keep secret. I wanted to tear it all open so badly—take her hands and look into her eyes and tell her all the things I locked inside. Just so I wouldn't be alone. Just so I could have someone with me who knew it all. Just so I could let down all the manners, all the images, everything Grace Hensley was supposed to be.

But I could never do that. "I can't."

Her hands fell to her sides.

"One thing at a time," Avia said. "I have to tell you something else. Another research discovery."

"I'm suddenly filled with a sense of dread." I smiled to let her know I almost didn't mean it. "What have you uncovered?"

"I've been talking to men returned from the Laneeri War," Avia said.

I went still.

"Not many, just a dozen or so. Their wives and mothers say they've come back with the brightest parts of their souls extinguished."

"It's battle fatigue," I said. "We were supposed to help them with the Veterans' Recovery Act. I want to reintroduce the bill as soon as I can—"

Avia touched my lips. "This is more than just battle fatigue, I think. Three young men came to the *Star* to see me. Once they'd had enough beer, they told me that they had nightmares, walking visions. They heard a voice speaking in their minds."

Miles would understand this. Miles would know. Maybe I could put them in touch. But Avia wasn't done talking, so I focused on her face and listened.

"They all fought urges, fearing they would lose control of their bodies to this voice. They all believed that if they lost the battle, they would succumb to what the voice wanted: to hurt the people around them."

I held my breath. Miles had told me about this. And now the men were talking, telling people what they had felt and believed was happening to them.

But Avia went on. "They told me of fellow soldiers who read the news, and they all knew those men who had killed their families had the same problem. Some were so terrified of what they could do if they lost control that they took the final resort, just to keep their loved ones safe."

"That's horrible," I said, but she shushed me again.

"They all had another thing in common," Avia said. "The voice in their minds always spoke Laneeri. And all of them reported relief from their symptoms, recovering on the same day—within an hour of each other. Do you want me to tell you what day that was?"

She didn't have to. I knew exactly what she was talking about. I knew when it happened, and how—I had been there when Miles nearly killed himself weaving the magic that freed them.

I sidestepped away from her and hurried to my coat rack. My colorful quilted tunic hung next to the black robes Ministers wore to sessions of Parliament. I pulled the robe from the hook and busied myself with settling it on my shoulders.

"I have to go," I said. "Session is in a few minutes."

Avia followed me and halted a few feet away, crossing her arms over her ribs. "I know you were there, Chancellor Hensley."

I lined up the front edges, careful to put the first of dozens of covered buttons in its matching buttonhole.

"You were at Bywell on the first of Frostmonth. The day the lights went out all over Aeland. The day the Great Haunting started. The day when our soldiers were cured of a madness that tormented them. The day the Amaranthines came to Bywell. I know you know what happened that day. You were a witness. Or maybe you were a participant."

I looked up from my buttons—oh, fool!—and Avia nodded, her suspicion confirmed by my careless gesture.

"Your wall of secrets has sprung a leak," she said. "Too many leaks for you to stop up. And those leaks will bring the whole wall down. There's nothing you can do to stop it. But there's something you can do, if you want to avoid being crushed."

My fingers stilled. "I can't."

"Trust me, Grace." Avia moved closer. "Trust me to share your story. I won't print anything you don't approve."

"What if I never approve anything?"

"Then at least you won't have to bear it alone," Avia said. "At least you'll have someone who knows what you're carrying. I promise you. I won't say a word without your permission."

I wavered. I pressed my lips shut and pressed my tongue to the roof of my mouth. Share my burden. Confess everything. Give it to someone else to carry. Trust her with the story of the century.

I gazed into her eyes and felt the words battering to come out.

"I have to go," I said, and crossed the bird-covered carpet to the door. I opened it and stood aside. "Thank you for your visit, but I'm going to be late."

She nodded. "If you want me, you know where to find me."

Avia walked past me and into reception, soft music from the pianochord weaving through the air. She exited on a glissando and looked back for one last glimpse before the door shut behind her.

NINE

The Strings on her Wrists

Avia's article worked. Albert Jessup tried to argue, but after a comparison of a full-page advertisement from the month of Leafshed to current costs, the Elected Members in attendance rolled over and pushed my motion through. The meeting dissolved, leaving me and Severin in the chamber alone. He offered me a hand and I took it, rising from the Speaker's seat with a tremble. We walked through the halls from the chamber of Parliament to my office at Severin's usual, unhurried pace.

"You were marvelous," Severin said. "They're angry. But if you hadn't skated around them, we'd still be there, listening to why price caps suppress competition."

I folded my edition of the *Star*. "They didn't even notice the bit about the smoke tax."

"Jessup dominated that session."

"Jessup dominates too many sessions," I said. "Do you remember offering me lunch? I am utterly famished—"

The rest of my sentence died on my lips as we rounded the corner leading to my office.

Raymond Blake lowered the afternoon edition of the *Star*,

staring directly at me. He inclined his head sharply, beckoning me over with the tilt of his chin as if I were a food server. Beside me, Severin stiffened, but I reached up to quell his ire by returning the shoulder-squeeze he'd given me.

"I think I'll be ordering from catering for lunch after all, Your Highness. My apologies."

I left the Prince behind me to greet my adversary with a smile.

Raymond tucked the newspaper under his arm and strolled through Government House's chilly halls, careful to stay abreast of my stride. We turned corners, moving past the offices of the Elected to climb stairs framed by a four-panel depiction of the seasons in stained glass, our breath puffing out in front of us.

What could he want? He hadn't originally waited outside the chambers because of the newspaper, though if he supported me in that regard I would fall down in a faint. He was here for some other reason.

It was Harriet's turn at the pianochord, and she played a softly layered work that drifted like the snow falling outside the windows. This was the last gasp of the storm, a final reminder of our failure to protect Aeland. I stretched my awareness wide, checking the state of the Cauldron. No storm grew from its fury, but what about the polar front? When would they meet and clash again?

Ray sighed and shook my shoulder. "Grace."

"Look at it, Ray. Just look."

"I don't have to," he said. "It's just the same in my garden. You can't even see the hedge-follies."

He saw a shroud over the landscape, the softening, anonymous layer. He saw snow. I saw the date, and all the days of winter to come. "It's only Frostmonth. It's not even halfway through Frostmonth."

My voice broke. I swallowed past the lump in my throat. This snow cyclone was only the first. How long did we have before the Cauldron spit out another? A month? A week?

Ray slipped his arm around my shoulder, his voice gentle in my ear. "Grace, put yourself back together. We have a country to run, and we need to get started. Don't crumble, now. We need you. You have to lead us. Do you want a drink?"

I forced myself back inside the walls encased by books bound in leather, tooled with gold. I took a deep breath tinged by the sweet aroma of resin-coated logs in the black iron fireplace. "I'm fine."

I broke out of his grasp and crossed the cream carpet. I sorted past the tinctures and tonics in amberglass to the cut-crystal decanters of brandy, whiskey, and glauce. Raymond's favorite. I put out two glasses, dropping honey balls into the bottom. "You had a reason to hunt me down in the Lower House, going five miles in the snow."

"I did some organizing this morning," Ray said. "You're managing the weather and the everyday business of Aeland. With everything that's happening, I realized you didn't have a minute to yourself."

"I have been at rather a run since my return." Just an eye-dropper of spring water to each, then the slightly green-tinged glauce, enough to cover the honey ball. I handed him the glass and sat in the chair opposite his. "What can I do for you, then?"

"I'm here as a service to you. I've had time to think." Raymond sipped, and held the drink on his tongue. "I've organized a list of the best candidates for appointment to the Cabinet."

Oh. Had he. "I'll be interested in your suggestions."

He smiled. "They're not really suggestions, Grace."

My head jerked up like it was on strings. His strings, winding around my limbs; he pulled them now, trying to teach me to dance. "Even without the usual scrutiny from the Lower

House, the Queen selects from a list that has more than one choice for each position."

"These are desperate times. The Lower House can't fulfill all the functions of government. Without a Cabinet—"

No. I had to get free. "The timing is all wrong for this. I need to propose at least three names for each position. I'll include your choices, but there are time-honored procedures we can't just throw out."

"You'll have these names in the Queen's hands by morning," Raymond said, "and only these names."

"I can't do that, Ray. Be reasonable."

His laugh was a single bark, loud as a duck gun blast. "Reasonable? I think you should look in a mirror. You want to interfere with the natural course of competition with a price cap, and march our progress back to gas?"

"Those are the least of the motions I would make. Have you any idea what the Jessup family is charging for necessities?"

Raymond shrugged. "It might be a tad unfair."

A spot of heat bloomed on my scalp. "Oh, a tad."

"But announcing this to the papers without a word to anyone? That's your idea of a sound plan? Obviously we need to work more closely. I didn't realize you were so impractical." He swallowed the glauce, glass upturned as he waited for the honey ball to roll down into his mouth.

He had never intended to step aside for me. I was the most powerful Storm-Singer of them all, but he didn't have respect for that status. He meant to hold all the power he could tie to his fingers. The Invisibles were his. He meant to possess the Cabinet, snatching away my opportunity to build alliances of my own and carve out my place at the peak. And he meant to own me, the one in the gaudiest robe, guiding the weather at his command.

He drew an envelope from an inside pocket and held it out. "Here are the Cabinet picks. We should get moving on this. The Lower House can only do so much." He bit down on the honey ball, smacking his lips as it crunched. "Richard and I will see you at the reception, I'm sure."

He left without another word.

I opened the envelope, the paper shaking in my hands. How dare he? He dared because he could, that's how. I read the list and laid a hand over my stomach. Most of the choices were naked pork-barrel appointments. Some names were the sons or daughters of the last Cabinet members to hold the post. The others were friends of his, cousins from in-country, even Richard was on this list. It was the youngest Cabinet ever suggested, ignoring most of the elder members in favor of cronies and family.

The Queen would never agree to a pack of children running the government. If I gave her this list, I'd look like a complete fool. But if I didn't, he'd set the Invisibles against me. I needed them ready to stand against the next storm. If they rebelled, everyone in Aeland would pay for it.

Two gentle taps on my office door tugged at my attention. "Come in."

Janet opened the door all the way. "His Highness Prince Severin to see you, ma'am."

Severin had waited? "I am delighted to receive him."

Janet stood back, bowing her head as Severin entered my office. She closed the door behind her, and I pushed myself half out of my chair when Severin stopped me with a gesture.

"Don't get up," Severin said. "May I sit down?"

"Of course. I am sorry I abandoned you in the hall, Your Highness."

Severin put on a smile. "I thought we were past 'Your Highness.'"

"My apologies. Can I fix you a drink?"

"I can fetch it myself." Prince Severin put his hand out for my glass. "It looks like you could use another. What did Sir Raymond want?"

I put the heavy-bottomed tumbler in Severin's hand. "To be a nuisance and a bother, honestly."

"Anything specific?" He stood at my selection and poured out another measure of glauce and the customary dropper of water for me, and some of my father's whiskey for himself. He made himself comfortable in the chair Ray had occupied, eyeing the folded paper I still held in one hand.

"This," I said. Ray's list of candidates went back into the envelope. "The others were in the middle of electing Raymond to the post of the Voice when I showed up with Queen Constantina's writ. He only appeared to take the defeat gracefully."

The Prince swallowed the whiskey he'd sipped while listening. "And so he was here with his countermove."

"Indeed. This is a list of his choices for Cabinet." I tapped the envelope with one finger.

Severin paused, his glass lifted halfway to the armrest. "Does he have that much of a hold on you?"

I laughed. Once, the noise sharp and bitter. "You know we were to be married."

Severin nodded. "Did he come to renew the engagement?"

I shook my head. "No."

Severin settled more comfortably in the chair. "Then I've interrupted your explanation. My apologies."

"Father arranged it. An alliance with the Blakes meant a significant number of votes in the Cabinet, as his father's coalition would cooperate with my father's. But he was even more popular among his peers—who are now the ones in positions of power."

"And his coalition is larger than yours."

"My coalition is nonexistent," I corrected. "I'm Voice because he withdrew his claim and supported mine. But I knew it wasn't going to be that easy."

"You can't bow to his demands, of course. What are you going to do?"

"Well. Marrying him is out of the question." I chuckled. It tasted bitter.

Severin scowled. "Would you want to?"

"Solace, no. It was a political arrangement."

Severin nodded, the furrows in his brow smoothing. "I'd hate to see you have to resort to such a measure."

"There's nothing in it for him," I grumbled. "Nothing but money, anyway."

"People have married for less."

That was certainly true. I had no illusions about marriage— the Hundred Families didn't concern themselves over such trivia as love. But in a way, Prince Severin had it worse. Hobbled by the need to secure his mother's royal approval, Severin's parade of beautiful women were little more than youthful romances. And honestly, Severin was on the near side of forty—past the age where he should be sitting down with a matchmaker who would present him with a collection of the daughters of the landed, to select a woman of suitable relative distance to court and marry. He should have done it years ago. Much longer, and Severin would go from charming to irresponsible.

I stirred from my thoughts and gave Severin an apologetic smile. "My mind wandered. Perhaps we should talk about what you need."

"Two things," Severin said, swirling the last sip of whiskey around the bottom of his glass. "Mother wants to know why you have a Laneeri diplomat sequestered in your suite."

"Oh, that. We're humoring her so she'll tell us what she knows about the Laneeri possession plot. She's young and a tiny bit grandiose, and Miles thinks flattery will be more effective than fear." I glanced at my glass. Tiny ribbons of honey dissolved into the glauce, and I swirled them away. "I wanted to speak to you about Sevitii an Vaavut, actually."

Severin grew thoughtful. "Is she royal?"

"Ninth in line to the throne," I confirmed. "She says she knows how the possession plot started, but she won't tell us unless we guarantee Laneer's independence."

Severin looked up at the ceiling as if he were actually considering it.

I had a sip of my glauce. Sweet enough to cover the powerful kick of the liquor, now. "There's no way the Queen would agree."

"No," Severin said. "But I wonder what the Amaranthine delegates would think if we showed Laneer mercy. It's a compromise point—and it might be a good one."

He frowned into his whiskey, and my glass hovered a few inches from my lips. "You're seriously considering it."

"Yes," Severin said. "If it'll save our skins, I'll let Laneer go free."

"Will the Queen?"

Severin glanced in the direction of my office's reception, listening to a snatch of music from the pianochord. "I think she would be difficult to convince."

What did he mean to do to her? I was to stand ready until he needed me, but I had no idea what his plans were. "Well then. I'll tell Miles. What's the other thing?"

"A simple message," Severin said. "Your father wants to see you."

I tossed back the last swallow of glauce, catching the honey ball on my tongue. "Do you know why?"

That was the most diplomatic thing I could imagine saying. Severin leaned forward, elbows resting on his knees. "I think he wanted to talk to you about the price cap proposal in today's *Star.*"

I didn't have time for my father and his opinions. "I suppose I had better make the trip," I said. "Is there anything else I can do, before I go see him?"

The lines on Severin's face shifted as he took in the breath that prefaces speech. But he closed his mouth, snatching back whatever he was going to say. "I wish you success in dealing with Raymond. If I can be of any assistance, please tell me."

"Thank you," I said.

We pushed out of the deep, too-comfortable seats and left the office together. But where Severin's path took him into the Amaranthine wing, I pushed on to Kingsgrave Prison, determined to get this summons over with.

There were a hundred other things I could be doing instead of climbing the steps to the highest cell in the Tower of Sighs, but up I trudged past the Laneeri in their cells, now furnished with plain blankets and thin pillows. Wool socks and fingerless gloves looked strange next to their filmy, layered robes and elaborate gold jewelry. Their head priest Niikanis wore a much-mended sweater over his brightly dyed silk tunic, his gossamer shawl draped over the knitting.

It wasn't the best Aeland had to offer, but they wouldn't freeze to death. I climbed past the luxury-stuffed cells of the First Ring, my thighs burning from the effort. Father's coughs echoed down the stairs. I emerged as he drank a tonic straight from the bottle with trembling hands.

The ghost of a Laneeri soldier drifted into the cell. He glared at us, but I didn't care about the hate of a being who couldn't do anything to me. I stood before the copper-plated bars, arms folded while I waited for the coughing to subside.

"I'm quite busy, Father. What do you want?"

He dropped a blood-spattered hemp handkerchief in the basket at the foot of his bed and leaned against the wall, trying to catch his breath.

"You should be in bed."

"It's not that bad." His suit jacket hung off his shoulders, and the collar of his shirt gapped away from his neck. "The storm overwhelmed you."

"You called me up here for that?"

"No." He shifted then, flicking a glance at my portrait, over the softly curved shapes of my hands painted at rest—I unclenched my clasped fingers before he looked back, the furrow between his eyes just a little deeper, just a little sharper as he lifted his chin and said, "Did I raise a fool, Fiona Grace?"

"You know very well that you did not."

"Then explain this." He turned back to his table, lowering himself into the spring-padded chair. Father stabbed his index finger into a folded copy of the afternoon edition of the *Star*. "You formed a specific alliance with a member of the press? And with Avia Jessup, no less? She's a flighty dabbler out to poke her father in the eye. I don't know what possessed you."

"It worked. I succeeded. The price caps will go through, and everyone in Kingston knows it was my idea."

"And now you owe a journalist a favor," Father said. "And these kinds of favors put demands on you that you can't afford to honor. What if she starts asking you too many questions about aether? Did you think about this at all?"

She had been asking too many questions even before I enlisted her help, but if I told Father that, he might have a paroxysm. And if he knew that she had offered to hold my secrets in confidence? "I made the decision I saw fit to make."

"I need you to be capable of the work put before you, Grace. The Hensley name—"

I hadn't climbed a hundred and eighty steps for this. "Aeland is facing a crisis neither you nor Grandpa Miles even had to imagine—and it's your mess I'm cleaning up, Father! Everything we're going through can be laid at your feet. It all comes back to aether—all of it."

"Destroying the network has brought Aeland to its knees—"

"Destroying the network was the only thing that stayed the Amaranthines' wrath! And even that might not be enough to save us. You know what judgment Aife is weighing, Father. I cannot be distracted by you summoning me up here to scrutinize my every decision."

"Then make better decisions," Father growled.

"I don't have time for this." I whirled away, pacing the tiny space before Father's cell. "Raymond tried to make a play for control of the Invisibles. I need to finish him. The Laneeri Miles and I are questioning wants Laneer's independence restored before she tells us who was behind their attempt at revenge. I still haven't reported to the Queen—instead, I'm up here, bickering with you."

"You're right; you don't have time for this." Father coughed and picked up a teacup, wetting his throat. "You don't have time for a single mistake, but you made one anyway. What will you do about your blunder with the journalist?"

"It's not a blunder."

He gave me an exasperated look. "Grace. Think. When have I ever allowed a member of the press exclusive access? You owe the Jessup girl, and it'll come back to bite you. End your association before it's too late."

I held back the urge to say no, to argue my choices. I let my gaze drift to the tiny window, where a scarlet jay pecked at a handful of seeds. "I can handle it."

"You can't fall into short-term thinking," Father said. "It will ruin you. You should be cultivating your relationship with the Prince, securing your future as his Chancellor."

"He's just as busy as I am, Father."

"You each have a part to play in this crisis, but you should learn how to handle him. He will be King, and it's never too early to start managing a monarch's expectations."

Did Father ever see anyone as a friend? "I'll see what we can schedule. Next time you tell Severin you want to see me, give him the reason. And it had better be good."

I turned away from the bars, ignoring the Laneeri ghost who glowered uselessly at my back.

I could have used this time in a hundred different ways, but what made heat race across my scalp was Father's order to stop associating with Avia. It was out of the question. She had put too many pieces together, and I had to keep her close.

I stalked past the Laneeri in their cells while a tiny voice in-truded. *Is that all there is to it?* The ghost of her hands smoothed the lay of my tie and trailed along my lapels as I thundered down the halls. I couldn't, I didn't dare, but that didn't stop me from imagining what it would be like if I did.

I took the twisting route out of Kingsgrave, tangled in my thoughts. I had to keep Avia close. Which meant I needed to keep offering her stories while keeping her away from the se-crets I needed to keep. I couldn't use the trick of telling her what I intended for Parliament again. I had to give her some-thing big.

A parade of liveried servants blocked the corridor, carrying music stands from a storage room to the largest ballroom in the palace. They were preparing for the ball welcoming the Ama-ranthines to Aeland. A ball! The Queen was a fool if she thought the company of the titled elite and the Hundred Families would soften Aife's disposition toward us. She wanted to know about the real Aeland, the Aeland of its people, its blemishes and virtues. She wanted the truth.

I couldn't get Aife access to ordinary Aelanders. I'd never get them past the guards. But I could invite a guest to accompany me to the ball. Avia would jump at the chance to speak to the Amaranthines. I hurried back to my office, already composing the invitation in my head. *Dear Miss Jessup: I humbly request the pleasure of your company at a reception welcoming the Blessed Ones to Rosemount Palace—*

That would do. I hurried past Janet and took up a pen, crossing out the seal of the Chancellor at the top of my usual stationery and concentrating on the pressure of the downstrokes, the featherlight touch of curves and curls as I wrote. I was no scribe, but I did well enough. The invitation lay on my blotter, the ink drying in a gently heated dome of air to speed the process.

I eyed the tray on my desk. New missives had arrived in the short time I was away from the office. I spied the soft cream-and-rose paper that signaled a personal note from the Queen on the top of the stack. Blast! I had forgotten. I picked it up and read a single line:

Attend me immediately.

Did immediately mean "after you've eaten, of course"? Probably not. I picked up a King Philip Pink from a bowl of apples and crunched into it. The invitation was still wet when I brought it to Janet.

"Have a messenger take this to Avia Jessup at the *Star* and wait for a reply," I said, and hurried out the door with a half-eaten apple in hand.

TEN

A Tangle of Hair

No guard attended the Queen's private library, a converted ballroom filled with a collection of books under ban in Aeland. Most of them were from foreign publishers, but there were plenty of dissidents with an argument and a press within our own borders. The distinctive yellow cloth spines of books published by The People's Press dotted the shelves, concentrating to a solid yellow wall in a section I wagered was about witchcraft—a particular specialty of the underground press.

Queen Constantina wasn't here, though I spied a dead noble-woman with bleach-pale hair and the torturously shaped waist-line and tiered skirt of a decade ago, fluttering an old-fashioned message with her handkerchief: *I am listening*.

All the tall windows were uncovered to let in the light, and every one of the fireplaces blazed—too far away for real comfort, but the sight of a fire is a cheery one. A book lay on the Queen's desk, and I ventured close enough to inspect a treatise on the unnatural and unpredictable nature of the weather in Aeland with detailed observational data, according to the hemp-bound cover.

Poor fellow, trying to make sense of it all—but did it show a pattern? Did it show in its columns and data the thing that I feared: that the weather we struggled against was growing more severe?

The book was heavier than it looked, the pages thin and crisp. I flipped past the bewildered ramblings of the scholar who tried in vain to discover what drove Aeland's climate and into the tables, which were divided by region. Tiny print crammed three hundred and sixty days onto a page. I needed a magnifying glass, or reading spectacles—

"Find something interesting?"

I shut the book with a quick thump. "Your Majesty." I took a knee on the spot, one hand over my heart.

"Rise." Queen Constantina was dressed in sporting wear, every stitch and pleat precise. Her son followed after, tortoise-shell glasses half down his nose, his arm tucked around an open document file. Severin smiled at me as I stood.

She plucked the book from the desk and returned it to the shelf. Her hair was drawn into a smooth knot clasped by a circular comb topped with rows of pearls. "The Grand Duchess had a particular question about our weather, according to my son. Do you know why she was asking about general, long-term changes in the climate?"

"I do not, ma'am. But after last night's storm anyone would wonder exactly what we survive each year."

The Queen swept one arm toward the windows, and the sight of everything so covered in snow that the ornamental garden was hidden under soft humps. "And this was the best you could do?"

That wasn't a question. I kept silent.

"Kingston lies under thirty-three inches of snow—thirty-three! It's record breaking. Did you know that? There has never been a recorded overnight snowfall of such height. People had to dig themselves out of their homes. You said you could slow this storm. You said you could lessen its effects!"

My right knee ached as I knelt. "Ma'am, every mage and Secondary in the Circle drained themselves so only thirty-three inches of snow fell." But it was still a failure. We hadn't protected Kingston, and it would be days before all the roads were cleared. People had died last night—and the counting of the dead wasn't done.

Queen Constantina shifted to stare out the windows, where everything was buried in white. "Only."

"We did everything we could. But we need more Storm-Singers. This storm will be the first of many. We need to prepare for that."

The Queen turned her head. "Severin. You've been quiet."

Prince Severin looked up from the document he'd been reading. "I'm reckoning. We should hire more people to operate tampers. We'll have to haul excess snow to the river and the Ayers Inlet. We'll have to hire a thousand people, easily. But if Grace had the First Ring—"

The Queen's eyes narrowed. "No. I will not buckle to their extortion."

Severin pushed his glasses up his nose. "What choice do we have?"

"I will not argue this with you, Severin. They remain exactly where I put them."

If not the First Ring, maybe there was another way. "Maybe there are Storm-Singers among the witches." They turned to me, and I went on. "There are hundreds of witches in the asylums."

The Queen's mouth thinned, her scarlet lipstick like a bloody line. "Impossible. They're held there for the protection of the people."

"Majesty, it's a lie," I said. "Witches don't run the risk of losing their reason any more than mages do. They're no different from us. And soon, the subcommittee reviewing the original sessions and supplemental evidence will determine that too."

She didn't seem impressed by my confession, dismissing it with a shake of her head. "If we parole the imprisoned witches, there's nothing stopping them from telling the stories of their experience. And those stories will spread from mouth to ear until the whole country knows the truth. And that will be one failure, one betrayal too many."

She was right, but the witches had done nothing wrong, and had had so many wrongs visited on them. Leaving them inside the asylums was one more injustice. But if they started talking, and they would, it would be a national outrage. And the men and women locked in the Tower of Sighs wouldn't be appeasement enough.

"The Amaranthines wish it done," I said. "That suggests to me that our choices are limited."

"They must be brought to reason," the Queen said. "Speak to them. Explain how it cannot be done—"

I fought to keep my expression calm. Had the Queen's voice quavered? Did she clutch at her armrests, white-knuckled and tense? "I will answer their questions about storm-singing, but I doubt it will sway them from wishing freedom for the witches."

"They want too much," Queen Constantina said. "We can't possibly—they'll upend the nation and shake every last coin from our pockets to pay Laneer—*pay* them! After they dared use necromancy within our borders. And you have one of them snug inside the suite meant for your convenience when you should be wringing answers from their lying mouths."

"My brother was a prisoner at Camp Paradise, ma'am, and he would never countenance torture. And we may not need to, as the subject we're holding in the Chancellor's suite is ready to tell us everything after a little diplomatic wrangling."

Queen Constantina tilted her head, skepticism scrawled across her mouth. "What does she want?"

"Laneer's independence."

The Queen scoffed. "Impossible."

"Mother," Severin said. "The Amaranthines want freedom for Laneer, and reparations paid to them. If we can lay the proof of the necromancy plot before them, we may be able to get away with withdrawing our people and restoring Laneer's independence."

Constantina pursed her mouth, her jaw tense. "I don't like it. We'll have to renegotiate our trade agreements, and that will raise costs."

When I was young, I had been awed by Constantina's majesty. I saw the fine clothing, the deferential respect everyone paid her, the porcelain perfection of her demeanor. This wasn't the first time she had shattered that girlhood impression with her stubbornness and greed. Gently, I pushed that button. "We have a chance of bargaining against paying reparations, which will cost us more than renegotiating trade."

She flicked her gaze toward me. She picked up a violet enameled pen and twisted it in her fingers, thinking. Thinking, and then a resigned sigh. "It's better than nothing. Get me that proof."

I bowed my head. "Yes, ma'am. Your Highness, would you consent to a visit with the prisoner? I can collect Miles, so we have a translator."

Severin pushed his glasses back up his nose. "Now? I think that's a fine idea. Mother? I can speak to you about expanding the Service Reserve later."

"Go." Constantina waved one hand, shooing us like midges. "I expect to hear of your results with the Amaranthines."

I bowed and left with the Prince, who offered his arm to

me as we walked together. The dead courtier drifted into the hallway and winked out of sight.

Severin turned to glance at me. "Did you ever get that meal?"

"I did not." I shrugged. "It's been busy."

"Let's fix that." Severin steered us toward one of the kitchens, where chefs and assistants dressed dozens of quail to roast. He waved off assistance from the chef with a smile.

"We need something fast to eat, is all. No time to sit down."

The chef bowed and crossed the kitchen. He dug into a warming oven and pulled out a pair of pasty pies. We leaned against a counter and ate without making clever conversation, and I devoured spiced, shredded lamb and vegetables baked in a folded crescent of pie dough.

"Another?" he asked, as I dusted the crumbs of the pasty off my hands.

"That will keep me for a couple of hours."

"We can discuss the meeting with your Laneeri informant over tea and something more fortifying," Severin said. We left the kitchen and headed for Miles's suite, finding him out of his wheelchair and moving lengths of firewood from the maid's cart to each hearth.

"Should you be doing that?" I asked.

Miles huffed at me, picking bits of bark off his shirt. "Activity speeds recovery— Oh, Your Highness. Good afternoon."

He bowed to Severin, who inclined his head in greeting. "We've come to ask your assistance. I wish to speak to the prisoner about her terms."

"All I had to do this afternoon was a bit of reading," Miles said. He moved to his wheelchair, but instead of sitting in it, he pushed it to the door. "I'll need it on the way back," he explained, "but right now I feel fine."

"How much have you eaten?" I asked.

He gave me an amused look. "Five marks says I've eaten more than you. Are you game for it?"

"No," I said. "I've been running full-tilt all day. I had a pasty—"

"Thanks to me," Severin said.

"Thanks to Severin," I said. "But you've got to make those stairs. Shouldn't you save your energy for that?"

"Fine," Miles said. "If you sit and eat where I can see you."

"Done." I took Miles's place behind the wheelchair and pushed. He climbed the stairs and waited for Severin to shove the wheelchair up the flight.

"See? I'm much better," Miles said.

"You're still too thin."

"It'll come," Miles said. "A few weeks, and I'll be well on my way to recovered."

He wheeled himself to the guarded door and was first into the suite, calling for Sevitii as Severin and I arrived. Nothing stirred in response.

I listened to the crackle of logs laid on the fire in an empty room. I held up a hand and crossed the sitting room to push open the door of the bedchamber. Light fell on the empty, rumpled bed, and I stepped inside.

"Sevitii?"

Pale sunlight glinted off a rippling tangle of hair spread across the carpet. I fell to my knees beside the sprawled body on the floor. Sevitii lay staring at the ceiling, her fingers caught on a snarl in her unbraided hair, the light in her striking green eyes gone dull against the lurid red of her sclera.

I gathered a breath, and my throat tightened as I shouted. "Miles!"

The hand brake creaked and two sets of footsteps hurried across the rug. Miles pushed me aside, his fingers at the soft, still column of her throat. He lifted one arm, inspecting the underside.

"Flexible," he said. "Hardly any lividity. Still warm . . . petechial hemorrhages." He set her arm down and rose to his feet. He walked all around her body, careful of the long, flaxen strands scattered all around her. "The way her legs are bent, she crumpled from a standing position."

I pointed at an oiled wooden comb on the carpet, a few inches away from her fingers. "She was combing her hair. I can hear water dripping into the bathtub."

Severin excused himself to the bath chamber, and the dripping stopped. He emerged. "The water's still hot."

"Blast it," Miles muttered. "That might have just destroyed evidence, Your Highness."

Severin looked back, and then at his hands. "Fingerprints?"

"Possibly. I need my medical bag," Miles grumbled. "I think it's been less than an hour, but without her internal temperature, it's just a guess. Whatever killed her, it was fast."

Severin stood well back from the body. "What could have done that?"

"From the look of her eyes, she couldn't breathe," Miles said. "I won't know until I've got her on the table."

"Does the palace even have a morgue?" I asked. I couldn't stop looking at Sevitii: at her wide, staring eyes; at her mouth opened on an unspoken word. She'd been combing her hair, and then she was dead. "There is one, isn't there?"

"There is," Severin said. "Do you mean to examine her, Sir Miles?"

"I do," Miles said. "We have to find out how this woman died."

Miles gently inspected Sevitii's body, poring over her hands in particular. "Grace."

I pushed myself off the wall I had been leaning against. "What is it?"

"She's missing a piece of jewelry. Do you see a gold bangle anywhere with planetary symbols engraved on it?"

I spotted some bangles on the side table next to her bed. "I see them."

"Good. Can you find it for me? I want to be sure to have it. They're important to Laneeri. Her survivors will want to have it."

Severin shifted his weight. "This is a troubling diplomatic incident. Should you be concerned about a piece of jewelry?"

"Yes, Your Highness." Miles straightened his back and rolled his neck. "It's of spiritual significance. They will want it. Grace?"

I crossed the room and sorted through the bangles, then sorted through them again. "None of these are engraved like that."

"Perhaps it's in the bath chamber."

I skirted around Severin to check, but there was no bangle on the vanity, or on the floor, or accidentally kicked under the bath mat.

"I can't find it." I left the humid bathing room and started opening drawers, searching. "You're sure she'd own such a thing."

"Yes." Miles swiped a hand through his hair, and all the carefully dressed curls sprang upward in response. "Poorer Laneeri have them in cheap metals, but everyone has them. They're engraved with the stations of the wandering thrones as they were in the sky at the moment of their birth. They're said to be the essence of that person's soul and destiny in this incarnation, and a Laneeri wouldn't easily be parted from it."

Severin cleared his throat. "The delegation did kick up a

terrible fuss when they were asked to surrender all their pos-
sessions for the ceremonial imprisonment, and they fought to
have their jewelry returned. You're saying it was over a bracelet?"

"Yes, sir. They're supposed to protect the wearer from bad
luck."

"Bad luck." Severin glanced at Sevitii's body, then quickly
looked away. "So what does it mean that we can't find hers?"

"I'm not sure." Miles rose to his feet, wincing as his knees
unhinged. "I wish Tristan were here."

Severin shook his head. "This has to stay secret, for now.
I'm sorry. I know you would appreciate his support—"

"Tristan's a trained investigator. It's part of his role as royal
bodyguard. He's quite good. I wonder what he would make of
this." Miles indicated the scene and Sevitii's body with a gesture that swept over the room.

"Tristan's also pledged to the Grand Duchess," I said.
"Could you ask him to keep this a secret from her?"

"Blast it," Miles muttered. "I wouldn't want to put him in a
fix. But if we could get his help officially—"

"I don't think that would be in Aeland's interests," Severin
said.

"I'm not sure how long we can hide it," I said.

"Let me discover how she died," Miles said. "Perhaps that
will give us some direction on how much we have to hide."

"And what, exactly, are we hiding?" Severin asked.

I bit my lip. "Sevitii's death."

"Her murder," Miles said. "I need to know what ended her
life. We need to find out who killed her, and what they stood to
gain from it. Don't we?"

Severin gazed toward the ceiling as he mulled it over.
"You're right. Find out what killed her. I'll arrange to have the

body discreetly moved to the morgue. When will you do the examination?"

"Tomorrow," Miles said. "I'm in no shape to take care of it right now."

"Very well," Severin said. "I'll have her moved."

"I'll get the ledger for everyone who has entered this room since we put Sevitii here," I said.

Severin nodded. "I'll leave you to your pursuit. We have to find who did this, and quickly."

Severin left the suite, and Miles grumbled at the room. "Nothing looks out of place. But her star bangle's missing. I don't like it."

"I don't either." I moved to the sofa where Sevitii had lounged when she made her bargain for Laneer's freedom. Nothing had fallen between the couch cushions, and the floor underneath hadn't so much as a dust ball. "You think she was murdered."

"Very few things kill a healthy young woman. Fewer still kill her instantly," Miles said. "I'll know more tomorrow. And you should go home. Don't stay here and work yourself to death."

"There's too much to do," I said. "And a murder inquiry on top of that. I need to see Grand Duchess Aife—"

"She can wait," Miles said. "Go home. Catch up on the meals and the sleep you skipped. The work will still be here when you get back. Doctor's orders."

I huffed. "Very well. You're right."

We left the suite with strict instructions—no one but the Prince and us could authorize anyone coming in. No maids were to touch anything. And they were to continue to guard the room until we relieved them of duty.

Avia hadn't sent back a reply by the time I returned to

my office. I could have found a reason to stay, to begin our investigation now, but Miles was right. I needed to rest and re- cover, and so I buckled on my skis and took the King's Way, my twenty-foot-long shadow falling along the freshly tamped road.

We had to know who'd killed Sevitii. She'd been the only one willing to tell us the truth about Laneer's plans to coun- terattack Aeland. She should have been safe. We had kept her a secret, hadn't we? No one had known she was in my suite—

Not true. The guards knew. Severin and Constantina, of course. But the guards could have gossiped about it, spread the story around all the Queensguards. The maids assigned to clean the suite knew, and the story could have traveled among them as well. And the Laneeri imprisoned in the Tower of Sighs obviously knew that their young leader was miss- ing, but they weren't reasonable suspects. They couldn't have done it.

I couldn't worry myself into circles. Miles would examine her. We had to start there, and speculation wouldn't help at this point.

My arms ached, but it felt good to ski and get fresh air. I could ask the grooms to put ice-spike tires on my bicycle, and let William and George pick me up in the evenings. Exercise cleared my head, and I hadn't been doing enough. I peered at the *Star* as I went past, but luck didn't bring Avia to me. I scowled at the dark, empty Edenhill Hotel and sped past it.

In all the excitement, I had forgotten about Ray's ridiculous Cabinet list. There was no way I was presenting his choices to the Queen. I needed him out of the way. I had too much to do and no time to play king of the castle. Ray should have been happy with being Finance Minister, like his father—

I dug my poles into hard-packed snow and sculled along, skis gliding with a soft, scraping shush. What if Ray needed that position? The Blakes had poured millions into the Eden-hill, confident that its modernity and luxury would attract not just the Hundred Families and the landed families whose complex lineages traced back to Queen Agnes, but also those who hadn't the benefit of good birth to go with the fortunes they had built through trade and enterprise. No one could have predicted the disaster of losing aether, but the Edenhill's finances must be swaying on a high-wire.

I grinned and skiied faster.

I knew how to get Raymond Blake out of my way.

I unbuckled my skis and strapped them together with my poles, cradled them in the crook of my left arm, and swept open the double doors of First Aeland Savings and Investment precisely five minutes before wicket closing. Every clerk and secretary in line to deposit their salaries gawked as I strolled across alabaster, black, and ochre mosaic tiles to rows of desks manned by account managers and loan officers. The branch manager rushed to meet me before I could find a seat.

"Mr. Fletcher. You didn't have to put yourself out. I could have waited."

"Never, Dame Grace, never. It's always such a pleasure to help you, I stole the opportunity for myself." He guided me down the long aisle between rosewood desks and furtive looks. "What may we do to assist you?"

I leaned my skis against one chair and took the other. "I've come to withdraw certificates for Blake Real Estate Development from my account."

The hum of voices around us fell to a murmur.

"Certainly, Dame Grace. What figure would you like to withdraw?"

"All of them."

The room went dead. Mr. Fletcher's tongue dabbed nervously at his lips. "All of them?"

"Every certificate I own."

His forehead shone. His imagination ran wild behind his eyes, made small by round black-rimmed spectacles. "I— Yes. Right away."

There was a game we used to play as children, building towers from waxed playing cards. The children with the steadiest hands and the right kind of cleverness could build towers so tall that they simply couldn't reach any higher. Miles could construct one that rose from the floor to his chin.

He used to let me topple them because it made me laugh.

"I'll start the paperwork immediately, but"—Mr. Fletcher pitched his voice to a soft murmur—"if you require funds, there's no need to deflate your capital."

Fletcher had to know better than to believe I'd divest capital without a reason. And he had to know that I wasn't a ninny. That was an invitation to explain my actions, if I cared to, but I wasn't inclined to spoil the fun this early.

"Oh, Mr. Fletcher. Thank you for your suggestion. It's lovely of you. But I'm not the one in need of money."

Fletcher's face went chalky.

I slipped a hand-carved ivory pen from my inside jacket pocket. "I'll be happy to sign the release and transit slips while we wait."

He blinked and pushed his rosewood chair back. "The forms are right here. Would you like some tea? Mildred, brew some tea for Dame Grace."

I sipped tea and dodged Fletcher's attempts to uncover my motive. A woman arrived with a tall stack of certificates, engraved and stamped on thick cotton-hemp paper. Every certificate in Ray's development company I owned lay there, taking up much less space than the currency they were worth.

The wrought iron clock suspended above the entrance to the vaults rang out the hour of four. Fletcher craned his neck to read the time, then turned hastily back to me. "I can finish your requests today, my lady. Leave it all to me."

"Thank you, Mr. Fletcher, but that won't be necessary." I finished the last sip of tea and rose. "See it done on Firstday. Have a pleasant evening."

I shook his hand and left the bank in an uproar.

ELEVEN

Examination in Progress

I spent the evening under the command of my lady's maid, Edith, who had done two weeks' work in days by restyling a white gown for the next evening's ball. I stood on a stool while she inspected every line of sequins and frowned over the seams, pinning last-minute tweaks and adjustments. We sorted through jewels, selecting glittering diamonds paired with more valuable pearls, and Edith set them aside to be cleaned and polished.

After a decent night's sleep and a hearty breakfast, William and George drove me through the Restday streets of Kingston. People in short white lace veils crowded the entrances to temples that exhaled sweetwood and luckgrass incense. Yellow ribbons fluttered from the elbows of those gathered, their wearers eyeing me and my ostentatious orange sled.

We drove past them and into the empty drive in front of Government House. I strode down empty hallways to my deserted office, where a note from Miles lay half-under my office door and Avia's response waited in the middle of my desk. I slit open Avia's envelope and unfolded a page that smelled like lilies and newsprint and read:

Dear Grace,

Thank you for your kind invitation. In spite of the late notice, I would be delighted to attend.

Avia

The page trembled in my hand. A shimmering elation rippled over my skin even as I reminded myself that I had invited her for our mutual advantage, and that she'd miss a chance to scoop the whole country with an interview with the Grand Duchess when they pried the camera from her cold, dead hands. I raised the note to my nose and breathed it in one more time before tucking it into my desk drawer and picking up the note with Miles's slanted, narrow hand in the script.

Grace,

We're in the mortuary. The examination will probably take several hours, but I can give you a report when you fetch us for lunch.

Miles

So Miles had told Tristan after all. I couldn't blame him—who wanted secrets between lovers? Tristan would be discreet. But that could mean that I had some explaining to do when I found Aife.

I sorted through the paper on my desk. There were reports I had asked for, but none of it was reason to delay my visit to the Amaranthines. It could all wait until Firstday, and so I abandoned it and locked the office door behind me.

The glasshouse Aife used as a salon was nearly empty. Aife sat with her long-necked instrument, picking out chords and melody with her nimble hands; above her head, gem-winged butterflies wobbled in the air. Black-and-silver-clad Ysonde stood by a window that let in the chill, intent on the scarlet jay perched on his finger. Tristan stood in a shabby tweed suit and Miles's Service coat, his long flaxen hair tucked under the collar and covered by a green knit cap, and if Tristan was here, who had Miles meant when he wrote "we"?

I stood quietly. Aife knew I was present, but she didn't cease playing her instrument. Her music shimmered; every string was its own melody woven around the others in haunting, ethereal harmonies. I could stand there for an hour, just listening.

Warm air billowed into the room as the door behind me opened. I glanced over my shoulder while I stepped clear, and a fully armed Aldis swept into the chamber, his wide-legged, calf-high trousers rippling with his steps. His padded jerkin was embroidered with a crawling rose briar of white blossoms and long thorns along the hem. A leather quiver of arrows slung across his back matched the longbow in his left hand. His single witchmark—the soul of Sir Percy Stanley—hovered near his left temple. He glanced at me for one sneering second as he passed.

"We're busy," he said, and the music ceased.

"This will only take a moment," Aife said. "You have your objectives, gentlemen."

Tristan pressed his fist to his chest and bowed. "I will verify Ysonde's findings, if I can. Are you ready to survey the damage, Aldis?"

Aldis cast another withering glance at me. "I am."

"Then allow me." Tristan extended his arm over his head, describing a spiral that smudged the air as if I peered through foggy spectacles. As the path of his hand spiraled tighter, the distortion in the air grew more intense, sparkling like the aura that clouded my vision when a bad storm triggered a dazzle-headache. But then Tristan's hand retraced its spiraling path backward, and—

—Sunlight poured into the room from a hole in the air,

afternoon-bright and blazing like a summer's day. It lined Tristan in gold as he opened the hole wider, and a scent like sweet running water and moss swept over my face.

I stood before the portal that led to the Solace. A brook babbled at my feet, the sunlight now filtered through the dappling shadows of leaf-laden tree branches. As I watched, the land turned from moss-covered stones bordering running water to a flower-strewn meadow, blossoms nodding in a breeze that flowed over our faces. Hills mounded upward, and saplings grew wide and tall, their papery white bark striped by black.

Ysonde watched the melting, transforming landscape with his brows knitted together. "That's not a good sign."

Aife glanced at me, then set her hand on Ysonde's elbow. "That is the Solace, Grace."

It was mesmerizing, but it made my skin shudder. "What—why is it changing like that?"

Tristan answered. "This land is unanchored. No one is here to believe in it."

The forest withered, thinned. Dry, golden grass clung to sandy ground, but the sand won and stretched across my view. A ruined city of shining white stone rose, making me wonder if its people had survived, if they had found safety. A river ran through the sand, turning golden ground to good black earth, sprouting grass once more.

"It's beautiful."

"It's dangerous," Tristan said. "Especially here."

"Why?"

Tristan glanced over my shoulder toward his Grand Duchess. She slid off the guitar stool in a whispering of skirts to stand next to me. "Stay safe. Come back in time for the ball."

Aldis's gaze softened when he looked at his liege. "I shall."

Aldis stepped into that other world, now a towering, misty

wood, noisy with birdsong. Tristan followed, and the passage between our world and the Solace sighed shut.

"Aldis is maintaining a patrol of the Solace here. Tristan is going to follow up on a lead in the city."

They had stepped out of this world and into another without using Waystones. How had Tristan done it? "Why does it do that? Why does it change like that?"

"Tristan told you. No one dwells in this part of the Solace. The land shifts because there is no one to believe it is still."

"You mean that no Amaranthines live near here?"

"That is also true," Aife said. "I'm sorry you didn't have time to talk to me yesterday, but I am glad you're here now."

So the business of the Solace was off-limits, then? I could ask Tristan later. He might give more than the Grand Duchess, whom I couldn't wheedle. "I understand you have questions about the storm."

"Yes." Aife returned to the guitar stool and picked up her instrument. It was strung with gut rather than wire, and its soft tones rose in the air, conjuring butterflies with every note. "This cyclonic blizzard. This is normal for your land?"

"Not exactly," I said. "I've faced a cyclonic blizzard before, but they don't usually come until we're deep into Snowglaze— next month, I mean, after New Year. Still, they're nothing like the storm we faced the other night. This one broke snowfall records."

"So too early, and too powerful," Aife said. "I'm sure you want to know who helped you that night. I did. And Ysonde."

Ysonde nodded and closed the window, having banished all but his roost of black doves to the outdoors. They billed contentedly within a wooden cote, the music of their murmuring calls blending with the circling, three-beat tempo of Aife's song.

Ysonde crossed the room in a fluttering of smoky black. He

wore the same voluminous calf-high trousers Aldis had been wearing, but with an embossed black leather kilt and jerkin, his wrists bound by sturdy leather armguards meant for working with birds of prey. He waved at one of a matched set of chairs in invitation, and I settled into a heavy armchair padded in red satin.

"We have never seen magic wielded in such a fashion," Ysonde said. "You must have numbered over a hundred, working in concert. How do you harness that many wills to one purpose?"

"Storm-Singers begin training as children," I said. "My father taught me to command the sky, and taught my brother to serve as my reservoir so that I could fight against the storms more effectively."

Aife's brows knitted together, but her fingers never ceased their plucking and fretting. "Necessity drove you to enslave your own, you mean."

I winced. "Yes. It takes immense power to tear apart a cyclonic storm," I said. "It's not just winter. Spring rains are easy to calm, but summer brings the cyclonic storms in-country, threatening our crops and towns. Autumn usually drags torrential rain and wind along the coast. We are on guard every day of the year. And storm years more than most."

"This is a storm year, then."

"Yes." I folded my hands in my lap. "And it's the worst one any of us have ever seen. Worse than the last."

"When was that?"

"Three years ago. It used to be every seven, in my grandfather's day, then five. Now three. And in the future?" I spread my hands and shrugged. "That's why I need to find out how to free the witches, how to end their persecution. If the storms are growing more powerful, there are not enough of us in the Hundred Families to stand against them."

"So you are ready to comply with my requirements?" Aife asked.

"It's not going to be that easy. We have done terrible things to the witches. We did everything in our power to keep it a secret. I don't know how to reveal the truth and save the Storm-Singers at the same time."

"And you will need both," Aife said. "You will need every last witch who can weave a wind if you're going to save your nation. Find a way, Grace."

Ysonde pulled a sloping lap desk onto his knees and carefully untwisted the cap of a black-and-silver filigree pen. I recognized it as a popular model from Wilson and Smith and not a marvel of Amaranthine design. He caught my eye and smiled, his cheeks plumping. "This is a far cry from dipping a quill. I quite admire this contraption."

He liked pens? I'd bring him twenty, and a quart of ink besides. "What are you writing?"

"Notes on our meeting. I've noticed that both you and the Prince are freer with your real inclinations when your monarch is not in the room."

I flushed. "We're doing what we can to ease Aeland's trouble."

"You and the Prince are a good team." Ysonde set his pen to paper and drew small ideographs, completely unreadable by me. They were beautiful curving shapes compared to the angularity of Aelander script. "I'd rather deal with the two of you than Constantina."

I swallowed. He couldn't be implying what hung in the air. He was simply stating his preference; that was all. I pushed myself from the armchair and bowed. "Thank you for seeing me. Did you have any more questions?"

"What do you know of the Stormbowl?" Aife asked.

"Samindan sailors call the Cauldron that," I said. "It's uncharted waters, hundreds of miles west of the Aelish coast. It's very warm water in an otherwise cold ocean, and it creates pressure systems that become storms. The trade winds push it eastward, and they funnel toward us. No one has returned from daring to explore the Cauldron."

"Who would dare to explore it?" Aife asked.

"Aelander ouranologists are deathly curious about the phenomenon. Samindan sailors steer well away from it."

Aife looked up at the gamboling troop of butterflies rollicking around the faceted glass dome. "That is wise," she said. "It's a dangerous place."

"How do you know?" I asked. "Is it dangerous in the Solace, too?"

Aife missed a note. Ysonde looked up from a smudge on the page. They glanced at each other, then realized I had seen their startlement and turned to me, speaking not a word.

I bowed my head and bobbed my knees in embarrassed courtesy. "I have an obligation elsewhere. My apologies."

"May it be a pleasure," Aife said, and I kept my mouth shut while I smiled.

The music ceased the second the door closed behind me, but I couldn't stay and attempt to listen. I hurried out of the ambassador's wing and found a page.

"I need to go to the palace mortuary," I told her, and the girl, probably a child of one of the palace's hundreds of servants, led the way.

The page wouldn't venture down the short hallway leading to the mortuary, but she had guided me to the right place without error. I regarded the wide double doors shut firmly before me, a message painted on each: "Mortuary—no admittance without authorization."

Tacked below this message was a note:

"Examination in progress. Thank you for your discretion."

I hesitated, my hand poised just above the door lever. Miles was in there, with a body, cut open with all its insides showing—a vision of the flashing blade of the huntmaster parting the belly of a slaughtered stag on my first hunt, the ropy entrails sliding out—

I snatched my hand away, then sneered at my weakness. *Don't be a child.* I scoffed at myself and pushed the handle down, swinging the door open.

A sickly, pungent bouquet of smells crawled up my nose— the odor of the butcher shop amid the high, gassy scent of alcohol and solvent through the medicinal smell of carbolic soap. The room was pale green tile sprinkled with black, and a noisy wall clock tocked every inevitable second. A long white porcelain table held spring scales with tall steel bowls perched on the trays, and I swept my gaze to the pebbled glass windows before the red things inside the bowls became recognizable.

"Come in; shut the door," Miles said. "Are you sure there's nothing wrong with it?"

"Positive."

Miles's mystery assistant was his friend Robin. Her hair was tied back and protected by a boiled linen head wrap. She was covered in a gray cotton smock with a black rubber apron, her hands encased in ochre-colored rubber gloves, and in those hands, she cradled a glistening human heart.

I choked down a cry of horror.

Miles twisted in his chair, concern arched across his eyebrows.

"We're nearly finished," Miles said. "Maybe you should wait outside."

"I'm fine," I said.

"You're green." He wheeled his chair toward me, offering a

small brown glass jar. "You can put some of this on your upper lip if the smell is too much."

He unscrewed the cap, and a whiff of menthol seeped out. I shook my head. "It's the gaslight. I'm fine."

I turned my gaze to Sevitii's body on the table, and gasped.

"Blast it, Grace. Don't look."

But I had already seen her. I saw the red flesh and white bone and the deep hole in her body where her heart should have been. I saw her face, bloodless and waxy and—

Miles pulled the hand brake and stood up, turning me around. "Steady," he said. "It's natural, what you're feeling right now. Adrenaline production has you shaking, ready to fight or run away. You have to learn to calm instinct when you learn how to do what we do."

I closed my eyes and tried to keep the sour taste flooding my mouth from becoming a complete loss of dignity. Footsteps sounded behind me, followed by the click of a cabinet door opening. The soft flutter of fabric unfurling came after, and then Robin said, "She's covered."

"I fainted during my first practical anatomy class." Miles patted my back. "I went down like a felled tree."

"You're just telling me that to make me feel better."

"I really did faint. You can turn around now."

Sevitii was draped in a white sheet, completely covered. I took a shaky step forward. "What have you found?"

"The only clue is the eyes," Miles said. "Her heart is perfectly healthy. Her brain is unblemished. Liver, lungs, all her internal organs show no sign of degeneration. We've pored over slides and tests, and they all say the same thing."

Robin shook her head. "She suffocated. But we can't tell you how it happened."

"There are no bruises around her mouth and nose. Her airway is completely clear," Miles said. "There is no evidence that someone forcibly smothered her, and there was no sign of a struggle at the scene."

"But what does that mean?"

Miles and Robin exchanged glances. Miles clamped his lips shut.

"I know you'd be guessing," I said. "But please, tell me."

"I can't say," Miles said.

"Give me something. You can't find a natural cause of death. That means her death was unnatural. Oh." I covered my mouth. "Miles, could magic do this?"

"Yes," Miles said. "If I touched someone, skin to skin, I could use my power to kill them."

"But you didn't."

"Of course he didn't." Robin threw her discarded gloves into a bin.

"And you know this," I said. "Miss Thorpe. I don't wish to alarm you, but I believe I should tell you that I know you're a witch."

"I'm aware of that." Robin moved to a deep porcelain-covered sink and turned the taps, scrubbing her hands with a scarlet bar of carbolic soap. She washed her hands as methodically as Miles did, turning to lean against the lip of the sink as she used a brush on her soapy nails. "Miles says you can be trusted."

"I can," I said.

Robin smiled, closed-mouthed and ironic. "As you say."

She wasn't one to give leeway. I fought the heat blooming in my cheeks with a clear, even voice. "I need to know something. Something of vital importance. There are witches in Riverside. They have the gift of being able to control the weather."

Robin switched the brush to her other hand, swiping it over her nails. She kept silent. Miles shifted in his chair.

I plunged onward. "Aeland needs them," I said. "That

storm was just the first of many. We need all the power we can get."

"And will these witches be your equal? Will they be invited to live behind the gates of the Western Point? Will they gain rich Cabinet positions, just like you?"

She knew. She knew all about the Royal Knights already, as if it wasn't really a secret. I stood speechless, unable to come up with a response.

Robin rinsed the nail brush under the flow, and running water washed soap suds away. "And will you ask them to stand by while examiners steal their relatives and friends while you spare them?"

I was back on the rolling deck of a ship, fighting to stand against her words, but they staggered me. "Aeland needs them. This is a crisis."

"Centuries of persecution has been a crisis. Decades of incarceration has been a crisis. Now a storm you couldn't handle pounded at the door, and you're talking about a crisis."

"You can't deny the problem we face!"

"You seem to be denying our problem just fine," Robin said. "If you want those witches to help you, how are you going to guarantee they won't wind up imprisoned? Why would they trust that you wouldn't bind their power, the way you do to your own families when they don't share your talent?"

"Binding is wrong. I want it to end," I said.

"The Witchcraft Protection Act is wrong," Robin said. "Do you want that to end?"

I looked at the green-and-black tiled floor. "I see what you're saying. I understand you. But I can't do it."

"Understand this," Robin said. "I'm talking to you because I trust Miles. And Miles trusts you. But I'm not going to lead you to a single witch, no matter how badly you need them. Not when all you can give me are promises not to tell."

"I can't give you any more than that."

"You could if you wanted to, Chancellor Hensley. You could give us a lot more than that."

"You already have something in mind," I said.

"People are questioning the law. The Elected's subcommittee scrutinizing the procedure behind the act have serious questions about the evidence."

"As the Chancellor, I don't strictly speak for myself. I'm the presence of the Crown—"

"I didn't say it would be easy." Robin stood by the draped body of Sevitii an Vaavut, her voice as even. "But it's in your power to do something."

Technically, that was true, and that's all that mattered to an idealist. I even had two routes I could take—the first was a prorogue of the law, suspending it until it had been examined by an advisory committee, and then seven more steps of argument, debate, and bargaining to revise, reenforce, or abolish. That would take the Lower House and the Cabinet . . . and I didn't have a Cabinet to appease, at the moment.

The second was to beg a decree. The Rose Crown was content to allow Parliament to guide the path of laws, with the Chancellor stating the throne's preferences one way or another. But the rule of the monarch was absolute. If I secured a decree from the Queen—

That would never happen. Queen Constantina would never agree.

But would King Severin?

I would do anything for Aeland, wouldn't I? I had already agreed to aid Severin, hadn't I? But my stomach wrenched itself into knots at the thought. Treason. I countenanced treason. I was no traitor. I had given my vow as a Royal Knight to—

—to serve Aeland always, to guard its people from danger, hunger, and darkness—

Solace, no. I couldn't step that far. Not unless I was desperate.

"I can attempt to persuade the Crown."

Miles let out a sigh. Robin regarded me a moment longer, and then nodded.

"That's a step forward. It's one of many. There's a lot of work to do if we're going to set Aeland on a moral path."

"Aeland is—"

I stopped. Robin waited, her expression patient, as my shoulders sagged and I looked at the floor. "Aeland is not on a moral path. Maybe it had been in the past. But today? You're right. We need to change direction. We need to dig deep and determine what kind of country we want to be."

Robin and Miles exchanged glances. "It helps to know your destination," Robin said. "The people have one in mind."

I looked up. "What?"

"Why do you suppose we chose yellow?" Robin asked.

I let my head fall back. "You can't just snap your fingers and make a kingdom into an Uzadalian democracy. That's admirable. It is. But I can't do it. That's too much."

"I'm not asking you to change it tomorrow," Robin said. "I'm telling you what the people want. What can you do to help them get it?"

"Honestly, I can't answer that right at this moment. I need to do an analysis. I need a hundred reports; I need a committee—wait." I looked at Robin, at Miles. "Member Clarke's subcommittee. The one looking into the Witchcraft Protection Act. That's you."

Robin nodded. "That's us."

"This is what I can do, then. I can open my door to Jacob Clarke. I'll ask for his committee's findings. If he wants me to consult with him, I will . . . and if there's trouble coming his way, I can warn them. I can't join Clarke's coalition, but I can support it."

Miles smiled at me, and I smiled back. "I can help you. It's hard to change course. But I'll do what I can."

Robin considered it. "It's a start. I know you can't just snap your fingers and make it happen," she said. "So let me show a little faith."

She lifted the corner of Sevitii's shroud, folding it back to reveal the pale knob of her shoulder. "I think I can call Sevitii's soul back, and then we can ask her."

TWELVE

To Summon the Dead

The wall clock ticked out the seconds it took for me to close my mouth and gather a response. "I think this might seem impertinent, Miss Thorpe, but if you could question Sevitii an Vaavut, why did you—"

I gestured at her still form, covered by the sheet.

Robin cocked her head. "I thought you wanted evidence that was actually admissible. The last time I checked, the testimony of the dead wasn't on the list."

"We had to determine how she died," Miles said. "If I had found a birth defect in her heart or a blood clot in her brain or lungs, then we wouldn't have a murder investigation, just deuced awful luck."

"The examination was necessary," Robin said. "Honestly I'd planned to keep quiet about what I can do."

"What can you do?"

"I'm a Deathsinger," Robin said. "I didn't know until the ghosts showed up. I spent my whole life crowned by magic. I had to learn to hide my aversion to copper. But I had no talent. Or so I thought."

I nodded. "That must have been an upsetting discovery."

"Perhaps we should delve into that part of it a little later," Robin said.

Avia had told me the other day how Deathsingers were the first witches to be arrested under the Witchcraft Protection Act. Talents were hereditary. Robin had probably lost someone in her clan to the asylums. "Of course. My apologies for bringing it up."

"Thank you." Robin laid her bare hand on Sevitii's exposed shoulder and closed her eyes. "I can hear them. Talk to them. I suppose I could command the spirits, but I won't work that way."

Nothing but the wall clock made a sound. It ticked on as Miles and I shifted our weight, glancing at each other while we waited for something to happen.

Robin opened her eyes. "This makes no sense. One moment."

Robin pulled two lockets out from under her smock. She opened one and pressed her finger to the coil of braided hair nestled inside, and an elderly Samindan woman in a dated, wasp-waisted gown materialized before Robin, transparent as any spirit.

"This is my great-aunt Joy," Robin said.

I had seen her before. She had been standing sentinel in Miles's suite in the palace the first time I had met Robin. I turned to her great-aunt and bowed my head.

"How do you do."

She returned the greeting with a grave expression.

Robin opened the other locket, and a younger woman in a knee-length frock with the piping trim that had been stylish three years ago appeared. "This is my cousin Mahalia."

"That's your middle name," Miles said.

"We were both named for my grandmother. She died in

an asylum," Robin said. "The examiners took her when I was seven."

I had been right. I bowed my head to Mahalia's ghost, but she lifted her haughty chin, her nostrils pinching in on an aggrieved sniff.

"Well. I had thought perhaps there was something interfering with magic. If the walls had copper behind them, for example," Robin said. "But that's not it."

"Maybe you can only call on your own relatives?" Miles suggested.

Robin shook her head. "I conjured up Octavius Green, and he's no relation. He told me where he'd hid his trove of pearls, and they were right where he said they were." Half of Robin's mouth quirked up and she went on. "After that he announced Jessamyn Brown of the Quickneedles was his secret daughter and that she was entitled to half the trove, and I left the clan house in an uproar. They're probably still shouting over it."

"So you should be able to call forth her spirit," I said. "And you can't?"

"That's correct," Robin said.

"Why would that be happening?" Miles twisted in his seat and pulled out a tobacco pouch. The sharp-cured scent of the fermented and flavored leaf blended with the smell of death and aldehyde, reminding me of its presence.

"If the spirit had passed over—"

"The ways to the Solace are sealed," I said.

Miles did some prestidigitation and rolled a perfect, if filterless, cigarette. "Right. It can't be that."

Robin gave him the eye. "You were trying to quit."

"I'm having a bad day," Miles said, and handed her his first smoke. "Grace?"

I gagged just thinking about it. "I can't smoke in this room."

Miles jerked his head in the direction of a black-painted door. "Leads to a drive for the funeral wagons."

"Thank all the Makers," I said. "Can we please go outside?"

Miles handed me his second hand-roll. "In a minute. Another possibility remains."

He looked up, and I knew he meant the crown of souls that shone in his aura. Robin saw it too, and her brow wrinkled. "Sevitii's soul could have been bound, you mean? I thought that had to be consensual."

"I don't know if that's true," I said. "I saw Aldis bind Sir Percy's soul at his execution."

"Really," Miles said. "So that's where it came from."

I nodded and blew out a sigh. "Can you hide a witchmark the way you hide your aura, Miss Thorpe?"

Robin put the cigarette between her lips. "I don't know. There's too much we don't know about magic. But if I had to guess . . ."

Miles popped another perfectly rolled cigarette into his mouth, leading the way to the exit. He stopped next to a lever, and when he pulled it, the black door swung open without him having to touch it. He rolled through the door and onto a covered driveway that was mostly protected from the snowfall.

Our breaths puffed out in front of us. The wind caught Miles's hair, tumbling it around his ears. I wrapped my arms around my ribs for warmth. Robin pulled out a gas lighter and flicked it out between lighting her own, then Miles's, then mine.

Miles smoked like a soldier, with the one end pinched between his thumb and forefinger, the burning coal hidden by his palm. He sighed out a long stream of smoke, musing to himself. "So she can't have gone into the Solace. She might have been bound against her will. What else?"

"I will look into it," Robin said. "I have old diaries hidden at home. I can do some research and tell you more."

"Thank you," I said. "You don't have to do this."

Robin exhaled in a plume of smoke. "I'm always willing to help a friend."

She meant Miles and not me, of course, but that didn't matter. "I don't know what you know about the victim."

"I know she's Laneeri—wait. Her star bangle. Where is it?"

"We searched the suite and couldn't find it," I said.

Robin nodded, as if she had expected it. "That might be significant."

"How? Miles never explained."

Miles rolled his neck, stretching the muscles. "Star bangles have hair inside them, cut on their fifth birthday, when a young Laneeri is named with their omen."

I was still a little lost. "And the bangle will tell you Sevitii's omen?"

"They're kept secret," Miles said. "But it's the hair that's important. You know how Father always ordered our hair and nails from cutting be burned, and cloths with our blood—"

"Every four weeks," I said.

"It's because they're sympathetic links," Miles said. "If you have the hair, you have the man. Or woman. Or kesi. If a magician had Sevitii's star bangle, it wouldn't matter if the door was locked and guarded."

"I still think we need to interview all the staff charged with guarding Sevitii or keeping up the suite."

"An excellent idea," Miles said. "I'll take notes for you."

"I have to be on my way," Robin said. "I have another engagement, and I'm going to be late. If you need me, Miles—"

"I'll write."

Robin bent to hug Miles around the shoulders. "You'll see

me soon," she said, and then turned to regard me. "Chancellor Hensley."

"Miss Thorpe."

We nodded to each other, and then she returned to the mortuary, her ghostly kin following behind her.

The guard station wasn't far from the mortuary, and a look at the duty roster revealed that one of the guards we had tapped to monitor Sevitii was on parade guard in the grand vestibule of the palace. He reported to us in an unused office in scarlet serge, brass buttons, and a spotless white cape, draped to accommodate the saber hanging from his hip.

"Corporal Sadler? Thank you for coming," I said. "Please sit down."

He planted himself in front of us but stared straight at a replica of the official portrait of Crown Prince Severin, the titular commander of the Queensguard, avoiding our gaze entirely. "Thank you, ma'am, but I should stand. How may I serve the Chancellor?"

"You were assigned to guard my suite and ensure that its occupant was secure, Corporal Sadler. I have the entry roster here, indicating that no one but maids, myself, and Miles ever entered the suite while you were in charge of its care."

Corporal Sadler's jaw clenched as he swallowed, but he kept staring down the opposite wall. "Yes, ma'am."

Miles leaned an elbow on his wheelchair's armrest and eyed me, just in case I hadn't noticed.

"Is it correct?" I asked.

He hesitated before answering. "I wasn't on all shifts, but yes, ma'am."

"Did anyone ever stop to ask you why you were guarding the Chancellor's suite?" Miles asked.

"Yes, sir," the guard replied. "Pages, other guards. Plenty of people asked."

"And what did you tell them?" I asked.

"That we had our orders, ma'am." He kept his gaze on the wall, his posture even stiffer than before. "But we never told them about the prisoner."

"Tell me about the prisoner," I said. "Did she ever try to communicate with you?"

"She couldn't speak Aelander, ma'am."

"How did you know that?" Miles asked.

He glanced at Miles before answering. "Because she tried to convince us to take a message to the other Laneeri prisoners, sir. We said no."

"But you weren't the only guards with a shift," Miles said. "If you had to guess, who would have been most likely to take her message?"

Corporal Sadler swallowed again. "She tried to give us gold, sir. Bracelets."

"Were they engraved, or decorated in any way?"

His brow wrinkled. "They were engraved, ma'am. I don't remember the pattern."

"She wouldn't have," Miles said. "Not her star bangle."

"I'm inclined to agree, but we need to check if any of the guards we were assigned had money problems," I said to Miles, who was already uncapping his pen.

"Private Fuller, ma'am," Corporal Sadler said. "He's got a grandfather who gets lost in his memories. They're waiting for a place at the care home, but it's a long wait and home care is expensive."

"That's a hard place to be in," Miles said. "Did anyone ever ask to see the prisoner? Someone you didn't want to write down on the roster. Maybe trying to bring a message back to the prisoner?"

Corporal Sadler's gaze darted off to the right. "No, sir."

"What if this person was important?" I asked, and Sadler closed his eyes. His shoulders sank a fraction of an inch. Then he pressed his lips shut.

"You know why you're not on that duty any more," I said. "You were there yesterday when we brought her out."

He opened his eyes, still staring at the wall. No. At the portrait of the Crown Prince. "I should return to my duties now, ma'am."

"Corporal Sadler," Miles said. "The Chancellor of Aeland is asking you a question."

"Regulations only allow a relief break of five minutes—"

"If it was someone less powerful than me, you could rely on my protection," I said. "You'd be able to tell me who wanted admittance to the Chancellor's suite. So that leaves someone more powerful. Someone I can't protect you from."

"Ma'am—"

"The Queen came to see the prisoner. Or Crown Prince Severin did."

"Ma'am," Corporal Sadler said. "Please."

Miles glanced at me. "Prince Severin."

"You're sure?"

Miles nodded. "Queen Constantina wouldn't have come alone—she would have brought the Guard-General. And she wouldn't have to demand secrecy."

Corporal Sadler licked his lips. Fear gleamed on his face. He didn't try to deny it, though.

"Thank you, Corporal. You may go."

His hand trembled as he pushed down the door lever and let himself out. Miles and I sat in silence, listening to the cadence of his footsteps as he retreated.

"Why would Prince Severin want Sevitii dead?" Miles asked. "He was ready to give her what she wanted, wasn't he?"

"He'd said as much." I reached for the duty roster and scanned it. "And he was with the Queen when I saw her that day."

"Was that an hour before my estimated time of death?"

I looked up from the roster. "Could it have been two? Corporal Sadler had reported in an hour before your estimate of Sevitii's death."

"The bathwater," Miles said. "Severin said it was still hot."

I closed my eyes and walked my memory back to searching the bathing chamber. "I never checked it for myself. But if he had killed her and then filled the tub with steaming hot water, and then went to turn off the dripping tap—"

"His fingerprints would be in the bathroom," Miles said.

"We're not really considering this, are we?" I asked. "We don't really think—"

"He's not the only suspect," Miles said. "Just the first."

Suspect. The Crown Prince, a suspect. I let out a shuddering breath. "He's not a mage. He would have had to leave evidence of how he killed her so suddenly."

"Sevitii could have been smothered with a rubber sack. He could have let her fall, then filled the bathtub to throw off time of death. It's possible."

"But why would he do it? What would he gain from it?"

"And how could we hold him accountable, even if he had?" Miles asked. "That's the part that worries me most."

"Sevitii tried to get a message to someone among the Laneeri," I said. "She was no mage, but every one of those star priests were. What if the bracelet wasn't a bribe? What if she gave her star bangle to someone in the delegation?"

Miles chewed on the idea and shook his head. "Maybe. They're supposed to allow a loved one to determine if the bangle holder is alive or dead. If she had a lover or— Her father."

"Niikanis," I said. "What if she gave it to him, to assure him she was fine? We have to question him."

"You don't have time," Miles said. "You have to go home and change, and then come back here for the ball."

"Blast it. We don't have time for this." But my ball gown waited for me at home, and when I returned, Avia would be my guest.

I'd introduce her to Amaranthines—to Grand Duchess Aife herself—and perhaps we'd get a moment where we could share a drink and talk about something that wasn't a scandal or a secret. Maybe I could make her laugh. Maybe I could have an evening, an hour, a minute where we could drop the press license and the Chancellor's robes to be Avia and Grace, the burden of our surnames discarded.

"Grace," Miles said. "Where'd you go?"

I shook my head. "I was thinking."

"It must have been good. Anyway, let's go. I promised Tristan I'd have a nap with him when he came back."

"A nap." I huffed out a laugh. "I'm sure it will be restful."

"Eventually it will be," Miles said. He gathered up our notes and the copy of the duty roster and led the way out of the guard office, humming to himself.

I walked with him to the ambassador's wing, then went outside Government House to wait for William and George to bring the sleigh around. I would see Avia tonight. I wondered if she would show up wearing red.

THIRTEEN

Edge of Night, Falling

Edith controlled every minute I spent in Hensley House before the ball, according to her schedule of resting, last-minute beauty treatments, and a carefully portioned meal (enough to satisfy without overindulging). She could barely contain herself at the moment of triumph as I descended the golden oak stairs clad in a snow-white gown covered in sparkling crystal beads, my neck and ears draped in silver-mounted diamonds and pearls, a full-length snow-weasel cloak around my shoulders.

She'd outdone herself. Every detail was perfect. Silver dancing slippers peeked from beneath my glittering hem with every step. My nails were carefully shaped and lacquered white with silver carefully painted along the oval tips. I moved in a cloud of white orchid perfume. I let William hand me into the sled, the soft white fur cozy around my neck as we dashed under a starlit night to arrive at the palace.

I tucked my check tag into the pocket hidden in the lining of my thin white gloves and strode the violet running carpet to the largest ballroom in Mountrose Palace. Dancing music grew louder, the three-beat time beckoning. Would we dance,

Avia and I, uncaring of the glances and speculation of titillated guests?

The entrance framed the scene as I walked in—whirling dancers cavorted before the Queen's dais while the monarch played a strategy game with Elsine Pelfrey, the two of them intent on a battle only one of them would win. The landed mixed with the Hundred Families, and together they eyed the tall, fantastic company of the Amaranthine cohort, whose attire was like jewels against the restrained, near colorless elegance of their mortal hosts.

I thought of dances hosted by King's Academy where all the girls hovered on one side of the room, so that trying to approach one was like accepting a dare. The only Amaranthines on the floor were Tristan, laughing softly as Miles taught him the basic step of a promenade, and Grand Duchess Aife, receiving the same lesson from Crown Prince Severin.

There were no clocks. I wore no watch. Time meant nothing at an Aelander ball—the musicians would play until after the Queen had retired, signaling to all that they were free to leave, and that was the only measure that mattered.

No. There was another, and that was the subtle collection of glances following me as I drifted through the crowd. Curious looks that cut away toward the same point in the room; slight, anticipatory smiles that couldn't wait for the fireworks.

So, word had gotten around, had it? I stopped a server and plucked a wide, shallow-bowled glass of sparkling wine from her tray. The bubbles kissed my nose as I picked a location that would afford my onlookers the best view while I watched my brother and my friend dance.

The crowd fluttered at my back, and I scarcely counted three before Raymond, garbed in the sober black and white of evening dress, planted himself in front of me. He smiled—or at least, he tried.

"Grace," he said. "I thought we understood the need to move quickly on selecting a new Cabinet."

"Did we understand that?" I asked. "It's best to do these things with the full consideration of everyone involved, in my opinion."

Raymond scoffed, amused at a feeble effort to resist his influence. "This delay is foolish. I thought you wanted to lead us."

I sipped excellent wine. "Your list was ridiculous, Ray. I know your father didn't apply himself to training you to make politically astute decisions, but I thought you were wiser than those choices."

"So you think your choices will warm you up to the others? Do you imagine that a mention in the Queen's ear is all it takes to sway them?"

Didn't he notice how interested the others were in this little exchange? I made him wait for my response as I held another fizzy mouthful of the Widow Vanier's Deer Valley on my tongue, the high floral tones dancing with a dozen partners, the flavors shifting like the sparkling reflection of water at sunset.

I smiled at him when I finally answered. "I imagine no such thing, my dear. I considered your list, and some of your choices number among my recommendations—not the foolish ones, of course."

"I see." Raymond gave me a regretful look made of pasteboard and paint. "Well. I suppose we'll simply declare no confidence and hold an election next week."

I nearly laughed. "No one told you. All those friends, all those admirers, and not a single one of them said a word."

He stared at me. "You've had rather too much of that vintage, I fear."

"Raymond. Listen carefully now; this is important." I

leaned a little closer, as if I were about to tell him a secret. "I withdrew all my stock in Blake Properties yesterday."

All the blood drained from his face. I gave him a moment to remember how much stock my father had purchased after he and I became engaged. After that, I let him have another, to remember that I sat on the board in my father's stead.

And then at last, I spoke. "I arrived too late to contact the transfer agent at the Royal Aeland Exchange, but my agent is taking them in when it opens on Firstday."

He licked his lips. Swallowed. "Grace. You can't."

"Can't I? The certificates are mine. I decide if they're worth keeping—or not." I let my focus slide from him to survey all the people watching us, too far away to hear. Richard Poole grinned at me and raised his glass in tribute.

Raymond Blake had forgotten one vital, universal thing: Everyone loves watching the powerful tumble from grace. Even the elite can't resist the drama of justice done—or revenge fulfilled.

Waxed paper cards fluttered in my imagination, spinning in the air as they fell. "I welcome your suggestions, as ever, but ultimately I must guide the direction of government soberly, prudently, and wisely. I make the decisions. Do you understand me?"

Hate shone on his face. He nodded, one tight jerk of his chin.

I returned his nod, a single serene dip. "I'll speak to my agent in the morning."

He unclamped his lips and twisted his mouth into a smiling grimace. "Enjoy it while you can, Dame Grace."

A server passed with a tray full of honeyed glauce, and I snagged a glass, presenting it to my enemy. "Here. You look like you could use a drink."

I didn't gloat when I walked away. It wouldn't do to appear graceless. But I felt seven feet tall as I moved from one vantage point to the next, scanning the crowd for the column of crimson I had half convinced myself I would see.

A young man in formal black and white stood in the entry to the ballroom. He was late, handing over his invitation, and raising his— No. I caught the sight of red-painted lips, a shining cap of bottle-black hair curved around full cheekbones, and stared.

Avia Jessup had arrived in full white tie, nipped and fitted to her figure, just like Dorian Salter in *Edge of Night, Falling*. She was a sensation. She was breathtaking. I set down my glass and crossed the room, helpless to do anything but get closer.

She bent over my hand, the light warmth of her breath kissing over the skin.

"I'm sorry I'm late."

Everyone was staring, but none of that mattered. "I'm sorry we're not dancing."

She winked and led the way as heads turned.

We took a place on the floor during the introduction that gave dancers time to arrive or leave. Avia rested her hand at my waist as if she led in dancing all the time. She could have danced like this a hundred times; often enough that her heart didn't pound in her chest at how she dared to stand with a woman and guide her through the weaving, complicated steps and turns of a promenade for two.

Flautists in the musicians' loft stood up and led the first tempo change, and Avia took so light a step, her fingers resting easy on my waist, guiding me with trust and the sparkle in her eyes. We were on air. The music pulled us, and we hadn't gone a quarter of the way around the floor before she spun me out, rising on her toes as I reeled back into her hold.

"You are very good," she said.

I was? "You're doing everything."

"You're letting me."

We changed to the circling step when we passed by the throne, whirling in a pattern that would trip me if I thought about what I was doing. I landed the fourth turn and we paused, catching the music's change to a slower tempo.

Her hair flared as we spun, falling back into place as we traveled, the locks curving lovingly around her cheeks as the music swelled. She held me in her hands, with her eyes—I looked at nothing that wasn't her, caught in her shining smile.

I should be making conversation, light and easy talk that had deserted me while I was busy being enchanted. I reached for a comment. "You look incredible. Like you came from the cinema."

She smiled, and murmured, so low I had to see her lips to be sure I heard her correctly: "I borrowed this suit. It was Nick Elliot's."

I kept my step even through the shock. "Was he your friend?"

"I'm glad you didn't pretend ignorance at his death." The flutes sang a melody everyone knew well enough to hum, and we danced on, never missing a step. "I regret that I didn't understand him, at the end. I wish I had known then what I know now."

Solace! All our meetings collided in my memory. All the questions she'd asked, all the research she'd dangled in front of me—she had been following in Nick's footsteps, tracing the path that had led to his murder. She wasn't searching for a connection between the events of Frostmonth 1; she already had them.

She spoke into my silence. "I hoped that you were different. That you were innocent. I was a fool to imagine that you weren't shaped from the same mold as your father."

"I'm not."

"Really." She sent me whirling in an open turn and caught me in the smooth, assured hold of an experienced lead. "I know what you made the witches do to make aether."

"Nick's manuscript," I said. "You have it."

The smile never left her face; her gaze never strayed from mine. "Nick figured it out. And he was going to publish it."

All those questions she had asked had been for a purpose. She wanted me to admit what had been done. She had wanted my cooperation, had hoped for it, but what she wanted was impossible. "Avia. You can't. Please, if you let this out—"

"I don't think you may tell me what I can and cannot do, my lady." She never missed a step. She never let me stumble. "How long have you known what they did in those asylums?"

"Since the day the lights went out."

"Why are they out?" she asked. "I want to hear you say it."

"Because I—" I caught the sentence and held it through an unwinding spin, tethered only by her gentle grip on my hand. I described an arc with my free hand, winding myself back into her hold. "We destroyed it. Me, Miles, and Tristan. Then the Amaranthines came and saved Miles's life."

That surprised her enough to break her smiling mask. "You broke it, not the Amaranthines? Why?"

"You know what it was," I whispered. "How could we have allowed it to exist? What would you have done?"

She kept silent. Thinking? She had to understand. She must! "I swear, Avia. I didn't know. And when I did, I couldn't allow it to exist. I couldn't."

The corners of her mouth pinned back, her face tight as she wrestled with my decision. "But you're trying to hide it ever happened. The witches aren't free. The dead walk among us. Your effort to deceive ends tomorrow, when the afternoon edition comes out."

The music sped to the final, breathless tempo. Avia twirled us through the circling step, coming to a halt on the final chord and bowing to me with one hand on her heart. Then she raised her head, high color in her cheeks.

"Thank you for the dance, Chancellor."

She led me to the edge of the parquet, then left me standing alone.

Avia had taken me off the dance floor with every courtesy, but I felt as if she had slapped my face and stalked off. I'd been a fool to think I could keep the truth from her. Yesterday I had been troubled, but still worthy. Now I was left trembling and alone in a crowd. I couldn't stand here much longer. Someone would speak to me of trivialities, or ask me to dance, and then I would have to smile and chat and no, no, I couldn't possibly.

I left the ballroom by the balcony doors, moving down the concrete stairs to the glasshouse, which glowed softly in the moonlight. The unlocked door slid aside at my touch, the casters grinding in the shocking, bone-deep cold to exhale warm air that smelled of rich earth, thriving greenery, and clean running water. I slid the door closed and let the damp warmth seep into me, so different from the stuffy, body-smelling heat of the ballroom.

From far away, the orchestra sounded another introduction to a dance. I picked out the steps along the winding path, caressing the large, waxy leaves of plants that had sailed across the Ayers Ocean to rest in this tiny patch of unreal summer shielded from Aeland's snow and frost.

Alone and away from curious stares. I could bite my lip, and did, focusing on the warm dull pain it gave freely. I could bow my head and wrap my arms around my middle. I could shake and tremble, sick at Avia's parting words. It would all come out tomorrow afternoon. Aeland would march toward the end as its citizens rose up in just fury, throwing over the order that had brought the Amaranthines who watched and waited to see what we did next, how we proved ourselves worthy of their mercy.

Would the Amaranthines have mercy for blood in the streets? Would they have mercy for the mob, that creature of violent mind and devastating purpose? I doubted they would. And then the merciless storms following the end of the Hundred Families would destroy whoever was left standing. If Avia revealed the truth, Aeland wouldn't survive the year.

I couldn't allow Avia to print that story. But how could I dissuade her? She had come clad in the suit of her dead comrade, her dear friend. Avia knew what Nick had been murdered for knowing. She could bring the whole card-tower down with the flick of a touch, and she was angry enough with me to do it. I imagined her vowing retribution as she knotted her white silk tie and promised her reflection that justice would come to Kingston.

And it should. It should. All the secrets she uncovered, the ones I tried so desperately to keep—they protected the people responsible from suffering any consequences. Oh, the First Ring was in prison, but that was to save Constantina's neck. Father might go to the hangman, but he would die for a tenth of the things he had done to Aeland.

The calculating, selfish part of my mind fixed itself on the First Ring. They were already locked up. Most of them were of my father's generation. Many of them were complicit. They could take the blame—they deserved the blame. If Avia named them, that might deflect anger away from those of us who worked to keep the storms at bay.

I had to find a way to convince her to follow my strategy, to be careful, and gentle, and guide the people through this devastating knowledge. I could bring her out here to this bit of summer, and—

"You're in the way."

I startled, bounced out of my thoughts. Aldis emerged from the shadowed canopy of banana trees, striding into the slice of moonlight where I had stopped.

I straightened my posture, bringing up my chin just a shade too high to be deferential. "I beg your pardon. I didn't know I wasn't alone."

Moonlight and shadow revealed his sneer. "I was alone until you came."

Oh, this ungracious, hostile man. "I apologize for the intrusion. If you will excuse me, I will go and seek solitude elsewhere."

He interrupted my retreat with his snide voice. "Is this what you imagine Laneer to be?" he asked. "Green plants and running streams, and nothing worthy of respect?"

"No," I said. "Port Walan was a vibrant, cosmopolitan city that had welcomed trade and the exchange of friendship, until the Magal overthrew the rightful ruler and closed off decades of trade with us."

He scoffed. "Is that the story they told? That a despot possessed the throne, and so you had to save Laneer from her?"

"Do you deny a coup took place?"

"I deny that it was a reasonable excuse to slaughter millions in your quest to strip everything of value you could find, down to consuming the souls of a country to fuel pretty lights."

I swallowed the lump in my throat. "I do too. The war was wrong. There's something we agree on."

Aldis cocked his head. "This is where you tell me that you were innocent."

"I was ignorant," I said. "That's not quite the same. But you know what I did when I learned the truth."

"I know that you haven't said a word in defense of the political prisoners languishing in your Tower of Sighs."

"Laneeri tortured my brother." My knuckles ached with the tension of my fists. "They kidnapped him. They kept him in the worst prison camp they had, and whatever they did, it was so unspeakable that he still hasn't told me what happened. And you want me to unlock those cells and serve his enemies tea?"

"You forgot the apology."

"I will never apologize to the people who came here to destroy innocents." I cut my hand across the air to swipe the proposition away. "I am sorry for the people who actually had to fight each other for the sake of greed, and power, and dominion. They didn't deserve what happened. To them, I am sorry. Now if you will excuse me—"

"I will not." Aldis towered over me, tall and red-faced. "You have taken an important diplomat from Kingsgrave Prison. What have you done with her?"

Blast it all to pieces! I couldn't answer him. We had given no word of Sevitii's death, made no announcement, and now their champion among the Amaranthines was asking me a perfectly valid question. "I do not have to tell you anything about our dealings with the Laneeri."

"They are diplomats."

"They are criminals." I wanted to twist the knobs of time and take that last word back, but I leaned into Aldis's space and made a dart of my finger, jabbing it in the air between us. "The details of prisoner interviews are none of your business."

Aldis caught my wrist, squeezing all the tiny, mobile bones against each other. "The welfare of the Laneeri is my business because I say it is. I won't ask you again. What has become of Sevitii an Vaavut?"

Aldis's eyes were dark and sharp. He stood so tall, taller

even than Tristan, and he was luminous, unearthly. My tongue slid back to shape the answer, to tell him what he wanted, anything he wanted, more. Aldis looked into me and knew the truth. I saw the truth in his eyes.

His eyes, too large to be human. His face, unearthly and delicate and utterly fascinating. He wound the spell around me, and a small part of me screamed in protest.

I caught the hem of his enchantment and ripped the web into shreds, shaking now.

"Let me go."

My whole body went hot. I burned, and my hair stood on end as that heat rushed through me, rising to the sky to erupt in jagged forks of blue-white light.

Aldis flinched and let go as a deafening crack split the air, thunder roaring. I backed away, my eyes shut against his bewitchment.

"Never touch me again." I raised my hand, fuzzy with the reverse-magnet feeling of lightning about to strike. "Never."

Voices cut through the haze. The grinding squeak of the glasshouse door sliding open made me drop the power and turn around. Prince Severin rushed to me, his hands on my gloved arms their own shock. "Are you all right?"

I stepped out of his grip, smiling. "Thank you. I'm just unsettled. I should probably go inside and see how Miles is—"

I smiled at the curious faces, the quizzical looks, and the frowns of those who knew the lightning for what it was. But the Crown Prince caught up to me, his palm warm on the plane of my back, just between the shoulder blades.

"I was looking for you anyway. Forget all this. Come and have a dance."

He meant to be my shield against the others. He would hide me in plain sight, protected by his presence. The onlookers

would have to adjust their assumptions by taking my friendship with the future King of Aeland into account.

It was a clever move. I let him lead me to the parquet, settling my hold—one hand on his shoulder, the other laid on his
palm—and had nothing to do but to look into his starry dark
eyes and mirror his pleased smile until the violins swelled and
our feet trod the measure.

Three minutes of refuge. Severin stood with me in hold,
and we waited for the opening theme to end.

"I had guards search the Laneeri cells earlier this afternoon," Severin said through his glad expression. "They found a
trove of star bangles in the cell of their head priest, Niikanis an
Vaavut. One was missing. I think we've found our murderer."

FOURTEEN

An Attempt at Strategy

I groped for something to say, something that wasn't incredulous or frustrated, but the music began at that moment. Prince Severin's movements became a dance. The braid on his shoulder scratched on my fingertips, the serge beneath it woven from the hand-combed undercoat of northern long-hair goats. I heard the orders of my dancing master—spine straight but not stiff. Shoulders down. Let the neck be free, the head balanced upon it, and glide.

A kettledrum boomed twice. Drums and brass chased winds and strings as we danced across the measures, his steps pursuing, mine retreating. He smiled at me, the lines by his eyes deepening with his pleasure. "It's good news, is it not?"

He'd put himself into the investigation the way Clarence Hawkes's character had in *Ten before Midnight*. Hawkes assisted the glamorous Phryne Davis's character—the sleuth who wasn't convinced that Darlene Charlesworth, cast as the lovely woman accused of murdering her grandmother to speed her inheritance, was guilty. He'd been there every step of the way, misleading them until the final realization. Was Miles right?

"Grace?"

"My apologies." My cheeks flared with heat. I shrugged and smiled at my absentmindedness. "The gears started turning. I was thinking about possibilities for motive."

"You never stop working," Severin said. "You're absolutely tireless. Have you any working theories?"

"Nothing but a basket of questions," I said. Why had he done it? "I wonder at motive, but I was wasting my time speculating. Is the prisoner in isolation?"

"Yes. He has no contact with his delegation."

At least he'd done that correctly. "That's perfect. Miles and I will interview him in the morning."

"And so we set that bit of work aside." Severin didn't look where he was going, preferring to aim all his attention at me. He whirled us through the circling step, fell into the simpler traveling step, but he never let go of me long enough to execute a turn. Everyone watching would wonder at so possessive a gesture, and the chances that I wouldn't be the subject floating over every breakfasting table in the Western Point plummeted to the ground.

This entire evening had torn the reins from my hands. Avia sat knee to knee with Grand Duchess Aife, their heads bent together in deep conversation. Ray couldn't stop watching me. His hatred blazed so strongly it should have melted the ice in his drink. Aldis wasn't anywhere in sight, and that could easily be cause for worry or relief.

"The work never stops," I said, "even when we don our finest and dance. Thank you for getting me away from Aldis."

"What did he do to incite your temper?"

"He demanded to know the whereabouts of Sevitii an Vaavut," I said. "When I wouldn't tell him, he dropped the glamor over his true visage and tried to compel me into revealing it."

"He what." There was something in Severin's eyes that made me think of the focused but pitiless stare of a falcon.

I fought the urge to lick dry lips. "I lost my temper. It was foolish."

"It was human," Prince Severin said. "I know you must sheathe yourself in the impenetrable armor of perfection, but imagine if he'd done that to someone who wasn't as strong as you. Imagine if he'd done it to me. I will speak to Grand Duchess Aife about this."

If Aldis had unleashed his power to enthrall on Prince Severin—it was unthinkable. "Thank you," I said. "But we have to report on the death. We can't hide it forever."

"We don't have to," Severin said. "We can say that we were negotiating with her, that her death was of unnatural cause, and that we already have a suspect in custody. The matter is in hand. We delayed announcement because of the timing."

I kept from surveying the curious faces turned toward us but tempered my smiles, hoping it would be enough to thread doubt among the inevitable gossip. Severin was too intent on our subject to realize how interesting his behavior was. "That should satisfy most people."

"I don't know if it would satisfy your friend. Inviting her here was imprudent."

"Aife wished to speak with an ordinary Aelander," I said.

"Avia Jessup is hardly ordinary."

"I happen to agree," I said. "But she was the best choice."

"She's a scandal," Severin declared. "That suit. As if the absurdity of cinema dramatics had any place here."

The Prince adored the symphony, the opera, the theater and dance presentations, but he had never once accepted an invitation to a cinema premiere. "I didn't give her enough notice to arrange a ball gown."

He shrugged, his mouth still sour. "At least her father bought her decent training in manners. She hasn't done anything unspeakable. But I don't think you'll get away with this without hearing from Mother."

"Certainly not. I expect she'll be displeased." When the paper revealed everything we'd worked so hard to keep secret, Queen Constantina would be furious. Maybe even angry enough to charge Avia with sedition.

My stomach did a slow roll. Before the uprising, Avia would hang, and there would be nothing I could do to stop it. I had to convince her to hold back. Everything would fall apart if she went ahead with the story.

"You look worried," Severin said. "I can be there, if you like. I'll put in a word or two about the foolishness of denying the Blessed Ones what they ask for, the generosity of your intentions."

"Thank you."

The music swelled to its final measures. Severin kept us in hold, our steps whirling us in circles until the very end. He smiled, his hand still at my waist.

"Thank you for the dance."

He stepped back, laid his hand over his heart, and bowed to me in front of the entire ballroom—gallant, elegant, his form perfect. A gesture of great respect hardly ever delivered from a royal to one of lesser station—even the shallow step down to the Royal Knights. It meant that an insult to me was one to him, and one that he would answer.

I wished that the intricately joined parquet would open beneath my feet and swallow me up. Instead, I bent my knee almost to the floor, bowing my head in complete respect for a royal heir. It was a gesture that returned all courtesy without a presumption of affection, the respect of a subject rather than the familiarity of a friend.

Let the gossips chew on that. I let Severin escort me from

the dance floor, watching a group of Amaranthines, including Avia among their number, who stepped onto the dance floor and clapped their hands for a fast-paced square-of-eight dance. The orchestra players glanced at each other, but one violinist stood up and played an energetic dancing tune, and the players who knew it joined in.

It wasn't done, playing square-of-eight or line dances at a formal ball. Instinct turned my head to look at the Queen. She watched me intently, and when I locked gazes with her, she raised her hand and beckoned.

I slipped my hand from Severin's arm. "It seems the Queen has no one to partner her at her gaming table. I've been summoned."

"Then you must go, and I must speak to Raymond Blake," Severin said. "I'll join you with Mother if I have time."

I turned my steps toward the dais where Queen Constantina waited for me, her mouth pinched tight.

No board game awaited my arrival. Constantina had no smile as I approached the throne, the seams of my skirt straining as I bent knee and waited for her to speak of whatever she wished to say.

"I wonder if you think before you act, Dame Grace, or if you just do as the whim takes you. What explanation have you for your actions this evening?"

"Majesty," I began, buying a moment to think. "My most sincere apologies for the disruption. Sir Aldis had taken serious liberties with my will. I ask forgiveness for my outburst. I was desperate to retain the integrity of my loyalties."

The Queen leaned forward. "Loyalties."

Oh, fool! "To you, ma'am. To Aeland. To the invisibility of our efforts."

She sat back. "Rise."

I was on my feet with hardly a wobble. "I am sorry, ma'am."

"I know." She tapped one finger against the arm of her throne, her hand resting on a carved gryphon's head. "What is your opinion of my son?"

My heart stopped for an instant. "Crown Prince Severin, ma'am?"

Her tone went dry. "I only have one son, girl. What do you think of him?"

"I think he's a man of strong conscience and integrity. A sober thinker, well-liked—"

"Do you think he's loyal?"

Behind me, Amaranthines stamped their feet and shouted. "I think he's deeply committed to Aeland and its way of life, ma'am."

"Hmph." Queen Constantina made a sour face. "He appears so to you."

I kept my face poised in attentive neutrality while a fraction of my mind screeched. She knew. She knew what Severin meant to do, and she knew that I swore to him, and she was going to make us both pay.

She picked up a cordial glass and sipped, but it didn't sweeten her expression one bit. "He's trying to bargain Aeland to these Amaranthines. Anything they ask, he nods his head and comes to me with the most ridiculous proposals. You'd shake your head if you knew what they imagine they can demand from us."

I didn't say anything. She didn't need me to.

"I want you to make him see reason. You're skilled in the art of compromise. You're keeping the Lower House in line, and you've made insightful choices for the Cabinet, considering what you have to work with. Make him see that we can't hand over the keys to the safe and empty it just because the Amaranthines threaten us."

So she was trying to deny what the Amaranthines wanted, and put the blame on her son, and wanted me to push her refusal. My plan would point a red-stained finger straight at her. How could the First Ring know something the monarch did not, after all? But Severin—Severin had been an infant, if he had even been born yet. Innocent. Idealistic.

I had to play this game of revelations exactly right, or she would kick me out of the Chancellor's seat. And I couldn't help anyone if I didn't have the power to push my changes into law. "Ma'am—"

The music ended to an outpouring of applause. The Queen looked to her left and nodded. The guards at that end of the dais marched onto the dance floor.

Gasps chorused, and murmurs played the counterpoint. Aife's voice rose above the hum. "Miss Jessup is my dancing partner, and I thank you to release her at once."

I twisted, but I couldn't see. "Ma'am, Miss Jessup is my guest. I invited her."

"Whatever possessed you to invite a journalist, much less a squinting gossip, to a royal dance?"

"She's my friend," I said, and winced as Avia came into view, her arms held by a pair of scarlet-coated guards. "Must she leave now?"

"She's been an embarrassment and a scandal all evening," the Queen said, "and I have had enough of her antics."

"But I need to— Ma'am, please excuse me, I apologize wholeheartedly, but I have to—"

The Queen stayed silent as a statue.

"I have to go," I gasped.

I whirled to dash across the floor, pursuing Avia and her

guards to the tune of outraged exclamations. They were half-way down the hall with her before I closed with them.

"I'll go quietly," Avia was saying as I clattered down the hall at a run. "You don't have to bundle me out like a ragbag—Grace."

"You two. Stop," I said. "Let go. Miss Jessup is leaving under my escort. You can go now."

The guards glanced at each other, but they released Avia's arms. She gingerly pressed her fingers on her upper arms and winced. "That's a bruise."

"I'll ask for a report on their records."

"Don't bother," Avia said, her tone weary. "What do you want, Chancellor?"

"I need to talk to you," I said, shaking all over.

She shook her head, and every bottle-black strand fell exactly into place. "Do you have anything to say that I haven't heard before?"

I glanced around, judging what the stationed ceremonial guards might hear even if I whispered. "Not here."

We retrieved our belongings from the attendants set to guard them. Avia eyed my snow-weasel cloak as I allowed the attendant to drape it over my shoulders. I shivered. She was probably thinking of how the price of it could feed a family for—how long, if milk was usually ten cents a quart? I shook my head, banishing the thought, and led her out to the palace steps. A page ran for the orange sled halfway down the line.

Behind a tall iron gate, protesters huddled around barrel fires, the flickering orange light dancing off their signs, some of which were too dark too see, others stark with a single word: "Shame." "Shame." "Shame."

They deserved better. They deserved to be safe and warm at home, snug in their beds, getting a good night's rest before earning a day's fair wages. They shouldn't be out here, screaming to get our attention.

They should have it. And we should be working to help them.

Avia buttoned up a felted wool coat. "What is it, Chancellor?"

Chancellor. It hit me low in the stomach, solid and cold. "Let me offer you a ride home."

"Let me invite you to tell me whatever you had to say."

My stomach writhed. Everything rode on this moment. Avia watched me with narrow eyes as I fought to loosen my tongue. I had to convince her to abandon her article. That meant I had to give her a reason. I had to tell her the truth.

My shoulders untensed. Relief was warm in my middle. There was only one thing I could do, and so I got to it.

"You're right. I should have confided in you. I'll start right now," I said.

But it wasn't that easy. My mouth dried up, and I squinted as the wind shifted to strike me in the face. I had to fight to say it, to look nowhere but at Avia's face as I told her the first of a long, long line of truths:

"My father killed Nick Elliot. And if you're not careful, he'll kill you too."

FIFTEEN

Mrs. Sparkle

Avia stared at me without saying anything as the sled pulled up. She stood where she was as William opened the half-door of the rear seat, watching me until a decision flickered in the depths of her eyes.

"Tell me the rest."

I hid a grateful sigh as she allowed William to assist her. I bundled in after her and we were back in my sled, our toes perched on the foot-warmer, our hands curled around steel hot-water bottles perched in our laps. William sat in the front with George, and I huddled close to Avia, keeping my voice down.

"Father found out what Nick was planning, and my father had him murdered to hide the truth about aether and the asylums. But there's another thing you have to know."

"More than one, I reckon."

I sighed and swiped my hand through my hair, and it flopped into my eyes immediately. "There's a hundred things you have to know, but please hold your story until I have told you all of them."

Avia regarded me with an assessing gaze. "And when will you do that, Dame Grace?"

I sucked in a breath of throat-chilling air. "Now," I said. "I'm a witch. We're all witches—the Royal Knights, I mean."

She didn't seem surprised by that at all. I plunged on. "Aeland depends on our magic to survive. You recall the storm?"

"Of course."

"We used our magic to calm it as much as we could. That's what you'll see—blizzards with winds that could tear off a rooftop. Snow as high as a man is tall, falling in a single day. Spring flooding destroying the first planting; famine, drought, late-summer hurricanes."

Avia looked up at me, understanding in her eyes. "So that's the noble reason for asking me to join your conspiracy. Because you protect the people with your magic."

"No," I said. "If you print a full exposé, Queen Constantina will have you arrested for sedition. Sedition is treason. Traitors are hanged."

"And you doubt I care enough about Aeland's people to become their martyr."

She made it sound like an insult. I clutched at the sled rug covering our laps and leaned closer. "Don't you remember what you told me? That you'd listen just so I wouldn't have to bear it alone? Did you mean that, or was it just something you said to gull me?"

Avia's gaze flickered to her lap. "I said that. I meant to gently persuade you to help me tell your story—"

"Exactly. And I accept. I will tell you my story. I will tell you everything you want to know, and I will let you tell Aeland. But gradually."

"How many years will it take?" Avia asked.

"One," I said. "The whole truth is a long story."

I'd caught her interest. "And what do you mean to start with?"

"The truth about Aeland Power and Lights," I said. "The

fraud we committed to write a law to imprison the witches. The fact that all the Royal Knights are witches, and what they do to keep Aeland safe. We need the people to understand that we must be kept alive. Their lives depend on ours. After that, you and I start telling the rest."

Avia rolled her neck, which popped loud enough to sound over the hiss of the sleigh running across hard-packed snow. "Does this mean you want to free the witches?"

"The Queen won't do it without intense pressure. Even the Amaranthines wanting it as a condition of their mercy hasn't budged her."

Avia nodded. "Aife told me that Prince Severin is much more amenable—that if he were in charge, her decision would be much easier."

I gasped, and the cold chilled my teeth. "I have heard that sentiment from her secretary. And they're right. This would be simpler if Severin had the power to agree to what they want."

Avia cocked her head. "We're talking around something important."

"We are," I agreed. "And I will continue to talk around it."

"But hypothetically—"

I shook my head. "Don't."

"All right." Avia sighed. "But I am holding you to your promise. You will start talking. Tonight."

"Where?"

Avia's gaze slid away. "There are things I want to show you. They're in my apartment."

"What things?"

"My files and research. The manuscript." Her shoulders rose. She darted a look at me. "I guess you'll have to come in."

I nodded. "I would be pleased to be your guest."

"It's not what you're used to. It's a tenement. Have you ever been in one?"

"I have not," I said.

"I'll give you a tour." She chuffed out an unamused laugh. "It'll be short."

Avia's building jostled for space in the middle of a block of buildings made of sooty red bricks and chipped white paint, every dingy window cracked open to let winter in. Black iron staircases scaffolded the outside, frost-rimed and hazardous.

Avia watched me take it in. I slipped the sled rug off my lap and caught her hand, squeezing it. "Are you ready?"

"You're going to pretend it doesn't bother you?"

I shrugged the fur collar a little higher on my neck. "Your landlord ought to be pilloried."

"My landlord is Blake Properties."

I pressed my lips together. I had come close to liquidating Avia's home as Raymond drowned in his debts. "Raymond ought to be pilloried, then. And there should be a law."

"How fortunate that you get to write them."

"Isn't it? Let's go in. I want to see your work."

It was a five-story climb, each floor a bouquet of cooking odors—I recognized boiled cabbage from my visit to the boardinghouse where Miles had lived. The third floor smelled of burning hashish, tinged with a sweetish edge that I imagined was opium. The floor creaked in agony as Avia turned down a dim hallway with crumbling green-printed wallpaper and stuck her key into a tarnished brass doorplate.

Avia sucked in a breath. "That's not right."

"What isn't?" I asked.

"The door wasn't locked. I locked it. I always lock it." She pushed the door lever and opened the door, her left hand twisting the gaslight to light up a hallway framed by hanging photographs.

The hem of my cloak brushed a tidy line of shoes that stubbed their toes on the green-painted baseboards. I slipped the fur from my shoulders, twisting to hang it on the one bare hook sunk into the wall. Coats draped shoulder to shoulder just above the shoes; a high shelf carried water-stained hatboxes. Two doors stood closed in the middle of the hall, and Avia passed them on the way to the room at the open end.

I followed her into a space that was a little smaller than my bedroom. A narrow iron bed crowded into one corner. A desk with a tall, heavy typewriter sat shoved into the other, squeezed by wardrobes standing in a row. A scarred wooden table with mismatched chairs took up the middle, standing on a carpet with worn patches.

Avia pulled out a wooden chair for me. I sat, but Avia turned in a slow circle, looking over her domain with a troubled crease between her brows.

"Something's not right."

"I don't understand."

She held up her hand, and I quieted. She opened all her wardrobes and pulled out a satin-covered box from under the hems of skirts and frocks. She set it on the table and opened it.

A gold-and-topaz parure sparkled in the gaslight. The work was exquisite, delicate filigree and brilliant-cut gems, carefully matched to progress from pale golden brown to a rich sienna. Avia touched each piece, but if anything, her frown deepened.

"All there." She closed the box and put it back. She turned to a filing cabinet next, picking up cameras of various sizes and complexity. "All fine."

"What are you doing?"

"Someone was in here while I was at the ball," Avia said. "But my jewels are still there, my cameras are fine, and they're the most valuable things I own."

"Are you sure someone was here?" I asked. "If they didn't take your valuables, what could they have wanted?"

"I locked the door. I know I did." She took out her keys, but stopped, shoulders rising as she regarded a filing cabinet. She reached out, and the scrape of the opening drawer made her shake. "I locked that, too."

And now it was unlocked. I fought a shudder and waited for her to sort through her files. She closed the drawer. "It's empty. Blast it to pieces."

"What's gone?"

"Everything. My research. Nick's manuscript," she said. The drawer slammed shut; another one opened. She hunched over a drawer that leaked the gassy smell of barrel-printing ink and the celluloid smell of film negatives. "My files are gone."

"What was in the files?"

"The research I was going to show you," Avia said. "It's all gone." She bumped the drawer with her hip and opened her desk drawers, searching. "My case notebook is gone too. My notepad—it's all missing."

"What does that mean?" I asked.

"Someone came in here and nicked everything. They took all my research, every photo I had on file . . . my expense reports, my bank quarterlies, everything. Including the article file I was going to hand in come morning—good news for you, I suppose."

I kept silent as she lifted the cover off her typewriter and froze. She sucked in a trembling gasp. I rose from my chair and went to her side, peering down at the silvery curve of the type-writer's key-arms. Shiny posts where the typewriter bobbins should have been were glazed with ink.

"They even took your typewriter ribbon?"

She dropped the cover and shook. "It's just like Nick. They took everything after they killed him—every scrap of paper, all his notebooks, and his typewriter ribbon."

I pulled her away. "We have to report it."

Avia laughed. "As if the police would do anything."

"I think they can be gently reminded of their duty by the Chancellor of Aeland, don't you?"

She shrugged and hugged herself. "Who did this, Grace? Your father is locked in the Tower of Sighs."

"I know. But he did this." How, though?

"I have ink on my hands." Avia turned away, disappearing down the hall. She pushed open a door, and a clean, lemony smell wafted out—the smell of scrupulously clean lavatories wiped down with Mrs. Sparkle's Cleaning Elixir. Under that, the scent of swimming pools, their water treated to kill germs.

Avia slammed the door shut and returned to me, her face white with terror. I stepped forward, ready to catch her, she was so pale. "What is it?"

She heaved in a strangled breath. "We have to leave. Now."

She pulled my cloak off the hook and thrust it at me. I swept it around my shoulders, but she didn't spare a moment. She grabbed my hand and pulled me out of her apartment, clattering down the stairs.

"Why are we running?"

Avia used her grip on the handrail to haul herself around the landing. "Booby trap," she said, leaping over the last three steps to thump down to the next curve. "They trapped my toilet."

"What?"

"Hurry," Avia said. "We need the police. Everyone in the building is in danger."

We shivered in my sled while emergency crews took care of the trap. Avia explained it between chattering teeth. Bleach in the tank, Mrs. Sparkles in the bowl. The gradual trickle would fill the bathing chamber with deadly toxic gas, and when the victim opened the door—

I rubbed her back as she broke into racking coughs. "We should take you to a doctor."

Avia shook her head. "It's purely psychological. The firefighters said there hadn't been much mixing. We probably missed my murderer by minutes."

Minutes. I shuddered to think of it. If I hadn't chased after Avia, if I hadn't delayed her progress home, she could have opened the door to a burglar who did murder on the side. I clamped my teeth together and resisted ordering the carriage back to the palace and climbing the hundred and eighty steps to my father's cell so I could—

What? What could I do? Accuse him of committing theft and attempted murder when he was locked in the highest cell in Aeland? How did he give the order? And to whom?

An image of the Prince sneering as he spoke of Avia Jessup crowded my mind. Would he have done such a thing?

He was already in my view as a suspect in Sevitii's murder. His motive to kill Avia and suppress her discoveries was clear as masterwork glass. Father read every page of both papers, taking his scrupulous notes. He could have decided that Avia's articles meant trouble. He could have told Severin, and Severin could have given the order when he saw Avia at the ball.

I tried to shake the thought away. The building was now completely evacuated. Tenants milled outside in the cold, their coats buttoned over sleep clothes. Yellow ribbons hung from plenty of sleeves, and the Hensley sled got plenty of side-long looks. Masked firefighters and police opened the tenement windows wide, freshening the tainted air. I caught a breeze and directed it into the windows, hoping to speed the cleansing so these people could get back into their beds. The curtains billowed as clean air blew into their homes, but I couldn't banish the notion of the Prince as my father's instrument.

It put a new cast on Sevitii's murder—instead of looking for a reason why the Prince would want Sevitii dead, I had to look at the reasons why Father would desire that end. And keep Avia safe from further attempts on her life.

Would he be satisfied with stealing her research? I didn't think so. Research could be duplicated.

"He took your story," I said. "What will you do?"

"I can get in early, recollect my research on APL. That's what you want me to tell first, right?"

"I think so. I need people to understand the motivation before everything else."

Avia coughed again. "I'll do my best to spare you."

"No," I said. "Father and Grandpa Miles were front and center in that scheme. The shares have come down to me."

"At least give me a statement saying you regret it." Avia fished a notebook and pen out of her jacket. "I can do that much."

"Thank you," I said. "Say, 'The incorporation of Aeland Power and Lights and its subsequent portrayal, designed to fool the people into assuming it was a Crown corporation, is one of the greatest deceptions—no, frauds—played on Aelander's citizens. I shall ask that an investigative committee take on the task of detailing this shameful deception and make recommendations to end this monopoly with haste.'"

"That's going to singe the page." Avia put the notepad away and watched her neighbors shivering in the street. "You think he was willing to hurt all these people, just to get to me?"

"Maybe you should hide," I said, and Avia laughed softly.

"I mean to do exactly that. As soon as I figure out where to go."

"You'll come with me to Hensley House," I said. "It's not exactly a fortress, but—"

A woman in a rubberized fire suit pulled an insectoid-looking gas mask off her face and approached the sled. "We're clearing everyone to go inside. The police want a statement, but I disposed of the tainted water myself. Your apartment is safe."

"Thank you," Avia said. "I don't know how I'll make it up to the neighbors."

"If you had waited an hour before opening the lav door you would have died—and not painlessly, either. The children on your floor would have had breathing problems for the rest of their lives. You and they were lucky," the firefighter said. The wind tossed tendrils of her nut-brown hair about, and she looked back at the tenement. "This isn't what you want to hear, but we found multiple fire safety violations. We have to report them."

Avia groaned. "So I just got everyone evicted, too. That's grand, just grand."

"Landlord might pay," the firefighter said. "If fixing the code violations is cheaper than the fines. And with the violations on record, he can't collect insurance if it burns. That's the law."

"Simpson!" someone shouted, and our firefighter turned her head.

"We're on our way out. You were lucky," she said, already moving off.

"He'll raise the rent to absorb the cost," Avia said, looking glum. "I don't have any friends in this building right now."

"It's not your fault someone tried to kill you, but I understand," I said. "Let's take William upstairs to collect some things for your stay."

Avia shook her head. "I can't."

"Yes, you can. You can pick your own guest room, or stay in the dower house—"

"You think your father was behind this," Avia said. "Your staff served him for a long time. How certain is it that all their loyalties have transferred to you?"

My heart sank. "They might not even believe loyalty to him and to me are separate things. But it's the middle of the night. Where can you go?"

Avia shrugged. "Princess Mary's Refuge for Women might have a bed."

"That's an itinerant shelter."

"Yes. But it's just on the next block."

"No. I won't let you sleep on a pallet on the floor. There has to be something we can do."

I knew of a perfectly good townhouse in Halston Circle. Tristan would help, but I couldn't ask him until morning. "I have an idea. But I can't arrange it until tomorrow. You can come to Hensley House with me tonight. You'll stay in my bedchamber. No one will try to harm you if we're together every moment."

Avia pressed her lips together, her gaze darting away. "You want me to spend the night with you in your bed?"

Oh. Heat flooded my cheeks. "I don't mean to imply that we would—"

She raised her kid-gloved finger and laid it on my lips. I hushed. "I would be pleased to share your bed." She grinned at my widening eyes. "Innocently, of course."

She lifted her finger from my mouth. "Of course. There was never any question of—"

"Wasn't there?" Avia asked, then slid across the sled's bench seat, nodding to William as he followed her inside.

SIXTEEN

A Better Bargain Than Marriage

Edith's warm fingertips feathered over the back of my neck, and the clasp of my diamond necklace came free, the skin-warm settings sliding along my collarbone. Behind me came the soft thump of a patent-leather dancing pump landing on the carpet, then silence as Jane undressed Avia, our backs turned for the sake of privacy.

Cool air touched my spine as Edith slipped satin-covered buttons out of their loops and the back of the gown opened. One strap slid off my shoulder, tickling my pebbled skin. I set my gaze on the fire dancing in the grate, its crackling burning crowding out anything I might have heard—the whisper of Avia's coat as she pulled her arms free, the clink of her silver cuff links landing in a wooden tray, a sigh as the stiff boiled shirt front and tall collar came away.

Edith slid the gown to the floor. I stepped out of it and moved into the glow of the fire, my skin heating from its radiance.

"Are you cold?" Jane asked Avia. "You're shivering."

A pause. "It's bearable."

"There are plenty of pans between the covers," Edith said. "My lady likes a warm bed and cool air."

She pinched the clasps holding my brassiere and it fell away. Next she popped the silk-cashmere gown that had been warming next to the fire over my head. I caught the hem and held it up by my hips as Edith unclipped my stockings. I sat on the edge of the bed to let her peel the delicate things off my legs and wiggled my bare toes while she rolled them up and slid them inside a protective pouch.

Behind me, the bed shifted as Avia sat on the opposite edge, and my heart pounded.

Jane spoke again. "Please be careful with the hem, Miss Jessup."

"I will," Avia promised. "Thank you, Jane. I think we can both turn around now, can't we?"

Her weight eased off the mattress. I stood and let the nightgown fall to my ankles. "Yes."

But I turned only as far as the small table where a pot and two handleless cups waited, filled with a sleeping tisane. I picked up mine, cradling the fragile vessel in my hand.

Avia had a handful of her borrowed nightgown rucked up so she could move without stepping on the hem. "You're a giant," Avia said. "Look at this."

She paused next to the foot of the bed and let go. The hem of the gown landed on the carpet, piling in little folds over her scarlet-painted toenails. Her face without cosmetics was pink in the cheeks and around her eyelids, her mouth rosy instead of red.

She picked up the hem again and came closer. "It's like a sleepover party, from when we were young."

I'd never had one of those. I summoned the will to smile. "It is rather like that, isn't it?"

Behind us, Edith and Jane slid warming pans out from between the mattress and the bedding. I gave Avia the other teacup, and she drank the tisane like medicine, getting it over with as quickly as possible. She poured herself another, and it disappeared just as quickly.

"Jessup Good Night Blend," she said.

"It is." I drained my cup and poured another. "A good night's sleep—"

"That's restful and deep," Avia finished. "I wrote that jingle. I was ten. I was a fiend for things that rhymed."

Edith carried a stack of warming pans as she bobbed her knee to me. "Will you need anything else, my lady?"

"That is everything. Thank you, Edith. I'll need a wake-up at five."

"Very good, my lady. Sleep well and dream sweetly."

Avia echoed my thanks to Jane, and they opened the door to my chamber. One of the footmen stood outside my door, guarding Avia from the rest of my household.

I stole a glance at Avia, but she was looking at the painting on the wall depicting our formal gardens in high bloom. She noticed my attention and gave me a smile and a shrug. "Should we retire?"

I nodded and swallowed the last of my tisane. Avia gathered up the front of her gown and circled to the side of the bed farthest from the door. We spent some moments sliding under the warm covers and twisting about, getting into a comfortable posture for sleeping. When the mattress stilled, I lay on my side facing the center of the bed, and so did Avia, her hands tucked under her chin.

"Just like a sleepover," she said. Her smile caught the starlight on her cheek. "I think the tradition is to talk about the boys we like."

"I'm already failing tradition," I said.

"Are there no boys you like? Poor boys." Avia tugged her pillow down and relaxed into it. "Girls?"

I swallowed. "There's one," I said. "What about you?"

Avia grinned into her pillow. "One."

I lifted my head. "Did you tell her?"

"I think she knows," Avia said. "Don't you?"

It stole my breath. I tried to find something to say, something appropriate. "Yes," I said. "I think she knows."

She reached out and caressed my hand with light fingers. "It's not as simple as that, is it?"

"Is it ever?" I asked. "Sometimes I wish . . . It's foolish."

"Tell me anyway."

"When I found Miles, I was a horrible snob about his home. He lived in a boardinghouse in Birdland with a dozen laborers, and I wouldn't hear of it. So I looked for a better flat for him. Something more appropriate. I even went on viewings walking through empty flats, deciding what was and wasn't good enough for my brother. But I never chose one. I kept going to viewings so I could imagine I was looking for myself."

"But you live in a—"

"I don't mean to sound ungrateful," I said. "But sometimes I wonder who I would have been, if I wasn't Sir Christopher Hensley's daughter. What would I do? How would I live?"

Avia turned my hand palm-up, tracing shivering little circles on the palm. "I think I understand."

"You did it. You walked away from it all. You knew who you were, and you did what you had to so you could be a reporter. Miles faked his death to get what he wanted most in the world. He knew who he was, and he fought a war to be able to do it."

She mulled it over for a moment. "You don't know who you are, if you're not Dame Grace Hensley."

I let out a breath. "I knew what I was going to be when I was a little girl, and I threw everything into that becoming. I studied. I practiced. Everything I did was in order to become what I am right now. Chancellor. A leader. But I wish . . ."

Avia reached out. We slipped into each other's arms, skin-warm and close.

"I don't know. I wish I had something that wasn't Dame Grace Hensley. Something that wasn't my father's daughter. Something that was mine, only mine."

"And if you had that thing," Avia asked, "would you give up everything for its sake?"

She waited patiently while I thought. Give up everything? What would be worth more than Aeland? Even thinking about it made me quiver with fear. "No."

"Then maybe that is what's yours," Avia said. "Maybe that's who you are. But does it mean that you are the successor to the Hensley legacy?"

I puzzled over the difference. "I need to think about that."

"All right," Avia said. She wriggled a little closer. "Close your eyes. It's already Firstday. We both have work to do."

I woke with Avia's head resting on the crook of my shoulder, my arm curled around her ribs. She looped one arm around my body, hugging me as if I were an enormous stuffed toy.

It should have been an agony of numb arms, but we'd slept comfortably, just like this. Fitted together, close and familiar. I didn't want to move. I wanted to stay right there, warm and embraced, breathing in the smell of the rose-scented wash she used on her hair and the last herbal whiffs of a fougère for men blended with her skin.

I refused to think about how I would sleep alone again after this. Being with her seeped into my skin, warm and soft and quietly euphoric. I breathed in time to the rise and fall of her chest; I marveled at the smooth, peaceful beauty of her face at rest. I was hers to sleep on, unwilling to move while she was comfortable and safe.

At some point I closed my eyes. The next thing I knew, Edith had come in with a pot of chocolate and started preparing for my morning toilet. She turned on the water in the shower to exactly the right temperature, and then her footsteps back paused before a wardrobe to sort through my outfits.

Avia raised her head from my shoulder. "It's five already?"

I had been released from my duty. "Good morning. Have some chocolate."

"Mm." She sat up and blinked at Jane, who offered her a tiny cup. She took it and sighed. "Is there coffee?"

"At breakfast downstairs."

Avia savored her cup of chocolate as if she hadn't had one in a long time. Edith led the way to the bath chamber and left me to wash and wrap up in a dressing gown. When I returned, my usual choice of three outfits lay on one half of the bed, while the other held ensembles for Avia, who almost ran in her haste to get in the shower.

I regarded the outfits, but really I was looking at the effect—hers on one side, mine on the other. Could it be like this every morning, instead of just one?

"Should I try new changes, ma'am?" Edith asked.

"My apologies," I said. "I was just thinking."

She darted a glance at Avia's side of the bed, and at Jane, who had coated one of Avia's shoes in tarry black polish. "I can change any of these ensembles, ma'am, if you need something more—"

"My black wool suit," I said. "The one with the gray pinstripes."

"Very good, ma'am. Your orange tie?"

I nodded, and Edith turned me to face the mirror while she combed and wave-set my hair. She left me broiling under a hooded dryer stand with the housekeeper's report, including staff shifts, my schedule, the week's menu, and a polite inquiry about Avia's diet and preferences. I balanced a lap desk on my knees and made amendments to the report. Beads of sweat rolled down my temples. My ears were burning hot.

I endured it. Avia emerged from the bathing chamber and moved out of my sight to pick an outfit. The noise of the windup fan muffled any conversation.

When Edith released me, Avia was dressed in a slip and stockings, sitting perfectly still while Jane applied her cosmetics. I turned to Edith's attentions, obeying all her directions as she powdered my face. After she had dressed me, I turned to regard Avia, clad in a slate-gray dress with a bell-shaped skirt and a ribbon bow on the neckline. Her hair gleamed, and her mouth was lined in red, waiting until after breakfast to be filled with her favorite shade of fresh-blood lipstick.

We took breakfast on trays in the library: coffee and eggs cooked to the precise moment where the whites cooked solid but yolk still ran, oozing and golden on buttered toast. Goose sausage, slices of cheese, and wedges of sugared oranges filled my plate.

Avia spent the better part of five minutes gaping at a painting. A woman dressed in the gleaming silk and lace excess of the twelfth century sat on an ornately carved divan, her hand captured by a gentleman in an orange coat that strained to stay buttoned over the years around his middle. While the gentleman devoted himself to kissing the woman's knuckles, she gazed over the gentleman's head at a soulful-eyed youth with long, curling dark hair and a plump, pink mouth.

"That's *A Better Bargain Than Marriage*," Avia said.

I swung my coffee cup away from my mouth. "Yes."

"It hung in the National Art Exhibition in Merrymonth. I took pictures of it."

I glanced at it. "Yes. That's supposed to be Bernard Hensley and Phillida Carrington, and of course her favorite lover, Eustace Harvey."

Avia's cup rattled as she set it on its saucer. "It's a Briantine."

"One of his juvenile works," I said. "Do you want to borrow a book?"

"Do I want to— No, thank you. I have one." She turned back to her plate and her swiftly cooling eggs. "What do you read during breakfast?"

I held up a copy of *Salterton's Hansard* from 1541. "Work."

She wrinkled her nose and pulled out a battered penny-book novel. "Miss Endicott is busy trying to choose between two suitors—the handsome man whom her parents adore, and the tempting, slightly wicked Diana who has jilted lover after lover after becoming a widow so soon after her marriage."

"That sounds more interesting than a word-for-word transcript of Parliamentary bickering."

"Oh, I don't know," Avia said. "They used to fight sword duels over policy, didn't they?"

"Great-Grandmother Fiona put an end to that," I said. "Now it's just underhanded subtext and debate as a sport."

We opened our books, reading while we ate. I familiarized myself with the transcripts of the final debate and vote of the Witchcraft Protection Act.

The committee was right. The Cabinet had voted in a law based on the most questionable evidence, and I noted the yeas and nays. I found Grandpa Miles had voted in favor, indicating King Nicholas's wishes. My father had voted to follow the Chancellor, as did every one of the men and women who were the first shareholders of Aeland Power and Lights. It was sickeningly obvious. They had jumped up a bad law to further their obscene scheme, making a fortune on the backs of imprisoned, enslaved witches.

Who had voted in the Lower House? I flipped back, looking for the relevant entry, when Avia's fork clattered on the rim of her plate.

I looked up. "Are you all right?"

She was back to staring at that painting. "I had imagined that coming here would be like returning to my past, in a way."

I imagined breakfast in the library of the Jessup house. What did they read over breakfast? Was it pleasant and peaceful?

Avia's mouth thinned as she concentrated on her half-eaten toast. I waited for her to speak, but the silence went on too long. "Was it?"

"I was a fool to think so," Avia said. "Your maid dressed me. Our lady's maid put out the clothes and the washing things, but she never did it for me. And this house . . ." Avia glanced up at the wall. "You have masterworks on the walls. As if they're just another kind of belonging instead of something you only see in a museum."

"It's a collection that spans multiple generations."

She flicked her free hand at it. "It's a Briantine."

"One of his earlier works."

"It's still worth enough marks to buy my whole building. And fix it. And rent to a better class of tenant."

I didn't know what to do. What would Miles do? Try to understand her feelings. "It bothers you."

"It discourages me," she said.

"Why?"

Avia cut off whatever she was going to say. "You've been very kind, inviting me here, and doing what I needed so I could feel safe enough to sleep. I don't want to throw that hospitality in your face."

"But?"

"Nothing."

I closed my book. "Tell me."

But she still didn't speak. She shook her head sadly as she looked at the painting. "All this money makes sure you can't see the truth of Aeland."

I gasped. "How can you say such a thing?"

"Because I fell from a very great height—and even then, your place is miles above where I once stood," Avia said. "It took me months to open my eyes after I left home. I stomped off and let an apartment in Wellston Triangle."

"But you don't live in Wellston Triangle," I said. "What happened?"

One corner of Avia's mouth curled up. "My father closed my bank account. I lost my apartment, they took the furniture, and I went east until I wound up in a tenement."

I shook my head. "I don't know why you fought with your father."

"I wanted to be a photographer. He wanted me to marry a transportation company."

I understood that. My father wanted me to marry eleven votes in the Cabinet. "And that's why you wore red that night. To say no."

Avia nodded. "I knew I was good enough for the papers. I was right about that. And I knew once I earned my byline, Father would want to reconcile. I was right about that too."

"But you didn't go home," I said. "Why?"

"Because it isn't fair," Avia said. "It's not right. The people of Aeland are exploited, and every time they try to improve their lot, the bosses and the politicians find a way to knock them down."

I had seen promising acts wither in the House with my father in the Chancellor's seat. But that could change, easily.

"I can help you. Those politicians? They answer to me." I was on solid ground again, and I lifted a hand as I spread the warm air from the fireplace around the library. "I can make things better."

"With laws and policy." Avia nodded wearily. "You'll start out with a proposal, and in negotiations, the law that comes out will be feeble compared to what the original bill had planned."

"We work out compromises—"

"It's not good enough, Grace. You'd have to legislate radical, sweeping change—and you can't get that past the House."

"A step forward is still a step."

Avia smiled. It stretched her lips as she conceded. "You're right. But do we have time for steps hobbled by compromise?"

I knew she didn't think so. And maybe she was right— the Amaranthines were deathless, but that didn't mean they wanted to live here while we inched forward, fighting progress as hard as we could. We had to do something big. Something clear-eyed and bold.

"I have to find a way to convince the Queen."

"And if you can't?" Avia asked. "What will you do if you can't?"

I dropped my gaze. "Something else."

"And what will that be?"

I raised my head. I didn't even try to hide my conflict. "Anything else is treason."

Avia stopped talking. She picked up her coffee, had a sip, and gave me time to repair my poise.

"Maybe this is the moment when you find out what you want more than anything else in the world," Avia said. She set down her cup and popped open a compact, filling in her lips with red. "Thank you for breakfast. I'm going to ride into work. Do you still have an idea where to stash me?"

I nodded. "I'll have an address for you by noon."

"Thank you. I know you didn't have to do this. And I didn't mean to—" She glanced at the painting again and sighed. "We were having such a nice morning."

Her shoulders slumped. But she drew herself back up and walked out of the library, shoulders back and head high.

I listened until I couldn't hear her footsteps any longer, then rang for a footman. Avia's life was still in danger, and I was still certain I knew who wanted her dead.

SEVENTEEN

The Promise
of Destruction

As I reached the topmost stairs in the Tower of Sighs, I heard the rush of many wings. I emerged to behold Father smiling at a flock of birds greedily pecking at seeds scattered across the floor. I counted sparrows, scarlet jays, one plump messenger dove, and winter thrushes. Father had a black-capped chickadee on his finger, sending the little passerine into bliss at being preened and petted. His own breakfast sat half-eaten, shoved across the table next to unopened newspapers.

He caught sight of me and shooed the little bird away. "Grace."

Loose feathers floated in the dusty air. "You tried to kill Avia Jessup last night."

"You invited her to the ball as your guest. After I told you to—"

"You don't tell me anything, Father. You don't get to push me around the game board. I am Chancellor. I am the Voice. I am the one who decides who is valuable to me—and you are depreciating your worth."

"You little fool," Father said, his voice as placid as a still

pond. "She knows everything. Everything, do you hear me?
There was a manuscript—"

"I know all about that," I said.

Father stood up, and birds startled, wings beating. "Then
why is she still breathing?"

"Because she's helping me." How did he know? How?

He must have subverted a guard. He had all the time in the
world to buy one. Just to send messages on to the person who did
the real mayhem. But who among the guards obeyed his orders?

"You have vision, Grace. You're capable of looking into the
distance where others keep their eyes on the path just ahead.
You have to forget these stopgap measures and look at the long
game."

My scalp prickled as if fire raced across it. "If you're so good
at this game, Father, why are you waiting to see if cancer or the
noose gets you first?"

He cocked his head. "Is that what you think I'm doing?"

That was a bluff. "I think you're meddling. I think you don't
know how to let go. And I think it's time that stopped. I have a
country to save, and you're getting in the way."

Father was the picture of calm. "And how will you put me
out of the way?"

"A word with the Queen should serve."

Father smiled. "And then when she tries to find my cocon-
spirators? When she discovers that Severin has been making
regular visits to my cell?"

She'd be furious, of course. She already hated how Severin
opposed her, no matter how gently he did it. If she knew Severin was meeting with the main instrument of the conspiracy
that had the Amaranthines weighing our fate, she could do the
worst. She could denounce him. She could accuse him of treason. And that would leave Aeland without an heir.

An heirless throne would bring the landed into the picture

as they squabbled over who had the strongest lines of descent from Queen Agnes. There would be no clear candidate. The struggle would be inevitable.

Father nodded. "You see now."

I couldn't handle the intricacies of a brawl over succession on top of everything else. I couldn't risk taking Severin out of play, and Father knew it. But I would go to chaos before I stood by and let Avia die. Father only valued one thing. All my leverage depended on convincing him I would destroy it just to spite him.

"You tried to kill Avia Jessup. You failed. She knows exactly who arranged to rob her home. In exchange, I told Avia to print her research on the founding of Aeland Power and Lights."

He stared at me from under the low, angry line of his eyebrows. "That will smear this family."

"That's the point." I unfolded my arms and squared off, hands on my hips. "Let me make this clear, Father. Avia Jessup is off-limits. I am guarding her life. And every time you try to hurt her, I will be there to protect her. And then I will tell her something that brings the Hensleys down. What shall I tell the papers the next time you get in my way? Attempt murder again, and you'll find out."

"It's your family too."

"It is. But I will disgrace you, Father. I will pull Grandpa Miles off his pedestal. I will make sure the two of you are remembered with contempt. Stay away from Avia Jessup."

"You ungrateful little fool," Father said, his voice soft.

"I have things to do, Father. Goodbye." I turned my back and strode to the stairs. "Finish your breakfast."

"Grace."

That single word pulled me out of my ruminations. I was on the main floor of Kingsgrave Prison, having automatically

STOR

made all the turns and choices that brought me to the heavy-doored cells where prisoners were held in isolation. There Miles waited, one eyebrow raised as I came not from the south end of the hall, the way that connected Kingsgrave to the rest of the palace, but from the north, from the Tower of Sighs. Miles gazed at me with the downward-turned mouth of disappointment, and it struck me in the heart.

"You were up there, weren't you."

It wasn't a question. "Yes."

He nodded, once, his gaze falling away from me. It ached to see him fold his hands together and smooth his features into a calm, observing aspect. It was so much worse than shouting or accusations.

I looked down at the smooth stone floor.

Finally, he spoke. "Does he advise you?"

"Only the one time," I said.

"Oh, Grace." His voice was so soft. So understanding.

"No," I said. "It's not like that. I don't want to see him. I don't want to look at him. I don't want to hear his voice."

"But there's always a reason," he said. "You don't want to, but you climb those stairs anyway."

"This is the last time," I said. "No more."

"Did you say that the last time you were up there?"

I lifted my head. "He tried to kill Avia."

Miles's gaze sharpened. "Why?"

"She was Nick Elliot's friend."

Miles nodded, listening.

"She has—had—Nick's manuscript."

"Had."

"Father had her flat robbed and trapped. He had the manuscript stolen, along with her research."

"Just like Nick," Miles said. "And you were up there to tell him to stop?"

"Yes." He understood. I could breathe again. "I don't take his advice. I don't ask him for help. He wants to run the country through me, but it's my job now, not his."

"I don't think I need to tell you that you should stay away from him."

"You don't. It's only that I need to keep an eye on him." How weak it sounded, coming out of my mouth. He called for me, and I came, no matter how much I blustered once I was there.

Miles nodded. "As much as he needs to keep an eye on you, I imagine."

I was playing into his hands, Miles meant. But he turned his head and regarded the door to the cell. "Perhaps we should get on with the interview. But if you need to talk, I'm here."

"Yes," I said. "We should get on with the interview."

He leaned forward, unlocking the cell door. Inside was the stink of humanity, rising from a hole in the floor. I sidestepped a tray of food—a bowl full of millet, a wrinkled King Philip Pink, and a waxed wooden cup and matching pitcher, filled with the day's measure of water.

I knew them from my own brief stay in Kingsgrave. I had choked down gluey, cold millet, hating every mouthful. I had made the apple last by chewing every bite down to mush, nibbling away at the core. I made the water last until the next meal—a soup without seasoning, watery fish broth, limp vegetables, plain boiled crab, usually cold.

Niikanis hadn't touched the tray. He sat on the narrow shelf in his robes with the patched sweater and rough wool gloves to keep him warm, staring at nothing. Miles rolled to a stop beside me, studying Niikanis thoughtfully.

"Grieving," he said.

Did that mean he was innocent, or did it mean that he regretted killing Sevitii? It could have been either.

"Niikanis," Miles said, and then continued in Laneeri, his voice even as he asked a brief question.

Niikanis raised his head and looked at Miles with nothing in his eyes. Slowly, he shook his head.

"Well, I asked him straight out if he'd killed Sevitii," Miles said. "I didn't really expect him to say yes, however."

"Why did you do that?" I said. "Aren't you supposed to try and catch him in a contradiction, or—"

"She was more than her omen," Niikanis said.

I startled at the fluent Aleander. Miles's shoulders went up. Niikanis looked down at his hands. "She was so much more. My youngest daughter had a face like the moon when she was born. Such a small thing—every finger, every toe perfect. I cast the omen. Halian the Maker and Menas the Just, rising in concert. Harmony with Lilia the Compassionate—and high in the sky, Amael the Traveler, square to Halian, to the degree. To the second. A long journey would be her making. Or undoing, as Halian wills. I thought I knew which it meant."

Miles glanced at me, and I kept my mouth shut. "You believed this journey would lead her to greatness. To ascend even higher. But not enough to let her go on her own."

Niikanis said nothing, but his shoulders sloped. His spine slouched. His arms wrapped around his middle as if it hurt. He rocked, swaying gently. "I was so proud of her destiny. To be so powerful—and when the Magal consolidated power, she stood on the ninth step to the Star Throne. I was so proud."

I looked to Miles. Miles listened. He watched as Niikanis kept his gaze on the floor.

"How I wish she had been ordinary, now."

"Halian's touch made that impossible," Miles said. "She had been negotiating, you know. She wasn't going to tell us a thing unless we acknowledged Laneer's right to be independent. She was brave. Ambitious. But she was going to betray the Star Throne to do it."

Niikanis shook his head. "She would not."

"The orders to the temples had to come from the Star Throne," Miles said. "It was a formality, asking who had told your Star Priests to ensorcel your warriors, laying the snare that would possess the Aelander who killed them. Who else would the temples obey for such a monstrous thing?"

Niikanis shut his eyes, shut out the sight of us.

I put my hand on Miles's shoulder and spoke. "If Sevitii had succeeded in negotiating Laneer's freedom from our rule, it would push her higher. If she had brought down the Star Throne, would she be chosen to take that seat?"

Niikanis went tense as I spoke. He peeked at me. He nodded. "She would have ascended."

Miles leaned his elbows on the armrests. "She bribed a guard to deliver her star bangle to you. To let you know she was all right, to give you a way to know if she was safe."

Niikanis shook his head. "No."

"And when you realized she was going to betray the Star Throne, you weren't proud of her anymore," Miles said. "So you used the hair as a link. You used magic to kill her. And then you dropped the bangle in the privy."

His face twisted. "She was my daughter."

"That's what made it hurt," Miles said. "That moment when you realized that she wasn't who you made her to be."

"No."

"She shattered that pride when she betrayed Laneer," Miles said. "When her ambition outstripped her loyalty and became a betrayal."

"No," Niikanis said.

He'd pressed enough. Miles was the club. Therefore, I was the honey. "She died two days ago," I said. "And you had no idea. You didn't have her star bangle. You didn't know if she was alive or dead, if she was safe or in torment. Isn't that right?"

"No one would tell me where she was," Niikanis said.

"What happened that day?" I asked. "What did you do, what did you see?"

"There is no amusement," Niikanis said. "A day in a cell is a year. I ate the sorry gruel and the apple. The Blessed One came to see if we had enough comforts. I saw guards. I saw your Prince, passing up to the tower stairs. I ate the watery soup. There were three pieces of fish. I was lucky. I watched the Prince come back after it was done."

I glanced at Miles. He caught the look, trading it for one of his own. "You saw the Prince before luncheon, and then you saw him again after you were done?"

"Yes." Niikanis said. "Why?"

"It's important," I said. "Did anything else happen after that?"

"Another wretched meal. Sleep," Niikanis said. "The Prince again, the next day. He had guards search my cell. He had me taken here. He accused me, just as you accused me. Now my days are nothing."

He raised his head and met my gaze. "There is nothing else to say but this: it should have been me."

It made something near my heart break open. This man had loved his daughter. He would have given everything for her; his life before hers.

Father loved me. But he would never do that.

He turned his face away. "I would like to be alone now."

Miles unlocked his wheel brake and paused just before the door. I pulled the cell door open, and Miles went through, passing me the key.

I locked the cell. "We'll have to give this back."

"And check the duty roster. I need to know when Niikanis and the other Laneeri got their lunch."

I nodded and walked beside Miles, who propelled his chair to the guard station. "Because Severin couldn't have killed Sevitii if he was in the tower when she died. But the timing would have to be exact. Prisoners only get twenty minutes to eat."

Miles halted his chair. "Do you know why Severin was in the tower?"

I licked my lips. "Yes."

"Is he visiting Father?"

Sick with it, I nodded. "Yes."

Miles watched me silently for a moment. "Do you know why?"

"He's taking Father's advice," I said. "I don't know the details."

Miles stared at an unseen distance. I bit my lip and waited. Severin, talking to Father. How often? About what?

No. I knew what.

Miles shook his head. "Severin's trying his best with negotiations. It would be easier if—"

"Don't say it."

But he didn't have to. It hung in the air, loud enough to fill my mind: It would be easier if Severin were King.

Miles wheeled to the guard station, signing the receipt of Niikanis's key. "I'd like to look at the duty roster," he said. "I need to verify when meals were served."

The clerk on duty handed over a green clothbound ledger, and paper slid and crackled as my brother flipped pages. The smell of boiled millet hung in the air. Miles bent his head and scanned a page.

"Here it is," Miles said.

But I already knew before he told me. "It clears him."

"Yes," Miles said. "Niikanis just gave an alibi to our other suspect."

EIGHTEEN

Tea and Correspondence

We kept silent as we passed through the prison, but my thoughts tumbled around, each of them competing for attention over the last. Severin was no longer a suspect, and for that I was relieved. But Niikanis's grief had been real. I feared we weren't even close to finding the truth.

Miles led me through the chilly passageway between prison and palace. Halfway between destinations, he stopped, spinning his chair around to face me. I stepped off to the right to give him a view of the door at the end of the passage, and I kept an eye on the door ahead of us.

He glanced at me, and I braced myself for another talk about dealing with Father. Instead he said, "Do you have a busy day today?"

I pulled a notebook from my pocket and consulted it. "No session," I said as I turned to the relevant page for my schedule. "No appointments. I am expecting some people will drop in on me, but nothing set on the schedule."

"That's better than I hoped. I need a favor from you, but it will take hours."

"Anything," I said. "What do you need?"

"I need you to be an accomplice," Miles said. "Aife wants to leave the palace."

"And she needs my help?"

"She wants you to come along," Miles said. "Will you do it?"

"I'd be happy to," I said. "But the Grand Duchess can't simply walk out of Mountrose Palace. You want to smuggle her out."

"Yes. Will you do it?"

"You know I will. Let's move; it's cold."

"Push me," Miles said. "We don't have time to dawdle."

A few minutes later, we were passing through the double-guarded doors that led to the Amaranthines' apartments.

"Straight on to the solar," Miles said, and I pushed his chair to the glass-and-iron chamber. I heard Aldis's voice as the door cracked open, and I squared my shoulders, prepared to wade into a fight.

"You are too tolerant," Aldis said, and stopped as the door opened all the way, his face turning to stone as he saw me. "You."

"Me," I said, striding along with Miles in front of me. "Were you just telling Her Highness how you attempted to control my will by dropping your glamor and interrogating me?"

Aife blinked. I did too, for Aife was not garbed in the shimmering, storybook gowns fit for a monarch. She stood tall and sharp in an Aelander chalk-stripe suit, her hair contained in a tall, intricately folded headwrap, bold in mustard yellow, orange, and black geometric patterns. Her blouse was of the same material, sporting a draped bow at the neck. She looked like a fashionable advocate on her way to an important meeting with a subcommittee at Government House. "Aldis?"

Aldis bowed his head. "At the time, I asked her what had become of one of the Laneeri delegation. Sevitii an Vaavut had gone missing from her cell at the base of the Tower of Sighs, where they were being unlawfully detained." Aldis shot me an ugly look. "I wished to hear Chancellor Hensley tell me where

Sevitii was, and how she fared. The Chancellor used her power to threaten and intimidate me instead of telling me the truth."

I couldn't shout. I clenched the handles of Miles's wheelchair and kept my voice even. "And that's justification for exploiting mortal weakness in order to get what you want? First you ask me to reveal information that I had no obligation to give you. Maybe that was out of concern for Sevitii—"

"Spare me your circumlocutions," Aldis snapped. "When I asked after Sevitii, she was already dead. Murdered. And you didn't tell me. I had to hear it from a guard when I returned to the tower to speak to Niikanis an Vaavut."

Aife turned her gaze toward me, now. "I would like to know the reasons for these removals."

"We were interviewing Sevitii," I said. "We had her moved to a different location in order to keep the subject of our discussions secret. We kept her under guard, but that wasn't enough to protect her. Someone wanted her silenced. They succeeded."

"And the reason for taking Niikanis into your protection?" Aldis hammered the last word full of skepticism.

I addressed my remarks to the Grand Duchess. "We suspect him in connection to her murder."

"How?" Aldis said. "He's locked in a cell."

"Recently, you requested that the Laneeri be given back their personal effects, along with warm clothing, blankets, and other comforts. We complied," I said.

"And warm blankets lead to murder?"

"We also struck off the copper-plated shackles we keep prisoners in. Niikanis is a powerful mage, made even more powerful with the addition of nine witchmarks bound to his will," I said. "Our examination of Sevitii's body raised the possibility she had been killed by magical means. We're questioning him in connection to her death."

"We have only your word on that," Aldis said.

"Yes," I said. "That's correct."

"You can't be trusted with the safety of the Laneeri delegation," Aldis said. "You must release them."

"Aldis," Aife said. "I recognize your perspective on the people of Laneer. You are their tireless advocate. Perhaps Grace can take suggestions on how they can be better protected. But for now, I believe I set you a task."

"You did. I'll take care of it," Aldis said.

He stepped away from Aife, dressed in the same wide-legged, calf-high trousers and padded jerkin. Armed with his bow, a sword, and multiple daggers, he stepped aside and waved a hole in the air. He walked into a scene by the seashore, the tide all the way out to the horizon. I let myself breathe a sigh of relief when the Way into the Solace irised shut.

"My apologies," Aife said. "Aldis is deeply attached to the Laneeri. He blames you for the war."

"That's fair," Miles said. "We're to blame, after all."

"And we are investigating her murder. We need to know that as much as we needed to know what she was going to tell us."

Aife's eyebrows rose with polite curiosity. "And that is?"

"I'm so sorry, Your Highness. Aeland wishes to level an accusation against Laneer, but we can't do it without proof, and I have no wish to make accusations without evidence to support me."

"And you're hoping to use it to negotiate with my requirements surrounding Aeland's treatment of Laneer."

I nodded. "Yes. So you see—"

"I do see," Aife said. "I see Miles has brought you. Does that mean you will help me?"

"I will. I know how important this is to you. And maybe it will even be fun," I said. "What do you wish to see? I'd be happy to show you around."

"I have a destination in mind," Aife said. "I've accepted an invitation to lunch in a citizen's private home. She also extended the invitation to my party, but I wished to keep it small."

A citizen's private home. Well. I suspected I knew who.

The door opened behind us, and Tristan sauntered into view. He cut a fine figure in a deep gray wool flannel sack suit and handmade shoes that gleamed with a painstaking polish.

"I know that suit," I said. "I designed that suit for Miles."

"You have a gift," Tristan said. "And the tailor you selected is a visionary. I am the height of fashion, and I could fight a duel in this."

"Do you anticipate fighting a duel?"

"It's my job to always anticipate fighting a duel," Tristan said. "But I don't think we'll come to any mischief."

"I am relieved to hear it," I said. "Actually, I need a favor from you. I need to hide Avia Jessup. Are you using your residence?"

"Only a little." Tristan reached into his pocket and produced a key. "I'll send a note to Mrs. Sparrow when we've finished our mission."

"Ah yes, the mission," I said. "What do you need me to do?"

"Simply lead us through the palace to your sleigh, and then accompany us for an outing."

"In Riverside?" I guessed.

"That is our destination," Tristan said.

"Oh, I knew it. You're going to have tea with a revolutionary."

"And you're invited," Tristan said with a twinkle. "Isn't that wonderful?"

"I know when I've been hoodwinked. Very well. Let's pay a call to Miss Robin Thorpe."

"Janet," I said, propping the door wide open. "I've had a change in my schedule."

"Good morning, Dame Grace. I have delivered your message

to cancel the sale of your shares in Blake Properties, and I have another message from that reporter, Avia Jessup."

I didn't know exactly where Tristan and Aife were, but I had given them plenty of time to hustle inside my office. I let the door swing shut and crossed the office to accept the note from Janet's hands, tearing the envelope open:

Grace:

APL story is go. You have until 11am to call it off. No second thoughts?

Avia

I slid my cuff back to look at my watch. Fifteen minutes. In fifteen minutes, Avia would have the story laid out on the front page of the paper, blasting the tale of deception and greed around the incorporation of Aeland Power and Lights. Included in the story would be profiles of APL's biggest shareholders, including me.

I had promised Father I would destroy our name if he raised a hand against Avia. This was a message to him as much as it was the beginning of my careful, measured delivery of the truth to Aeland.

"Thank you, Janet. Please rush a reply to Miss Jessup."

Janet had notepaper and a clipboard ready, and I wrote my note back:

Avia:

Congratulations on another front-page story. The address for the attached is W. 1703 Halston Street.

Grace

The clipboard and Tristan's key went into an envelope. Janet hid her consternation. I fetched my sable coat and swung it around my shoulders before I wondered if the hem would strike anyone, but it flew free. I opened the door and stood with it propped open, allowing my companions to pass through.

"I'm going out," I told Janet. "I expect to return this afternoon. Can you get some reports for me about whatever the subcommittee investigating the witchcraft act has been looking at? I'd like to know what they've uncovered."

And if they hadn't investigated every corner, I would point them in helpful directions. Satisfied that I had given Tristan and Aife enough time to duck out of my office, I stepped into the hallway and began my journey through Government House.

I fastened a sable fur cap over my carefully set waves, listening to the tripled echo of footsteps ringing off the marble. The sound made my heart leap with anxiety. What if someone noticed?

Well, they probably wouldn't suspect invisible Amaranthines. I smoothed my hands over my coat, trying to soothe my jangled nerves. I was bad at being surreptitious. I didn't know anything about sneaking about and doing mischief. Did it make your hair stand on end, waiting for someone to raise an alarm? Was it supposed to feel this frightening? If we were caught, there would be so much trouble.

But excitement bubbled inside me too. I was part of a mission to disregard the strictures that kept Aife cooped up in a single wing of the palace. It was an adventure. I was rebelling, just as I had when I'd invited Avia to the ball. I had to restrain my smile as I delivered sober nods to the clerks and scribes traveling the halls. When I reached the front doors, I was ready to jump for joy.

"Well done." Tristan and Aife emerged from behind one of the massive stone pillars that held up the pediment fronting Government House—a bas-relief of the first gathering of Parliament. Anyone stepping out would assume I'd met them on the steps. Anyone coming in would assume I'd walked out with them. We had made it.

"The carriage will take a few minutes," I said. "How are you, Tristan?"

"I'm well," he said. "I wouldn't mind a snack."

After concealing himself and Aife for some ten minutes? I couldn't imagine how much power he could wield, just by himself. But Aife was breathing in great lungfuls of cold winter air, her smile like a small sun.

"I've never been so cold in my life," she said, still grinning, "as I have been in Aeland. All this snow. I wonder what Elondel would look like, if it was ever permitted."

I blinked. "You have such control over the weather that you can defy winter?"

Aife and Tristan exchanged hasty looks. "It's never winter in Elondel," Tristan said. "It's sometimes cool. Sometimes warm. Rainy, when it needs to be. But never winter."

Just thinking about it gave me a headache—or perhaps it was the glare of the low-hanging sun, shining in the southern half of the sky. I slipped my hand inside my coat and produced a pair of snow goggles, sighing in relief as the dark lenses soothed my vision. I should have put them on earlier. I was going to have a headache for at least an hour, now.

Tristan and Aife slid matching pairs of snow goggles over their eyes, and Tristan pointed. "That one's yours, isn't it?"

A pumpkin orange sled and four matched grays pulled into the drive. We descended the stairs together, climbing into the black leather bench seat. I gave a West Water Street address, and George took us on a route that zigzagged the steep hillside dotted with enormous houses, built to shelter grand-aunts and first cousins and entire packs of niblings.

We passed by shops open for business, corner dining halls and public houses, then switched direction on the next block, easing our way down to the flat, colorful streets of Central Riverside's main shopping promenade, traveling along Water Street.

Everywhere I looked—on oldsters, on children, even on shop awnings and light poles—yellow ribbons fluttered, each one a silent message of liberation, reparation, and conciliation. I should have expected it. While black Samindan Aelanders were slightly better off than the average white Aelander, being more highly represented in scholarly and professional fields, more Samindan citizens had been convicted for witchcraft by a significant margin. This was the heart of the movement that wanted justice and equality for all.

Neighbors cleared the walks in front of clan houses with wooden exteriors painted yellow or green or sky-blue or orange— bright and cheerful against white snow and brilliant blue skies. West Water Street was lined with sleds—many of them bearing the lamb and scroll of the Parliamentary fleet, manned by drivers in tall hats and black coats. There were politicians here. I glanced at Tristan and Aife. Aife shrugged.

"I wanted to meet them."

That made sense. I would greet Jacob Clarke and his committee inside the wide, maroon-red clan house with windows full of curious faces. Thorpes, all of them, watching as William helped Aife out of the sled and onto the hard-packed street.

Almost as one, the Samindans bent in respectful bows, hands over their hearts to relay deep respect for the Grand Duchess. Shoveling walks, indeed—I inspected the men and women outside the clan houses and recognized the posture and bearing of soldiers and guards on every one of them.

Aife touched her heart in return, and smiles broke out

among the makeshift security force spread throughout the
street. I led our party up a cleared sidewalk, and my headache
throbbed to a different rhythm as the house's shadow protected
us from the harsh glare of sunlight on snow.

The door swung open before we had even set foot on the
wide, wraparound porch that skirted the main floor of the
clan house. Music heralded a wizened, white-haired man who
stepped out on the greeting rug in his slippers and held the
door for us. Aife shook hands with him, and his decades-lined
face went serenely happy.

"You are welcome in this house," he said. "Have you eaten?"

The smells that carried on the warm air of the house were
enough to make me moan. Rich, complicated spices, slow-
cooked meat, the smell of baked bread and burnt sugar—I could
have wept. I had anticipated perching on the edge of a parlor
chair, politely taking no more than two cookies. Instead, I would
sit down to a full luncheon and a belly full of home cooking.

We left our footwear at the door and followed the old
man—the eldest of the house, who only answered the door
for the most esteemed guests—through a double-wide hallway. Hundreds of photographs of Thorpes—depicted alone, in
pairs, in clumps and assemblies—stared solemnly at me, their
gaze following even as I moved away.

The music grew in volume and clarity as we ventured
deeper into the house. A string ensemble played with skill and
precision in the front parlor to a quiet, appreciative group of
listeners, the voices of their instruments winding around each
other in harmony and countermelody. I recognized the cellist
as Ramona Thorpe, who had entertained all of Kingston with
her wireless performances. She kept her gaze on the music in
front of her, however, so I kept moving.

We passed parlors full of men and women in conversation with Elected Members. Member Clarke was here somewhere, of course, but as I counted and named each of the Parliamentarians in attendance, I tallied them against a mental list. This was Clarke's coalition, but it was more than that. This was the committee who had investigated the origins of the Witchcraft Protection Act—the committee expected to stand in the domed rotunda of Government House and announce their findings to the press later today, after they had taken lunch in the home of a noted abolitionist.

I was tired of all the things I had to do, all the balls I had to keep in the air. When we stopped at a chamber with two hearths and a conference between Robin Thorpe and Member Clarke, our host rose to her feet and smiled.

Bows, and a grave exchange of nods between me and Member Clarke. Robin rang a bell to signal everyone to come and sit for lunch in the clan's dining hall, a gracious room with silver-and-crystal chandeliers hanging from the mullioned ceiling. A staggeringly long table with enough room for everyone spanned the length of two chambers. A set of young Thorpes acted as ushers, bringing us to assigned seats. I was near the foot, with Member Clarke at my right hand, and the white-haired old man who had let us in took the seat at the foot of the table.

Other children brought in platters of food even as we shuffled about getting seated, and dishes started passing hand to hand the moment the last guest sat down. Samindans put all the courses on the table at once, rather than serving them one at a time, and I had a sugar-crusted brandy custard in my possession before I had laid down a bed of sweet-pickled cabbage to hold delicately fried fillets of star-back trout. The food kept coming, passed to my hand by Elder Thorpe. I was taking too much. Everyone was.

I spread slow-roasted garlic on a slice of goose breast and got down to the business of eating. Forks and knives clicked on bone-clay plates. Goblets and stemware thumped on the bare, silvery wood. Grunts and sighs of satisfaction sounded around the long table as we sampled dishes, swooned over flavors, and filled our stomachs. I ate every last scrap of trout—and looked up in surprise as the Eldest slid another piece on my plate, nodding. "Go ahead and eat, girl."

Had anyone else noted my appetite? Member Clarke regarded my emptying plate with some bemusement, but plenty of Thorpes were already helping themselves to more.

We ate without need for dinner conversation. Eldest kept filling my plate, grinning with every one of his ivory teeth, gesturing for me to go on. He gave me pickled beans, and I ate all six. He slid another slice of goose breast on my plate, offering me sweet mustard sauce to spread on top. He laid down another fillet of the beautifully spiced fish. I broke open a crusty roll and used it to catch every last drop of sauce on my plate, echoing the actions of the Thorpes, and Eldest lifted a ceramic bowl of roasted skirrets.

"Oh please, I beg you, no more," I said, and the bottom half of the table burst into laughter, Eldest included. It made the aching across my scalp flare, but I laughed with them.

At last Robin rose from her place at the other end of the table, lifting a glass. "Welcome, all of you. It is my profound honor to introduce the Blessed Grand Duchess Aife, heir to the Throne of Great Making."

Applause rained from clapping hands. Aife smiled and stood up. "Thank you for inviting me. And thank you for your efforts in abolishing the law that turns the gears of horror in Aeland. I have brought you Dame Grace Hensley, an ally in the push to bring freedom and safety to the starred ones."

She had what. What. She lifted her hand and I rose to my

feet, buttoning my jacket even as I scrambled for something to say.

"Ahoy." I smiled around the table. "Thank you for inviting me to your wonderful home. And thank you, Eldest, for stuffing me full of fish."

I searched my mind while the assembly laughed. "I haven't yet read your findings, but I have done a little poking around myself. The Witchcraft Protection Act is a bad piece of legislation, based on questionable evidence—and, I believe, poisonous greed."

The assembly nodded, a few murmurs of "That's right" and "I knew it."

Now I had to put my foot on the tightrope. "I am with you, esteemed friends of the Lower House. If you wish it, I will attend your press conference this afternoon to stand beside you in support, but the Queen is not disposed to striking down this law."

A Thorpe dropped her napkin on her plate. Her aura was smooth, generic, noticeably unremarkable. I dragged my gaze away and kept talking. "She believes that it will harm Aeland to admit there is no merit or truth to the idea that witches present a danger to society, and my voice in Parliament is merely the instrument delivering her will. She must be convinced to agree with your findings, or she will force me to vote against my conscience."

Smiles faded. They had wanted me to defy Constantina. I hadn't said what they wanted to hear. But Aife, still standing, picked up her goblet and drained it.

"Then she will listen to me," Aife said. "I will summon the Queen to me. She will not refuse me. And I will make clear my wish to see an end to the monstrous practice of imprisoning witches for life."

Now the assembly cheered. It thudded across my scalp with

a bright, red-tinged thud—and a dazzling, crystalline distortion bloomed in the center of my vision. I pressed my fingers against my temples and closed my eyes. The dazzle spun on the red-black darkness of my eyelids.

Oh no. Oh, oh no. I reached out, sending my perception westward. How had I missed the signs? I wasn't at the Western Point, but I didn't need a weather kite for the vision I beheld—

Clouds. Great, thick, spiraling clouds spinning around the empty, unblinking eye of a storm. Vast and pitiless, it stretched farther than I could see.

Another storm, as bad as the last one. Worse. Standing at the table and swaying dizzily, I opened my eyes to dozens of people watching me.

"My apologies," I said. "I suddenly don't feel well."

I bent my knees, aiming to retake my seat, but the headache redoubled. It struck so hard I heard myself whimper in pain before I landed in the chair and my vision went gray.

I didn't pass out. If I had, maybe it wouldn't have hurt so badly to hear the shocked exclamations that ringed the table.

"Quiet," Robin said. "It's hurting her."

She rounded the table and pulled my chair back and away so she could kneel in front of me. "Squeeze my fingers."

I cracked open one eye so I could find them.

"Good. Smile. Make a smiling face. Good. Now say 'Just Truth Youth Dust.'"

I repeated the words, my eyes still shut. "What are you doing?"

"Checking for cranial paroxysm. Good news. You're not having one."

"It's a dazzle headache," I said. "I get them sometimes."

"So you need dark and quiet?" Robin asked. "Amos. Get a pair of snow goggles."

Amos's scampering feet thumped away, and then back. Robin handed me the goggles. "I think you should take something for the pain."

The lenses were a deep-smoked gray, and it was almost enough to dial down the pain. Treatments for dazzle headaches made me groggy, but I could stand that.

"Please," I said. "And if I could have a word?"

"Up you get."

I felt gangly and huge next to Robin, who led the way into a tiny, windowless room. A narrow iron bed crowded one half of the room; the other side housed locked cabinets. Robin produced the keys and soon had a thimble of sweetish-smelling tincture under my nose.

"Samuel's Mixture?"

"I didn't think you wanted any morphine," Robin said. "It'll take the edge off, at least."

I took the thimble and choked it down—honestly, the attempt to sweeten it made it infinitely worse—and Robin answered a soft scratch on the door.

"Eldest wants to know if the lady needs ice," a high, too-loud voice asked.

"Thank you, Amos, but we're fine. Go and tell Eldest we have it in hand."

The door clicked shut. Robin sighed. "Go, Amos."

Footsteps thumped away.

"That should start working soon. What did you want to tell me?"

"There's a storm coming," I said. "Worse than the last."

The floor creaked as she shifted her stance. "Worse."

"Warn your Circle in Riverside," I said. "I don't know if you have anyone who can sense it yet."

"That's why the headache?"

242   C. L. POLK

"Yes. It happens fairly often. I'm used to it."

"All right. Was there anything else you wanted to tell me?"

"It hurts to think," I said. "Please tell your people to be careful. I can send details of the storm's heading—"

"We can do that," Robin said. "Thank you for telling us."

"You probably didn't need me to," I said. "I can see the snow didn't fall so hard on Riverside."

"It was kindly meant," Robin said, "and you were mindful of keeping our people a secret."

"I'll be glad when all this is over," I said. "All the secrets. They're exhausting. Persecuting people to keep those secrets. It's horrible. It has to end."

Robin closed cabinets and locked them. "How do you think it will happen?"

I bit my lip. Miles trusted Robin. She was a leader in the action against the government. "I think there can't be any real progress while our monarch doesn't want it." I could barely manage to whisper. "I hope Aife can sway her opinions."

"What if she can't?"

My throat went tight. "Then there will be blood."

"You fear that. Even though the blood will most likely fall from our veins."

"I don't want any blood to fall," I said.

"It's like surgery," Robin said. "When a patient will die without the surgeon's knife, then you need to cut into the body. Blood falls, but the patient is saved."

"And Aeland needs a surgeon." I sat up. My head pounded, but it was a muffled thump, at least. "To cut out the thing that's killing it. That's what you're saying."

"Do you disagree?"

I didn't dare shake my head. "I don't. But—"

"Every patient fears the risks. And only the worst doctors pretend there aren't any. People die in surgery. It's dangerous,"

Robin said. "But if you just leave it, the patient will die without that intervention."

It made sense. I knew it did. And she was right. "I think I can make it back to Government House now. I have a committee to support."

NINETEEN

The Cabinet

last this stupid sled. It had the yellow-ribboned crowd making ugly noises as we passed the temporary fence holding them at a distance from the long, shallow steps leading to Government House. They raised their signs and chanted in one angry voice: "Free them now!"

Permitted past the fences were reporters and photojournalists, milling about and smoking in the frosty afternoon air. One look at my ostentatious orange contraption and the scrum of newshounds in pinch-fronted hats came flying, cameras raised. Beside me, Tristan groaned.

"That's our cover blown out of the water."

"I'm sorry." I stood and let William hand me down. "I'll distract them."

I plunged into their midst and kept moving up the stairs, every shout drilling straight into my skull. "Citizens. I have a terrible headache. Please take this statement and ask no questions. I do not yet know what will come of Miss Jessup's investigation. It must be decided on by Parliament."

"But where do you stand?" one voice asked.

I nodded toward the group gathered at the top. "Behind

Member Clarke, who has an announcement for the press today. Member Clarke?"

Member Clarke shook back his lock-braided hair and let me pass into the bulk of his committee. I couldn't exactly hide, but I let them shield me. Tristan and Aife weren't anywhere in sight. Had they escaped without being photographed? Solace, let it be so.

Across the street, the protestors shook their signs, but they quieted as Member Clarke raised a bellower and shouted his message. I set a small charm that would project his speech a little farther, standing in the back behind the real members of Clark's coalition. He'd picked up more members in the crisis, as common-born Elected from Aeland's cities broke away from trying to ingratiate themselves with the landed who dominated the seats from in-country.

"The committee has reviewed the records of *Salterton's Hansard* and related supplementary documents entered into consideration during the debate and approval of the Witchcraft Protection Act," he said, letting his trained voice ring over the crowd. I tried not to look like I was being murdered by the pop of flashbulbs.

"It is the conclusion of this committee that the evidence is questionable, the debate inadequate, and the vote suspicious," Member Clarke went on.

A ragged cheer rose from the protestors. Clarke let them have a moment, then continued. "This law should never have been confirmed."

Cheers from across the street, jubilant and earsplitting. I smiled like I would die if I stopped. Clarke addressed the reporters in front of him. "Our findings led us to investigate key members of the vote, and our discoveries have prompted an audit and investigation into the finances of seventeen members of the Lower House who voted in approval."

"Are you saying they were bribed?" a reporter asked.

Member Clarke's tone was patient. "We are asking that their finances be investigated so we can determine if they were bribed."

"But what does this mean?" another reporter asked. "Are you siding with the abolitionists who claim that witches aren't dangerous?"

"This committee was formed to investigate the claims made in an independent report. This report detailed serious abuses of ordinary citizens supported by propaganda and myths surrounding the magically talented. The report was researched and written by a team of historians, lawyers, and medical experts. The story that the magically talented become mentally unstable and violent can boast no evidence of anyone actually doing so. It uses documents on public record. You can read it for yourselves."

He lifted a hand, and clerks handed out bound volumes to every reporter who put out their hand for a copy. A pretty young woman handed me a soft-bound book. I noted R. M. Thorpe among the list of authors, along with names I didn't recognize. I tucked it under my arm and waited for Clarke to finish.

He lifted the bellower to his mouth once more. "Based on this report, and the failure of this committee to refute its claims, we are introducing a notice of prorogue concerning the Witchcraft Protection Act. We ask that it be immediately suspended. We wish for every inmate of the asylums to be emancipated on Snowglaze one, 1584, to be returned to their places in society."

Screams of joy from the protesters. But a reporter yelled, "That's too soon!" and the whole group went into a tumult. I clenched my jaw and kept my hands by my sides.

One voice rose above the din to shout, "Chancellor Hensley, will the Queen approve this action?"

I raised my hand and the scrum quieted. "I have only just learned the findings of the committee," I said, but waves of pain knotted my forehead. "I shall have to meet with Her Majesty and discuss it."

"Do you approve this hasty action, Chancellor?"

That was it. That was the question they'd all been waiting for. I scanned the reporters, hoping that my snow goggles weren't making me look too distant.

"I've read about the Cabinet vote in the Hansard," I said. "I suggest you look at it yourselves—and then compare the yea votes to the list of major shareholders in Aeland Power and Lights."

"But does that mean—"

"Yes," I said. "I believe we should set the Witchcraft Protection Act aside. But my vote in the House will not be my own, but the Queen's. I stand before all of you and I say yes. It's a bad law, forcing a terrible injustice on Aeland's people, catering to the lies and fear surrounding the magically talented. I hope it is torn to shreds. Excuse me."

I couldn't stand in the low, slanting light beaming onto the south steps any longer. I couldn't bear the voices, loud and demanding. I took the stairs and moved through Government House, desperate for a quiet, dark place to rest and a healthy dose of the tonic I had from the chemist.

Janet gasped when she saw me. "Dame Grace."

I held up a hand. "Quiet, please. No typing. I need to lie down and—"

A woman rose from the padded depths of the couch and walked into my view. Muriel Baker, the Queen's personal amanuensis, was smart in her wool skirt-suit, but her presence in my reception room made me want to fall on the floor and cry.

Muriel stood with perfect posture, her arm curled around a writing board. She checked off an item and announced, "Her Majesty wishes you attend her immediately."

I closed my eyes and sighed. "Of course."

"This way."

Muriel's route led not into the palace where I had expected to go, but along the narrow hallway that served as a shortcut to the House of the Elected and the Queen's Cabinet chambers. What were we doing here? There was no Cabinet. We neared the tall doors carved with a bas-relief of Good Queen Agnes and her lamb, and the buzz of voices rose from inside the chamber.

Voices. In the Cabinet. Scarlet-coated guards draped in gold braid and tassels emerged from alcoves on either side of the door. The Queen's personal guard barred the way as the sharp crack of a gavel pounded through the thick wood and smacked me in the forehead.

The doors opened, and I beheld disaster.

The Queen sat on a dais at the bottom of the chamber, clad in the violet robes that weren't quite her most formal, crowned in a circlet of gold oak leaves, her scepter nestled in the crook of her elbow. Beside her in the junior throne, Crown Prince Severin wore one of his beloved bespoke suits, with violet snugged at his throat and peeking from his pocket square, amethyst cuff links winking at his wrists. He noticed me first, and Constantina fought the cruel edge of a smile when she laid eyes on me. She beckoned me to her.

I moved down the steep stairway bisecting the half circle of tiered seats filled with people dressed in black robes and violet-trimmed caps, the formal attire of Cabinet members. Familiar faces turned to watch my progress. I tallied up the faces, matching them to their positions by their chosen seat: Sir Jonathn Sibley, sitting in the seat for the Minister of Agriculture. Dame Irene Stanley, Minister of Labor. Dame Sarah Varley, Minister of Transportation—

Dame Elsine Pelfrey, seated in the place reserved for the Minister of Finance.

I knew their faces. Many of them occupied the seats held by their mothers and fathers. Elsine regarded me with spiteful triumph. I had been so busy crushing Raymond, I'd missed that she was the real threat.

"Chancellor," the Queen said, and the room leaned into a hush. "You were expected an hour ago."

Blast it. I descended the final stair and went down on one knee, the joint pressed against cold marble.

"My apologies, Your Majesty." There hadn't been any notice. Janet would have told me if there was something this big going on. I'd been sandbagged. "As I was unaware of this emergency session, I took the time to meet with some Elected Members who wished to speak of Parliamentary matters."

"I hope it was not Elected Member Clarke and his coterie?" The Queen cocked her head, looking so innocent.

She knew who I had been with already. "It was, ma'am. They wished to speak to me about their investigation into the Witchcraft Protection Act."

"And you recommended the law stay in place. Correct?"

Oh, the deuce! "Their discoveries are cause for deep alarm, Your Majesty. Public questioning of the case made in favor will inevitably—"

"Do nothing," the Queen said, "as there will be no suspension of the act. Which you should already know. How is it that you don't?"

My knee ached with the glowing burn of being made to kneel and never given leave to rise. All stares were on me, drilling into my back and shoulders. My head split open at the scalp, fire pounding over my skull. "Ma'am, there are compelling, urgent reasons to ensure the matter of the witches be handled with care and attention. The charade has to come to an end, guided by our hand—we have the threat of the people's deep anger, on one side—"

Someone behind me loosed a brief, scornful laugh.

"And the wishes of the Blessed Ones on the other. We're being squeezed between them. Our best chance is to control the release of the witches, and to do it with our own narrative thoroughly in place."

"And you have a plan."

I raised my chin. "I do."

"I'm in an indulgent mood," Queen Constantina said. Severin bit down on a corner of his lip. "What is this plan?"

I steadied my voice. "We use the media to release stories that emphasize that the decisions of forty years ago were made by those men and women currently held on charges of treason. That the reason for their current imprisonment is connected to those past actions. You had no part in them, Your Majesty. Your signature isn't on any of those laws. You weren't even the heir—"

"Enough." The Queen held up her hand. Reminding her of the horrible accident that had taken her husband and brother and made her the Crown Princess—that was thin ice I skated on, cracking under me as I tried to find a different angle, a better one.

The Queen steepled her fingers together. "So. You propose to put your father in a noose."

Damn it. "They can be sentenced to life in prison."

"The crowd prefers blood," the Queen said, one finger tapping on the arm of her throne. "The most wicked participants should be punished in order to wash us clean of all offenses for the fullest effect. Tell me, would you send your father to the gallows for the sake of your own comfort?"

I was supposed to say no, and look weak, or say yes, and look cruel. "I say this to you even knowing that Sir Christopher Hensley was instrumental in the choices that have brought the Amaranthines to Aeland to judge us for our trespasses against them. That if there were a list of the worst offenders, his would be the first name on it."

"So you would." Constantina injected that phrase with fascinated wonder. "Shall we ask the Cabinet to volunteer their own parents to your plan? Say aye if you wish to see your father kicking at the end of a rope. Your mother choking to death like a murderer. Well, which of you will offer up a sacrifice?"

The room may as well have been empty for all the noise the Cabinet made behind me. Constantina bestowed a smile on them, praise for the correct answer.

"I think you need to come up with a plan that doesn't ask others to desert their parents as readily as you are, Dame Grace. You are my voice in Parliament. You do not have a vote of your own. You do not get opinions of your own. They are mine. You are simply the messenger."

I would never survive the Cabinet at my back, not after a declaration like that. Confound it, when had she had time to contact them all?

I had to do something. Get control of the situation.

"This is a mistake," I said. "My job is to advise you with a clear-eyed evaluation of what is right for Aeland. My advice isn't just opinion. I am describing the extremely narrow path we must follow if we are going to survive this crisis. If I tell you otherwise, I am not doing my job as your Chancellor."

"I don't want to hear any more of this plan," the Queen said.

I had had more than enough of the Queen's petty attempts at humiliation. I rose to my feet, slowly unbending the knee that throbbed at being mashed into the marble floor for so long. "That is a very great pity, Your Majesty," I said, "because it's the only choice you have left."

Behind me, a liveried herald struck the floor three times, announcing a visitor to the Cabinet. I swiveled in time with the noises of surprise from behind me. That only happened when the Queen visited a Cabinet meeting. The Crown Prince would wait for a break in the proceedings, the same courtesy he gave stage performers and ice-hurley players.

Whoever wanted entrance to the chamber stood higher than any monarch.

The doors swung open, and Ysonde Falconer strode inside, garbed in fluttering black smoke and glints of silver. A huge black eagle rode on his gauntleted wrist, its eyes piercing and intent. Ysonde's gaze was just as pitiless as he pinned the Queen down with a look.

"Constantina Isobel Mountrose," he said. "You are expected to attend Blessed Grand Duchess Aife, Hand of the Throne of Great Making, First Daughter of Elondel, Watcher of the Dead. She who weighs Aeland's violations requires your presence in the glass hall tomorrow at nine. You are invited to bring your heir, Severin Philip Mountrose, and are permitted no other guests."

Queen Constantina's face blanched. "I regret that my duties—"

"Fail to attend and Aife will deliver her judgment on Aeland on that very noon," Ysonde said. "No clemency will be given."

The Queen opened her mouth, and Severin spoke. "We hear and obey the Grand Duchess's every wish. We shall attend her promptly on that day."

Aife would change Constantina's tune on the witchcraft act. She had no choice but to do the right thing.

How it galled her, even as she shrank away from Ysonde. Her white knuckles on the arms of the throne spoke of her fear, but her eyes smoldered. No one told Constantina what to do, but not even she dared defy an order from the leader of the Amaranthines. And with Aeland's fate on the line—she'd show up to that summons.

I wished I could be there to see it.

"Dame Grace," Ysonde said. "Aife would like to thank you for your help today. Your service is gratefully received."

"Please give the Grand Duchess my thanks for trusting me with the task," I said. "It was my honor to assist her."

Ysonde nodded to me and went out of the chamber, leaving us all in silence.

I returned my attention to Queen Constantina, who sat with wide, unsettled eyes. "Your Majesty."

She swiveled her gaze back to me. I kept my tone firm, skirting the edge of commanding. "I suggest you prepare yourself for facing the First Daughter of the Solace, Your Majesty. Aeland is balanced on her judgment, and she has asked for three concessions from you. I would start thinking of how to cooperate with her."

"Leave me." The Queen's voice quavered. "All of you. Now."

A shuffling and thumping behind me as the newly appointed Cabinet hastened to obey. I didn't quite dare put any weight on my right knee—a limp wouldn't do, after I had seized the moment. Severin hopped off the dais and was at my side in moments.

"You can't walk on that." He offered me his shoulder. "I'm sorry. I tried to find you, but you weren't anywhere."

"I wasn't in the building," I said, gritting my teeth as I tried to put my weight on my knee.

"Come to my office. It's closer," Severin said. "There are things you should know."

We used the secondary corridors to navigate through Government House, avoiding the media and anyone trying to get a word with the Prince. Severin was a patient crutch as I hobbled beside him past walls laden with displays of lesser works of art, too sentimental to be much more than decoration seen mostly by clerks and servants.

We went right instead of left, and a few steps later I was inside the reception room of Severin's office. A recording of the principal soprano of A Strand of Stars for Your Hair singing a difficult passage made me groan in pain.

"Turn that off," he said, and the windup audiophone went silent. "Just a little farther. You can do it."

A secretary rushed ahead of us and opened a door. Behind it, Severin's sitting room waited to serve his comfort. A black-and-white carpet, bold with interlocking circles and squares, lay spread beneath white leather sofas gathered around a leaping fire. Severin helped me to one and stuffed cushions beneath my knee, letting it rest while slightly bent. Severin's book of meditations and a pen rested on the low table next to the sofa. What had he written? No one was ever supposed to look inside. The writings in one's Book were sacred communications with the Makers. They were private.

That book made my fingers itch.

"Don't move." A fringed rug of royal purple silk settled over my legs, and he crossed to his sideboard. "You have a light-headache."

"Yes."

He plucked up a blue bottle and poured a familiar treacle-dark liquid into it. I caught the whiff of Samuel's Mixture as he brought it to me. I quaffed it, hoping this time I'd swallow it so fast I didn't have time to taste it.

No such luck. I tried to straighten my leg and gasped. "Oh, the deuce! This hurts!"

"Like someone slowly crushed it." Severin moved away, raising his voice to be heard. "Just give your knee time to rest. You can rub it. It makes it hurt more, but it feels like you're doing something."

It did, but somehow it was better. I rubbed, and it hurt, and I kept rubbing.

Above me hung an arrangement of photographs. Severin was in all of them, standing with one beautiful woman after another. The Prince posed with opera sopranos, principal dancers, and the divine stage actress Hyacinthe Chalk, who would neither confirm nor deny the rumors that they enjoyed a tender friendship. I suspected they had, but I wouldn't stoop to celebrity gossip.

Severin came back into view with two bags of ice. He handed me one, and the cool soothed my knee. I took the other and put it on my head. I sighed in relief. "You know this punishment."

"Intimately. I once suffered it in front of your father." He huffed out a laugh. "How did you work out how to time Sir Ysonde's arrival?"

"I didn't," I said. "That was pure magic."

"Or the Makers on your side," Severin said. "I am sorry I didn't hear about Mother's plan to spring the new Cabinet on you. I dropped in to warn you, but you were gone."

I sank into the black and gray pillows cradling my head. "I was with Member Clarke."

"And the Grand Duchess?"

I nodded and regretted it. "She wanted to leave the palace. I obliged her. But the new Cabinet is a disaster. They'll strike down the prorogue in a heartbeat."

Severin perched on the edge of the sofa, sitting near my hip. "They might not even get the chance. Mother might intercede and strike it down before the matter even reaches them. Either way, it's doomed to fail."

"It can't." I shielded my eyes with one hand. "Everything will go straight to blazes if we don't free the witches."

"We need it to fail," Severin said, "if we're to get what we really want."

I lifted my hand from my eyes. "You want it to paint the Queen in a bad light. To turn the people against her, specifically. But the Amaranthines—"

"Will be lenient, if we act swiftly."

I caught my breath. The promise I had made in Kingsgrave Prison—this was how Severin wished to use it. "There will be rioting."

"I know. We will quell those riots by overturning the old order. I'll begin my reign by rooting out the corruption of the old guard, just like you said. Then when we release the witches, they will blame dead traitors, not us." Severin's dark eyes were alight with the plan. "We can do this, Grace. We can save Aeland."

How many people had quietly hinted that they wanted this? Enough of them to ensure a smooth transition from one crowning to another. I had told Constantina we had to walk a very narrow path. This one was even more dangerous. But it was our best chance. We could survive it all, if we pushed the right story, with the handsome, charismatic Prince acting out of love for his citizens. I lifted my hand away from my eyes. Outside the tall windows, a mottled gray messenger dove lighted on a feeding platform and pecked at millet.

"We need your support of the prorogue on record," I said. "If you talk to Avia Jessup, she can interview you. She takes wonderful pictures. I can get her here tomorrow."

Severin glanced up at the gallery of photos. "What time?"

"It will have to be in the morning, if we want to make the afternoon deadline. Ten o'clock?"

"I think I can have everything arranged by then," Severin said. "This plan depends on you taking a strong personal stance against Constantina, emphasizing your support and her disapproval. We need the vote in the Lower House to be the one everyone hopes for, so when it fails, we're the heroes the people need."

A coup. We were planning a coup. It was what was best for Aeland, but that didn't stop the constriction of my breath or the wobbling, fluttering fear that raced around me. "I wish the timing was better. This headache? It's a storm warning. We're about to get a full cyclonic blizzard again."

"Again?" Severin asked. "That's so soon."

"I fear it might be like this all winter. I have to plot its progress and calculate when the Invisibles will need to do the ritual."

"Then you should go home," Severin said. "Get a good rest in."

"There's too much to do."

"You'll get a bit of a reprieve," Severin said.

I squinted at him. "What do you mean?"

"I mean Mother will be angry with you. Toweringly angry. She'll probably denounce you as her Chancellor."

I bit my lip. That wouldn't help me with the Storm-Singers. Not one bit. "But if I'm not Chancellor, I can't help."

"It won't be for long." Severin clasped my hand, squeezing it gently. "I can't imagine running this kingdom without you. I need you by my side. You'll only be out of play for a short time."

Inside I was screaming. I squeezed Severin's hand in return. "But if I'm not here, how can I—"

"The Amaranthines will demand your presence. You were right, earlier today. It's the people on one side, and the Deathless on the other, and I'm going to use them to crush Mother's rule. Trust me, you won't miss a thing."

TWENTY

Birdseed

I stayed long enough to reassure a worried Janet and write to Avia care of the *Star*. I asked her to meet with me and the Prince the next morning—me at nine, to brief her, and then the Prince would join us at ten, to give her the real story.

To brief her. I couldn't even pretend to believe that. I watched for the sight of Tristan's townhouse as William and George took me home, my hope leaping as I saw the lights shining in the windows. I wanted to stop and determine if she was well, but I couldn't selfishly reveal where she hid from my father's assassins. I couldn't stop, even if I trusted my driver and footman implicitly.

I ate supper and surrendered myself to Edith, who knew everything that worked to ease my headache. She dosed me with tonic, washed my hair with lavender-sweetwood shampoo, served me the blandest food to avoid a spice that might prolong the pain, barred chocolate and wine from my diet. I could not read, or do any correspondence, though I did win five minutes with my amanuensis, instructing him to write a message to every member of the Invisibles. Warning of the new cyclone sent, I lay alone in my bed, breathing in the incense that promoted peaceful sleep.

I dreamed of storms and woke alone. I went down to breakfast and gazed up at the painting of my many times great-uncle Bernard. I tried to see it as Avia had until my eggs grew cold. I huddled in the back of my sled, watching all the people who had yellow ribbons fluttering on the sleeves of their coats. William handed me out of the sled, third in line behind two bright green cargo haulers stuffed with sacks of mail.

I tilted my head. Just how much mail did Government House get in a day? Much more, with the telephones out of service, but two cargo sleds' worth, for the 7:00 a.m. post?

Sleigh bells jingled behind me. A third cargo sled parked behind us, loaded with sacks of mail. A mail carrier jogged down the steps from Government House, circled to the back of the sled, and hoisted a sack over his shoulder, again climbing the steps to the entrance.

I stopped the mail carrier behind me. "Excuse me, do you also have a sack of letters bound for Government House?"

She squinted, as if she needed spectacles. "They're all for Government House, ma'am." She said it like "mum," the way Riversiders did, taking in her sled and the other two with a sweep of her arm.

I blinked. "All three sleds? Is this normal?"

"Not at all, ma'am," she said. "One, maybe two bags at seven. More at ten. But this is more mail than I've seen in one place."

What in the world? "Thank you," I said, and hurried inside.

A full sack of mail rested outside my office door. Inside, Janet stacked envelope after envelope from a second sack, trying to sort them all into categories. Her silver-streaked hair was coming loose of its bun, wisping all around her head.

"What is this?" I asked. "Janet, what's happening?"

"All these letters are from constituents," she said. She slit open an envelope with the loopy handwriting of a child and pulled out a single folded page. "They're all about freeing the witches, so far. Some of them are heartbreaking."

She handed me a letter from a stack, and I unfolded it to read:

Dear Chancellor Hensley:

Auntie told me to write what it was like to hide. It makes me sad. I can make plants grow. If I could tell people, then I could make everyone's plants grow and tell them when they have cutworms and bad beetles and help them grow lots of food. But I can't tell anyone because they'll take me away and I'll never see my family again.

Sincerely,
Anonymous

That signature had halting spots where the pen paused before writing the next letter.

"This is from a child," I said.

Janet nodded. "That's a heartbreaking one. Some of them are blisteringly rude."

I took a stack of letters Janet had sorted and sank into reading them. I read the story of a boy who could heal animals and who had "a good job" but couldn't say what it was. I read a letter from a mother who cried the first time she realized her child was speaking directly into her mind, because her child was too young to know that their talent wasn't safe. I read about a girl who was in love with a boy who didn't have witchcraft, and how her parents forbade her to be with him, because the risk of discovery was too great.

We had hundreds in each asylum. Kingston sheltered thousands more, living small and in fear. I sat surrounded by letters when Avia stepped inside, lifting her camera to capture the sight of me and my staff reading letter after letter, sorting them into piles.

"The *Star*'s been buried in them," Avia said. "Whoever organized this is a genius."

I extricated myself from the sofa. "I'm glad you came. Do you want coffee?"

"Please." Avia sighed. "The *Star*'s run out. We're on rebrew."

I stopped at the potbellied silver urn and poured us each a cup, aromatic and dark. Avia took hers black. We were nearly out of sugar anyway. She followed me into my office, smiling as I stirred the air to spread the heat from the fireplace around the room.

"One day, I want to watch while you make it rain."

I barely had to consult my senses. Clouds hung heavy and low in the sky, their bottoms dark with unfallen snow. I pointed out the window, and Avia watched as tiny flakes danced in the breeze.

"Are you doing that?"

"I am," I said. "Though it's going to snow for real in a few hours."

Avia watched out the window, her coffee cupped in both hands. "How does it work?"

"I can feel it. You feel it too—cold, warm, humid, dry, windy. It's only I feel it more strongly, with finer details. Like a tailor who knows their cloth with a look and a touch, I suppose."

"And you can tell when a storm is coming, like last week."

"Yes," I said. "Like last week. Like now."

She turned to examine me. "Another storm is coming?"

"It's a bad one," I said. "Vicious. Tell Mrs. Sparrow to stock up the house. She has about three days before it hits."

"That makes my story more important than ever." Avia pulled a file from her satchel, and I opened the familiar goldenrod-colored paper cover to find a typewritten article headlined "The Hundred Witch Families—How Aeland's Elite Kept Their Power a Secret."

Cold trickled down my spine. Were we ready to reveal this so soon? I scanned the neatly typed page and read Avia's crisp style detailing the facts: that what we had characterized as one of the most common delusions of witches, the one guaranteed to prove that they were already surrendering to a loss of reason, was in fact true and that the most powerful families of Aeland—the wealthy, powerful, insular members of the Hundred Families—were witches themselves.

Then the article introduced me, giving a biography of my life and a romantic account of how I could command the elements of air and water, to make the weather do what I willed it. I read all the way down to the line "Grace's interview goes here" before I shut the folder and dropped it with others just like it, piled on my desk.

Avia set down an empty coffee cup. "I wanted you to see it first."

"You want me to just tell it." I lifted my hand to cover my throat. "Not an anonymous source. Me, admitting the truth."

"I think it's our next move," Avia said. "I want to run it in the morning edition on the day of the vote."

Oh Solace. I trembled all over. I could barely breathe. If I did this, I could kiss my place as the Voice goodbye. I was guaranteed to lose my seat as Chancellor. I'd be poison to the touch. Maybe even too much for Severin to handle.

But maybe it would work. Maybe I could use my notoriety to help the witches, once I was reappointed the position of Chancellor when Severin took the throne. It was a huge risk. Could we chance it?

Avia's shoulders rose, huddled up by her ears. "You don't want to do it."

"I didn't say that."

"You're not saying anything."

"That's because I'm terrified," I said. "This could blow up in my face."

"I think it will win you the Lower House," Avia said. "If you support it, you could swing votes."

"But that might not be enough." A sour taste rose in my mouth, flavored with lies. The easiest kind of lie: the one mixed with so much truth it went unnoticed. "Queen Constantina has appointed a new Cabinet. They're sure to strike down the House's vote."

Avia's eyes flew open. "What? Without letting the House interview the choices?"

"Legally, she doesn't have to involve anyone in her decisions."

"I have to teach you what's worthy of a headline," Avia grumbled. "Dropping a story on me like that."

"I'm sorry," I said. A thumping knock sounded on the main door of my office. More mail, probably. "Maybe there's a way to tie it in with Severin's story."

She cocked her head. "You call the Crown Prince by name?"

"He insisted," I said. "We work together. I see him more often than I see the Queen, these days—"

Heavy footsteps. Janet protesting "You can't go in there!" just as the door to my office opened and Queensguards barged inside.

"Miss Avia Faye Jessup," a beaky-nosed guard said. "We arrest you in the name of the Queen. The charge is sedition."

"What?"

We said it simultaneously, and Avia stared at me, hurt burning in her eyes.

"No," I said. "Avia, I didn't do this. I would have never—

you can't take her!" I shouted. "I am invoking the rule of legal shelter."

"You can't shelter her from the Queen's charge," the guard said. "She's above your authority, don't you remember?"

"What is your evidence?" I demanded. "What proof leverages this charge?"

"Miss Jessup was in possession of seditious material, including a fraudulent manuscript accusing Her Majesty's government of a conspiracy designed to inflame the temper of the people. Included with it were documents written with the intent of publication."

My stomach hit the floor. I had thought I'd found the weapon that would keep Avia safe from Father. I had relaxed my guard, thinking him defeated. I had underestimated him.

"You set me up," Avia said. She looked at me with hurt hollowing out her expression, the warmth of friendship and trust banished from it. Gone, it tore at the center of my chest. I would have fallen to my knees, if it would have put everything back together again.

"No. I didn't. I swear to you, it was Father. He did this."

She stared at me, incredulous. "How?"

I didn't know. All hope dulled, crumpling inside me. I didn't know how. I had no proof.

The guards clapped manacles on Avia, their hands impersonal and blunt as they searched her, taking her camera, her pen, her press badge. She watched me as she endured all their indignities. She turned her head and kept my gaze as they hauled her out of my office and marched her to Kingsgrave Prison. She would stand trial for sedition. The court would treat her research as lies. Disgraced as a traitor, she would hang.

I thought I had protected her, but only a fool would underestimate Sir Christopher Leland Hensley.

Janet came in when they were all gone. "What did she do?"

All I could see was the look on her face when they took her away.

"She told the truth," I said, "and she'd barely gotten started."

I sent a message to my advocate, along with a check that should pay for every minute of her time devoted to interfering in Avia's incarceration for a month. That would keep her safe and as comfortable as she could be while I did the one thing that would save her from the noose: put Severin Mountrose on the throne.

The messenger nearly bumped into Severin when she opened the door to dash up to the offices of Naismith and Brewster. Severin bent down and picked up an envelope with a boot print on it and handed it to Janet.

"I see they letter-bombed you as well," the Prince said. "But something happened; I can see it on your faces."

I nodded, my throat tight. "The Queen had Avia arrested for sedition."

Prince Severin's face pulled into pensive lines. "Over the article in the *Star*? It's flimsy."

If only it had been the article in the *Star*. "I'm sorry. Maybe if you had been here, you could have invoked legal shelter for her while we figured this out."

Severin huffed out an ironic chuckle. "I don't outrank my mother."

Yet. "I think they would have paused."

"Then I'm sorry I didn't get here earlier," Severin said. "Is there anything I can do?"

"I need to keep her safe," I said. "It's only for a few days. I assigned my advocate to block every process with court orders, so that will slow matters down."

I hoped. The Queen could order her into a trial right away. And if she had the manuscript and Avia's research, she had enough evidence to prove her guilty. And once guilty, the sentence of death by hanging would be carried out on the very next noon.

Dorothy had to get there in time. She had to.

Severin rested his hands on my arms, curling around my biceps. "It will be all right," he said. "A few days at most—you'll see."

I nodded. The plan was on. Severin's help would keep Avia alive.

"I want to go see her."

"It'll be a few hours to process her," Severin said. "But I will have the Guard-General understand that she's to be treated well. Do you want to send her anything?"

"Blankets. A change of clothes, warm clothes—what she needs to not freeze to death. Better meals. Something to write with?"

"She can only have quills."

"Good enough," I said. "Thank you, Severin."

"It's the least I can do," Severin said. "Go on with your day. You can probably see her in a few hours."

I nodded. "Solace knows there's a lot to do." But I had no idea where to start. "Severin, can you do one more thing?"

"Whatever you wish," Severin said.

"Can you shuffle the guards currently on duty in the tower? Rotate them out with guards who haven't been on the tower's roster since Leafshed?"

Whoever Father had in his pocket, I had to break that connection. He couldn't be allowed to influence the outside world for the sake of his plan.

Severin cocked his head. "I can do that. How soon do you want it done?"

"Today?"

"Very well. I'll summon the Guard-General." He rubbed my arms, raising his grip to my shoulders and squeezing. "It'll come out right."

"I know," I said.

"I'll send a report," Severin said, and he left my office.

All three of my secretaries hastily returned to what they were doing. I sighed. The Crown Prince of Aeland wasn't an everyday sight in the offices of Government House.

"I need to go over my agenda," I said. "I'm not receiving guests at present."

I shut myself inside my office and stared at nothing out the window. Everything rode on getting Severin on the throne. I had thrown in my support for the prorogue. I hadn't found another lead in Sevitii's murder—

Blast it, how had he done it? A guard in his pocket? A meal attendant? I had to know which one. I needed to look at the duty roster for the guards and see which ones had been working when Avia's flat had been burgled. But how had he known Avia wouldn't be at home that night? I had told no one of my plans to bring her to the ball—

Except Janet.

Janet had been my father's secretary. She'd been with him since before I was born. I'd never considered replacing her for an instant. She handled every visitor, knew my every working minute, read and wrote my correspondence. She ran the office of the Chancellor with efficiency, order, and poise. I leaned on her for rock-solid support through this crisis.

She didn't like my meetings with Avia Jessup. She'd never said so, but I knew Janet well enough to know when she was choosing not to speak her opinion. If Janet was informing Father of everything I did in this office, if she believed that loyalty to Father was the same thing as loyalty to me, she wouldn't even think she was doing anything wrong.

But that meant my office was compromised.

How were they communicating? Father only had two visitors. Janet was just as bowl-eyed over the Prince as anyone outside of his circles, but there were messengers and pages all over the palace complex. They could have moved messages that way. It was possible. But it was traceable. Pages and messengers had to account for their movements in duty rosters. It would take hours, but if I found a trail of messengers to and from the Prince's office, I would have them. That couldn't be it.

A plump-breasted messenger dove landed on the ledge feeder next to a hinged window. Father would let birds hop all over his office. Perhaps this one expected Father to open the little porthole and let him track feathers and seed-dust everywhere. Poor bird.

Chilly air radiated from the windows. I moved closer to feel for a leak and stopped.

The messenger dove didn't startle as I came near. It spread its wings and cocked its head, exactly as if it were waiting for me to open the porthole.

It had a tube around its leg.

I backed away carefully, watching the bird. Better than messengers, who could be interviewed and questioned—birds. Birds trained to carry messages and small objects. Birds, who were utterly unremarkable outside the window of the Chancellor's office, or the window of Father's prison cell.

Or the window of the office of the Crown Prince.

What part did Severin play in Avia's imprisonment? Had he just gone along with my plan to use the paper to push the prorogue, looking like he was cooperating but secretly sabotaging me? Just like he'd interfered in the talks with Sevitii an

Vaavut—but Niikanis had cleared him, by saying that he had been in the prison when Sevitii had most likely been murdered.

That didn't tally correctly. I had to speak with Niikanis again.

I eyed the window. The dove was still there, bobbing his head and peering in the glass. I could probably find the seed, feed it, and intercept the message—but that might reveal that I had guessed at Janet's treachery. I had to act as if I didn't know what was happening.

I couldn't let them know that their conspiracy had been uncovered. I had to outmaneuver them. And if I didn't knock my father off the board, I wouldn't be able to save Avia.

I spied Avia's file on my desk. The guards hadn't known it was special, piled atop other folders just like it. I couldn't keep it here. Janet was privy to all my files. I picked it up and read it again, hearing Avia's voice patiently telling the story that introduced my part of it. I stared long and hard at the final line.

Grace's interview goes here.

I pulled out a school pencil and a lined pad and began to write. I let the sound of the pencil scratching at the paper lull me into a light trance as I wrote without pausing to think or judge my words, filling four pages by the time I was finished. I thought of all the letters sent to my office. They had been brave, to write to me and fight for their right to be safe.

I wrote this letter for them. Because that little boy should be Kingston's greatest gardener when he grew up, not a fugitive. Because Healing was a gift. Because that girl should have a chance with the boy she loved. Because we'd robbed them of happiness, of safety, of opportunity.

I pulled out a pen and better paper, transcribing my rough draft into something more polished, managing to take the essay down to three pages. I let the sheets dry on the desk and

took the scratch pad to the fireplace, feeding my rough draft—
and the pages indented with the pressure of my writing—to
the flames.

Paper curled and blackened in the grate. I poked the remains
into powdery ash. I gathered up Avia's file and my portion, slipping them in a pile of files containing economic reports, all the
covers exactly alike.

The messenger dove was still there.

I draped my sable coat over my shoulders and sailed out.
"I'm in need of the Parliamentary Library," I said to Janet. "I'll
get lunch from the cafeteria. If anyone comes by, can you set
them an appointment?"

Janet nodded, and I swept past as if nothing was at all
wrong, walking halfway down the hall before turning back
and reentering my office.

Janet's chair was empty. My office door was closed. I opened
it to a swirl of cold air from the open window, and Janet gave
a start.

"I forgot my pens," I said, breezily. "I'm sorry I startled you."

"It's all right, Dame Grace," Janet said. "These poor birds.
They still don't know he's gone."

She held a bag of seed in one hand. Behind her, the dove
pecked greedily at a pile of seeds. The tube was missing from
his leg.

"Please keep feeding them," I said. "I'm sure Father would
smile to know that the citizens of the air have a refuge here."

She smiled at me, that beam of pride that used to warm my
heart when she thought I'd been particularly clever or dutiful.
"I'm sure he would."

I picked up my pen box and smiled again, masking the dull
warmth that spread over my scalp. "I'll be back later."

I turned my route to the rotunda. I didn't have time to

wait for my own sled—I hailed a cabbie driving a rough coupe seater and paid him with two crisp mark notes.

"I need to go to the main office of the *Star of Kingston*," I said, "and I'll have five more marks for you if you wait."

TWENTY-ONE

Four Paths Cross

The *Star of Kingston* used to be the giant of Main Street, a full two stories higher than its competitor, the *Kingston Daily Herald,* headquartered directly across the street. But when Ray had built the Edenhill, it soared a full twenty-eight stories into the sky and reduced the *Star* to "the building next to Main Street Station." It was still a lovely building, fronted by a message spelled out in brass: "Accurate, Interesting, Timely."

The cabbie pulled out a penny-book and huddled in a plaid wool blanket, content to wait in the cold for five marks. I hopped out of the back seat and crossed the wide sidewalk past full racks of bicycles and smokers huddled against the wind, their shoulders hunched and collars raised.

A directory placed Headline News on the second floor, and I climbed polished limestone steps into the rattling of a hundred typewriter keys. I found the frosted glass door with "Headline News" on its face and swung the door open.

Solace, the din. Lines of desks had typists drumming out stories. The smell of developer, sweet and chemical, seeped from an empty photo booth to my left. I took three strides down the central aisle, and with each step, the racket of keys thumping against platens died as typists looked up and gaped in recognition.

I made three more steps before a woman stepped into my path, notepad in hand. "Chancellor Hensley, are you truly in support of the prorogue of the Witchcraft Protection Act, even though the Queen herself is against it?"

The others did her the courtesy of letting her get the first question, but all bets were off after that. I could barely make out individual words as reporters babbled question after question, trying to be the one who got the response.

"I am here to speak with the editor," I said. "Where might I find her?"

Fingers pointed to the glass-walled office. A woman stood before the glass, hands tucked behind her back and as watchful as a rook, her dark eyes locked on my face. She nodded when I met her eyes, and I passed through the chatter of reporters and climbed the stairs to her domain.

The door stood open and I passed through it, my right hand extended to shake. "Ahoy. I'm Dame Fiona Grace Hensley."

"Ahoy," she said, with a voice like honey and smoke. "Mrs. Delora Gardner. It's an honor to meet you."

Mrs. Delora Gardner cared not a thing for beauty in her surroundings. The wall behind her office was a chalkboard, scribbled all over with overhead views of project tasks. I spied Avia's name next to "Investigative Series—WPA, Trains, aether, 1539–1541."

I remembered myself and looked back at Avia's boss. "I seem to recall your face," I said. "Were you a reporter about five years ago?"

"I was. I'm surprised you remember me. What can the *Star of Kingston* do for you today?"

To the point. No time for pleasantries. Good. "I'm here

because Avia Jessup is imprisoned in Kingsgrave on charges of sedition."

"Sedition," Delora echoed. "Because of the exposé on Aeland Power and Lights? I recall you enjoyed a tidy profit from that particular deception, for all your angry words against it."

"That article spurred a search on Miss Jessup's home. I should say, a robbery of Miss Jessup's home. They stole—"

"All her files and photographs," Mrs. Gardner said. "She told me. She also told me that she was headed to Government House to interview you, Chancellor. Was she arrested at the meeting you arranged?"

"Yes." Mrs. Gardner saw a story in everything, and in this one, I was a heartless, greedy manipulator, out to intimidate and suppress. How true a likeness was it? "But I wasn't the one who had her arrested."

She set her weight back on one foot and crossed her arms, watching me through a squint. "Then—forgive my bluntness— why are you here?"

"Because when the Queen's guards arrested Avia—at the Queen's orders—she had come not just to interview me and the Crown Prince, but to invite me to speak about a secret the Royal Knights have kept since the time of Good Queen Agnes."

Delora cocked her head. "But she's in prison. Why come here and complain to me about it?"

I was gazing at the ceiling before I could stop my eyes from rolling. "Because I wrote the rest of the article."

Now she straightened her spine. Now she looked at me. "About this secret. You mean to reveal it."

"I wanted to ask you to publish it in the morning edition. That's just before the prorogue vote."

"And this article will—you hope—sway the prorogue in a certain direction."

I fought a sigh. "Yes."

She pursed up her mouth, shifting it left, and then right. "I print news, not propaganda."

"Very well," I said. "Good afternoon, Mrs. Gardner. Do you happen to recall the name of the editor at the *Herald*?"

"Now, hold on, that wasn't a no," Mrs. Gardner said. "What did you write?"

I opened the folder and turned past the typewritten pages to the ones I'd done in pen. "I was four years old when I passed one of the most important childhood skills among the Hundred Families. Where most children were praised for reading picture books, I stood in the back garden of Hensley House and, with an act of will, made the sky pour down rain at my command."

Mrs. Gardner said not a word. I read on. "This is the first duty of every Royal Knight: to give their talent to command the weather and protect Aeland's people and crops from catastrophic, violent storms."

I looked up. "I'm a witch, Mrs. Gardner, and so are every one of the Royal Knights of Aeland. We designed the Witchcraft Protection Act to protect our secret. The time for such secrets is over. That's what I want you to print on the morning of the prorogue vote. The people deserve the truth about us. And if you won't do it, I'll get Farley Hart instead."

"And what do you get out of it?"

I didn't know if she was insightful or just cynical. "I'm trying to undermine the case against Avia Jessup," I said. "I've hired her an advocate—"

"Who?"

"Dorothy Naismith."

Delora looked impressed.

"She'll fight tooth and nail to delay the trial, get evidence tossed out, protect Avia's interests. You can help by reporting

Avia's arrest and incarceration by an increasingly tyrannical government—"

"It'll be your neck," Delora interrupted. "What's to keep the Queen from locking you up in the cell right next to her?"

"That is something I can't reveal," I said. "I'm taking an awful risk, but I can't stand by while the Crown puts Avia in a traitor's garb and makes an example of her to the people—and the media themselves."

Delora studied me for a long moment. "You mean it."

"I do."

"Very well," Delora said. "It's a deal. Freelance journalists are paid on publication, if you care about that."

"That's all right," I said. "Just getting the story out is enough. Do you want me to give a statement about Avia's arrest for sedition?"

The cabbie was still outside when I escaped the clutches of a charming, handsome Samindan man Delora had assigned to write about Avia's arrest and incarceration. I bundled into the back seat, planting my feet on the warming box. "I need the east side of the palace complex. Kingsgate Prison."

He put his book away and jumped down, retrieving a bucket of horse feed before we were on our way, bouncing across sled ruts and turning down the King's Way. I hunched the collar of my coat higher, tucking my hands into the sable fur muff that doubled as a winter handbag, and bore the wind freezing me and the people in the streets.

It was bone-chilling outside. The protesters still gathered. They huddled for warmth, but their presence filled half the square. Yellow banners flew over the crowd, the pennant ends sheeting in the wind.

Those yellow flags were unadorned, but if they'd borne a

ring of fifteen stars, they would have been the flag of Uzadal, the
league of nations settled by the Samindan people. I paid the cabbie seven more marks, nodding as he touched his cap in thanks.

I walked into the main entrance of the prison, battered by
facts. Samindans didn't oppress witches. They taught magic to
their talented citizens.

I fished my identification out of my hand-warmer and
passed it to the gate guard. She looked at it, and then at me.
"Your business?"

"Visiting a prisoner," I said, accepting my card back.

"Which one?"

"Avia Jessup."

The gate guard looked it up. "She's still in processing."

"I will scrutinize the processing, then. Please provide an escort to her location."

The guard stepped out of the booth and unlocked the
prison doors. "Howard. Take the Chancellor to see Avia Jessup. Prisoner 25318, Sedition."

Howard barely made the height requirements for guards,
but he was wide across the shoulders. He led the way through
stone halls to a lower level, and looked at a clipboard next to a
heavy door marked "Medical." He nodded and opened it, ush-
ering me in.

I walked into damp, chilly air and the smell of carbolic soap
doing its best to fight the swampy aroma of mildew. Avia shivered on a table, clad in a thin hemp shift, the shoulders dotted
from droplets falling off her wet hair. Her bare feet dangled
above the floor, her makeup scrubbed off. She watched me
walk in and her shoulders rose.

"What do you want?"

"Leave us," I said.

Howard shut the door, grinding the lock closed.

I came closer. Avia shied away. I stopped, holding up empty hands. "Did they hurt you?"

She rubbed one shoulder. "They would say no."

"And you would say?"

"They stripped me," she said.

I nodded. "And then they scrubbed you. Louse control. The water was ice cold, and they soaked you. No towel. Then they gave you those charming garments to put on."

"They did it to you?"

"The whole drill," I said. "It tears your dignity away. Strips you of your citizenhood. Humiliates you, knocks you down. And if you struggle—"

Avia winced. "You struggled."

I let that pass. "I had to know if you were all right."

She scoffed. "The guilt got to you?"

"I didn't do this," I said. "I know you don't believe me."

"It's hard to prove a negative," Avia said, "but try."

I reached into my pocket and handed her typewritten sheets of paper scattered with red ink. She held them up and read her own words, her lower lip caught between her teeth. She flipped the page, her eyes tracking over the lines.

"You lean on passive voice."

"Occupational hazard," I said.

"Shh." She read more slowly now that the words weren't hers. She glanced at me. "So if you're not a weather mage, you're a weather mage's lackey?"

"It's a terrible system," I said.

She nodded and read on, the light flaring in her eyes. "This is everything. You told them everything."

It made me warm to see hope in her eyes. "I also talked to a very handsome man who asked me questions about your arrest. They're doing a story about it."

"Samindan? Ivory beads in his hair, likes bow ties, dresses like he's teaching at university?"

"Yes."

"John Runson. He's my competition. He's good." She crossed her ankles and shivered. "You know, they could look at this new article and use it as evidence."

"I thought of that. I wondered if you would want to run it anyway."

"Out there, I would have said yes." She looked away. "Feels different, once Kingsgrave swallows you whole."

"Was it a mistake?"

She clutched the paper to her chest. "No," she said. "I'm going to hang. I might as well go down swinging."

"Don't be so sure," I said. "I hired Dorothy Naismith."

Avia whistled. "She's expensive."

"Money's got to be good for something," I said.

She looked at me again, trying to push her hopeful expression into something neutral. "You really didn't have me arrested?"

"I didn't." Please believe me. Please.

"Who did?"

I bit my lip. "My father."

"You said that before," Avia said. "But you didn't say how he managed it, up in that cell."

"My first thought was that he subverted a guard," I said.

"Logical," Avia said. "But traceable."

"Right," I said. "I think it's even wilder than that. I think he used birds."

Avia gave me a bemused look. "You're going to have to explain that."

Behind me, the door swung open. Two guards and a clerk entered. The clerk blinked at me. "What are you doing here?"

"Seeing to the accused's welfare," I said. "You need to supply her with warmer clothing. The prison's unheated."

"She'll be warm enough in the courtroom," the clerk said. "We're taking her to enter a plea."

"But her advocate isn't here yet."

"An advocate will be assigned to her."

"No," I said. "She hasn't had a chance to be consulted. Her advocate is on the way here—"

"The assigned advocate can do that."

"You don't listen very well," I said. "What is your name?"

"Daniel Swan."

"Daniel Swan. I am declaring myself Avia Jessup's interim advocate. I will act in her interest as needed."

The corners of his mouth pulled down. "This is highly irregular. You can't do that."

"Can't I?" I asked. "Am I not educated in Aeland's laws?"

"But you're not a jurist. You—"

"Write the laws jurists employ in the pursuit of a fair and uncorrupted pursuit of justice. Are you implying that I am unqualified?"

He went pale. "No, but—"

"Avia Jessup," I said. "Do you accept me as your advocate in the interim, while you wait for Dorothy Naismith?"

"I do."

"It appears I've been hired, Mr. Swan," I said. "And as Miss Jessup's advocate, I charge the court with misconduct."

Swan spluttered. "What?"

"By law, an accused person gets six billable hours, not including time for meals, rest, and exercise, to consult with their advocate before a plea hearing. It can only be waived by the advocate and the client together—which is why you were trying to hustle my client out of here."

"You can't—"

"I can." I looked at my watch. "Oh. It's four hours after noon. The legal business day is over in thirty minutes, and then the clock doesn't start again until seven thirty tomorrow morning."

"Chancellor," the clerk protested. "That's why we have to get her into court."

"Not today, Daniel." I gave him a tight smile that invited him to go straight to the void. "Tomorrow's not looking good either. I suggest you let the court know that they're going to have to answer for misconduct before they can hear a plea."

The clerk shrank back. "No one told us she had an advocate—"

"Did you ask?"

"They never asked," Avia said.

"It's time to go, Daniel," I said. "Goodbye."

I watched him hang his head and leave. I counted to three before I let out a sigh and turned back to Avia. "You're not leaving my sight until Dorothy gets here," I said.

"You—" Avia's muscles tensed, and then paper crackled as she pressed right against me, her face buried in my sable fur. I wrapped my arms around her and squeezed.

"You didn't do it," she said.

"I didn't."

"You went to the *Star* and told them everything."

"I did."

"So now you're a seditionist too," Avia said. "For me."

"I won't let you die." I buried my nose in her wet, liniment-smelling hair. "I don't care. I'll spring you out of jail if I have to."

"Why?"

"Because," I said. "Because I want to be who I am when I'm with you."

"I don't know if I can handle all that responsibility," Avia said.

"It's not just you. It's Miles too. And Tristan. All of you make me want to be better. All of you know exactly who you are, even if it's not what you're supposed to be."

She stood in my arms, her cheek resting against my shoulder, just as she had when she was asleep. I stood there with her, swaying gently as I held her close.

A knock came at the door, and a guard opened it. "Prisoner Jessup, your advocate is here to see you."

Avia stepped away from my arms then, swiping at her cheeks. "Thank you. Please let her in."

"I'll tell Dorothy's assistant what happened. Here." I stripped off my coat and settled it on her shoulders. "So you don't get cold."

The hem touched the floor, settling on top of her bare feet.

There was something I should say here, something that would mean everything I wanted it to. Cold air prickled at my skin while I searched for the right words.

"I'll let you and Mrs. Naismith talk," I said.

"Thank you." Avia curled the coat around her, giving me one last smile before she shook Dorothy's hand.

The cold in Kingsgrave Prison sank into your bones. I climbed stone stairs to the well-lit, labyrinthine halls of the main floor, and stopped at a hallway where all my routes into the prison crossed: the way that led to the palace, the way to the isolation cells, the way to the Tower of Sighs.

I still burned to climb the tower and confront Father. But that was exactly what he wanted, and I wouldn't give it to him. He'd find a way to further his schemes if he did—and I knew exactly what he wanted. Severin on the throne. Himself freed from prison—hang everyone else, but he would walk free, ready to weave his web back together again. He'd want the Chancellor position back, and he already had a plan to get it.

I could go back to my office, where nothing I did was safe from the eyes of my secretary—Father's secretary. I could pretend nothing was wrong, that I'd lost my coat somewhere—no, I wasn't about to return to that particular den.

The noise of marching boots echoed off the stone, and scarlet-coated Queensguards accompanying a gray-suited stranger strode past me and into the hall where we kept Niikanis. A premonition prickled against my spine, and I followed them, straight to Niikanis's cell.

"Stop! What are you doing?" I let my voice bounce off the stone. "No one is to interfere with this prisoner."

"Queen's orders," the lead guard said.

"To do what?"

"The Queen wishes to employ alternative methods of persuasion." She nodded toward the man, who had cold blue eyes and lines that frowned on a clean-shaven face. "This is Examiner Johnson. He'll be handling the questioning of the prisoner."

An examiner. I felt slime dripping down my neck. This man specialized in extracting confessions from witches. He used their own talents to torment them. He was going to use all those skills on Niikanis. He'd get his answers, or Niikanis would break like an egg.

"You're talking about torturing a diplomat," I said. "You're talking about committing an act that will plunge us straight into war with Laneer again—and the Queen told you to do this?"

"She needs him to talk."

She needed to be able to blame Laneer for their attack on

Aeland. She wouldn't want to walk into Aife's presence with nothing. "Do you want to do this? Do you want to hurt this man, listen to his screams? Will you enjoy it?"

She glanced away. "It's an order."

"Let me try," I said. "Give me a few minutes with him. One last chance."

"Ten minutes." She lowered her voice. "If we've spooked him, it might work."

I nodded. "Ten minutes."

They let me into Niikanis's cell. A tray of food lay untouched by the door. He watched me with dull eyes.

"I suppose you heard all that," I said.

"Let them take me," Niikanis said. "I deserve to die."

And he deserved to suffer? I wasn't going to ask him. I already knew the answer. "Is the ruler of the Star Throne more important than your daughter?"

He looked at me, unspeaking.

"I have a father," I said. "He's a power-hungry manipulator who was directly responsible for the reason Aeland declared war against Laneer. And he loves me."

He shrugged his shoulders, a defeated little smile on his face. "Fathers love their daughters."

"I believe you didn't kill your daughter, even if she was going to betray the Star Throne. I'm positive you didn't. But that means someone else did, and I don't know who. But you might."

"Do you really care about that?"

"Yes. Because Sevitii was about to negotiate peace between us. She was going to tell us who orchestrated the attempt to devastate Aeland with a necromantic attack. And in return, we were going to recognize Laneer's right to govern itself. I don't think Sevitii's killer meant to prevent that peace, so it must have been to keep a secret."

He listened. He sat up straighter when I told him about her bargain but slumped when I mentioned secrets. He shook his head.

I softened my voice. "Sevitii an Vaavut had a glorious destiny ahead of her. Her omen said so. Someone cut that destiny short. And I don't believe that it was because Laneer would be better served by her silence. I think someone was saving their own skin. I think you know the person who killed Sevitii. You may not know that you know. So I'm going to tell you how she died."

Niikanis looked away, but he nodded.

"When we found her, there was no sign that she'd fought an assailant," I said. "Her chambers were locked. She was a prisoner. No one could get past the locks, or the guards at her door. She suffocated. She couldn't get any air. We know this because of her eyes. They showed the signs of her fighting for air; she couldn't breathe. But there were no signs of anyone covering her mouth and nose to keep her from breathing. No bruising around her mouth or her nose or her throat. Her airway was clear."

He glanced at me. "How did the murderer get in, if the doors were locked and guarded?"

"We think that the attacker used magic to paralyze her lungs," I said. "It's just a guess. But we think it was done by means of the hair inside her star bangle, providing a magical link to Sevitii. So we know it's a magic user. What we don't know is which of the priests in your delegation had the most to lose if Sevitii talked. But one of them did."

He shook his head and looked at the floor.

"What? I'm missing something," I said. "Please. If I know who killed Sevitii, that's the key to everything we need to know. One of your priests was involved in the decision to use the spells that bound Laneeri soldiers to the Aelander soldiers, so they could come here and fulfill the plan to usurp power here. You know who it is. I know you do."

He shook his head again, his gaze far from this room. He licked his lips, opened his mouth, and closed it again.

I took a tiny step closer. "You know who it was," I said. "Now you know exactly who it was, because of what I told you. Who pushed the plan forward?"

He crumpled, bowing his head. He wrapped his arms around himself. "It's no use," he said. "Send in your torturers."

"Niikanis. Don't you give up on me, not when we're this close. Avenge your daughter. Tell me who pushed the plan."

He sighed and rubbed one side of his face. "We all did," Niikanis said. "All of us were in agreement. All of us learned the spell and then taught it to the other priests. We all persuaded holy people to commit this terrible act."

"That's not what I mean," I said. "This idea started with one person. One person with the knowledge of necromancy saw the potential for this spell to save your nation from the soul-engines. You know who it is. And you're protecting them, even though they killed your daughter. They killed Sevitii. Her murderer denied her the air she needed."

Niikanis rocked back and forth, shaking his head, his eyes shut tight.

"It took three minutes," I said. "Three long minutes where Sevitii couldn't breathe, no matter how hard she tried. Three minutes where she was terrified. Three minutes where she saw her death coming and couldn't do anything to stop it."

Tears rolled down Niikanis's face.

"I'm so sorry she's dead." I crouched in front of him, looking into his face. "Not just because she was going to work on the side of justice. I liked Sevitii. She was bold. Brave. She had confidence in herself, complete faith in her abilities to serve a country she loved with all her heart. I thought we were a lot alike, and if I had been in her shoes, I would have done the hard thing to save the country I love too, because that's what my father taught me to do."

His voice cracked on a sob. He took a deep breath, sat up straight, and gave me a tiny, sorrowful smile, the tears drying on his cheeks. "There's nothing you can do. Sevitii will never be avenged. Her murderer cannot be punished."

"Why?" I said.

Behind me, the cell door opened. "Time's up," the guard said. "Did you get an answer?"

"One more minute," I said. "Please."

"No," Niikanis said. "Thank you for trying, Dame Grace Hensley. I will not forget that you tried."

"He's one of your delegates," I said. "What makes him so special?"

Niikanis rose to his feet. He held his hands out. "I am ready."

"No!" I tried to get between him and the guard, glaring hard at the examiner. "I'm so close."

"We'll handle it from here," the examiner said. "You did a good job opening him up."

I shuddered at the compliment. "He's not going to tell you," I said. "He's going to suffer at your hands because he wants to be punished."

"Then we'll try the next one," the examiner said with a shrug. "I will get answers. I always do."

Guards pushed past me to seize the Star-Priest. They clapped copper manacles around his wrists. Niikanis gritted his teeth, but he fought the horrible sensation to look me in the eye once more.

"You can't stop him. None of us can."

The guards led him out of the cell. I followed, keeping up with the tangle of red coats.

"At least tell me who," I said. "If I can't stop him, I can expose him. That's what he was trying to prevent. Exposure will hurt him. Let me do that, at least."

"You cannot extinguish a star," he said. "Turn away from this. You cannot reach that high."

A guard turned around, barring my way. "You're done," he said. "It's for the examiners now."

I stopped in the same intersection of hallways where I had met the examiner's guards. I stood there, listening to the party march away.

You cannot extinguish a star. Sevitii's murderer stood too high. I didn't know what it meant. And then I did.

I ran through the halls, desperate to get to Miles.

TWENTY-TWO

Plans and Preparations

Tristan was there. I'd expected that. They were sitting down to a candlelit dinner. I ought to have expected that. But seated at the table, twisted to peer at me still in my hat and hand-warmer, was Robin Thorpe, and that wouldn't do. That wouldn't do at all.

"Grace," Miles said. "Good to see you. Come and eat."

I put my arms around Miles's shoulders in greeting and whispered in his ear. "I know who killed Sevitii an Vaavut."

He squeezed my shoulders twice, our old signal of "talk later," and brought me to the table. "There's plenty. You're going to eat where I can see you do it."

I couldn't wait! This couldn't wait. But I took off my hat and hand-warmer to sit before gold-rimmed serving bowls filled with mouthwatering stews and unfolded a thin pancake, spooning lamb cooked in cinnamon onto it. I tried to hide my impatience with a hand-feast, a meal consumed with leisure and conversation, only ending after hours had passed. There was no clock in my line of sight. I couldn't look at my watch.

The wine was amber colored, and I tested it against the lamb. Peach wine, heady and sweet with a bit of toasty flavor in the back. I eyed the other stews with renewed appetite, as a serving of peach wine promised hot and spicy dishes.

"Where is your coat?" Miles asked.

I spooned up pepper-roasted skirrets in ginger sauce, letting it cool on another pancake. "Kingsgrave Prison," I said. "The Queen had Avia Jessup arrested for sedition this morning. It's cold there."

"She was arrested? For telling the truth?" Robin's brows furrowed together.

"I've hired her the best advocate in town," I said. "She'll stall the courts for weeks over this."

"Stalling isn't the same as freeing," Robin said. "Does the court have anything besides that one article?"

"Yes," I said, "but Dorothy can get it thrown out. She can cut the Crown's case to shreds."

"No one has ever walked away from a sedition trial in all of Aeland's history," Robin said.

I was trying not to think of that. "I just need time."

The moment I said it I wished I could take it back. I stuffed lamb dara into my mouth and made an appreciative noise over the flavor.

Robin's mouth slid sideways, and her shrug was sympathetic. "You may not get it."

She was right. "I still have to try."

Robin scooped up fiery hot prawns in stewed chili sauce, the kind that made your eyes water and your nose run. "It's lucky that you're here. I was just telling Miles that we've gained five more votes in favor of the prorogue. That puts us at forty-six."

So many. Robin was the best lobbyist Aeland had ever seen, having pulled off that feat in so short a time. "So if five people abstain, you'll have it."

It had already started snowing—not the storm, but the

storm's herald. Maybe if it snowed enough, some of the object-
ing members would stay home, thinking the vote a sure thing.

"It's so close," Miles said. "I'm getting a bellyache just thinking about it. And with Miss Jessup in jail, we've lost our voice
in the papers—"

"I've spoken with the editor," I said. "If that will help."

"What will help is your support in the House," Robin said.
"But the Queen's tied your hands."

But Ysonde had appeared in the Cabinet and summoned the
Queen to Aife's presence. They were meeting tomorrow. The
prorogue vote was that afternoon. If Aife laid down the law
with Constantina, she might change her tune.

"I'm going to try one more time to persuade her," I said.

"Tomorrow. After Aife gets through with her," Tristan said,
echoing my thoughts. "That's your best chance."

"Who is going to be at the summons?" I asked.

"Aife and her advisors, of course. Guards. Prince Severin.
The Queen herself."

Robin dabbled her fingers in a crystal bowl of hot water.
"How many advisors does Aife have?"

"Me," Tristan responded. "Ysonde and Aldis."

"And the session will begin at nine," I said. "Will you be
there early, to discuss things?"

"We have a meeting half an hour before. Why?"

"I want to know when to start pacing in my office," I said,
my heart beating fast. I drew a circle on the tabletop and then
an "N" inside it, waiting for Miles to notice. It meant, *I have to
tell you something now.* "N" was a hint about what.

"Just tell us, Grace." He lifted his glass. "I told him. Tristan
knows."

I didn't quite thump the table. "That's a national secret!"

"He's going to be my husband. Husbands don't count."
Miles smiled around the rim of his glass. "Robin may as well

hear it too—she was at Sevitii's examination. Go on now, you're ready to burst."

I glared at him. This was supposed to be a secret! But I didn't honestly expect him to keep it from Tristan, and Robin had been at the examination, just as he said. I sighed and told them. "I think I know who killed Sevitii an Vaavut. It was Aldis."

"The deuce," Miles said.

"Who is Aldis?" Robin asked.

"Aldis is one of Aife's advisors, as Tristan said." I nodded to Tristan, who had gone very still, his mouth open but silent. "Tristan, whatever is the matter?"

"Why do you think it was Aldis?"

"Niikanis an Vaavut, Sevitii's father, said as much. You cannot extinguish a star, he said."

Tristan leaned back in his seat. "And you took that to believe that the one Amaranthine who actively champions the Laneeri here in Aeland murdered one of them."

"He told me that he was a steward of souls. That's a Deathsinger. Right?"

I directed that last at Robin, who nodded. I went on. "I think he uses the palace ghosts as spies. That's possible, isn't it?"

Robin nodded again. "They avoid me. They avoid Mahalia and Joy, too. You could be on to something. And that could be why I couldn't contact Sevitii's spirit."

"There. You see?" I picked up my glass and drank fruity, floral-smelling wine. "Do you disbelieve?"

"No. But you can't fling an accusation like that at an Amaranthine." He grimaced. "You'll need a way to prove it."

"Can't we just tell Aife?"

Tristan shook his head, his blond hair gleaming in the candlelight. "If you accuse him without proof, he can challenge you to fight him for the insult. Did you learn the sword?"

"I think you can guess the answer to that," I said. "How do I prove it?"

"You need to produce evidence of his deeds, or you have to force him to confess," Tristan said. "I don't think you can force him to confess without fighting him first."

Damn Amaranthine custom! I knew nothing about it, but I knew the history of duelling in Aeland. Plenty of crooked leaders had gotten away with murder by declaring their honor smirched by an accusation. If Aldis did the same, I couldn't defend myself. Drat Great-Grandmother Fiona for outlawing the practice! If she hadn't, I would have been as fast with a blade as I was with calculations. Father would have seen to it. "Blast it. How do I do that?"

"I do it," Miles said. "I'm a bit rusty, but—"

"You are not fighting an Amaranthine duel," Tristan said. "Not that Amaranthine. He's better than me, and I'm quite good. Besides, you could be brilliant, but Cormac hasn't declared you healed."

"If he can beat you, Tristan, then you can't do it either," I said. "That leaves finding proof."

"Look for Sevitii's star bangle," Robin said, touching the lockets at her neck. "It's an anchor. He'll have it hidden somewhere no one else goes."

"I think I know where," Tristan said. "He won't let anyone in his room. Not even the maids. They leave him firewood and fresh linen by the door."

That only made my instincts sharpen. He had something hidden in there, all right. "Then I absolutely have to search his room." I rolled up the spicy roasted skirrets. "And I know when he won't be in it—while you are meeting with Aife, before the Queen and the Prince arrive. Then if I show up before the summons, we're set."

"It's too dangerous. He locks the doors. You can't get in."

"Tristan, my lamb," Miles said, leaning against Tristan's shoulder, "you said there wasn't a lock in this palace that would keep you out."

Tristan looked up at the ceiling. "The both of you," he declared. "Foolhardy adventurers."

"I'll do my usual hallway constitutional," Miles said. "When I see him leave, I'll come in. Then you will take Grace through the service door, pick the lock to his suite, and then dash off to the meeting so you're not suspiciously late. Grace and I—"

"No," I said. "I'm not risking you."

Miles huffed. "Two can search faster than one."

I rubbed my temples. "Fine."

"Jolly! We'll bring this villain down in no time," Miles said. "Now that we've settled all that, will you stop picking at that rolly and eat something? We can fill Robin in on the rest."

I usually tried not to make William and George suffer through a long day of waiting for me to finish my business at the palace— and then there were days like these. I hurried through the halls of Government House with the collar of Miles's Service coat turned up, an incongruous mix with my hat and hand-warmer, but it would do to get me home. Most of the temporary gas-lights were extinguished, their fuel hoses bundled against the baseboards. I rushed from one pool of light to another, pausing at my darkened office.

I could go inside and search Janet's desk. I could confront her with the evidence of her conspiracy— No, I couldn't. I couldn't let on that I knew of it. I had to keep operating as if I were ignorant while I looked for a way to tear it apart—

But did I want to? Father was working toward putting Severin on the throne. That was something we desperately needed if Aeland was going to survive the judgment of the Amaranthines and the ire of the people. But something was missing from my understanding of Father's scheme—namely, what was in it for Father.

There was no way Severin could pardon the Cabinet for treason. No one would abide Father walking free, not after everything he had done. Did he really do this simply to save Aeland from destruction?

He wouldn't stand by and do nothing. There had to be something in it for him. But what was it? What?

I moved through the half-lit hallway, my ten-foot shadow stretching in front of me. At the end of the hall, the door to the stairwell opened, and Prince Severin stepped out.

"Grace. Oh, this is luck from the Makers! You're exactly who I wanted to see." His smile lit up the hallway as he came to me, a goldenrod-colored file folder in his hands. "I've just been rooting around the archives."

"I see you found something."

"I found the key." The stars in Severin's dark eyes danced. "I'm so glad you're still here. But I shouldn't be too surprised. The correct path sings in harmony, after all."

"I had dinner with my brother," I said. "Rollies."

"Oh, I do love a hand-feast," Severin said. "No wonder you're here so late. You're going to find a letter from me at home, informing you that I convinced the Grand Duchess to include you in the summons tomorrow."

Oh, the deuce! Blast it to pieces! I smiled. "I wasn't expecting that."

"It only makes sense to include you," Severin said. "And I wanted you to be there."

"Thank you," I said. "I have a conflicting event that must be attended a quarter hour before the meeting. I can't reschedule, but I think I can be finished in time to accompany you if I run like the blazes."

"Is it magic?" Severin asked, alight with curiosity. "To do with the storm?"

Only the truth would do. "The safety of Aeland depends on it. I am deeply worried that I will be late."

"I know you'll do your best," Severin said. "Now let me tell you the best part. The time has come to end Mother's rule."

I froze. "Has it?"

Severin scowled. "She still thinks she can kick and fight when it comes to the Amaranthines. She is going to explain to them one more time why their demands are impossible. And that is when I will make my move."

Tomorrow. He was starting the coup tomorrow. I took a dizzy breath. "So you'll use the Queen's resistance to contrast with your willingness to work with the Amaranthines. Will you tell them that she plans to quash the prorogue if the vote goes through?"

"Yes. But this is the final blow. Look."

He offered me the folder. I held it in my spread hand, the spine cradled against my palm, the leaves buttressed against my fingers. The first item was a photograph that made me cock my head.

Constantina Mountrose was a handsome woman today, but as a newly wed princess, she was luminous. All her dark hair was carefully, securely dressed in an upswept style that wouldn't have budged even had she done cartwheels down the aisle of the private train car where she stood beside her equally handsome husband, Lord Pearson Hayes of the Duchy of Red Hawk. They were the perfect couple—beautiful, wealthy, poised on the threshold of a match made for love and not dynasty.

This Constantina was merely a royal daughter. She had a life of setting fashion and championing worthy causes ahead of her, able to live in luxury with none of the burden of a kingdom on her shoulders. I stared at her clear skin, her brilliant smile, the way she tilted toward Pearson as if he were her lodestone even with her eyes on the camera.

Pearson hadn't even bothered to try to look less than besotted. He gazed at the Princess in open adoration, a little smile on his mouth that said, *Ah! How fortunate I am, how blessed we are.*

I flipped the photograph over, reading the date. She'd been pregnant with Severin by then. She'd only had six more months before the accident that killed her husband and her brother upended her life.

It hurt my chest to flip through these photographs of her highly publicized national honeymoon, where she and Pearson had traveled the length and breadth of Aeland by the newly constructed, monstrously expensive railway network. She cut ribbons. She kissed babies. She rode bicycles in a dozen Main Street processions, the figure of fashion in a calf-length split skirt that fit close to her hips, a peplumed jacket making her waist look a handspan wide, the tops of her buttoned boots disappearing under the hem of her skirt legs.

She had been so happy.

I turned a page, and there was Constantina in a smart, tailored traveling suit, squinting at the tall spires and whitewashed walls of an asylum. I narrowed my eyes and read the wrought iron sign over the entrance—Talonlocke Hall, in Red Hawk.

I looked up at Severin then, openmouthed. "She knew."

"She did."

I turned the pages, and she was observing patients who had been washed and combed for her visit. I studied the inmates. Most didn't look at her, or at anything. But there were sidelong glances: watchful, distrusting, even hostile.

There were no pictures of her inside the basement room where they forced witches to channel the dead into soul-engines, but did Severin really need one? She had been inside an asylum. It was hard to pretend she didn't know what was going on inside it.

"If you reveal these to Grand Duchess Aife—"

"She'll denounce Mother," Severin said. "It will be over at that moment, but we'll do it properly—we'll call an emergency session, call a vote of no confidence, climb every step."

If this went the way Severin thought it would, and I couldn't see an alternative, then we'd hold the government in our hands. We could fix everything. And the key had been hidden in the basement of the archives, forgotten, unused promotional material.

"Severin," I said, closing the folder, "how did you know to find these?"

"Your father told me where they were," Severin said.

Disquiet slithered around my middle. I smiled. "That makes sense. Father makes it his business to know where the bodies are buried."

"All my faith in him was soundly placed." Severin gestured down the hall, in the direction of his office. "Shall we celebrate with a drink?"

"That's pushing the Maker's luck too far," I said, still smiling. "And I called for my sled some time ago, so my men are freezing out there. We'll have time to offer thanks to the Makers when it's all said and done."

"Always so pragmatic," Severin said. "The New Year will dawn on a better Aeland. But you're right. We wait to celebrate at the proper time." He laid a hand on my shoulder, beaming. "I don't know how I'm going to sleep tonight. I'll see you at nine."

I nodded. "At nine."

He looked at me for a moment longer, his hand still on my shoulder. But he smiled and squeezed once, letting me go. He turned and walked away, the folder tucked under his arm, and I hurried to the sled, an anxious flutter in my middle.

What did Father get out of this? What?

I was awake before Edith came in with a cup of strong tea and the newspaper. I glanced at the *Herald*'s headline: "A Reckoning: Anticipation Builds for Amaranthine Meeting."

They'd licensed Avia's photo of Aife astride her antlered heera and gazing curiously at the camera. Beside Aife's tiny smile lay a past photo of the Queen, her lips a thin angry line. I read it while I was under the blazing hot hair dryer.

Someone in the Cabinet had told of Ysonde's arrival to the Cabinet to summon the Queen, finishing with, "How can she defy a Blessed One? They command, and woe on she who resists. But what if their demands are dangerous for the country?"

The *Star* was a different headline, and Edith handed it to me with shaking hands.

"The Hundred Witch Families—How Aeland's Elite Kept Their Power a Secret."

"You told them," Edith said.

We had never spoken of this, never. Edith had been my maid since I was sixteen, and she never so much as commented on the weather in my presence. None of the servants ever had, keeping their silence as part of the job. "Yes."

"Was that—" She shut her mouth, going red. "Ma'am. Excuse me."

"It's time, Edith," I said. "Times have changed. We can't fight it any longer."

Edith bowed her head and left my bedchamber to turn on the shower.

I skimmed the story—I already knew it, after all. The article below the fold made hay with a story about John Runson being denied access to the *Star*'s very own Avia Jessup, locked in Kingsgrave Prison and accused of sedition by the Crown. They tantalized the reader with coy details of Avia's attempt to investigate the actions of the traitor Cabinet, saying that she was at the edge of a story too large to tell without an extensive series.

Edith had three outfits on the bed, just as if I hadn't told the most important secret in the Western Point. I dressed in flat shoes, tall strand-knit socks with small bands of geometric patterns rising up the calves, a pair of tweed knee-breeches and a jacket cut by the same tailor Tristan had praised for flexibility and daring. My vest matched the socks. I covered it all with a woolen coat, dressed for a day on skis or breaking and entering.

I was pleasant to Janet when I arrived in the office and fought to keep my focus on my tasks. I was shaking like a rattle by the time I left my desk to walk—calmly!—down the corridors leading to the Amaranthine wing, where Miles was already stumping up and down the hall, obeying his healer's orders and serving as lookout.

"Go in, have a tea, I'll be there in a minute," he said cheerfully, and not at all like a man about to burgle the suite of a Blessed One. I let out a sigh as the door to Tristan and Miles's suite closed behind me and Tristan put a mug of Amaranthine tea in my hands. I drank, and blinked as my perception sharpened, focusing on the thistle and sparrow embroidery on Tristan's waistcoat.

"That stitching is incredible," I said.

"Thank you. I'm pleased with how it turned out," Tristan said. His hand snapped up. A blur raced straight for my face. I snatched a leather hurley ball out of the air, then boggled at how unthinkingly fast I had caught it.

"What the blazes is in that tea?"

Tristan looked innocent. "Nothing. Well, herbs and such. You're riding the excitement. Are you a thrill-seeker?"

My laugh was a weak, unconvincing thing. "No! I'm no daredevil. But we're about to solve this. We're about to fix everything. Wouldn't you be excited?"

The door lever clicked, and I faced Miles as he came in. "Now," he said.

A feeling rushed over me like sea surf, and every nerve came alive. "I can do this on my own," I said.

"I know you can," Miles said. "But I'm going, regardless."

"All right."

Tristan led the way to the cleverly hidden door servants used to come and go, and we were in a narrow hall, tiptoe-ing to Aldis's suite. A stack of rumpled bedding rested next to the door; he'd probably already taken in the firewood. A duty roster next to the door had "Do not enter this suite" written in red ink across the top. I read the initials and dates tallied by the servants, tracking their movements throughout a workday.

Tristan crouched in front of the doorknob and slid two nar-row probes inside the lock, wiggling them. I should learn to do that. I should know how to pick locks and have adventures. I kept a rein on my tongue. There would be time to ask later.

The doorknob clicked. Tristan stood up. "There. Be care-ful," he said, and with a kiss on Miles's cheek, he was striding down the servants' hall, intent on not being too late to meet Aife.

"All right. Here we go," I said. Anticipation fluttered in my chest, excited and avid to get on with it. I was not a thrill-seeker. I was not.

I pushed the door lever down and felt the barest resistance as the door swung open, as if I had snapped a thread. A high-pitched whine sang out deep in my ears, as if aether was still working on the other side of the door, but it faded as I stepped into the room.

A Laneeri soldier stood in a room that was the green-and-ivory mirror of Miles and Tristan's suite. He whirled and melted through the opposite wall, and I ran as if I could catch him or hold him.

I knew, then, what the ringing in my ears had been. An alarm. Aldis had trapped his suite, guarding against intruders.

"Grace," Miles said. "That's it, we're sunk. Get out of there."

But I ran deeper into the suite, dashing past the sofas to cross the room. We had one minute? Two? Better not push it.

I shoved my shoulder against the door and it gave way, putting me face-to-face with a wide-eyed Sevitii an Vaavut, her spectral hair unbound and trailing on the floor. She pointed, her lips moving as if I could hear her, but I leapt on the bed and bounced to the floor, landing on a pile of laundry.

I opened the drawer of the nightstand, and gold winked up at me, round and shining. I snatched it up, the engraving on the tube deeply inscribed. Sevitii's star bangle. Her omen.

I could hear her then, as if someone had switched on a wireless. She was crying and shouting in Laneeri, and I didn't understand a word. I didn't have to. I shoved the bangle onto my wrist and hopped on the bed again, taking the straight-line route across the bedchamber and out the door.

I had gone two steps past the threshold and into the parlor when the Laneeri soldier was back, passing through the wall as the door to Aldis's suite opened. My stomach lurched. *Run!* But I was already going full tilt when he collided with me, knocking me to the floor, his hands around my throat.

"You." All the hate in that word dripped.

I clawed at his fingers, forcing my eyes wide, loudly gagging on my lack of air. He smiled, gentled his grip, and I sucked in a great lungful of air, coughing on it.

Then Aldis squeezed again, and I kicked my feet, feebly attempting to free myself. Three minutes to death, if he had only cut off my air, but his hand squeezed the blood supply to my brain. I might have a minute.

All at once, I went limp, as if I were overcome. He chuckled. One cynical huff.

"I can tell you're faking," Aldis said. "I rule death, little meddler. You can't gull me as simply as that."

Keep talking, you fool. I opened my eyes, stared deep into his, and grinned as I coiled up my power and struck.

TWENTY-THREE

Crimes and Justice

I dug my fingers into Aldis's skin. Some magic needed touch. This magic needed touch. I slipped my power under his flesh, enveloping his being, melding with the magic in his soul, the power of his witchmark.

Even as I stretched my power around him, I faltered. I had done this to Miles. I had learned better than this. But it was my life. He was going to kill me if I didn't do this.

Aldis reared backward, releasing me. I gasped in air. Miles had leapt on his back, one arm crooked around his throat, his hand curled around Aldis's chin. The other held Aldis's shoulder, ready to snap his neck.

What had happened to my gentle, sweet brother over in Laneer? I pushed the thought away as I grabbed Aldis's hand.

"Don't kill him."

"I will if he—"

Aldis did something—rolled his shoulder, ducked his head—and freed himself from Miles's grip. He tore his hand out of my grasp and spun, his fist clenched and jabbing straight for Miles, aiming below the belt. Miles doubled over and crumpled to the ground.

I had to bind him. I had to, or he was going to kill us both. I dove for Aldis again, scrabbling to get my hand on his bare skin. I poked at his eyes, but he wove away from my fingers, coming back with a ringing slap to my face. The impact flared purple against my cheek, then melted to hot red. I tasted blood in my mouth, bright red metal washing over my tongue—

And then I couldn't breathe again. Aldis got to his feet, walked over to Miles, struggling to rise on his hands and knees, and kicked him in the ribs.

Miles fell back to the ground. Aldis turned away from Miles, his mouth small with anger, his jaw set, and his hands coming up to hit me again. We weren't any kind of match for an Amaranthine trained in the art of violence. Miles groaned as he struggled, crawling away.

I thrust out my hands, directing a violent, fast wind. Aldis stumbled in its grip, trying to fight its relentless push. Miles swung his legs around, hooking one of Aldis's ankles. It was enough. Aldis fell into the wind's grip, arms flung out in a desperate bid for balance.

I spread the wind wider. A lamp slid off a side table and caught the air, sailing straight for Aldis's face. He screamed and clapped a hand over his nose. An armchair toppled, tumbling toward Aldis, and I punched the air, sending it flying. Aldis fell over, howling as the chair hit him.

He shouldn't have tried my brother. Hot anger spread across my scalp. I had to press my advantage. I stepped out of the corner, hooking a ceramic figure of a dancing couple with a gust and aiming it for his face. He flinched, throwing his hands up to protect his face, and a bright scarlet triumph flooded my senses. I picked up another lamp, yanking the aether cord out of the wall, and threw it into the wind.

He was a defensive ball in the corner. I let the wind die and reached, my power sliding up his nose, down his throat. Air and water were mine to command. Aldis gasped out a long whoosh of breath and clutched at his throat. His staring eyes went pink around the irises.

"Grace," Miles said. He fought to get to his feet. "You'll kill him."

But what else could I do? If I stopped, he'd be on us. "I can't stop."

"Yes, you can. I've got it."

He stumbled to where Aldis huddled and fought to breathe. His witchmarks flared as he slapped his hand on Aldis's cheek. A brief flare of power shimmered against Miles's aura, and Aldis stopped struggling so abruptly I flinched. He thumped to the floor, his eyes shut, his breathing even and slow.

I stared at Miles, who was breathing hard, cradling his arm around his middle. "You shouldn't have—"

"Save it," Miles said. "We won."

The door to Aldis's suite slammed open. Tristan dashed inside, followed by Amaranthine guards. "Miles! Are you all right? Grace, oh no."

I tried to smile before I realized that it would be an awful, bloody sight. I composed myself and addressed the guards. "I accuse this man of the murder of Sevitii an Vaavut, leader of the Laneeri delegation to Aeland. Please arrest him and take him to Grand Duchess Aife for judgment."

Amaranthines in tunics and trousers came forward, seizing Aldis by the arms.

"What did you do to him?" one of the guards asked, her gaze taking in the wrecked room.

"He wasn't disposed to coming quietly," I gasped. "I ask for the judgment of Grand Duchess Aife. Aldis Hunter murdered to hide a great crime."

"And you shall have it," the commander said. "Take them both to the Grand Duchess."

There stood a throne in the glass ballroom meant for Grand Duchess Aife. Carved of a red-orange wood, deep grained and enchanted with the illusion of butterflies fluttering along the flowers carved and painted into the frame, realistic down to the dew sparkling on petals, it was a seat out of a Guardian tale, the kind of chair that cradled a pitiless ruler of death's kingdom.

Aife sat in that throne, clad in a gown split down the front, her legs encased in enameled leg guards depicting butterflies in flight, but the margins of their wings were torn, as if these creatures battled each other to the death. A bow and quiver rested nearby, in case she needed her weapons to hand.

A queen and a prince knelt before that throne, heads bowed as the guards dragged Aldis into the room. Miles touched Aldis's cheek, and he came awake all at once, struggling in the grip of the guards, but going still as he realized where he was and who witnessed him.

I moved past Aldis, my coat torn and my face bloody, taking my place next to Prince Severin. I bowed my head, bent my knee, and covered my heart with one hand.

"Water," Aife said. "You have blood on your face, Grace Hensley."

"I'm sorry. There was no time— Thank you," I said, as Ysonde brought me a silver-chased crystal basin and a cloth. I listened to the trickling song of the water as I wet and wrung out the cloth, and then shivered. Wait—where had it come from? I wiped my face and tried not to gape as Ysonde took the basin, covered it with one of his draping, black sleeves, and vanished it.

"How did you come to be injured?" Aife asked, and Ysonde moved away before I could ask how he'd done it.

"Your Highness," I said. "I accuse Aldis Hunter, who slew

Sevitii an Vaavut. I discovered the proof of his crime in his suite." I slipped the bangle off my wrist, and Sevitii popped into view. "This was in his room. I suspect he used his power to trap Sevitii in place, so another Deathsinger couldn't learn what he had done to her."

Aife gazed at Sevitii, who kept talking, trying to explain what had happened to her, I guessed. "And what motive had he to murder this woman?"

"When Aldis was in Laneer, he taught the Star Priests a spell that would allow Laneeri soldiers to inhabit the bodies of the Aelanders who killed them," I said. "In this way, over fifty thousand men returned home to Aeland, unable to stop the Laneeri spirits from possessing their bodies and using them to commit terrible violence. They planned to kill Queen Constantina and occupy Aeland. I argue that this is a war crime, and a hideous one at that."

Aife stared at Aldis, who kept his eyes on the floor. "Is this true?"

Aldis sealed his lips shut, refusing to answer.

Aife's face went ashy pale, her golden-brown skin bloodless. "Your refusal to answer is troubling, Aldis. We should not have to ask you if you indeed slew Sevitii an Vaavut, the diplomat who threatened to expose a terrible deed you are accused of doing in Laneer. But we compel you to answer—did you teach the Laneeri the soul-taking spell, and did you intend them to enact the plot Grace described?"

"It was meant in defense," Aldis said. "The Aelanders had terrible weapons, and every death went to feed their monstrous soul-engines. The Laneeri needed a way to survive."

"I did not ask for your excuse, Sir Aldis. Did you teach the spell?"

Aldis's lips writhed, but he answered. "Yes."

Aife's lips pressed together, her nostrils flaring. "Did you play a part in the plan to attack Aeland with possessed soldiers?"

"Yes."

Aife went very still. She gazed at Aldis, who faltered under that gaze, his chin dropping as he bowed his head.

"The penalty for murder demands the punishment of service, but the crime you have committed is far more heinous than even killing. The crime you have done is nearly unspeakable." She was calm as a still pond, frozen into glass. "There is a fate for you, and you will not escape it. Do you submit to service, Aldis?"

He looked up and bowed his head. "I swear to serve, Your Highness, until you see fit to release me. May my every infraction add a year to my service."

"You will serve, Aldis Hunter. You will be punished, as justice bids us. You murdered Sevitii an Vaavut. You committed thousands of souls to an abhorrent crime. They have died, and your actions touched all of them. You have done murder. You attempted genocide. You advised me to bring down the harshest justice on the people of Aeland in order to hide those crimes, and because I trusted you, I entertained your counsel."

Aldis bowed his head, crossing his arms over his chest. "I have done all that you have said. I am guilty of all of it. I deserve your justice."

"And so you shall serve, Aldis Hunter, until I deem your service is done." She rose from her throne and beckoned. "Come here."

Aldis rose to his feet. A single sob escaped him, but he went bravely, kneeling before his Grand Duchess.

What was she going to do? What could she do? Make him serve, but how? Surely she wouldn't bind his power as I would have.

Aife reached out, laying her hand on Aldis's head. "It shall be done."

Under her hand, Aldis wept. With a gasp he fell forward, his hands landing on the stone floor. His fingers curled into fists, then—

I covered my mouth with one hand as he screamed in pain. The borders of his body stretched, growing misshapen under Aife's touch. He screamed, and the noise sounded like a thousand agonies as bones lengthened, altered, changed. His clothing hung in tatters as his skin sprouted hair thickening into a russet pelt, curly under his chin and feathering over the wrists, his hands hardening into tough hooves, cloven down the middle.

I was going to be sick. I couldn't look away.

Aldis kept screaming, his human voice giving way to a beast's panicked squeal. Horns burst from his head, which flattened, lengthened into muzzle and cheek and squared-off teeth, his rolling eyes now set a handspan apart, skin filling in with short, ruddy hair. The horns grew and split, curving into branched, fuzzy antlers under Aife's touch.

A tail grew, glossy with rippling hair. Aldis's cries were all animal now as the beast rippled with its transformation and then shuddered with heaving, labored breaths, its becoming complete.

It wasn't a horse. It wasn't a deer. But the heera was a creature out of daydreams, and the little girl inside me who thrilled at horses clasped her hands together even as I fought nausea at the sight of it. It—he—sighed and put his nose in Aife's hand.

She petted Aldis, as if he were a prized beast. "Take him out to the stables," she said, and took her hand away.

A glamor settled over Aldis. His hooves melded. His antlers faded. His body slipped into the seeming of a strong, glossy chestnut horse, and a guard looped a rope fashioned into a lead

over Aldis's head. Aldis went quietly, his unshod hooves clump-
ing on the floor. Aife waited until the door closed behind the
guards and the new horse, then turned her attention to Constantina and Severin, both of them pale and clammy. They
stank of terror. They uttered not a word.

Aife regarded them both a moment longer. "You wished to
negotiate?"

Constantina ran. She tore open the doors and dashed past
the guards, who stopped her and marched her back inside.

She tried to kick, to wrestle herself loose, but they brought
her back to the throne. Constantina wailed, terrified. "No!
Please!"

"Calm yourself," Aife said. "I asked you a question."

Constantina screwed her eyes shut and shook her head. I
wanted to look away, to try to preserve some of her dignity. I
glanced at Severin, who stepped a little closer to Aife's throne.

"Your Highness," Severin broke in. "I wish to show you
something. Constantina should properly be counted among
the imprisoned traitors in the tower. She knew that the asylums were using witches to power the aether network. I have
pictures of her inside the asylum at Red Hawk."

Aife put out her hand. "Show me."

Severin offered the folder, and Aife glanced through the
presented photos—a handful of the ones Severin had showed
me. Only the important ones made it to Aife's hands.

Constantina wilted. "Foolish boy," she said. "Aeland will
never be ruled by your hand, no matter what crown you put
on your head."

"We have no interest in controlling Aeland's government,"
Aife said. "We wish to see justice restored to this land. We will
give you a year to change your ways."

"Then I'll be King?" Severin asked. "With your leave of
course, Blessed Highness."

"We can't put the crown on your head, Severin. You'll have to do that yourself."

Severin smoothed away his consternation. "Mother. I ask you to abdicate your throne and make way for my rule. If you do this, I will see you comfortable in the duchy of Red Hawk. I don't want to hang you."

But he would. If that's what it took, he'd send his own mother to the gallows with Father and all the rest. Perhaps he should—would the people countenance mercy to his mother?

Constantina raised her head. "You may have to, Severin. But not because I will resist your efforts. I abdicate the throne in favor of my son, Severin Philip Mountrose. May he reign with wisdom and strength."

Severin bowed his head. "Thank you. Grace, take Mother to the scriptorium. Get that abdication in writing. Meet me in my office in the palace afterward. I have something I need to do."

TWENTY-FOUR

The Strings on His Wrists

Ending a reign with legal documents was strangely peaceful. Constantina wrote the abdication, then read a penny-book novel while we waited for the master penwoman to scribe her declaration, a process that transformed official documents and writs into legal existence.

For the time between Constantina's declaration and the signing, Severin's rule was in limbo—not real until documented, signed, and sealed, like any legal agreement. We had typewriters and printing presses to produce text, but a document of law still had to be scribed.

When it arrived, Constantina took out an engraved silver pen and signed it on the spot. She glanced sideways at me as I signed, declaring myself as witness.

"I don't fancy taking the trip to Red Hawk in sleds and tents. I'll take the train after it thaws."

So Constantina was going to stay a while—and if she played the hand dealt to her, she meant to influence her son's decisions. My head throbbed. I could deal with her opposition—I could even use it to my advantage. But I wanted to get on with the business of setting Aeland back on its feet. Constantina was promising to hinder that progress.

"Shall we go to your apartments now? I think you'll wish to consult with the head housekeeper about moving to another wing."

A flock of junior scribes looked up from their calligraphy, wide-eyed at the gossip. A glare from the master penwoman put them back to work. A muscle in Constantina's jaw jumped, but she strode out of the room as if I hadn't insulted her.

"How long have you both plotted against me?" Constantina asked, as if this were a comfortable, boring conversation for hallway talk.

"Not long." I owed her the truth. "When Severin fetched me out of the jail cell you ordered for me."

"You pulled me from the throne in a little over a week." Her mouth went sour. "Severin had better remember how easy it was. Do you really think he'll do a better job?"

"Severin has the proper respect for the Amaranthines and their wishes."

"Severin relies on the judgment of others. It's a dangerous trait in a king."

"Severin has his own mind," I said. "And he's very good at considering the needs of others. He tries to make balanced decisions. That means listening to people he trusts."

"Countries tremble when a weak king takes the throne." She looked straight ahead, giving me a brief glimpse of her profile, recognizable as the same elegant nose and curving chin on the coins in my pocket. "It's a wonderful monarch for an ambitious Chancellor, though. Isn't it?"

Oh, Constantina was not going to be eliminated so easily. "Honestly? I had never thought about it in those terms."

"Spare me," the Queen scoffed. "As if a Hensley would ever overlook an opportunity for power."

But I had. I had never really thought of Severin as a king, even though he would certainly come to the throne in my lifetime. Even when Severin had come to me, asking for my support when he made a bid for the throne, I had never thought of how to take his need to be likable and shape it for my own ends.

I turned the notion around in my mind. As Severin's Chancellor, I stood to influence many of his decisions. I could manage him easily enough. But thinking about it put a sour taste in my mouth. Severin had ideas of his own, a vision of his own, and it was my job to push those ideas and that vision into policy. I wanted to do that job, but Constantina was going to turn him into a string-doll and squabble over who got to make him dance.

I had to get rid of her.

"This is where we part," I said. "I suggest you contact your dressmaker as well. It's going to take a while to adjust your wardrobe."

Only a monarch wore more than a splash of violet, and Constantina had draped herself in purple. All those gowns and suits had to go. Constantina puffed up angrily at the reminder but composed herself. "You think of everything, Dame Grace. You have the knack for being an able assistant."

I curved my lips. "Thank you. I'll consider it if I find myself looking for a new job."

I bowed my head—a mere dip of courtesy from a Royal Knight to one of the landed—and walked away from her, not requiring her leave to go. It was a short journey from the royal quarters to the wing that housed the Crown Prince, and servants already buzzed through the hall, carrying crates and packing material to move Severin's personal belongings. A guard bowed to me and led the way to Severin's office, the only room left in peace from the industry of porters and maids.

"Do you have a pen, Your Majesty?" I asked as I walked through the door. "I can lend you mine if you haven't got one handy—"

I stopped midstride as the floor shifted under my feet. My stomach plummeted, as if I sat inside a roller coaster that had taken its first, terrifying plunge.

Father stood next to Severin, his hand on the new King's shoulder.

Severin waited for the abdication in my hands with barely contained excitement. He tried for a casual smile, but it stretched too far, betraying his joy. "I'll borrow yours. It makes for a better story."

Father stood by his side, pride curling his lips. "Excellent work, Grace. You made this happen. I couldn't be prouder."

Oh, Solace, no. This was not going to happen. "You can't free him, Severin. Everything the Amaranthines deplore us for doing stems from his schemes. The people won't stand for it."

"The people are nothing," Father said. "They complain and wave signs and want everything handed to them, but once we turn the lights back on and their jobs are waiting for them, they'll go home and stop this nonsense."

"Do you hear him, right now?" I asked Severin, whose smile had faded. "The people aren't just complaining. They can't just be soothed by a ten-hour shift six days a week for bad wages. And when the witches come home and start talking—"

"It will all be handled," Severin said. "My reign will right all of that. Apologies will be made. We'll task the government to institute reforms. But this disruption from protests and strikes can't be tolerated. As King, I will—"

"Think about this, Severin. You'll be King, I'll be Chancellor, and Father will be—what? What will Father get? If you pardon him there will be a revolt."

"I'll return to my post as Chancellor," Father said.

"The deuce you will. You're going back into a cell." I turned my attention to Severin. "You might get away with not hanging him, if you say he's too sick to face an execution."

Father went on as if I hadn't said a word. "I'll take on a proxy to attend the sessions and the events I don't have the energy to do. You will be doing something quite different."

Father's voice distorted, sounding like he spoke into a well. I blinked, trying to clear the feeling of unreality that blanketed me. "Different? You honestly thought I'd let you push me aside, and then use someone else as your proxy? That's not going to happen."

"I'm not pushing you aside, Grace." Father shook his head. "Maybe I should step back and let Severin explain."

He did exactly as he said, taking three steps away. He roamed along the naturalist displays, pausing to gaze on a specimen dome containing a black guardian butterfly, mounted as if it had just lit on a branch.

I looked back at Severin. "What do you have to explain? What story did he cook up, and why do you think the people will fall for it?"

Severin stepped close to me, taking my hand. "It's not a story. It's— Ah, blast it. This isn't how I wanted to do it," Severin shook his head and licked his lips, smiling at me with warmth. "I had something very different in mind."

"What?"

"This."

Severin let go of my hand and sank to one knee.

The roller-coaster sensation lurched to the right. He slipped his hand inside his pocket, and my hands trembled.

He couldn't be. It wasn't done. It was never done. Every moment of that dance at the ball came back to me, every second spent dancing in his arms, the Prince never letting me go. This couldn't be happening.

Severin produced a band of silver, mounted with— Oh, Solace shelter me. The Prince held out a ring with a sapphire the size of my thumbnail, surrounded by tiny sparkling diamonds. He held the Heart of Aeland, passed from royal bride to royal bride for generations.

"Please take this ring," the Prince said, "and consider. Will you consent to become Her Royal Highness Princess Grace of Aeland, Royal Knight of Aeland, Duchess of Red Hawk, Marchioness Westfjord, and my wife?"

His wife. My heart pounded. This was beyond imagining. This was impossible. "We can't."

"I checked. There is no law that says a member of the royal family can't marry a Royal Knight. There never has been."

"It's understood. Royal Knights don't marry out. And neither do you."

"King William married his secretary."

"King William wandered off to the country to have a dozen children while his cousin did all the work."

"And his eldest son was my great-great grandfather," Severin said. "I need you, Grace. Aeland needs you standing for them."

This was what my father wanted. This was what he had worked for, behind the bars of the prison that barely held him—a way to elevate the Hensley legacy to unimaginable power. We would forever be a step above the Hundred Families—we would be royal, part of the bloodline of Good Queen Agnes. After Severin, a Hensley child would take the throne. Magic would run in the veins of Aeland's rulers forevermore.

It would be the greatest achievement in our family's history,

outdoing even Great-Grandmother Fiona. This was the ulti-
mate climb to power. This was an achievement to take a sick
old man peacefully to his grave.

And this was his wedding gift to me—a handsome, weak-
willed King who wanted to be liked. A man I could easily control as Princess-Consort, the most powerful woman in Aeland.
I could do almost anything.

I could lead reform. I could dismantle the worst of the Royal
Knights' legacy of greed and cronyism. I wouldn't have to hob-
ble radical legislation with compromise after compromise—I
could simply decide what was best, and Severin would sign his
name. It was the answer to everything.

All I had to do was accept duty and responsibility over selfish wants, just as I had done my whole life. To accept that marriage was about the advantages of partnership, about alliance
and legacy. This was best for Aeland.

I stared at that ring, sparkling and dark with all the potential to put everything right. I could do everything I wanted. It
made sense to say yes. Say yes.

My lips wouldn't move.

"Please allow me to confess something," Prince Severin
said. "This is the solution to our problems, but political expedi-
ency isn't my only motivation."

What? I blinked and looked at him instead of at the hyp-
notic depths of the sapphire in his hand. "It's not?"

"I admire you. Fervently." He tilted his head, gazing at me.
"You never guessed?"

"No," I confessed. "I never thought about it."

"I think you're brilliant," Severin said. "I've always been in
awe of how quickly you see the undercurrents of a situation."

"Except romantic interest, it seems."

"Do you doubt my sincerity?" The light sparkled in his
night-dark eyes. He wanted to marry me. This wasn't just an

alliance for political influence. This wasn't just Father's strings making him dance. He wanted this. He would love me. He would adore me—he already did.

It solved all my problems. It cut through the tangle. But I couldn't open my mouth.

Miles would never— No, he would understand. He would understand completely. And he would still love me, even though he could never trust me. Tristan would probably understand too, but my heart wrenched at the thought of losing his friendship, however cordial we would be with each other. I would stop the crackdown Severin planned for the protesters, but I'd never be welcome in Robin's house—she would be my critic, my honored scrutineer, and never, never my friend. Avia—

The roller-coaster took another plunge. We hadn't promised each other anything. But Dame Grace Hensley would take that ring, and rule, and do her best—

And the person I was when I was with my brother, Avia, Tristan, when I could shed Dame Grace like a coat—that woman would never become anything. I didn't know who she was, but I would never learn with the King's ring on my finger. Every person I loved, admired, and respected would be on the other side of the line. The right side of the line, no matter how much good I did, how pure my intentions would be.

And so I smiled at Severin, and he knew before I opened my mouth.

"I'm sorry, Severin. So sorry. I am deeply honored by your proposal, but I must decline. This is a line we must not cross."

He took it in the heart. It bowed his shoulders, dimmed the light in his eyes.

"I'm sorry," I said.

He nodded, silent and sorrowful.

Behind him, Father stared at me, incredulity in his eyes. "You what? You're sorry?"

Severin stood up and turned around. "It's her choice, Sir Christopher."

"All of those years I taught you," Father said, his voice simmeringly angry. "Everything you learned, everything you dedicated yourself to, and you— Severin. Lock her up."

"I will not," Severin protested. "She hasn't done anything—"

"She willfully destroyed the aether network. She is responsible for all the jobs lost, the widespread hardship Aelanders suffer, every poor soul frozen to death in their homes. She lied on the front page of the paper about the Royal Knights. All because she's been subverted to a dangerous ideology dedicated to destroying the government and our way of life."

How quickly he moved through the game of power. Father always had an answer. He always had an attack. His body was weak, but his mind was as sharp, as dangerous as ever.

Severin blinked. "None of that is true."

"All of it is necessary," Father said. "She's the greatest threat to our nation, and she must be contained."

That was quite enough. "You can try explaining that to the Grand Duchess, if you like. I'm sure she'll give that the response it deserves." I folded my arms and turned my attention on Severin. "You know what the Amaranthines want. You told me that you would satisfy their requirements. Imprisoning the woman who liberated the dead from the crime that they're considering withering us over won't look good to them."

"She's right." Severin touched his lips and swallowed, the memory of Aldis's transformation plain on his face, but I wasn't done.

"And there's no way Sir Christopher can appear to have won freedom from consequences. He's losing his ability to reason if he thinks he can take over the position of Chancellor. You should march him back up the tower stairs and stop up the window so he can't will his birds to be his messengers.

You should try him for the crimes he has done, just like the Crown did to Percy Stanley, but the Amaranthines don't like killing."

"I thought you'd be happy," Severin said. "He's your father."

"And he's the reason why the Amaranthines are judging us. He's no use to you, Severin. He probably still thinks that you should stop the prorogue."

Father quivered with the urge to speak. "I can guide Aeland through this crisis."

I went on as if Father hadn't spoken. "You need to step into a bold direction, Severin. You need to show Aeland that you're not your mother's son. You need to act in favor of progress and change. And that's why you will stop the prorogue vote this afternoon."

Severin blinked. He looked at me, perplexed. "What? But you just said—"

"You're going to abolish the law by royal order," I said. "Today, in the Lower House. It will be your first act as King. It will mark the beginning of Aeland's reconciliation. Do that, and you will stun the people. Extend your hand to them. It will earn you some respect."

"I see your argument," Severin said. "But royal orders should be rare. We should allow the natural process of government to operate."

No. I had to convince Severin on this, and I had to do it now. Aeland depended on it. I had to convince him to listen to me, not Father. "You need to abolish the witchcraft act, and you need to do it right now," I said. "We have a terrible storm headed our way. It's worse than the previous one, and we couldn't stop three feet of snow from falling on Kingston last week. It will bury us—unless I get more help."

"The First Ring stands ready to assist with this storm," Father said. "All I need to do is give the word."

Now I acknowledged his presence, with a tight smile and little more than a glance, fit for an underling speaking out of turn. "Thank you, but that won't be enough. We need more than just the First Ring and their conditional cooperation, Severin. We need the witches in hiding all over Kingston."

He cocked his head. "I didn't know there were Storm-Singers outside the ranks of the Royal Knights."

"They didn't want you to know," I said. "They kept their secret well. I can get in touch with their leader, but I must have that law abolished if I'm to convince them. I need proof they won't be taken and locked up. I need you to make them safe, Severin, so they can save us. We need them. Desperately."

Severin went pale. "The storm is that powerful?"

"I'm underestimating," I said. "The truth is I can't really imagine how bad it will be. I will need to leave the palace to ask them in person—and I need to do that with a guarantee that they'll be safe, that their families are coming home at last."

Severin looked up, and I averted my eyes as he asked for the guidance of the Makers. Father kept his mouth shut, watching me with thin-lipped anger. He knew I hadn't been exaggerating about the cyclonic blizzard headed our way—he could still sense the winds, even if he was no longer strong enough to pit his will against it. He knew we needed all the help we could get. But he couldn't let me win here. We both needed the first victory, to be the person Severin listened to.

Father cleared his throat. "Properly, these alleged Storm-Singers should have been—"

I cut him off. "In an asylum, where they certainly couldn't help us now. It's a blessing of the Makers that they're here, able to turn the storm and save the city—we must show them that they are needed. Valued. You must show the people that the sun will rise on a better Aeland—one that you will defend to the last. Free them. Earn their trust."

"It would mark my reign as King," Severin said. "I must act in the defense of Aeland. I will abolish the law and declare it in the Lower House."

"Thank you." I had won. I was the Chancellor. I was Severin's better advice. The tight band around my chest loosened. Severin may have wanted to marry me, but he didn't value my expertise any less. I almost breathed a sigh of relief. "The next act of goodwill would be the release of anyone currently jailed for protest activities. Say that they were against the Queen's government, not yours, and so they ought to go free."

"She doesn't care about some rabble in a yellow ribbon," Father said. "She wants you to free those charged with sedition."

Severin's expression turned sober. "Sedition is a serious crime."

"Against the former Queen," I said. Drat Father! He knew what I was up to, and he wasn't going to sit back and let me take control.

Fathe scoffed. "They're vandals and thugs trying to overthrow the government, and releasing them won't change their minds. They want our traditions and way of life destroyed, and anarchy in its place."

"Were any of them violent? Did they destroy property?" Severin shook his head. "No. I have to look at each individual first. We'll discuss it after the session in the House. After the danger of the storm has passed."

"What about Sir Christopher? You can't let him free." He had to go back to the tower. He couldn't traipse about, getting his schemes everywhere.

"Hospice. I have arranged for a room and medical care," Severin said. "A final act of compassion for the dying,"

No. If Father wasn't sent back to his cell, if he wasn't cut off from the world, Avia would become a pawn in our game. He'd use her to check my efforts or arrange for her to suffer an accident of some kind. I couldn't risk that. But there was no time to argue it.

"Then let him be taken to his bed. There's been quite enough excitement for one day, and you need to get to the Lower House before the brawling over the prorogue really starts."

"No time for that," Father said. "There is much to discuss—" His own words died on a fit of coughing.

"Too much exertion." I resisted the urge to cluck my tongue. It would have been petty.

"You need to rest, Sir Christopher. Sit. I'll tell the guards to bring a wheelchair." Severin stuck his head out the door and spoke to a guard, who followed him inside. He returned, standing beside me as the door opened again and a guard pushed a wheelchair into Severin's office. "I had better get to the Lower House. Will you accompany me?"

Father seethed as a guard took him away. I shook my head. "That snow is coming down too fast already. I must get to Riverside immediately. We'll meet again, after the storm. I have much to do, Your Majesty."

"Including planning my coronation." Severin walked me to the door, then caught my hand again. "Grace. Is there any way you'd reconsider—"

"No." I smiled to take the pain away. "I think you know why it's not possible. I'm better as your Chancellor, not your wife."

Severin nodded. "All right. We have work to do. You have my leave to go."

I bowed my head, but I left Severin without delay.

Once outside, I let myself exhale. Relief unkinked my shoulders, released the stiffness in my spine. I hadn't won it all, but Severin had listened to me. And I could neutralize Father's next move, but I had to do it now. I moved through the hallways at a brisk walk. I had one chance. I had to get Avia out of Father's reach. I had to get to Riverside as fast as I could, and hope that Robin would trust me with the knowledge of Riverside's Storm-Singers.

If I could have run without a guard stopping me, I would have run as fast as I could, down the halls and through the chill of a window viewing one of the palace gardens, where the wind rattled the windowpanes. I would have run through the enormous foyer, my footfalls ringing off the intricate marble tilework. I would have run down the wood-paneled halls to the ambassador's wing, where I stopped to greet the guards stationed there before passing through and knocking on the door to Miles and Tristan's suite.

I held my breath and listened to the footsteps, sighing in relief when Tristan opened the door.

"Grace," Tristan said. "You're white as a sheet."

"Thank the—stars," I said. "I'm glad you're here. I need your help."

TWENTY-FIVE

Escape

We left the suite after Tristan had dressed himself in a formal robe, unbinding his hair and holding it back with a silver diadem. He put on the enthralling, sinister demeanor of a Blessed One in a temper and strode through the palace with a tight-lipped stare that made guards shrink back and find something else to do.

I tagged along in his wake, my hand on his shoulder to keep the spell that hid me from view active. No one saw me carrying a bundle of Miles's clothes as Tristan glared his way across the palace and into the long, cold stone hallway that connected it to Kingsgrave Prison. I couldn't be connected to breaking a prisoner out of Kingsgrave, but Tristan was an Amaranthine, prone to doing as he pleased.

We came to the long stone passageway connecting the palace to Kingsgrave. The wind howled around us, whistling through the gaps in the masonry. A guard stationed at the door stepped in our way, and Tristan stopped long enough to growl, "Move."

The guard plastered himself against the wall, and Tristan stalked off. I squeezed his shoulder once, our signal for left, and Tristan turned into a stairwell, down into the lower cells.

"Which way?"

"That station."

Tristan strode for the end of the hall as if he knew exactly where he was going, and Solace help anyone who got in his way. When I asked him how he planned to get past the guards, he pointed out that the story of Aldis's punishment had been deliberately spread to the Queensguards who had stared pop-eyed at a horse being led out of the Amaranthine wing to the stables. There had been a shift relief not long after. Nobody wanted to cross a Deathless One today.

And so we came unmolested to the cell block where Avia had been incarcerated. Tristan planted his fists on his hips and said, "We wish to see the accused herald. Open this door," to the guard stationed in front of it.

That guard, scared as he was, shook his head. "She's due to be transferred."

"I don't care about that," Tristan replied. "I will see her."

"No one is permitted—"

"Do you think you'd make a good hound?" Tristan asked. He put his hand on the guard's wrist, and I sucked down a gasp as the guard's hand grew glossy black hair, shrinking into a fist, then a paw—

"Please!" the guard cried. "No, please! I have the key!"

"Use it," Tristan said.

The guard cradled his hand, flexing his fingers to assure himself that they were all there, working as fingers should.

"Now."

The guard knocked over the high stool in his haste to fumble a key into the lock, holding it open for Tristan, who swept inside in a shimmer of silk and embroidery, his hair a shiny cape falling half down his back.

"I do not wish to be disturbed," Tristan said. "Let no one inside until I am done."

The guard thumped his chest with one fist and closed the cell door.

I let go of Tristan's shoulder. "Here."

I handed him a pasty pie, and he tore into it. I moved past him and to the only occupied cell, where Avia stood with the hem of my fur coat puddled around her bare feet, gripping the copper-plated bars, her eyes alight.

"What are you doing here?"

"We're rescuing you," I said. "I told you I'd break you out if I had to, didn't I?"

Avia eyed the pile of clothes in my arms. "Did you bribe the guard?"

"Tristan threatened him. He was going to turn him into a dog—"

"Just an illusion," Tristan said. "I don't have that kind of talent. Scared him silly, though."

"Then how are we getting out of here?"

"The easy way," Tristan said. "One moment."

He licked his fingers and pinched a set of lockpicks from his sleeve, kneeling on the rough stone floor in his fine robe. He set his fingertips on the lock plate and jerked them away, gagging.

"Copper. Faugh! That's horrible." He shook his hand as if the sensation would fling itself away like water droplets. He set the picks back in the lock, careful not to touch the lock plate, and worked.

Avia clung to the cell door, tense with the need to shove it open, to get free. Tristan gently worked the lock open and turned the barrel, wresting his picks free.

Avia burst out of the cell and into my arms. I dropped the

bundle of clothes to hold her, and I didn't care about her stringy hair or the musk on her skin. I squeezed her tight and fought the tears welling in my eyes.

Avia chuckled and tilted her head back to smile up at me. "How are you going to explain this, Chancellor?"

"I'll think of something later." I thrust the bundle of clothes at Avia. "Put these on. Sorry about the fit."

"Do hurry," Tristan said. "There's a pair of double-quilted socks, and hopefully they'll help you fit into Miles's shoes. Let's save the reunion for the escape, shall we?"

"Tell me what happened," Avia said. "Dorothy said we had a good case. We even planned a series to release with the *Star*, explaining her motions for the court, what they meant, how they worked in a just system—"

"Queen Constantina abdicated," I said.

"The deuce!" Avia hopped into Miles's trousers, landing on tiptoe. The legs were too long, and I knelt to roll them up. "When?"

"At about twenty past nine." I handed her a shirt. The fur coat fell to the floor, and she turned around to remove the hemp shift, showing me the contours of her back.

"So Severin's the King. Weren't we all saying how much easier it would be if Severin—"

"He asked me to marry him."

Avia froze, one arm half in its sleeve. "But you're breaking me out of jail. He'd just let me out if you asked him to. If you're marrying him, couldn't you just—"

She turned around, sliding her arm the rest of the way into her sleeve. Her eyes were wide as she stared at me, her mouth open.

"You're not marrying him," she said. "You said no."

"I said no."

"You said no. Because—because of me?" She seized my hand, clasping it to her breastbone. "You could have been the Queen. Are you sure you want this?"

"Am I sure I want you?" I lifted a hand and drifted my fingers down her cheek. She tilted her face into my touch, and it sent furry-soft shivers over my skin, to see her eyes slip half-closed. It felt like the hair-raising, aetheric charge in the air before lightning flashed hot and blue-white across the sky. It felt like the warm rain of summer, breaking the spell of long, hot weather.

"I want to know everything about you," I said. "I want to make you laugh. I want to learn about your photographs, your art, exactly what to get you for a New Year gift and your birthday. I want to dance with you again. I want—"

"I want to kiss you," Avia said.

A storm whirled up inside my head—a swift, unbearable pressure that wasn't the cyclone outside. It was Avia's eyes, the soft parting of her mouth, her hands on the back of my neck, pulling me down to meet her kiss.

I touched her lips with mine, and my heart thundered as she brushed a kiss across my lower lip, holding me captive in her gentle grip. Soft, like the first kiss of rain on parched ground, until she opened her mouth and took more.

Her mouth on mine. I was lighter than air—only her touch kept me earthbound, the sensation in my head fizzy like double-yeasted wine.

She drew back and touched my face. "You want this."

"Yes."

She swept my hair out of my eyes. "My birthday is the thirty-eighth of Applebranch."

"Sixteenth Firstgreen."

"I'll get you something nice," Avia promised. "Just as soon as I'm not a fugitive."

Tristan coughed. I glanced his way, and he stood with his back turned, facing the door. "I don't mean to ruin the moment. But the sooner we're gone, the better."

Avia buttoned her shirt askew and didn't bother to fix it. She bent down and picked up a lamb's wool sweater and finished dressing, pulling the belt tight around her waist to keep Miles's trousers from slipping down her hips. She settled the Service coat on her shoulders and picked up the fur. "Sorry. It smells."

I slipped it on. It was still warm from her body. "It's fine. We're ready."

"Here are the rules," Tristan said. "Don't step off the path I choose. Don't dawdle. Stay close to me. I'll answer what questions I can, but the point is to get you out of here."

"How are you going to get me out of here?" Avia asked.

"The easy way, as I said." Tristan smiled and lifted his hand. "We're taking the way through the Solace."

"The Solace!" Avia exclaimed. "But don't you need to do that at a Waystone? The stories say—"

"Tristan can open a Way anywhere," I said.

"Indeed I can. Observe."

Tristan described a spiral with his hand, and reality shimmered, opening on a hot, dry breeze and the peculiar green sky I had only seen once in my life—the sky that heralded a tornado poised to tear its way across the fields.

Tristan lifted one hand to his mouth. "Oh, no."

I peered at the sky, looking for the funnel cloud that would rip its way over the land. "What is it?"

"Shifting storm," Tristan said. "This is a disaster."

The golden plains heaved themselves upward, becoming an endless land of nothing but sand, billowing into the sky on the fingertips of a howling wind. The sand turned to snow, cold and fading into a wall of white streaking across the sky. The portal closed as Tristan pulled it shut.

"We can't travel through that," he said. "I survived a shifting storm in the Tiandran Marches once. I can't chance it with the two of you."

"Then how are we getting out of here?" Avia asked. "If we can't travel through that, what do we do?"

Tristan swiped one hand across his brow. "I didn't make a contingency plan," he said. "Blast it."

Avia worried at her lip. "There's no way the two of you can bluster me walking out of here."

"No. It's now or never. We have no choice, Tristan."

Avia's expression wilted. She put on a brave smile. "The trial will make the papers. Dorothy can pass on my last articles for the *Star*."

"You'll never get a chance to see trial," I said. "Father has two choices—either he'll arrange for you to hang yourself in your cell, or he'll keep you in here until you rot and use you to control me. No glorious end. No final words."

"I'll have to go on the run."

"Yes," I said. "You absolutely have to hide. But I know someone who can help. We have to get you out of here. Tristan, can you vanish both of us?"

"What do you mean, vanish us?" Avia asked.

"Tristan's an illusionist. Tristan, if you keep us invisible while we walk out of here, we'll get to Halston Street ourselves. Can you do it?"

"Not for long," Tristan said. "Not if I'm to do this."

He pointed, and a dejected figure sat on the hard bench inside Avia's cell. Its chest rose and fell with the illusion of breath, its features so like Avia's it was uncanny.

"He'll want to look in when we walk out. It'll give us a head start." Tristan headed for the cell block door. "Avia. Hold on to my shoulder, keep up, and whatever you do, don't let go."

We were in the middle of the drafty stone hall connecting the prison and the palace when the bells rang, tolling out the message to Kingsgrave's guards: a prisoner has escaped.

"Blast it," Tristan said. "Run."

We picked up our feet and dashed for the palace. Avia's too-big shoes clomped on the stone, but we were through the door just in time to dive to the left and hide in a service corridor. It didn't matter where it went, so long as we weren't found strolling out of Kingsgrave whistling innocently.

We dodged a stack of broken chairs with a work order tucked in their lashing ropes. The halls had never been upgraded to aether, and so our shadows stretched and pooled as we bolted down the hall in dim, greenish light.

"Where are we?" Avia asked.

"I'm not sure." I dug my fingers into a terrible pain in my right side. My shins ached from the impact of running on stone floors. My lungs were a bellows, sucking up dusty, dry air—but we kept running until we came to a sign that said "Exit—be discreet!" as a reminder to palace servants that they should be mostly unseen. Tristan listened at the door, then swung it open.

"Where are we now?"

Avia vanished from sight as she touched Tristan's shoulder. I gripped his other shoulder, and trusted that I was invisible once more. "Public area. The main exit's just ahead."

"Too busy," Tristan said.

"We don't have a choice." I fussed with the lay of the fur, trying to smooth it. Edith would cluck her tongue when she saw my coat in such a state. "I say we pull out the stops and put on a show."

"Fine. But grab me if there's trouble." Tristan slipped out

the servant's door and got back into his persona, already roll-ing his steps into an arrogant strut. I pressed my fingers into my side, trying to squeeze the knifing pain in my guts.

"We could just walk around with the crowd."

"I don't think I'd blend in very well," Tristan said.

"In that case, go right. We're headed straight for the Royal Gallery."

The public areas of the palace—including the gallery, the palace temple, and the mirrored hall where tour guides met their flocks of tourists—were nearly empty of people. Staying home and not braving the wind and snow—Makers, just this snow front threatened to drop a foot or two. The storm com-ing in behind it would be colossal.

We had to escape the palace. After that, Avia would be hunted by every constable and guardsman in Kingston. I would have some explaining to do, but that wouldn't matter until later. I had to get to Robin before the storm struck the coast. I had to convince her to let me meet the Riverside Storm-Singers, now that I could promise that witchcraft was no lon-ger illegal. I needed every hand against this storm, tonight. I needed Avia safe.

"Which way?" Tristan asked. Onlookers stared at Tristan as he sailed through the grand foyer, where servants were unpacking candles for the vigil of lights at New Year. His step faltered as a swarm of red-coated guards filled the room with shouted orders, running to circle Tristan with their rifles raised.

"Halt!" a captain cried. "What is your business?"

"Do you point guns at me, sir?" Tristan asked, his posture reaching for every inch of his formidable height.

"We are in search of an escaped prisoner and her accom-plice," the guard said. "Aim."

At his command, rifles swayed into position. Twenty guns

aimed at me and Tristan, who glared back cold as ice. "You threaten an Amaranthine with death? Do you have the slightest idea what you invite by threatening me?"

Guards faltered, at that, the barrels wavering. One guard dropped to his knees, his hands clasped in front of him. Their commander bristled, but another guard lowered her rifle, bowing her head.

The others still trained their guns on us. Shoot a Blessed One? Aife would never forgive that, never. Her wrath would be a legend before the blood of Aeland even dried on the stones. I gathered my power and drew down the moisture in the air.

It was the simplest act of magic for a Storm-Singer. I knew how water felt, hanging in the air. How it tasted when you breathed it in. How it made your clothes feel damp, how it made the cold seep through your best winter coat.

The guards lowered their rifles, staring at the condensation that had formed on the bolts. I directed my will at the rifle in the hands of a child-faced guard who looked like he wanted to scream. I clenched my fist, and his posture jerked up and back as his rifle froze.

He dropped it with a yelp, and as the other guards turned toward the noise, I hit every rifle I could see. There. There. Every rifle barrel was rimed in frost, tiny spikes of ice growing on the bolts. Guards dropped their rifles, clutching frost-nipped fingers to their chests. Shouts of alarm erupted down the line.

I blinked my dizziness away.

Tristan flung his arms out with all the drama of a prestidigitator on a stage. "You dare."

Guards stared at him, awe and terror etched on their faces. Tristan loomed, dropping the glamor that hid his true countenance from the mundane eye. He stood before them, majestic and wrathful, pointing an accusing finger at the commander.

Then the air shimmered in front of him. The Way to the

Solace opened, and rain spattered on the marble tiles. Wind blew through the Way to the Solace. I caught it in my hand, whipping it in a tight, violent spiral.

Some of the guards tried to flee. Others exclaimed as Tristan flung his arms out again. The forces were routed, wide-eyed and stumbling at the wind and the hole in reality. Tristan seized the moment. He pivoted left and ran straight for a gap in the guards' line, headed for the Amaranthine wing.

"Hurry," Tristan said. "I just caused a diplomatic incident."

I let go of the wind and ran, Avia stumbling along beside me. We dashed through halls I knew as intimately as the passages through Hensley House until Tristan slowed, his energy flagging.

"Drop the spell, Tristan."

"Can't. I have to get us to Aife," Tristan panted.

"You are going to Aife," I said. "We have to get to your house."

"Aife can protect you," Tristan said.

"I can't stay in the palace," I said between gasping breaths. "I have to get Avia to safety."

"All right. Halston Street it is." Tristan said. "Which way do we go?"

I led the way to an unassuming green door. I pushed the bar-latch, and a cold wind whipped me in the face.

"We're out," I said. "Thank you, Tristan."

"It's not over yet." Tristan stepped outside with us. The snow was ankle deep on the path. I buttoned up my coat against the wind's assault. "I'm coming with you."

Avia raised her collar and stuffed her hands in Miles's coat pockets, pulling out a pair of gloves. "Tristan. You can't. You don't have a coat."

"No choice," Tristan said. "I doubt I can fight my way through the palace guards inevitably stationed at the door. You're stuck with me for a bit longer."

TWENTY-SIX

Mending

We walked on numb toes by the time we stumbled down Halston Street. We walked with our arms around Tristan, trying to shield him from the wind, but his teeth had stopped chattering two blocks ago, and that was a bad sign.

"We'll carry him if we have to," Avia said.

"No need," Tristan said, a little breathlessly. "I think I've gotten used to it."

My heart thumped. "You're not cold?"

"Not really. But I'm very tired."

"Oh no," Avia said. "Tristan. You cannot stop moving. You can't sleep yet. Talk to me."

"I was thinking," Tristan said. "Miles is frantic."

I twisted from the waist, trying to keep my coat collar close to my neck. "How do you know?"

"We're still tethered to each other from Cormac's healing spell."

"So he knows where you are."

"Yes. And he's scared."

He should be. We had to make it to Tristan's house, but we could hardly see.

"You can hear each other's thoughts?" Avia asked. "Keep moving. Keep talking."

"Not as such," Tristan said. "I can feel him. I can tell when he's happy, or angry, or scared out of his wits because I've done something foolish. He can feel me."

"Oh," Avia said. "That sounds terrifyingly intimate."

"It is," Tristan said. "It's rare that Amaranthines tie themselves to anyone this way."

Much less a mortal man like Miles. I kept silent. I had the excuse of maintaining the spell that held the wind away from us, of peering through the snow at rows of townhouses on each side of the street. We could knock at any door. No one would turn us away. But we picked up our feet and sank shin-deep in the snow, looking for Tristan's house.

But inside I felt stained. I had forced Miles into that bond with me, but it was one-sided, giving me everything and my brother nothing. I had done a terrible thing to him, and he went on loving me anyway. It didn't matter that I had let him go. I shouldn't have ever done it.

Tristan described a kind of closeness that felt too special to do lightly, a precious thing that you gave yourself to. A year ago, I would have never understood what I had done to Miles—and now I didn't know how he forgave me.

"Grace?"

"Can't talk," I said. "Too hard."

Tristan squeezed my hand, but only the sensation of pressure registered. "There."

Seventeen oh three. We had made it.

Tristan dropped the keys in the snow, trying to get them out of his pocket. I bent and scooped them up, shoving the key into the lock and twisting the door open. We piled inside the entrance, the air smelling like baking bread.

"Mrs. Sparrow," Tristan croaked. "I'm afraid I've been on a bit of an adventure."

Tristan's housekeeper bustled out just as Tristan's weight sagged between us.

"We need hot water bottles," I said. "He just walked here from the palace with no coat."

Mrs. Sparrow wheeled about, dashing back to the kitchen. I picked Tristan up, swinging him into the cradle of my arms. "You weigh a ton."

Avia shoved the low table in the middle of the parlor off to one side, snatching fringed lap-rugs from where they draped over chairs. "We've got you. When you warm up, it's going to hurt."

"That's all right," Tristan said. "It's only pain."

Mrs. Sparrow bustled in with a teapot and cups. "I'm boiling more water. I made crab chowder—can you eat?"

"Please. I could eat a horse," I said, pressing a heavy clay mug into Tristan's hands. "Drink that. How are your feet?"

"I assume they're still there," Tristan said.

"Blast it, I'm not a doctor," I said. "Avia! Where are you going?"

"Take his socks off." Avia knelt in front of the parlor fireplace. "Are his feet red, or black?"

I knelt and stripped Tristan's feet bare. "Red."

"Good," Avia said. "It's just chilblains, then. He'll be fine."

"Stop fussing," Tristan said. "I'm going to sit here and complain and try to convince Miles I'm not cuddled up next to death."

"When you're warm enough, you should have a bath," Avia said. "It will help."

Tristan grunted in agreement and sipped more tea. "Talk to me about your plans, Grace."

"I'm supposedly in Riverside right now, recruiting witches to aid us," I said. "I should head out that way, now that you're safe."

"It can wait until morning," Tristan said. "What will you do?"

"Robin told me about the movement," I said. "The people are tired of the system. They want something new. I have a brand-new King who's willing to cooperate. I'm going to make a deal."

Mrs. Sparrow returned, carrying a foot-warmer on a thick wooden tray. She set it before Tristan, who stretched to rest his heels on it. "Thank you. Have some tea. Grace is just telling me how she's going to rescue the country."

"Oh, I never heard this part," Avia said. She sat on the settee next to me, a mug of milky tea in her hands.

"I'm going to Robin. We need to organize the emancipation now that the Witchcraft Protection Act is struck down. With no law to oppress them, the witches will help us turn the storm—not without their conditions, but I'll deal with that. Elsine will be leading the Storm-Singers, but when we're all facing the same storm, we'll come together."

Avia gazed into her teacup. "And me?"

"You're going underground," I said. "I'm so sorry, Avia. You have to stay hidden for now. I'll be working to exonerate you."

"If you imagine I will give up reporting, you can forget it," Avia said. "I'll mail my articles if I have to. This is a story, and you can't stop me from telling it."

"I'd never dream of it," I said. "I need your byline on the front page. I'm just sorry that you have to hide."

"You have tonight," Tristan said. "At least you have that."

"And we have to figure out how to get you back into the palace," I said.

Tristan waved that away. "Through the doors, I imagine. You're going to support Robin?"

"Yes. No one else understands what Aeland needs better than she does. She'll keep me accountable and hold my feet to the fire if I stray."

Tristan nodded. "That should be enough for Aife."

I pressed my lips together. "If she's satisfied, then you'll be leaving. Going back to the Solace. You and Miles."

"If she sees fit, yes. But she'll need an envoy representing her in Aeland. I'm supremely qualified. Don't imagine you're getting rid of me anytime soon."

I sighed out a relieved breath. "You and Miles are staying here."

"Miles and I are staying here," Tristan said. "Mrs. Sparrow would miss us if we left."

"That I would, Mr. Hunter," Mrs. Sparrow said, standing in the threshold of the parlor. "I've put together a supper. Come and eat, all of you."

"And then I think it's early to bed," Tristan said. "I apologize for the lack of heat in the master suite, Avia. I trust the guest room was comfortable?"

"She fixed it," Mrs. Sparrow said. "Miss Jessup took a screwdriver to that radiator upstairs, and she had it steaming in minutes."

Avia shrugged. "The landlord doesn't fix things in my building when they're broken. You learn a trick or two."

"I'll take the guest room, then." Tristan hugged the hot water bottle close and grinned. "The master suite is more romantic."

Tristan's collection of wall mirrors didn't extend to the long silver-and-violet bedroom, but twin fireplaces crackled behind iron screens, casting warm firelight and dancing shadows over the deep-piled sheepskin rugs and the bed, a soaring whitewood frame draped in creamy sheer curtains. A plush velvet coverlet was pulled halfway down the mattress, inviting us to slide under the blankets and get cozy.

"It's the nicest safe house I've ever seen," Avia said. She stood on a rug, curling her scarlet-painted toes into the pile. Tristan's dressing gown was belted lazily at the waist and gaped open over bare skin, showing me the pale flesh stretched over her sternum, shadows playing along the spread wings of her collarbones. She carried two crystal brandy glasses in one hand, and grasped the neck of a bottle of peach brandy from the orchards of Norton in the other. "You're nervous."

"I'm not." I sprang out of my seat by the fire. "Shall I pour?"

"Your hair curls," Avia said. "Left to its own devices, you're a curlyhead."

I hadn't the art of hairdressing, even if Tristan did possess curling tongs and a hair dryer. My hair had dripped on my shoulders while I'd tried to read a novel by lamplight as I waited for Avia to finish her bath.

Avia set the brandy down and picked the volume up. It was another one about Miss Hambly, a well-loved lady sleuth who lived in a county where a truly alarming number of murders occurred. The latest victim had been found tied to a waterwheel, but I had read the same page five times.

"You're nervous," Avia said. "You ride herd on Parliament members, you can stop a media scrum in full bawl, you literally run the country, and you just rescued me from Kingsgrave Prison." She set the novel on the small table and poured us each a puddle of brandy. She handed me one and watched me over the edge of her glass.

"I'm fine."

"Mm." She tipped her glass back, downing the brandy in three quick swallows. She set the glass down and pulled on one tail of the satin sash that held her dressing gown closed, one shoulder slipping free. "Do you know how long I've admired you?"

"I don't know," I said.

"Do you remember the Kingston Charity Wicket Championship of '81?"

"I do," I said. "I won."

"You were brilliant. You played the most cutthroat game of wicket I had ever seen. You were merciless. And when you won, I wanted to go to you so badly it ached. I wanted to congratulate you. I wanted to take you away to get ice creams and then you would have liked me, even if I was just a grocer's daughter."

"You cut your hair shortly after I got engaged," I said. "You cut it to the way it looks now, and dyed it shining black, and you were surrounded by people—I was, too, but it wasn't the same. They were Ray's friends, not mine. I wanted to tell you how glamorous you looked. How captivating you were. How you caught my breath with every smile. But we never crossed the floor."

Avia shook her head. "We never crossed the floor. And then Father threw me out—"

"And you flew," I said. "And to the void with what the world expected of you. That freedom, to do exactly as you wanted— do you have any idea how much I wanted to do the same?"

The other shoulder of Avia's dressing gown slid away. "You can do exactly what you want right now. What do you want, Grace?"

I remembered the brandy glass, cradled in the warmth of one hand. I set it down before I drew closer, before I traced the curve of her cheek with my fingers and tilted her chin a little higher.

Avia's robe puddled to the floor. Borrowed silk slid off my shoulders and spilled at our feet. She led me to the wide, cool bed, and allowed me to show her exactly what.

ACKNOWLEDGMENTS

Writing your first book is hard, but nothing really prepares you for the roller-coaster ride that is the second book in a series. Drafting was an experience, and I want to thank A. J. Townsend for reading every draft she could before MAXI J1820+070 started getting ornery and interesting. Eaving Hardy's observations on my first draft helped shape the revisions. Elizabeth Bear saw the beginning and its consequences before I did, and Stella Sauer and Alex Haist read the final draft and kept me going to the end. Mary Robinette Kowal's monthly Patreon lessons were eerily prescient about what I was facing in drafting so many times it's like she knew what was going on.

No one writes a book alone, and I'd like to thank Kimberly Bell, Alexis Daria, and Robin Lovett for our Friday chats where we kept each other steering toward what we wanted. Online for me every day, the zoo and the isle joined me in the daily ins and outs of writing a novel: keeping up accountability, breaking through stuck points, and reminding me that work/life is supposed to be balanced.

When the story is done, there's a whole team of people waiting to make the work everything it can be. I'm grateful to

Tor.com and their genius, excellent people, especially Carl Engle-Laird and Ruoxi Chen, for vision and insight. Together we dug deeper into the story, its settings, its themes, and had great conversations about what this book should aim for. Irene Gallo, for the clear direction and unwavering belief in the Kingston Cycle series and the gift that is Will Staehle's breathtaking covers. Thanks to the production team for their expertise and making the book look great: production editor Megan Kiddoo, production manager Steven Bucsok, and interior designer Nicola Ferguson. I'm grateful for Mordicai Knode's tireless work in promotions and that excellent story from forensic science that inspired a scene in the book. Thank you to Amanda Melfi, whose efforts promoting *Stormsong* on social media kept me enthusiastic and cheery. I owe much to Deanna Hoak's precise and skillful copy editing, and explaining that that thing I do is called a misplaced modifier.

Finally, I want to thank Caitlin McDonald, my agent and champion, who was there every time I emailed just one more question, explained everything I didn't understand, and who kept it all together even when I thought I couldn't.

ABOUT THE AUTHOR

C. L. POLK wrote her first story in grade school and still hasn't learned any better. After spending years in strange occupations and wandering Western Canada, she settled in Southern Alberta with her rescue dog, Otis. She has a fondness for knitting, bicycles, and single-estate coffee. Polk has had short stories published in *Jim Baen's Universe* and *Gothic.net,* contributed to the web serial *Shadow Unit,* and spends too much time on twitter at @clpolk. Her first novel is *Witchmark.*